A Tale Ripper Street: Inspector Edmund Reid's Hunt for Jack the Ripper

JOSEPH BUSA

josephbusa.com

ISBN-13: 978-1507782378

To Michelle

A TALE FROM RIPPER STREET

CONTENTS

A TALE FROM RIPPER STREET

A TALE FROM RIPPER STREET

CHAPTER ONE

Another Horrible Murder in Whitechapel

THE PRIORITIES OF THE FALLEN WOMEN of Victorian London were alcohol, food and a bed for the night, often in that order. The four pence required for a bed, if the wooden cots could be described such, put many women at the mercy of evil men. Amongst the men that sought to exploit them was a man made for the times in which he lived. Unlike the capitalists, he had no wish to sweat their feeble bodies for profit. No, he wanted more than that, much more. What he sought from them were their souls, and he intended to rip each and every one from the body of any woman forced into prostituting herself before him.

ɗ ɗ ɗ

The weather in 1888 had been dismal, with many cool cloudy rainy days; it was going to be another tough year for the people of Great Britain. The unemployed in London had organised mass rallies against the conditions in which they had to live in the autumns of 1886 and 1887, and for all intents and purposes looked as if they would do so again in the autumn of 1888. The Government of the day were hoping for something, anything that would distract the minds of the masses away from hardships that they were forced to endure. They say that you should be careful what you wish for. Soon the Government's wish was to be granted, but once out, this particular genie was never going to return to his lamp.

❧❧❧

None of the gloom that hung over the country like the London smog, had stopped Inspector Edmund John James Reid's family from enjoying their seaside holiday at Margate. Saturday 8th September was a fine sunny day and Reid's wife Emily had taken their children – Elizabeth, aged 15 and Harold, aged 6 - for a walk along the beach. Emily had her own timepiece and would allow the children to see the spectacle at the appointed time.

The years had been kind to Reid; although now 42, he looked younger than his years and was still physically fit. At 5 feet 6 inches in height he was the Metropolitan Police Force's shortest policeman; not that this had stopped him from rising rapidly through the ranks. Fortune tends to favour the brave and Reid had bravery sown into his DNA. He had light brown hair, a moustache and full beard, with thinned-out sideburns. By all accounts he did not look like an officer of the law, but more like a member of staff one might find in a bank; only with better manners.

Prior to joining the Met, Reid had tried his hand at seventeen other trades; including that of: a watchmaker's apprentice and a steward on a fast steamer that took passengers to and from London Bridge to Margate. He had married Emily Wilson back in 1868 when they were both aged 22 but knew then that he had not found a vocation in life that would allow him to start a family. He wanted a job that he would excel in; something that he would stick with until retirement age, something that would provide him with excitement. In 1872, he got his chance when the officers of the Met went on their first ever strike, a number of men were sacked and this resulted in a manpower shortage. Keen to fill the gap in police numbers the Met waived its minimum height restriction of 5 feet 8 inches and a few men like Reid, possessing qualities other than brawn and physical stature were recruited into its ranks. Right from the start Reid felt completely at home in the police; the unsociable work hours were not always to Emily's liking but being a police constable provided secure employment and paid relatively well. Life in Victorian Britain was hard, but happy with their lot in life the Reids had their first child - Elizabeth - in 1873. In 1874, Reid joined P Division's Detective Department and in 1878 he qualified as a Sergeant 3rd Class in its Criminal Investigation Department (CID). In 1880 he passed the examination that made him a 1st Class Sergeant, the extra financial security afforded by his promotion helped ease the way for the Reids' second and only other child - Harold – who was born in 1882. Three years later, Reid qualified as an Inspector 2nd Class and transferred to Scotland Yard, otherwise known as A-Division.

Edmund Reid was an unconventional man. He had always been something of a showman and combined his working life as a married policeman with a passion for what were at the time considered to be the very dangerous sports of ballooning and parachute jumping. With Reid it was a case of do it all or nothing at all. In the 1870s he performed a parachute jump in front of thousands at a fete in Luton and in 1883 he received a medal for achieving a record height for a balloon ascent. In 1886 Reid was transferred to be the Local Inspector CID at the newly created J-Division covering London's Bethnal Green. It had taken him 14 long years to get there but he had finally found the role that he loved. However, his unconventional nature came back to bite him in 1887 when ignoring orders to the contrary he got involved in an altercation with a local dignitary. Reid had good reasons for what he did but this did not stop him from being reprimanded and transferred to the adjacent policing district of Whitechapel, otherwise known as H-Division. He had been very fortunate not to have been demoted and very nearly lost his job. But the transfer proved to be punishment enough, because as luck would have it his new job placed him in the unenviable position of filling the shoes of London's most successful detective; one Frederick George Abberline.

Inspector Abberline had spent 14 years in Whitechapel and had received a large number of commendations, including one from the head of the Met for his part in capturing and helping successfully prosecute two members of the Irish Republican Brotherhood (IRB) who had planted and exploded a bomb in the Tower of London on 'Dynamite Saturday' back on January 24th 1885. That was the day that the Fenians went to town, planting three bombs in London; one in the Houses of Parliament, one in the Banqueting House and the one that actually exploded, in the Tower. For his efforts, Abberline had received a bonus of £20 - well over a month's wages – on the personal orders of the then Home Secretary, Sir William Harcourt. In 1887 he had been promoted to Inspector 1st Class and transferred over to Scotland Yard; leaving the gap that Reid was forced into plugging. Reid knew that Abberline would be an impossible act to follow. He knew how things were going to pan out for him from then onwards. No matter what he did, he was always going to be found wanting in comparisons with the man many in the Met nicknamed the 'Bank Manager'. Abberline had received the name, as he just like Reid, tended to treat people with great respect – even the criminals! His general demeanour was much better suited to that of a bank manager, than a mid-ranking policeman. Life at H-Division turned out exactly as Reid had imagined it would. Whatever he did, it just wasn't quite good enough; with 'Abberline did this' and 'Abberline did that'. What he needed was to get transferred out of H-Division or to solve his own big case, something that would finally lay the ghost of the 'Bank Manager' to rest.

***

The weather that week had been atrocious, with a lot of heavy rain, but the day that Reid had chosen to make his parachute jump was fine and sunny. He had promised Emily that it would be his last ever jump and he hoped that his little boy Harold was at an age where he might remember his father's feat of daring into his adult life. The balloon's pilot checked Reid's backpack and gave him the all clear.

"Anytime you are ready, sir."

"Thank you," responded Reid.

Reid looked down at the ground below him. He loved the view and the sense of power that it gave him. As a member of Her Majesty's Constabulary he had often thought what great assistance to crime fighting might be had if the Met were to use tethered balloons over the city. It was true that the narrowness of the streets and the smog would make seeing the ground difficult, but he felt that the knowledge of a pair of eyes looking over the city's streets would be enough to deter a large proportion of the miscreants from committing any criminal activity. He had witnessed many changes and was sure that someday a new-fangled invention would be found that could record and monitor criminal activity. As it was, he had seen the invention of the telephone, the bicycle and even the police had moved-on from carrying rattles to whistles; who knew where it would all end?

Reid checked his timepiece, it was 1.00pm, the time he had informed Emily and the children to watch out for him. He climbed over the basket, took a breath and jumped. He pulled the cord as he fell to earth and took another deep breath as he waited for the parachute to exit the backpack and open. He'd jumped from only a few thousand feet, so only had seconds to prepare for his landing. However, all went as planned and he landed safely in a field.

Emily and the children were ready to witness the scene and a number of other onlookers gasped in amazement as the man leaped from the basket that hung under the balloon. The first UK ascent in a balloon had taken place back in the 1780s and the first parachute jump in 1838, but the sight of a man falling to earth was still a novelty and held the attention of anyone fortunate enough to witness it. Harold was much impressed by what he saw, he could not be sure that the man floating to earth like a bird was his father but his mother ensured him that it was. He knew like all small boys that his father was a giant of a man, but how many other fathers could fly? Emily and Elizabeth both gave gasps of relief; they were also proud of Reid's daring but had no wish to end up in the workhouse should the family's main breadwinner have fallen to his death.

Emily and the children continued on with their picnic. Reid would be a few hours yet, as he had to return the parachute and would no doubt engage in conversation with any fellow balloonists back at the balloon base camp.

❦ ❦ ❦

Reid was on his annual holiday; the week was almost at an end, but he could not keep himself from thinking about work. As he trudged through the fields his mind wandered back to April, a fallen woman named Emma Smith had been murdered on his patch. She had been attacked in the early hours of the morning of the 3rd April. Before she died, she'd informed her friends and staff at the hospital that she had been set upon by three men who robbed and beat her. However, not content with beating her physically, one of the men took it upon himself to ram an object up into her passage. The damaged tissue became infected and she died the following morning. Reid and his colleagues had only found out about her murder on the 6th April when the coroner reported the death to the police. All of this felt a bit strange to Reid; the sexual nature of the assault was far from usual and none of the PCs on duty that night had recorded any unusual disturbances in their notebooks. There were no reports of any street gangs or for that matter even the small group of women who had assisted Emma Smith on her agonising walk to the London Hospital. Reid had a mind to think that the woman had not been attacked by a gang at all, but had instead been set upon by a punter that she might have taken down an alleyway for sex. However, he and his men had investigated the murder thoroughly enough and there was no proof of what had really happened to the ageing London prostitute. The coroner recorded the death as being committed by the yet to become infamous 'wilful murder by a person or persons unknown' and that was the end of the matter.

Reid took the time to admire the beauty of the countryside as he walked. The air was so much cleaner than in the city. In only a few short days he'd felt his lungs clear and he hoped that the smog in the city wasn't having too harmful an effect on his children. He decided that even if the family could not escape the city on a regular basis, he and Emily should make more effort to take the children to London's parks. His mind then wandered back to a second unusual murder, on the morning of the 7th August another murder of a fallen woman had taken place on Reid's patch. On that occasion a woman named Martha Tabram had been stabbed 39 times. Again, the murder was far from the usual sort of crime that one might expect in London's east end, in that such a murder would have been unusual in just about any city on earth. However, much was known about Tabram's last night in the world. She was a well-known prostitute and had spent the night in the company of fellow prostitute named Mary Ann Connelly - aka Pearly Poll - and two soldiers whose identities were to remain unknown. Connelly had made a statement describing how she and Tabram had gone off for sex with their respective 'partners', deposits for their services having already been paid for in kind by the 'free' drinks that the men had purchased for them over the course of the evening. The group had frequented a good number of Whitechapel's numerous public houses as the night had gone on and even hardened alcoholics like Connelly and Tabram had had more than their fill of beer and rum. Tabram was said to have taken her soldier into a street called George Yard and was not seen alive again. Reid had spent many hours investigating the crime. Initially, he was confident that it would be relatively easy to solve; the murder likely committed by one of the soldiers; most probably the result of an argument over the price Tabram wanted for performance of the sexual act. Meticulous logs were kept by the military with details of all soldiers' absence from barracks, so it should have only been a matter of time before Connolly was able to identify the two men that she and Tabram had spent the night drinking with. However, it was not to be. After a number of line-ups conducted at various barracks Connelly was only able to pick-out two men that went on to produce cast iron alibis proving that they were not in Whitechapel on the night of the murder.

Reid might have been able to let this all go, but three weeks later another fallen woman was murdered. This murder had not been committed in Whitechapel but in Reid's old patch, in the neighbouring police district of Stepney, the Met's J-Division. The murdered woman's name was Mary Ann Nichols and she had been killed in the early hours of Friday 31st August. Reid had been grateful that she had not been killed on his patch as he most likely would have had to defer his annual leave. As it was, Emily was just about putting up with his night-shift duties; there would have been hell to pay if the family's annual holiday had had to be rearranged because of his work. Nichols had been murdered in Berner's Street, but this time little was known of her movements on the final night of her life and the coroner recorded yet another verdict of 'wilful murder by person or persons unknown'. Nichols' death appeared to be yet another unusual sexually related murder. The murderer had slashed her throat and then set about her person, eviscerating her lower body with a long bladed razor-sharp knife. Reid felt sure that the murders were connected - especially the last two - and thought that it was going to be just a matter of time before another woman was killed. There was talk in the police ranks of a man named John Pizer – aka Leather Apron - being the culprit and this had been leaked to the press. Stories had been written in newspapers circulating the globe carrying descriptions of the evil man/monster.

Anyway, all that could wait until Monday as Reid intended to enjoy the rest of day before making the return journey home.

❦ ❦ ❦

"Hello, dearest," called out Reid as he approached Emily and the children.

Emily did not respond as she was engrossed in a story carried in a newspaper. Harold called out to his father and started to tell Reid all about how he had seen him flying like a bird.

Reid was pleased to see the pride in his young son's eyes, however, he was concerned that Emily had not spoken to him. "Now, dearest, there is no need to be upset. Did I not tell you that this was to be my last parachute jump? I meant what I said. I won't put you and the children at risk again."

"No, Edmund, that is not the cause of my discomfort. Look at this," said Emily as she passed Reid the newspaper. It was then that he saw the headline 'Another horrible murder in Whitechapel'. Another fallen woman had been murdered, details were scant, but it seemed that this latest murder was even more gruesome than the last, and appeared to have been committed by the same hand that had slain Mary Ann Nichols.

Reid, though a hardened officer and well used to murder, was genuinely shocked by the atrocity. However, he had spent the last year in the shadow of the Bank Manager and now was sure that he had found the big case that he had been praying for. All he had to do now was solve the murders so that he could finally free himself from the curse that was Inspector Frederick George Abberline.

CHAPTER TWO

The Bank Manager Returns

ON MONDAY 10TH SEPTEMBER Inspector Reid woke earlier than usual. Unlike the end of his other holidays he was keen to get back to work and wanted to get up-to-speed with details of the latest murder. The newspapers had been quick to spot what appeared to be a pattern of sexually motivated murders and had lumped them together under the banner of the 'Whitechapel Murders'. The death of the unnamed woman was linked to those of Emma Smith, Martha Tabram and Polly Nichols. Reid had given further thought to the whereabouts of John Pizer; the man's family were known to live in Whitechapel but he was not thought to live with them. The Inspector wondered if anyone had actually taken the trouble to search the man's family home for him.

There were four police stations in Whitechapel, located at: Leman Street (the Division Headquarters), Commercial Street, King David's Street and Arbour Square. Reid made his way to the Leman Street HQ where he hoped to find Sergeant William Thick on duty. Thick was one of Abberline's old trusted sidekicks, but Reid had found him to be a forthright man of integrity who displayed great courage in physically demanding situations. Thick was also a man of great strength who was more than a match for most of the east end's petty criminals, who'd nicknamed him Johnny Upright.

The Lehman Street nick was pretty much representative of the other London police stations. The ground floor contained a spacious reception area - that was usually manned by a desk sergeant - there were a few large rooms with enough desks to accommodate an inspector, a sergeant and a few constables, with three interview rooms. The cells were in the basement and the station's lead man - the Superintendent – had a separate office on the first floor of the building, which also housed a large briefing room.

Reid was in luck; Sergeant Thick was on duty. The sergeant was a large man; at least six feet tall, broad shouldered and of a large build. His hair was dark and he had a large dark moustache, but had neither a beard nor sideburns. He was also a family man with two daughters and son and was not long back from his own holiday away from the smog of the city.

Sergeant Thick saw Reid enter the station. Thick greeted him as he made his way to his desk.

"Morning, sir," called out the Sergeant.

"Morning, sergeant," replied Reid.

"I trust that you had a good holiday, sir."

"Yes. Mrs Reid, the children and I enjoyed our time away from the city. Now, Sergeant, tell me, what do you know about Saturday's murder?"

"It is thought, with some certainty, that the murdered woman was a known prostitute named Annie Chapman. She was found murdered at around 6am in the backyard of 29 Hanbury Street. Inspector Chandler was the first man on the scene and is giving a briefing to the men from Scotland Yard at midday today."

"Thank you, sergeant," replied Reid. "You say a briefing of men from the Yard. What do you mean by that?"

"I'm afraid that I have no other details, sir. All I know is that Chandler has been told to be ready with full particulars, and there is talk of Superintendent Keating and Inspector Spratling of J Division attending. Inspector Chandler will also be attending the opening session of the inquest into Chapman's death, which is being held later this afternoon. My guess is that you will also be requested to attend the meeting, sir. The Super instructed that you were to report to him on your arrival at the station."

"Is Mr Arnold currently in his office?"

"Yes, sir."

"Sergeant, have you been involved in the search for Pizer?"

"Yes. Officers from Y-Division have reported that he has been harassing unfortunates in the Holloway area."

"Has anyone actually visited his family home in Mulberry Street?"

"No, sir. Officers from J-Division are leading the investigation into the Nichols murder and they have been concentrating the search in and around Holloway for him."

"Do you have anything pressing to do at the moment?"

"No, sir. Why do you ask?" replied Sergeant Thick, wondering what the Inspector could possibly want him to do.

"Well sergeant, I know that Pizer is in the habit of extorting monies from the local fallen women but I am not aware of his ever having badly injured a lady. Would you agree with that?"

"Yes, sir."

Reid fixed the sergeant with a blank stare. It was his habit to unpick a problem and then have his men try to think of the solution before he steered them into the direction that his thoughts had taken him.

"Now if you were Pizer," continued Reid. "and you were aware of stories in the newspapers stating that you were the prime suspect in a series of gruesome murders, and that half the coppers and every East End mob were looking for you. What would you do?"

"Well, sir, being in fear of getting lynched, I'd be inclined to seek refuge somewhere."

"Now if you were unable to work and had no means of procuring a room in a lodging house. Where would you go?"

"In those circumstances, I'd likely lie low at my family's

home."

"That is my reasoning exactly. So if you have some time available to you. Why don't you and a few PCs take a walk around to Mulberry Street to see if our man has taken refuge there."

Thick was not keen to follow-up the request. He knew that Chandler's involvement in the case would likely cause Reid complications and he did not want to get caught in the middle of any ensuing crossfire. "Well, sir, Inspector Chandler is leading the investigation and he is out interviewing a witness at the moment and -"

"I can appreciate that, sergeant. Now be a good fellow and take a quick look so that we are able to confirm this to the men from the Yard, should they ask if all Pizer's known haunts have been searched. I reason that it will be better for us to have done so, rather than be instructed to do so at the briefing."

Yes, sir, I'll attend to it immediately."

With that Sergeant Thick rounded-up a few PCs and left the station for Mulberry Street.

Reid did not immediately go to Superintendent Thomas Arnold's office. He was a bit taken aback that the Yard would intervene so quickly in the investigation. He had assumed that he - as the most senior ranking Detective Inspector - would automatically takeover the running of the investigation. He hoped, that with luck, the men from the Yard only required an appraisal of the investigation, the detail of which might be included in a report to the Home Office. Reid spent a few minutes scanning his notes of the Smith and Tabram murders before finally knocking on the Super's office door.

"Come in," responded Superintendent Arnold.

Reid entered and found Arnold seated behind his desk. Arnold was a large man, he was taller and broader than Sergeant Thick, and that was saying something. He had light brown hair, that was not matched by his grey/white beard and moustache.

"Good morning, Reid. I trust that you enjoyed your holiday?"

"Yes, I did, sir. Sergeant Thick told me that you wanted to see me."

"Yes, that's right, we are having a meeting with a team from the Yard at twelve, members of J-Division will also be in attendance. I want to be sure that everyone is fully conversant with the detail of inquiries into the murders of Emma Smith, Martha Tabram, Mary Ann Nichols and Annie Chapman - the woman murdered last Saturday morning. J-Division will provide details on Nichols' murder, Chandler is currently following-up some information relating to Chapman and I trust that you are able to report on Smith and Tabram?"

"Yes, sir, I have my notes and all is in order."

"Now, Reid, I doubt that all these murders are actually related, but the press has connected them and the Home Office has instructed that a full report be submitted to them by Wednesday. So be sure that you report on all salient points, do not concern yourself with any theories or other extraneous data. We will leave it to A-Division to coalesce the facts of the matter."

"Yes, sir."

"Please be in the briefing room by 11.50am, I want everyone in place well in advance of the meeting."

"Will that be all, sir?"

"There are two new cases waiting in your in-tray, please come back to me if you have any questions. I will see you later."

Reid returned to his desk. He decided to leave the rereading of his notes on the Smith and Tabram murders until 10.30am. In the meantime he acquainted himself with the new cases waiting in his in-tray. He was already investigating a fraud case and there was a note from the

Super with the details of two new cases that he wanted investigated. The first was to identify the cause of a surge in illegal gambling that had taken hold around the Spitalfields market; the second related to information provided to a constable by a local informant, that a local house was being used to produce a particularly hideous type of pornography. Reid decided to refresh his mind on the detail of the fraud case, he planned to make a start on the gambling and pornography cases later that afternoon.

❦❦❦

At approximately 9am, Sergeant Thick and his fellow PCs arrived at 22 Mulberry Street. The sergeant did not expect to find 'Leather Apron' in the building but had instructed his men to draw their truncheons just in case of trouble. Pizer was a small man, standing only 5 feet 4 inches, but was very powerfully built, with a huge head and neck and was known to carry a knife with him at all times.

Unknown to the policemen, the occupants of the house had already seen them making ready to enter the building. They were all more than a little surprised when the door was opened to them by none other than John Pizer.

"What can I do you for, officer?" asked Pizer.

"Are you the man known as the Leather Apron?" asked Sergeant Thick, who knew Pizer by sight but needed an answer by way of a formal confirmation.

"I am," replied Pizer.

"Then, sir, are you aware that you are wanted in connection with a series of murders?"

"I am, sir."

"Then I trust that you have no objection to accompanying me and my men to the station?"

"I do not, sir."

The sergeant noticed that Pizer was casting a wary eye over passers-by who'd started to gather in the street behind him. Thick could see a hint of fear in the man's eyes and thought that Pizer, usually no friend of the law, looked glad to see him and his police escort.

"May I collect my jacket?" asked Pizer.

"Yes, you may, but be quick about it man as there are only four of us and I am keen to get you back to the station in one piece."

Pizer grabbed his jacket, said a quick goodbye to his relatives and stood in the middle of his police escort, with two officers to the front and the back of him. Someone in the crowd shouted 'THEY'VE GOT LEATHER APRON, STRING-UP THE BASTARD'. A few men tried to block the group's path and Thick shouted at them to move away or be arrested. Pizer and his escort picked-up the pace and made good speed to the safety of the police station. The sergeant instructed his PCs to stand guard at the front door and not to let anyone in unless they had had good business to be there.

Reid could not help but notice the commotion in the station's reception. "I take it that we have our man. Good work, Sergeant!" he called out through the din.

"Thank you, sir," replied Sergeant Thick before escorting the suspect to the safety of a cell.

Whilst the sergeant was placing Pizer into a cell, Superintendent Joseph Keating and Inspector John Spratling of J-Division arrived at the station. Keating informed Spratling that he would have private meeting with Superintendent Arnold, and would call him in after a few minutes. Keating knocked at Arnold's office door and went inside.

"Good morning, Joseph, please take a seat," said Arnold.

"Good morning, Thomas," responded Keating.

"I have a very bad feeling about this sorry business," continued Arnold "As I understand the matter, Her Majesty herself telephoned the Home Office yesterday to harangue the Home Secretary. She has requested a full report on progress made into all four murders since April and has stressed that she expects the culprit to be in police custody before the end of the month."

"Do we know A-Division's requirements?" asked Keating.

"No, all I have been told is that we are to provide them with a comprehensive briefing, they are formulating a course of action this morning."

"What is Reid's involvement in the case?"

"He was the lead investigating officer into the Smith and Tabram murders, but was on leave when Chapman was murdered. He returned to duty this morning."

"Just a word of advice Thomas, Reid's not a man to be trusted with a case like this one. He likes to go his own way, and in a matter such as this you need somebody who will do exactly what you tell them to do."

"Reid has done good work for me, but in view of his past I must agree with you. Inspector Chandler is investigating the Chapman murder and I will have him assigned full-time to the ongoing investigation. Reid will be taking a supporting role."

"Excellent," replied Keating. "Inspector Spratling is outside, would you like to speak with him in advance of the briefing?"

"Yes, ask him to come in".

Keating called Spratling into Arnold's office, after which the Inspector provided H-Division's Super with a summary of his investigation into the murder of Mary Ann Nichols.

Inspector Joseph Chandler arrived at the station at 11.35am, he had just returned from interviewing a Mrs Fiddymont, the landlady of the Prince Albert public house. The woman had reported that she had details of a possible suspect.

Reid saw Chandler enter the station. "Good afternoon, Joseph, can we speak before the briefing with A-Division?"

"Sorry, Edmund, I've just returned from an interview and need to update my notes. There is nothing useful that I can tell you now that will not wait half an hour."

"Thank you, Joseph. In that case I will let you get on. However, just to inform you that Sergeant Thick has apprehended the Leather Apron, he's in the cells."

"Excellent, thank you for letting me know."

At 11.50am Reid entered the briefing room, followed by Sergeant Thick and Inspector Chandler. The room resembled a school classroom with a few rows of desks facing a chalkboard at the front of the room. Before the men had the opportunity to speak they heard the gentlemen from the Yard arriving in the station's reception. Superintendent Arnold met the men at the front desk and directed them to the briefing room. In all, six men entered the room: Arnold, Keating, Spratling and three men from the Yard. The lead man was Chief Inspector Donald Sutherland Swanson and with him were two Detective Inspectors.

CI Swanson immediately took the lead. He requested that the officers from H and J Divisions be seated and he introduced himself and his team. CI Swanson was another large man; he had dark brown hair and a medium sized, greying moustache.

"Good afternoon, gentlemen. As you are aware, I and my men are here today as a result of the series of unsolved murders being reported in the newspapers under the banner of the 'Whitechapel Murders'. Commissioner Warren was summoned to a meeting with the Home Secretary yesterday evening, where it was decided that a special taskforce would be established to focus solely on the investigation into the murders. The Commissioner has instructed that the efforts of your two Divisions are to be coordinated by a team from

A-Division. Ultimately, all reports pertaining to the case are to be forwarded to my office. I have established a team of three Inspectors, two of which are with me today. The Inspectors will act as conduits of information for all local inquiries made into the case and will make round the clock inquiries. A duty roster will be prepared so that you know who the Duty Officer is at any particular time of the day. For those of you that may not know them, may I introduce Inspectors Moore and Andrews. These gentlemen will be led by a man that I trust you all know very well, Inspector Frederick Abberline. Unfortunately, Abberline could not attend this morning because he is in Gravesend, interviewing a suspect. In Abberline's absence you should report to Moore and Andrews.

Inspector Moore stepped forward. "Gentleman, I think that the best way to proceed is if you can provide us with a summary of your investigations to date. Abberline will arrange private meetings with each of you to ascertain the fine detail. In order not to hinder the operational functionality of H-Division, with Superintendent Arnold's agreement, Inspector Reid will from today be taking a much reduced role in the case. Inspector Chandler is currently leading the inquiry into Chapman's murder and is to remain the local lead Inspector until directed otherwise. This will allow Inspector Reid to focus his energies on H-Division's other ongoing investigations."

Reid could not believe the words entering his ears. Not only was his best chance in laying the ghost of Abberline to rest being taken away from him, but the man had returned in person to haunt him. Reid wanted to protest, but knew that he had no means of influencing CI Swanson. The man's decision was final and he would just have to live with it.

Moore continued, "Right, gentleman, I would like to address the inquiry in chronological order. So can Inspector Reid come up to the front and start us off by summarising his investigations into the murders of Emma Smith and Martha -."

Inspector Chandler interjected "Sorry, sir, but could we not reverse the order of events as I am due at the Chapman inquest which commences at 2pm?"

"That is not ideal," said Swanson, scratching the back of his head "but yes it makes sense to let you get on with your business."

"Thank you, sir," replied Chandler "I'd also like to draw your attention to another matter."

"And what would that be?" asked Swanson.

"I have some good news, sir. Sergeant Thick has this morning apprehended Pizer, the man known as Leather Apron. He is currently residing in one of the cells in this station."

The briefing went on about an hour. Reid was embarrassed to admit that he had no firm suspects for the murders of Smith and Tabram. Spratling confirmed that his best lead for the Nichols' murder was John Pizer, aka Leather Apron. As for Chandler, he had been pleased to report that earlier that morning he had interviewed the landlady of the Prince Albert public house, a Mrs Fiddymont. She had reported that at about 7am on the morning of Chapman's murder, a crazy looking man had entered the pub and asked for a glass of ale. She said that the man had bloodstained hands and a frightening appearance, further describing him as being about 5 feet 8 inches in height, with red to ginger hair, and a red to ginger moustache. She added that he had a slight build but wild blue eyes. His gaze was so scary that she had avoided looking into his eyes when serving him but took the liberty of further inspecting his appearance using the bar mirror. She noticed that he was wearing a bloodstained torn shirt under his jacket. However, the man noticing what she was doing, quickly finished his drink and left the building. The man's manner had aroused the interest of the pub's regular patrons and a few of them followed him up the road, but none felt safe in tackling him before he disappeared into Bishop's Gate.

CI Swanson was pleased that he now had three possible suspects to report on and was especially pleased that two of them were already in custody. He was most pleased by the capture of the man known as 'Leather Apron', the one the press had created the hullabaloo about. Inspectors Moore and Andrews were also pleased with the capture of Leather Apron and informed that they would question Pizer in Inspector Chandler's absence. Swanson reiterated that all future reports were to be directed to Abberline, Moore and Andrews, with copies made for his information. He added that a daily summary of activities was to be telegraphed to A-Division at the end of each of the Inspectors' shifts.

CI Swanson returned to the Yard and Inspectors Moore and Andrews got to work on interrogating Pizer.

ჭ ჭ ჭ

At 2pm sharp, the coroner of the South Eastern division of Middlesex, Mr Wynne E. Baxter, opened the inquest into the death of Annie Chapman, at the Working Lads' Institute, Whitechapel Road.

Inquests were unusual in not having fixed buildings assigned to hold them in. In the main, meeting rooms were rented on an ad hoc basis, the size of which usually reflected the interest taken by the press and the general public into the death. By now the 'Whitechapel Murders' were creating quite a stir and the meeting room at the Working Lad's Institute - although capable of holding about sixty people – had nowhere near the capacity required to accommodate all those who wanted to attend the inquest into the latest murder victim, of the man, the locals had dubbed 'The Knife'.

Baxter was very much the showman. He loved holding

court over the inquests and was in the habit of wearing loud colourful waistcoats under his jackets. Inquests could take several days to complete, but even by the standards of the day, Coroner Baxter's were thought to run on the long side. That said, he was a devil for detail and would thoroughly interrogate all witnesses who took the stand.

Coroner Baxter started proceedings by calling the first witness, a Carman named John Davies, who was resident at 29 Hanbury Street along with his wife. Davies explained how he had discovered the body of the woman at 6am when he entered the yard at the back of the building. He went there to use the outside convenience before making his way to work. On discovering the body he ran into the street to get help and sought the assistance of two men who happened to be standing close to the entrance of the building. Davies said that the men returned to the yard with him and then all three of them raised the alarm.

Baxter asked Inspector Chandler if he had managed to ascertain the names of two men that Davies called to assist him with his gruesome find. Chandler explained that unfortunately he had not been able to do so because he was waylaid with other work. Baxter was not impressed with his first exchange with the Inspector.

Next up was a lady named Amelia Palmer. Mrs Palmer informed the court that she knew the deceased very well and had been on friendly terms with her for about five years. She added that she did not know of anyone holding a grievance against her friend. Mrs Palmer's testimony was followed by that of the deputy of the common lodging house at 35 Dorset Street, the last location that the dead woman was known to have resided in. The deputy, a man named Tim Donovan, informed the court that he had turned Annie Chapman out into the street at about 1.50am, on what turned out to be the morning of her death, because she did not have the necessary four pence to pay for a bed.

Coroner Baxter adjourned proceedings until

Wednesday 12th September in order to allow the police more time to make further inquiries into Chapman's death.

❧❧❧

Inspectors Moore and Andrews were already seated in the interview room when Pizer was brought in from his cell. Pizer was calm and controlled; a feat in itself considering the shouts heard from the crowd, of about 50 people now gathered outside of the station, calling for him to be lynched.

"You are John Pizer, the man known as Leather Apron?" asked Inspector Moore.

"I am, sir."

Moore continued, "We are investigating the murders of a number of women in the locality and are specifically interested in knowing where you were on the nights of 30-31 August and 7-8 September?"

"That's an easy question to answer," responded Pizer. "On the night of 30-31 August I stayed at a common lodging house in Holloway, at a place called the Round House, it's on the Holloway Road. I believe that's when the unfortunate, Polly Nichols, met her end. I heard it said in the newspapers that it was me that did it for her. I got scared for my life and wanted to return to the place I know best, being Whitechapel. But I was afraid to come back here, so I stayed a few nights in a lodgings house in Peter Street, in Westminster. Not feeling safe there, I returned to my family home on Thursday and have laid low there ever since."

"Can you prove what you say?"

"Yes, sir, if you check at the Round House, I am sure they will remember me there as I was in conversation with the deputy about the dock fire. Everyone was talking about being able to see the flames from where we were standing. As for my family; they are good people and will speak the truth when asked."

"So you are saying that on the night of 30th to 31st you were in Holloway and from the 6th until the 10th September you were resident in Mulberry Street?"

"That's what I have told you, sir."

Inspector Andrews left Moore to finish interrogating Pizer whilst he sent a telegram to Y-Division, in which he requested officers be sent to the Round House to check Pizer's story.

ŧ ŧ ŧ

Reid had only been back at work for one day and he already felt in need of another holiday. He was pleased that his order to the sergeant had resulted in Pizer's capture, but knew that the credit would ultimately go to Abberline. Not being able to concentrate on his work he decided to return home early. He informed the desk sergeant that he was going in search of suspects thought to be involved in gambling around the Spitalfields market area and left the station.

ŧ ŧ ŧ

Earlier the same morning, Inspector Abberline had been informed that a man named William Henry Piggott had been arrested in Gravesend on suspicion of being involved in the Whitechapel murders. The man had been in the Pope's Head public house, noisily expressing his hatred of women. That in itself would not have warranted Abberline dashing off to interview him, but soon after Piggott's arrest a package of his was found at local fish shop. On opening the package the police found a number of items of clothing including a torn, bloodstained, shirt. The officers then noticed that Piggott's hand was injured; he had a large deep bite mark on it. On further questioning

Piggott claimed that he had received the bite from a woman he'd encountered in the yard of a common lodgings house in Whitechapel. He went on to explain that he'd defended himself by punching the woman who'd bitten him; the altercation supposedly observed by two policemen before Piggott fled the scene.

Abberline had not seen a police report matching the incident described by Piggott, but was aware that the landlady of the Prince Albert public house had reported seeing a man in her establishment at 7am on Saturday morning with a torn, bloodstained, shirt. Abberline's gut instinct told him that this man might prove important to the case, and so decided that he himself should go to Gravesend to interview him.

None other than the local Superintendent, a man named Berry, met Abberline on his arrival at the Gravesend police station. Superintendent Berry informed Abberline that he had interviewed Piggott and that, in his opinion, the man was suffering from a form of homicidal mania. Abberline had Piggott moved into an interview room in the company of two constables, one standing either side of the suspect. He recorded into his notebook that Piggott was in his early 50s, with light-brown receding hair and a light-brown moustache; adding that the man had wild eyes and was in a very agitated condition.

"Be seated," instructed Abberline.

Piggott sat down and Abberline commenced his line of questioning.

"What is your name?"

"It's William Piggott, sir."

"Is that your full name?"

"No, sir, my name's William Henry Piggott."

"Do you know why you are here Mr Piggott?"

"Well, sir, I think it is to do with my causing a nuisance in a pub hereabouts."

"Tell me what happened."

"Well, I'm in great pain, you see," said Piggott showing Abberline his injured hand.

"That looks nasty Mr Piggott, it must be causing you some discomfort."

"Yes, sir. Well this woman, she bites me you see, for nothing. They are all the same ain't they? Anyways, I goes to a pub because of my great thirst after having walked 'ere from London, Whitechapel way. My hand's 'urtin and I start cursing the blooming woman for 'avin bitten me. Next thing I know I'm in here."

"You say you walked all the way from Whitechapel?"

"Yes, sir, I was staying in a lodging house you see and had to leave it sharpish on accounts of the whore that's bit me."

"You say a lady bit you?"

"Yes, sir, flaming whore it was, some sort of witch or something. I found her in the lodging house yard acting all peculiar, like she was having some sort of fit. So I goes over to help her like, and she bites me for me trouble. I gave her a wallop to fend her off, then I saw the rozzers and I made a run for it."

"You saw the policemen in the lodgings house yard?"

"No, I sees them in Brick Lane after I've hit the witch. Then I made a run for it on account of my being scared like. The pain's all bad you see? All them whores is the same, I'd smash 'em all."

Piggott started to get very agitated at that point and the two officers made ready to restrain him in case he tried to attack Abberline. Abberline, although aware that Piggott was deranged, wanted to know if the man was in Whitechapel at 7am when Mrs Fiddymont reported seeing a man of 'frightening appearance' in her pub.

"I see, Mr Piggott. Now tell me if you please, when did you set-off for Gravesend?"

"What do ya mean, sir?"

"Did you set-off after sun-up or maybe you decided to

wet your whistle before embarking on such a long journey?"

"I get your meanin', sir. I was still hiding like from the rozzers until sun-up, then I found myself a pub and had a drink before setting off."

"Do you remember the name of the pub that you drank in?"

"No, sir, one's much like another."

"Mr Piggott you have been most helpful but I'd be very grateful if you would accompany me back to London. You see, I'm working on a very important case and I think that you might be able to help me solve it."

"How do you mean, sir?"

"Well for a start, I'd like to be able to find the woman that bit you. It sounds to me like no man will be safe from attack until we apprehend her. What do you say?"

"Well, sir, it was not just her, I've seen many witches and they all need sorting."

"Well we need to start somewhere, so we could start by finding the lady that bit you. What do you say?"

"Okay, sir, that sounds good to me if it gets me out of here like."

"Yes, me, you, and a few of the officers from the station can take a trip to London to find the woman. I'm sure that we will all feel safer knowing that she has been taken off of the streets."

"That sounds grand, sir. I would be pleased to help clear the likes of her off the streets."

"I will go and make ready our arrangements. The officers here will look after you in my absence."

"Thank you, sir."

Abberline informed Superintendent Berry that he wanted to take Piggott back to London, by rail, on the next available train. He requested that two experienced officers be selected to accompany him on the journey. He made a point of adding that the Central Office at the Yard would reimburse all costs, and that he would personally inform CI Swanson of the insight and cooperation provided by Berry and his staff. Berry made the necessary arrangements and soon Abberline, Piggott, and their police escort set-off for London's Whitechapel.

Abberline made for the Commercial Street Police station on their arrival in London. Piggott's behaviour on the journey had been erratic and potentially violent, making Abberline feel glad that he had requested an escort. The longer he spent in Piggott's company the more he thought that he might have stumbled upon the Whitechapel murderer.

No further progress was made with Piggott that day. Abberline issued instructions for an identity parade to be arranged for 11am the next morning, with Mrs Fiddymont and other eye witnesses from the Prince Albert pub in attendance.

⸸⸸⸸

Reid walked slowly through the streets of Whitechapel. All about him were downtrodden people living in decrepit housing blocks. For his part, he felt much like his surroundings. He didn't want to go home in such a state of melancholy, so he decided he'd venture into one of the numerous public houses to have a drink and spend a little time thinking about the hand that life had dealt him. He then noticed that he was close to Hanbury Street and the Prince Albert public house. The pub in which the landlady had reported seeing the wild-eyed man on the morning of the Chapman murder. He entered the pub, ordered himself a pint of ale, and sat in a corner observing the other patrons of the establishment. Numerous conversations made mention of 'The Knife' being seen in the pub but his being too fierce to tackle. Then all went quiet as two constables entered the pub and requested to speak with Mrs

Fiddymont. Reid heard them inform her that a man was being held in custody and that a Detective Inspector Abberline, of Scotland Yard, required her presence at an identification parade to be held the next morning. Reid felt like ordering himself another drink, something a little stronger than ale, but he thought better of it and decided to return home to Emily and the children.

When Reid got home he told his wife all that had happened. Emily took the view that their family, although far from well-off, were able to live comfortably on her husband's income. Also being a Detective Inspector provided secure employment. So, even if her husband's future prospects of promotion now seemed remote, she was content with what they had. Emily was pleased to hear that the authorities were taking the Whitechapel murders so seriously. As a mother with a young daughter she wanted the culprit or culprits brought to book as soon as possible, even to the detriment of her husband's personal ambitions.

ϕ ϕ ϕ

At 8pm that same evening, 16 men met in the Crown public house, 74 Mile End Road, off the corner of Jubilee Street. The men were a mixture of Spitalfields and Whitechapel tradesmen, most being of the Jewish faith. They had decided to meet with the intention of forming a committee, the purpose of which was to assist in the apprehension of the Whitechapel murderer or murderers. Their main concerns were as follows: firstly, a maniac or maniacs were wandering their local streets slaughtering women; secondly, the police appeared to be making no progress in their investigations; and thirdly, they were becoming aware of increasingly anti-Jewish feeling in the east end as rumours were rife that the killer was a Jew. The lead man in the group was named George Lusk. Lusk was a large, well-built man with fair hair and a light brown moustache; he was a builder by trade and lived in the Alderney Road, Mile End. At the end of their first formal meeting the committee had agreed to: naming itself the 'Whitechapel Vigilance Committee', had elected Lusk as its chairman, and elected a man named Joseph Aarons as its secretary and treasurer. Its primary aim being to get the authorities to sanction a reward for the capture of the murderer or murderers. The committee had also decided to put up its own funds for a reward and it was agreed that fund raising measures would be enacted in due course. They also agreed on the wording of a notice to be issued the next day, informing people of the committee's creation, and offering a reward for information leading to the bringing of the murderer or murderers to justice. The notice also stated that the committee - from then on until further notice - intended to meet at the Crown public house at 9pm every evening and would be pleased to receive the assistance of residents of the district. The WVC was not the only vigilance committee to be established in response to the murders, but it was to play an unexpected part in the ensuing mystery.

CHAPTER THREE

Profile of a Serial Killer

REID DID NOT SLEEP WELL and had trouble rising for work on Tuesday 11th September. The only silver lining in the dark cloud that had descended upon him was that, if he was not investigating the Chapman murder, he was not obliged to report to Abberline. Reid normally made his own arrangements for breakfast, what with his working unusual hours, but that morning Emily tried to bolster his spirits by cooking him a hearty breakfast. Reid wasn't particularly hungry but ate all that Emily had prepared as he did not want to hurt her feelings. He then made his way into work.

On arrival at the station, Sergeant Thick informed Reid that Abberline was already in the building and holding a meeting with Inspector Chandler. Reid asked the sergeant if he was aware of any new intelligence relating to his fraud case and went on to inform him that he was going to start investigations into two new cases. The first, relating to illegal gambling around the Spitalfields market; the second, to a premises supposedly being used to create and distribute pornographic materials. The sergeant informed Reid that his own priorities over the next few days lay with the Whitechapel murders and helping Abberline and the other Inspectors from the Yard with their inquiries, but promised to pass-on any intelligence he might receive relating to Reid's cases. Reid went to his desk and began reading the reports into his new cases. About an hour later he felt the presence of somebody standing behind him.

"Good morning, Inspector. I'd be grateful if you can spare me the time to go through your inquiries into the Smith and Tabram murders?" asked Inspector Abberline.

Reid was tempted to tell Abberline that he was too busy to see him, but thought better of it.

"Good morning, sir. Yes, I have time now if you would like an immediate meeting?"

"Excellent Reid, please see me in meeting room A in five minutes."

Reid had read all his notes the day before and knew the detail inside out. He decided to freshen-up in the outside convenience before his meeting. He then collected-up his notebook and went to see Abberline as requested.

❧❧❧

At the same time that Reid was meeting with Abberline, two men, Joshua Engels and Levi Greenfield, entered 24 Finch Street. The house had previously belonged to a short line of silk weavers and their families, the rooms having large windows that allowed a lot of natural light into the building. An abundance of natural light had been a necessary requirement of the silk weaving trade. That industry had collapsed as a result of foreign competition and the Government's policy of free trade, now a more lucrative business was being conducted on the premises. The new business also required a lot of natural light; the photographic plates needing light in order to produce the most visually pleasing images. However, Engels was not your common all gardener photographer. No, Engels specialised in poses of the human form, as Engels was a pornographer.

Both men could be described as being 'Jewish' in appearance, meaning that they were dark skinned, had very dark hair and Jewish facial features. Engels was the taller of the two, being about 5 feet 11 inches in height but he possessed a skinny, weak, body and weighed about 10 stones. In contrast, Greenfield was a powerfully built man, standing about 5 feet 9 inches in height, weighing-in at about 13 and half stone, all of which was solid muscle. Engels had inherited money and the property he lived in from his family, who had been in the silk weaving industry when times were good. However, over the years the property had fallen into disrepair, as Engels never seemed to find sufficient funds with which to maintain it. As for Greenfield, his family came to England when he was a young boy, they had been peasant farmers back his native Poland and had struggled to make ends meet in London.

Engels had just returned from one of his more lucrative transactions. He'd just sold ten photographs, at a pound apiece, to a new west end client. Engels not wanting to take any chances on being robbed had gone straight to the bank to deposit seven of the ten pounds notes that he had received that morning. He employed Greenfield as his fixer. Greenfield first and foremost provided Engels with physical protection, but he could also be relied upon to find photographic models and help deal with the day-to-day administrative tasks relating to the running the business. That morning Greenfield had been required to provide him with security, as Engels wanted to ensure that his client would pay for the photographs and then wanted to deposit his money at the bank without the risk of being molested on the way.

"A good morning's work, Greenfield. I have no further need of your services today. I trust all is in readiness for tomorrow?" asked Engels.

"Yes, sir. I am meeting the models at the Ten Bells and we will be with you by 11am as instructed."

"Excellent, Greenfield. Please remember that the models are fine in wetting their whistles, but I expect them to be clear-eyed for the photographic session…" Engels paused and then continued. "and I trust that they have made arrangements for our younger models?"

"Rest assured, sir. All has been arranged as you instructed."

"In that case I will see you tomorrow."

Greenfield let himself out of the building and disappeared into the crowded east end streets. As for Engels, he decided to make ready for the next day's photo shoot, double-checking his photographic materials. Once sure that all was in order and with a good day's work behind him, he headed into the city to purchase himself a decent lunch.

❦❦❦

Greenfield was quite the entrepreneur. His work for Mr Engels, although lucrative, allowed him quite a bit of free time and he made use of it wisely. In his spare time Greenfield bred fighting dogs and had recently become involved in illegal dogfights around the Spitalfields market area. Greenfield always marvelled that no matter how poor a neighbourhood was, men always seem to find the money to service their base needs, which he thought consisted of alcohol, sex and gambling. He now had his fingers in two of these three pies. Whitechapel and the surrounding area had more than its fair share of public houses, so short of buying a pub, he could not think of any way of making inroads into the market for alcohol. He had hopes of selling drinks at the dogfights, but he was a patient man and knew that the time was not right for him to do that, as he didn't have the muscle required for a turf war. He had been very fortunate with gambling, a police crackdown had resulted in the previous controllers of the business either going to prison or moving onto pastures new. So no one had had any problem with his providing a few fighting dogs to the new controllers of the gaming events. Greenfield was heavily involved in dogfights being arranged for the coming weekend and he went off to a pub, to literally see a man about a dog.

❦❦❦

Also meeting that day were the Home Secretary, Sir Henry Matthews, and the Commissioner of the Metropolitan Police, Sir Charles Warren. Warren was a tall man, standing at about 6 feet 1. He was every inch a military man, standing straight, his movements crisp and sharp. He had dark brown hair and a large dark brown moustache to match. He had been waiting in the Home Secretary's outer office for over half an hour but had refused the invitation of Sir Henry's staff to take a seat. Warren was an ex-army general and had been brought into the Met to instill some military discipline into the men of the force. However, being from a military background, he was not inclined to treat any occurrences of public disorder with kid gloves and fully endorsed his men wading into crowds with their truncheons drawn. However, his was a thankless task. If he had been too soft on demonstrators the press would have labelled him as 'weak', however, by dealing with matters as he saw them 'firmly but fairly', he had been labelled by some of the left leaning newspapers, such as The Star, as an 'enemy of democracy'.

Eventually he was called into the Secretary of State's office. Warren entered the room and as usual found Matthews seated behind a large mahogany desk. Seated at a small table to his left was a young man in his late twenties, whom Warren assumed to be a Home Office aid. Unusually, there was another man in the room, a middle-aged gentleman who had the appearance of a military man, but the shabby manner of his dress did not befit a man of the officer class. As for Matthews, he was also a tall man, but of slight stature. He had brown wavy hair and unusually, for the times in which they lived, he was clean shaven with no hint of any whiskers.

"Take a seat, Sir Charles."

"Thank you, sir," replied the Commissioner.

"Have you any progress to report on the murder investigation?"

"Yes sir, the man named by the press as 'Leather Apron' was apprehended yesterday and there is another promising suspect in custody, but we have nothing conclusive at this time. I have set-up a special unit under the direction of Chief Inspector Swanson, with three Inspectors overseeing the work of the Met's local divisional Inspectors -."

"One of your Inspectors is Abberline?" interrupted the Home Secretary.

"Yes, sir. His involvement in the case is already paying dividends."

"That is good to hear. However, intelligence has been received indicating that Abberline's involvement may come at a cost to us."

"What do you mean by that, sir?"

"The Secret Department are of the opinion that the Fenians may be inclined to have their people withhold information from any police unit including Abberline. They have not forgotten his involvement in the arrest and prosecution of the men responsible for planting the bomb that exploded in the Tower of London back in January of 85. However, I am of the opinion that we are better to include him in proceedings at this stage. His local knowledge and contacts being far more likely to outweigh the costs of any IRB organised resistance."

"Yes, sir," said Warren looking over at the man sharing the desk with Sir Henry's aid. He was in no doubt that the man belonged to the Secret Department. Warren's experience told him that the man was someone who gave the appearance of looking at nothing in particular but observed everything about him. For what it was worth, Warren agreed with the department's assessment of the situation. "Swanson is reporting to me tomorrow at 1pm, in good time for our afternoon meeting."

"Excellent, Sir Charles. I hope that your men are able to shine some much needed light on this murky business."

"Thank you, sir."

With that Warren got up from his chair and left the room, leaving the Secretary of State to continue his meeting with the man from the Secret Department.

ççç

One of Sir Charles' first actions when taking over as Met Commissioner, had been to instigate a recruitment campaign with an unofficial height restriction of 5 feet 9 inches, one inch taller than the Met minimum of 5 feet 8. This policy had ensured three things: firstly, that the new recruits had a greater physical presence on the streets; secondly, that most of them were from the countryside, where the quality of food was better, allowing for better growth; and thirdly, that there was a detachment between the politically 'right leaning' new recruits and the more 'socialist' orientated city dwellers. An unintended consequence of Warren's policy was that although the new recruits could be moulded along military lines, a lot of them were not very streetwise and lacked the street smarts required to deal with the local villains inhabiting the rookeries. A relatively small man, like Inspector Reid, would never have been accepted onto the force during Warren's tenure, no matter what other qualities he might bring to the job.

ççç

Reid, although still smarting at his exclusion from the newly formed 'Whitechapel Murder Squad' was now beginning to settle into his caseload. An informant had provided one of the sergeants with the names of two men thought to be responsible for uttering counterfeit money.

The men's names were Harris Marks and Harry Clements aka Mad Sailor Harry. Reid had never heard of Marks but Mad Sailor Harry was a name that he knew well. He had investigated a murder that had taken place close to the Ten Bells public house at the end of 1887. A Spitalfields market worker had gotten into an argument with a dockside labourer inside the pub and the dispute had been settled outside on the street. To all intents and purposes the cause of the man's death was his hitting his head on a kerbstone. Eyewitness accounts originally pointed to Clements being the murderer, but all the witnesses were sailors and they set sail from the London Docks before the Inspector was able to amass a compelling case against him. Reid knew that Clements was not a Whitechapel regular, but he was known to gamble in the locality of the Spitalfields market. He had an inkling of where he might find the man and planned to seek him out later that afternoon. In the meantime he could not get his mind off the Chapman murder. There was no sign of Sergeant Thick, but another sergeant, Leach, was manning the reception.

"Sergeant!" called out Reid.

"How can I help you, sir?"

"Where can the doctor's report into the Chapman murder be found?"

"All the information is on Inspector Chandler's desk, but he is not in the station at present."

"Thank you, sergeant, that will be all," said Reid before walking over to Chandler's desk. The desk was covered in files, but one caught Reid's eye, it was labelled 'Chapman'. Reid quickly found the document he was looking for, a report by the divisional surgeon, George Baxter Phillips. He scanned the pages, picking out the doctor's main observations which read as follows: 'I found the body of the deceased lying in the yard on her back... The left arm was across the left breast, and the legs were drawn up, the feet resting on the ground, and the knees turned outwards.

The face was swollen and turned to the right side, and the tongue protruded between the front teeth, but not beyond the lips; it was much swollen. The small intestines and other portions were lying on the right side of the body on the ground above the right shoulder… The throat was disserved deeply. I noticed that the incision of the skin was jagged, and reached round around the neck… There was an abrasion over the bend of the first joint of the ring finger, and there were distinct markings of a ring or rings – probably the latter.' It appeared to Reid that the victim had been despatched by first being strangled, then, possibly before her death, having her throat cut. After her death, the killer mutilated the lady's body and removed some of her body parts and a few rings from her fingers.

Reid compared the details of Chapman's murder to the earlier ones. The murder of Emma Smith did, in all probability, appear to be the work of a gang. He thought that the fatal injury, the insertion of a blunt object into her passage, although hideous, was not likely to have been intended to cause death. There was no disputing that Martha Tabram had deliberately been killed, having been stabbed 39 times, but there was evidence that she had been strangled before being stabbed. As for Mary Ann Nichols, J-Division's case, she too may have been strangled, her throat cut before the mutilation of her lower body. None of her body parts had been removed, but it was thought that the killer might also have taken rings from her fingers.

Reid tried to think of a motive for the murders. There were too many of them to be related to the usual quarrels between man and wife or a jealous lover. Such savage murders were also very unlikely to have been committed for profit, as the dead women were unlikely to have had much more than their four pence doss money. However, the killer took away some of the dead women's possessions: their rings and parts of their bodies. The Inspector had been involved in a few murder investigations in his time but he had no benchmark with which to compare these murders to. He knew that without a motive he had no foundation on which to build a case. He was left with eyewitness descriptions of suspects seen in the locality on or around the estimated times of death, but none of these descriptions was specific enough. He reasoned that logic alone was not going to be enough to solve this case. He decided to pay Dr Phillips a visit whilst walking the streets in search of Harry Clements.

Reid was in luck, Dr Phillips was at home and able to spare him some time for a meeting. He was shown into the doctor's study, two of its four walls covered by bookcases filled with what looked to be well-thumbed books.

Dr Phillips was a very clever man, he was descended from a long line of doctors, and had bright intelligent looking blue eyes that sparkled in the light. The doctor was fascinated by the workings of the human body and never failed to find the gruesome task of performing autopsies interesting. He had recently turned his attention to thought processes of the human mind and had spent many an hour discussing mental health issues with his peers in the field of psychiatry.

"How can I help you, Inspector?" enquired Dr Phillips.

"Well, sir, before we start, I wish to make clear to you that I am not currently an investigating officer in the Annie Chapman murder. But I would be very grateful if you could provide me with your thoughts on the type of man responsible for her death and the other murders recently committed in the east end?"

"Very well, Inspector. At the risk of some duplication, I am happy to provide you with my thoughts on this matter. But before we start, would you like a cup of tea?"

"No, thank you, sir."

"Now please bear in mind that one man's views on a subject may not bestow greater insight than any others.

However, as you should already be aware the perpetrator's motive does not appear to be robbery and he does not appear to have any emotional attachment to the women. His motive appears to be the need to kill for killing's sake and he is likely gaining some level of satisfaction from the physical act of murder. Now Inspector, you are a man famed for exploits in air balloons are you not?"

"Yes doctor, but what has that to do with a case like this?"

"Well, Inspector, how did you feel when making your record ascents into the heavens?"

"Not that I appreciate the relevance, but I found them a wondrous experience."

"I believe that in recognition of your great achievements you were presented with medals, were you not?"

"That is correct, sir, but with all due respect where is this leading?"

"Tell me, Inspector, have you handled your medals since your courageous endeavours?"

"Yes, I have."

"What were your emotions upon holding and looking at the medals?"

"Well, thinking about it, I'd say that when handling my medals I started to relive the experiences in my mind. All the sense of pride and excitement returned back to me," said Reid, finally understanding what the doctor was alluding to. That the killer's feelings toward the act of murder were likely to be similar to those that he himself felt towards his hobbies of ballooning and parachute jumping. There were no medals to be won for the slaughter of innocent women, so the killer would need to collect his own trophies - the dead women's possessions, their rings and parts of their bodies. At that moment his eyes lit up like the doctors.

"I can see that we are now on the same page,

Inspector," commented the doctor.

"So, what you are saying is that the man might kill for satisfaction and that he takes trophies to relive the events?"

"Well, that's my theory. Unfortunately, it sheds no light on how he chooses his victims. You might have noticed that the physical acts are evolving. At first, the sheer act of murder was sufficient to appease his bloodlust, but now the act of murder appears to be playing a secondary role to the evisceration of the victims' bodies."

Reid was pleased, he thought that he finally had a handle on the mentality of the murderer. "So returning to the ballooning analogy. I achieved a great sense of satisfaction from my early balloon ascents but then I moved onto parachute jumping, an experience that provides far greater excitement and joy to me. So the act of evisceration could be the key to unlocking the mind of this madman?"

"Yes, Inspector, we may well be dealing with a man with pretentions of being a surgeon. He might possibly be a failed medical student."

"Tell me, doctor, have you shared your thoughts with any of my colleagues?"

"No, Inspector. No one has asked and I did not think it proper to propose a theory that has absolutely no basis on fact."

"Thank you very much for your time and your views on the matter. Finally, doctor, before I let you get back to your business, in your view, what might have triggered the first murder?"

"That is a good question Inspector and is one that has many possible answers."

"That might be so, but grateful to you if you can provide me with your thoughts on the matter."

"Returning to your hobby of ballooning, if I may? I trust that you first became aware of the activity during a conversation or by reading about it in a newspaper. Then, once the seed was implanted in your mind, you started to give more and more thought to making your own ascent."

"So what you are saying is that our murderer may have harbored feelings of murder over a period of time, possibly following and attacking other women before going on to commit his first murder?"

"Yes, Inspector. However, it is likely that his first attack on a woman would have resulted in his murdering her. If our killer attacked a woman who knew him personally, even if he had not intended to kill her, he would no doubt have been aware that she would report the attack to the police. So he might have felt that he had no other choice other than to kill his first victim to ensure her silence, no matter what his original motive might have been. More than this I cannot say, I have already delved too deeply into the realms of fantasy."

"Would it be possible for me to spend some time mulling over what you have told me and speak with you again about the case?"

"I should really dismiss such a suggestion out of hand, Inspector. However, I have an ill feeling that this matter will not soon be ended. So unfortunately, we may yet have ample opportunity to discuss this and other possible theories. So yes, feel free to contact me again."

The Inspector left the doctor's house and started making his way to the docks. The doctor's theory seemed plausible enough to him, but did not explain why any man would enjoy murdering a fellow human being and it did not shed any light on the preferred method of murder. Reid thought that identification of the first murder victim might provide a way into the mind of the killer. He decided that the murder of Emma Smith could be ignored; so was Tabram, Nichols or even another woman the first victim? He was in agreement with Dr Phillips that there would be other murders. He knew Inspector Chandler to be a good man but didn't think that he was up to the job in hand. He thought the man too sloppy and that he left too many loose ends. However, Abberline had chosen Chandler over him, so he would let them get on with it for now.

❦❦❦

At 11am Sergeant Thick had seventeen men lined-up in the Commercial Street Police station ready to be viewed by Mrs Fiddymont and the other witnesses from the Prince Albert public house. All the men in the line-up had their hands behind their backs, but one of their number was wearing handcuffs. That man was William Henry Piggott.

"Mrs Fiddymont, if you would like to go first," said Abberline. "Now remember to take your time. If you don't recognize the man with the torn shirt and bloodstained hands, who took a drink in your public house on the morning of the 8th September the first time around, please feel free to walk back along the line. If you see the man, please stop and point at him."

Piggott stood out from others as he was constantly fidgeting and muttering under his breath, but to Abberline's disappointment Mrs Fiddymont walked the line and failed to pick anybody out. The other witnesses went along the line and only one of them, a Mrs Chappell, identified Piggott as 'possibly' being the man that she saw in the pub, but she would not swear to it.

Abberline thanked the witnesses for their time and then ordered that Piggott be detained in the Whitechapel Union Infirmary pending further inquiries. He also worded a telegram to CI Swanson to inform him that, unfortunately, Piggott was not likely to be the man they sought.

❦❦❦

Reid had by now visited a number of public houses but Clements was nowhere to be seen. He then noticed one of his informants leaving the Princess Alice pub and decided to tap him for some information. Michael Riley didn't see the Inspector as he left the pub, he'd been there to discuss arrangements for illegal dogfights planned for the coming weekend.

Reid didn't challenge Riley until they were well out of sight of the pub. "Stand firm, Mr Riley, I would like a word with you," he ordered.

Riley immediately recognised the dulcet tones of Inspector Reid. He was tempted to make a run for it but thought better of it. The last time he'd tried that he'd been chased down by Reid's attack dog, Johnny Upright, and received a bit of a hiding. "What can I do ya for Inspector?" he asked.

"I'd welcome some information concerning the whereabouts of a man known as Mad Sailor Harry."

Riley thought that this was one of the Inspector's ploys, as Reid only spoke to him when he was well into a case and already knew most of the facts relating to it.

"Okay, Inspector, times is 'ard and we all got ta make a living. I'm just trying to earn a crust to keep a roof over me head."

"Look, Riley, you know how things work, the police can turn a blind eye to a certain level of villainy but when you people start to take liberties we have no choice but to intervene," said Reid, not having the faintest idea what Riley was referring. He hope to make the man sweat a little before disclosing his hand.

"You know me, Inspector, I'm small fry, I don't go making any arrangements. I'm just advertising, if you like."

"No, I don't like," responded Reid. "Maybe you will be a bit more forthcoming down at the station?"

"Look, Inspector, it's like I says. I just lets the men know what's happening. I helps out a bit on the night, looking out for the rozzers, but I ain't done no planning."

"So what's Mad Sailor Harry got to do with all this?"

"He's just a punter, but he's been betting big like. No one knows where he's getting his dosh from. He's flush with sovereigns and there's men planning to rob him."

"When's the next event planned for?"

"Come on, Inspector, you already know the crack? There's two of them, one this Friday night and the other on Saturday."

As Reid understood it, Riley was putting the word out to men in the local pubs that two gambling events were being held over the coming weekend. Clements seemed to be regarded as a big hitter but was unlikely to have been able to finance any substantial bets with legal tender. Reid could not envisage a man like Harry Clements ever having much in the way of ready cash. He concluded that Clements was betting with snide, fake money. If that was the case, the quality of the forgeries must have been very good. As the money handlers at betting events were experts in the identification of legal tender.

"So when is the Mad Sailor expected to come up from the docks?" asked the Inspector.

"He won't be round these parts till Friday. Most likes, he'll be drinking in the Ten Bells. That being his regular when he's around here."

"Who's planning on robbing him?"

"Sorry, Inspector, I don't know now't about that. All I know is that somebody's out to rob him."

"Now, Riley, since you've been so helpful in this matter, so I'm going to do you a favour. Tell me when and where these events are being held and you'll earn yourself a half crown and your freedom."

"They are both taking place in Spratt Alley off George Yard at 8pm. They're going to dig a pit for it on Friday morning."

"Alright, Riley. You be sure to keep away from the Ten Bells and George Yard this weekend. Else we'll be forced into taking you into custody with the rest of them."

"Can't do that Inspector. If I don't show and the rozzers do, it will look all suspicious like, if you gets me meaning? I has to be there."

"Alright, Riley, my men will let you escape, but you need to wear something distinctive so they will be able to identify you."

"What do ya mean by that?"

"Could you wear a red neckerchief, so they know who to lookout for?"

"I gets ya meaning, I'll get myself one…" said Riley pausing. Reid sensed that the man wanted to tell him something, something serious but not related to gambling or street robbery.

"What is it, Riley?"

"Inspector, there's something that I can tell ya for nothing. I knows you been looking into the murders like and well words got round that we ain't to tell ya nought about it, if ya gets me meaning?"

"I don't understand what you are referring to. Come on, out with it, man!"

"The murders like. Our boys back home in the Emerald Isle says we ain't to tell ya nothing what we knows. There'll be a punishment in it for those that do. None of the unfortunates will be telling ya truths; they been told to spin ya a yarn like."

Reid wasn't certain that he understood what Riley was telling him as the man seemed to speak in nothing but riddles. However, there was a lady killer loose on the streets of Whitechapel and if he understood Riley correctly, the Irish community were being instructed to withhold information from the police. Reid decided not to pursue the matter as his interest lay in illegal gambling and fraud, but he wondered if Abberline, Chandler or anyone else back at the station was aware of what Riley had just told him. He gave Riley a half crown for his trouble and decided to return to the station to update his notebook before returning home for the day.

❧❧❧

Abberline had had a long day and was just about to head off home as a telegram was received at the station. The telegram was from the Central Office of the Scotland Yard, who were forwarding a report received from Detective Inspector John Styles of Y-Division, Holloway. The report stated that a Dr Crabb had visited the Holloway station house at 11pm on Monday night to report his suspicions about a man lodging at 60 Milford Road, who he thought might be the Whitechapel Murderer. The man's name was Joseph Isenschmid and he was reported as leaving his lodgings at 1am every morning and not returning until 9pm each evening. Styles informed that Isenschmid had recently separated from his wife and was in the habit of carrying large butchers' knifes. Styles added that he took this information seriously and had directed one of his officers, PC Cracknell, to keep Isenschmid's lodgings under observation.

Abberline looked around the station for someone to send to Holloway. Inspector Chandler was nowhere to be seen and the only other man that Abberline trusted to provide him with a thorough assessment of the situation was Sergeant Thick.

"Sergeant!"

"Yes, sir, what can I do for you?"

"Are you able to go immediately to Holloway? I need someone to go there to gather intelligence on a man that might prove to be a very good suspect in our case."

"Yes, sir, I can do, as long as you are fine with my popping home first to inform my wife."

"Yes, sergeant, that will be fine. I will have a telegram sent to Holloway letting them know to expect you. The suspect's name is Joseph Isenschmid. Officers have already interviewed his wife but I'd grateful if you can re-interview her. By all accounts she has not seen her husband in over two months and I am keen to know how dangerous she thinks he might be. Be sure to make a record of the man's mental state."

"Yes, sir, I will find out all that I can. I will see you at the Working Men's Institute tomorrow morning for the Chapman inquest."

Abberline had forgotten that the sergeant was also required to attend the inquest session being held under the authority of Coroner Baxter. He felt bad in insisting that the sergeant go to Holloway but he had no one else at his disposal.

Sergeant Thick was met at the Holloway Road Police station at 6pm by Detective Inspector Styles.

"Hello, sergeant. Inspector Abberline's telegram said that we should expect you," said the DI by way of a greeting.

"Good evening, sir. I'm hoping that you can provide me with details of Isenschmid's antecedents? I am hoping to be able to interview the man's wife and inspect his lodgings before returning back to Leman Street."

DI Styles went on to inform the sergeant that Isenschmid was Swiss in origin, a butcher by trade and had a history of mental illness. Their meeting was disturbed by a commotion in the station reception. A man was screaming at the top of his voice. Shouting words in several languages, none of them English.

Sergeant Thick entered the reception to see a wild-eyed red haired man being dragged along the ground by four constables. The man was of slim build and only about 5 feet 8 inches in height, but it was clear to Thick that it was taking every ounce of strength the PCs possessed to drag the man across the room. Finally, after a fierce struggle, the PCs managed to get the man into a cell.

One of the constables reported to DI Styles that the man, thought to be Isenschmid, had been picked-up after returning to his lodgings. The man had a bag with him containing three large bloodstained butcher's knifes and was thought to be deranged. His having tried to resist all the officers' efforts to get him to the station.

Sergeant Thick asked if the man could be restrained in order that he could take a closer look at him. He hoped to inspect the man's clothes for bloodstains and for any tears and rips that might indicate that he had been in a struggle with a woman. He was surprised to find that in spite of his frenzied struggle with the constables, Isenschmid's clothes were quite clean with no obvious signs of blood. Also, the man had no scratches on his face, hands or neck. There were no obvious signs that he had been in any sort of a struggle with a woman. As for the knives found in his bag. They were large, sharp and stained with blood, but there was nothing to suggest that they had been used to assault a woman or women. However, one thing was very clear to the sergeant. The man before his eyes was definitely a lunatic and that even a tall, powerfully built man, such as himself, would not have been keen to tackle Isenschmid, alone, in one of London's ill-lit back alleys.

As per Abberline's instructions, Sergeant Thick found and interviewed Mrs Isenschmid before searching Isenschmid's lodgings for clues.

CHAPTER FOUR

Suffer Little Children

ON THE MORNING of Wednesday 12th September Abberline, Inspector Chandler and Sergeant Thick arrived early at the Working Men's Institute where the second session of the Chapman inquest was to be held. Inspector Helson of J-Division arrived shortly after them.

"Sergeant, what is your assessment of the suspect Isenschmid?" asked Abberline, eager to know what his sergeant had discovered about the new suspect.

"He has the look and manner of a madman. I could easily imagine him being responsible for the gruesome acts."

"Did you check his clothing and possessions?"

"Yes, sir. I was somewhat surprised by the absence of blood on his clothing, especially considering his trade. However, he was in possession of three large bloodstained butcher's knives."

"What makes you think that this man could be our murderer?"

"He is clearly mad and highly aggressive. Let me put it this way, sir. I myself would not want to meet such a man, alone, in a poorly lit alleyway. He is not large in stature, but he is very strong. I could not imagine a lady being able to put up much of a fight against him."

"Were you able to interview his wife?"

"Yes, sir. She informed me that she had not seen him for two months. She felt that he was capable of murder, but said that he would likely murder her first before any other woman. She added that he had been committed to an asylum at the end of last year."

"Will Y-Division allow us to transfer the man to

Commercial Street for an identity parade?"

"I am afraid that there might be a problem with that, sir."

"What do you mean?"

"A doctor attended him and recommended that he be transferred to an infirmary or asylum. He was saying something about him being not mentally stable enough to undergo interview or any other such process. I left this matter in the hands of DI Styles. He said that he would send you a telegram with full details of the doctor's medical assessment."

"Very good, sergeant. With luck the assessment will be waiting for us back at the station."

"Chandler, tell me, who are the main witnesses today?" asked Abberline, the detail relating to the new suspect dealt with.

"John Pizer, the Leather Apron, is being allowed to speak in order to prove his innocence to the press and mob. Most of the others are residents of 29 Hanbury Street. Also in attendance will be the local workmen called into the yard by John Davies, the man who discovered the body. The key witness is a gentleman by the name of John Richardson, a Spitalfields market porter whose mother lives and runs her business from the building."

"Why is Richardson of interest again?" asked Abberline.

"He looked into yard where the murder was committed on his way to work at approximately 4.45am. He went there to check that the cellar door was secured and had not been broken into. He will say that he did not see Chapman's body at the foot of the steps at that time. My opinion is that his evidence is of little value as it was still quite dark at 4.45am and the door to the yard opens outwards, so Richardson would not have been able to see a body from where he was stood."

"You are certain of this?"

"Absolutely, sir. I arrived at the scene at 6.10am and spoke to him within 30 minutes of my arrival."

"Excellent. Well gentlemen, it looks as if we are to have a wasted morning but make the most of your rest as we have another busy day ahead of us."

"Yes, sir," replied Chandler and Helson in unison.

Coroner Baxter started proceedings and called-up various witnesses who all explained how they had been made aware of the murder. Eventually John Richardson was called upon to give his evidence. He made his oath and started describing the events of early Saturday morning.

"I assist my mother in her business you see? I went to 29 Hanbury Street between 4.45am and 4.50am on Saturday last. I went to see if the cellar door was secure, as some while ago there was a robbery, some tools were taken. I have been accustomed to going there on market mornings since the time when the cellar was broken in."

"Was the front door open?" asked Baxter.

"No, it was closed. I lifted the latch and went through the passage to the yard door."

"Did you go into the yard?"

"No, the yard door was shut. I opened it and sat on the doorstep and cut a piece of leather off my boot with an old table-knife. The knife is about five inches long, I usually keep it upstairs at John Street. I had been feeding a rabbit with a carrot that I had cut up and placed it inside my pocket. I do not usually carry it there. After cutting the leather off my boot, I tied it up and went out of the house and onto the market. I did not close the back door. It closed itself. I shut the front door."

"How long were you there?"

"About two or three minutes at most."

"Was it light?"

"It was getting light but I could see all over the place."

"Did you notice whether there was any object outside?"

"I could not have failed to notice the deceased had she

been lying there then. I saw the body two or three minutes before the doctor came. I was then in the adjoining yard. Thomas Pierman had told me about the murder when I was in the market. When I was on the doorstep I saw that the padlock on the cellar door was in its proper place."

"Did you sit on the top step?"

"No, on the middle step, my feet were on the flags of the yard."

"You must have been quite close to where the deceased was found?"

"Yes, I must have seen her."

Inspector Chandler did not listen to the rest of the exchange. He could not believe his ears as Richardson had contradicted the statement he'd recorded in his official report. He knew that after the session was over he would have some explaining to do to Abberline.

Eventually, John Pizer was called to the stand. He was able to confirm that he was otherwise known as Leather Apron. He denied any wrongdoing and claimed that he had alibis for his whereabouts on the nights/mornings of both the Nichols and Chapman murders.

Next up was Sergeant Thick, who stated that he was Pizer's arresting officer, adding that Pizer's whereabouts had been verified and that he had been released from custody without charge. All this appeared to be a great disappointment to the members of the press and the mob in the hall, but was hopefully enough to save a lynch mob from trying to take the law into their own hands.

John Richardson was recalled to the stand, he had been allowed to go home and collect the knife that he said he used to cut the leather strap off his boot. Having shown the court that the knife was unsuitable to have been used to commit the murder he was allowed to stand down.

Coroner Baxter then adjourned proceedings until the next day and informed Inspector Chandler that he would definitely be required to give evidence to the court at the next session. In addition to Chandler, the common lodging house deputy, Tim Donovan, the man responsible for turning Annie Chapman out into the street on the morning of her murder, would also be called to the stand.

As the hall emptied out Abberline instructed his men to remain seated.

"What just happened here, Inspector?" asked Abberline.

"I do not know, sir. I spoke with Richardson within an hour of Chapman's body being found and he was adamant that he did not enter the yard," replied an embarrassed Inspector Chandler.

"He no doubt also made no mention of carrying a large knife upon his person?"

"Em. Well er, em, no sir."

"We are lucky that Baxter has spared us great embarrassment today. He is obviously aware of the implications of what could have happened if he had taken issue with the man's evidence in front of so many members of the press."

"Yes, sir," replied Chandler.

"Anyone can make a mistake, Inspector, but from now on can you please be sure of your facts when interviewing key witnesses. I know that we are all under great pressure and things are most likely going to get worse before they get better. But if you are in any doubt as to the facts in hand, please make me aware and we will have them rechecked, no matter what the delay to proceedings. This applies to you too Inspector Helson. Now gentleman, have I made myself clear?"

"Yes, sir," replied the men in unison.

Abberline dismissed his men and went off to see if he could have a private word with Coroner Baxter. He was beginning to wonder if a mistake had been made in removing Inspector Reid from the case but there wasn't much he could do about it at the present time.

❦❦❦

It was close to 11am when Greenfield arrived at 24 Finch Street. With him were what looked like a very down at heel family consisting of a man, a woman and two children. The children were aged between ten and twelve and the adults must have been in their mid-twenties. Greenfield escorted them all to the top floor of the building where Joshua Engels was waiting for them in his photographic studio. He had a washtub ready to clean the children up and an assortment of goodies that he hoped to trade with them, in the game of dare which he had devised for them to play. Failing that, he had a few alcohol laced beverages and opiates at the ready, just to ensure that the children did all that was required of them.

Greenfield has no interest in what happened over the next hour or so. His job was to procure people for the photographic sessions. This wasn't the first time that he had provided children for Engels. He hated doing it and unlike many other things in life, it wasn't getting any easier with repetition.

Engels' business was pornography. It had all started innocently enough, with his specialising in what could be called 'soft porn' and he was making a decent living from it. Everyone seemed happy with the arrangement. The clients were happy with the photos, the 'models' were happy with their pay and even the police appeared to be happy, content to turn a blind eye to the somewhat sordid industry. However, things had gradually changed for the worse when one of Engels' customers requested what he had referred to as 'risqué' photographs of women in different forms of bondage. Engels had not keen on the arrangement, but the client had been willing to pay a lot of money for the images. Without consciously being aware of it, Engels had moved into a higher-class niche market, his new clients being well-heeled men living in London's West End. These men would purchase their materials through an agent, not risking dealing directly with the likes of Engels.

One of Engels' clients had decidedly strange tastes. The images he wanted were not what one could call pornographic, in that he liked his women fully clothed. What he wanted were images of women in various states of physical assault. His expressed preference was for the woman to face the camera, with her 'attacker' standing in front of her. The attacker was to hold the lady's chin with his left hand and place his right hand behind his back, holding a series of medical implements. The client had been most specific that the attacker was to be fully clothed, seen from the back or side and must have a moustache, but no beard.

In recent months some of Engels' clients had started requesting photographs containing children. Greenfield had refused point blank to source them himself, but finally agreed to do so through the models involved in the photo sessions. For the latest session, Greenfield had approached two of Engels' regular models and offered them three times the going rate if they would be willing to pick-up some street urchins for a special photo shoot. That task was easy enough as Dr Barnardo, and other likeminded citizens, could only take a small fraction of the abandoned waifs off of the streets, so there were plenty to choose from.

When the session was over Greenfield had to carry the children down the stairs as Engels had given them a combination of alcohol and drugs. He told the couple to return the children to where they had found them, reminding them that there would be severe consequences should the police find their way to Engels' door.

The couple led the children slowly through the front door onto the bustling street, stopping for a short while whilst the young girl vomited on the doorstep. This drew no undue attention and they started their journey back to the street from which the children came. The couple were tempted to dump them around the corner but knew of Greenfield's reputation for violence and did not want to risk being on the wrong end of a beating.

❦ ❦ ❦

Reid had had an uneventful day and was expecting to make little progress in the forgery and gambling cases until Friday evening, and had told Emily that they could spend Friday morning and afternoon together. He was now determined to make some progress with the pornography case as he'd made little headway with it. Word had it that one of Sergeant Baugham's informants knew of an illicit photographic studio working out of a building somewhere in the Whitechapel area. The informer's name was Michael Marne, an underemployed labourer who periodically resorted to petty crime in order to make ends meet. Marne's last known address was a common lodgings house in Flower and Dean Street.

The lodgings houses only tended to keep records of their regular customers and turned everyone out onto the streets at 11am each day so that the squalid rooms could be cleaned. Reid decided to check the lodging house registers in the hope that Marne, a local man, might be registering under his own name when purchasing cots for the night. Marne had been described to him as being a small powerfully built man, standing about 5 feet 3 inches in height. His physique forged by years of labouring in the London docks and local Spitalfields market.

Pornographic photographs were expensive, meaning that there were very few men local to Whitechapel affluent enough to afford them. Baugham's report stated that Marne had heard rumours about a building used to take 'orrible' photos, some of which included 'little uns'. Marne didn't know where it was or who was involved but wanted

Baugham to 'get it sorted'. Ordinarily such scant information would never have found its way onto an Inspector's desk, but reports had been sent directly to the Yard from CDivision – Mayfair and Soho - stating that the production of pornographic materials 'of the worst kind' in Whitechapel were finding their way onto the salubrious streets of the west end. As yet no arrests had been made, most likely due to the high social status of the recipients of the sordid images. It being agreed that best way to deal with the matter was to stop the flow of material at its source.

Reid had visited a number of lodging houses without any success. He had not told the deputies who he was searching for, but had found most were unusually keen to help him with his enquiries, not realising that they assumed he was searching for the Whitechapel Murderer. Eventually Reid found what he was looking for. The register at 27 Flower and Dean Street contained entries over the last three weeks in the name of Marne. There was no first name or initial, so Reid would not know whether he had the right man until he saw him. Many lodging house tenants made use of the kitchens for their meals, but as there was no sign of anyone matching Marne's description, Reid decided to return back there at teatime.

ǂ ǂ ǂ

Sergeant Thick had rushed to the station to complete his report on the suspect Isenschmid. Shortly after his arrival he was passed a telegram from Y-Division stating that Isenschmid's doctors had transferred him to the Bow Infirmary, deeming him too mentally unstable to take part in an identity parade. The sergeant had come across many maniacs over the years but he had a strong feeling in his water about this one, and his report reflected his instincts.

❦❦❦

George Crawford had returned early from work to his home on the Marylebone Road. He had not been able to concentrate on his work, his mind consumed by other thoughts. He was not a large man, at 5 feet 8 inches in height, but was broad shouldered and had the muscle tone of an athlete. He was 35 years old, had medium brown hair and a large red to ginger moustache. If it hadn't been for the colour of his moustache, his face had no distinguishing features and once seen was easily forgotten. However, Crawford was no ordinary man. He was an American by birth, born into a poor family. His father had been a struggling farmer but had been forced to give that up due to ill health and had become a preacher. Crawford was highly intelligent and did very well at school and with the help of his family he managed to go onto further study at college. However, his life took a completely different course when he took a chance and headed out west, to try his luck with thousands of others in the 1870s American gold rush. He'd struck lucky and with the money he made from the sale of his small gold mine he went into the import export business. America was a fast expanding country but the centre of the universe for trade was England and its capital city London. So being young, free and single he travelled to London in 1880 setting himself up in a very lucrative business, exporting wool and importing spices and other precious commodities. His business went from strength to strength and he made many influential contacts. Now in the year 1888 he was a man of great wealth and influence. However, monetary success did not come without its costs and the stress of his business dealings had taken its toll on his health. Physically, he appeared normal enough but he was drained mentally and was subject to bouts of depression, he had not taken a wife and had little to do with women.

As with many wealthy people of the age, Crawford had developed a taste for collecting curios. A large number of well to do households contained mini collections of historical artefacts, with some of the larger private collections matching those of the London museums. Crawford's collection was in this latter category. He sent money back home to his family in America but he had no family in England, so tended to spend what spare money he had on collecting medical artefacts. One of his uncles was a frontier surgeon whom Crawford, when still only a young boy, had sometimes assisted in his often gruesome work. Crawford's childhood experiences had left him fascinated by medicine and surgery and one of the rooms in his house was dedicated to his collection of weapons, death masks and surgical implements.

More recently Crawford had taken to collecting items of an even more objectionable nature than his curiosities. He had amassed hundreds of pornographic photographs and his taste in these had deteriorated in unison with his faltering mental health. Late in 1887 he had started to develop a taste for photographs with distinctly sadistic overtones. Such material was difficult to come by but he'd struck lucky when he'd obtained the details of a supplier working out of the east end of London.

Crawford had left his business early that day to view his foul collection of pornographic images, laid out amidst his macabre collection of medical artefacts.

⸸ ⸸ ⸸

Abberline had now lost interest in William Piggott. He had tasked Sergeant Leach with ascertaining Piggott's whereabouts on the nights of the Nichols and Chapman murders but was expecting the man to hit a dead end. Leach had not relished the task allocated to him, as Piggott was a mad man with no fixed abode and could have been just about anywhere on the nights of the murders. Even if Piggott had stayed at a doss house he was likely to have provided the deputy with a false name. However, Piggott's insanity gave Leach something to work with and he had been in contact with a number of asylums in the hope that one of more might have records on him. Leach had struck lucky and had discovered that Piggott was safely tucked away in an asylum on the night of the Nichols murder. So barring an administrative error, it looked very much like Piggott wasn't the man they were after. Piggott might have been a potentially dangerous lunatic but in Whitechapel he was just one of a multitude. Leach completed his report and placed it in Abberline's burgeoning in-tray, on top of Sergeant Thick's report on Isenschmid. Leach didn't envy Abberline. About ten men had been brought into custody following Chapman's murder on the Saturday morning and the Whitechapel Murder Squad were slowly working their way through more leads than they had the capacity to follow. The local girls were living in fear and had started to report any man that they didn't like the look of. All these reports had to be followed-up and Abberline was responsible for making sure that nothing was missed. If that wasn't bad enough, journalists were everywhere and other interfering busybodies were setting-up what they called Vigilance Committees. Leach had witnessed Abberline's rise following his capture of the Irish Republican Brotherhood bombers but he had a feeling that this case might prove to be a reputation breaker.

Shortly after arriving at the station Abberline was told the news about Piggott. He instructed Sergeant Leach to double check that the asylum had their facts straight and seek medical opinion on what to do with the man. Abberline was now very much interested in the suspect named Isenschmid and sent a telegram to CI Swanson informing him that he had a good feeling about the man. He also sent a telegram to Y-Division informing that every effort must be made to get the doctors to agree to Isenschmid taking part in an identification parade. He added hints should be dropped that failure to comply would result in his going over the heads of the doctors by involving senior members of the Department of Health.

❦ ❦ ❦

Reid struck it lucky on his return to the common lodging house at 27 Flower and Dean Street as he spied Marne in the packed out kitchen. He did not immediately inform Marne that he was a police officer and instead tried engaging the man in casual conversation.

"How goes your day, sir?" asked Reid.

"Wot, mine?" replied Marne, somewhat surprised that the relatively well-dressed man had condescended to speak to him.

"Yes, you. We've have had some fine weather and my own day is going rather well."

"Wot do ya care for my day, guvnor?" replied Marne with a hint of menace in his voice.

"I'm just trying to make conversation on this fine day."

"Well you can bleedin' make it somewhere else."

"Don't be like that my man."

Marne felt inclined to give Reid a slap, but it crossed his mind that the man in front of him might just be a plain-clothed copper.

"Okay, wot do you want mister?"

"Like I said, I'm just making conversation. It's noisy in here so why don't we take a walk in the fresh air after you've finished your tea?"

"Alright Mr, s'pose we could. Wot's ya name and wot's ya business?"

"My name's Edmund, it is a pleasure to meet you, sir, and you are?"

"The name's Marne, Michael Marne."

"What have you been doing this fine day Michael?"

"Well it's been as much as usual. Been to the docks today and got the call-on early this morning like. I put in a good shift and I'll be going for a couple of drinks to quell me thirst."

Marne looked Reid up and down. He thought that the man who called himself Edmund seemed too short to be a rozzer and didn't dress like a peeler. The only thing that Marne felt sure about was that Edmund didn't have the build of a man used to physical labour.

"So wot 'ave you been doing today Edmund? By the looks of ya I'd say that you ain't a working man," said Marne looking down at Reid's callous free hands as he spoke.

Reid had quite small hands for his size and never gave much thought to how they looked. Now that he did so he couldn't help but think they looked very much like the hands of a woman in comparison to Marne's shovel like dukes.

"How very astute of you Michael, you strike me as a very observant fellow. I'd wager that you are a man who doesn't allow much to get by him. I am afraid that I am a slave to a desk and gaslight but my work can involve some honest labour. I tell you what Michael, after you finish your meal I'd be grateful if you would allow me to buy you a pint."

"Alright, Edmund. You let me finish-up and I'll meet you outside shortly like."

As Reid turned to leave the kitchen he noticed the lodging house deputy in the far corner of the room. Reid gave him a nod of acknowledgement and went on his way. The deputy had expected Reid to lay hands on Marne and had lost interest in the men's conversation when it was apparent that no arrest was to be made.

Ten minutes later Marne met Reid outside the lodging

house.

"Okay, sir. Wot's this all about then? Wot do ya want from me?"

"Why don't we take a walk, Michael?"

"I'm guessin' you're a rozzer. You didn't come to arrest me, else I'd be in the station by now. So what is it that you want?"

"Sergeant Baugham says that you passed him some information regarding the whereabouts of a house of pornography."

"What?"

"What I mean is that you told the sergeant that you know of a building in Whitechapel being used to take unholy photographs of children."

"That's not strictly true, sir. Ya see, I tells him that I knows that young uns are being photographed, but I don't know where."

"And what did you want done with the information that you gave him?"

"I wanted 'im to catch the beggars who are takin' the photographs."

"Well the sergeant has told me and now I'm trying to find the people responsible. What I need to know is if you can help me do this?"

"Well I don't know where the 'ouse is but I knows a street where they be catching the young uns from."

"Can you take me there?"

"I can't be doing that, I'm no squealer, ya see? I'll give ya the name of the road and you can search for the little uns yourself. I only knows where they are because one of the street brides seen them being dropped-off."

"How am I supposed to identify them then?"

"Don't know that guvnor, you is a rozzer, so you'll be finding a way. The best place to be searching is around Pearl Street and Great Pearl Street."

"Do you know when the last children were taken?"

"No, but I hear that they're being taken quite regular like."

Reid was glad of Marne's information and decided that he'd take a walk around to Pearl Street. He wasn't expecting to find anything out of the ordinary and had the feeling that his efforts were going to come to nought.

"Thank you very much for your help, Mr Marne. I will do what I can about this sorry business. Here, take something for your trouble."

"No, sir, I don't need nothing from ya. I'm 'appy to try and get the evil bleeders for wots been 'appening like." Marne thought for a moment and decided to ask Reid for a favour. "Tells you wot, sir. Me reward would be to knows that you ketched someone for this. Can't say that I'll always be lodging in Flower n Dean Street, but the sergeant knows me. So grateful like if you can gets me a message if ya get the bleeders."

"I promise you, Michael, if I arrest the man or men responsible, I shall try to tell you in person."

"Thank you, sir. One last thing, I don't knows ya name."

"It's Reid, Inspector Reid".

With that the two men parted and Reid made his way to Pearl Street.

❦ ❦ ❦

Back at the station Abberline and his team were in the briefing room discussing the case.

"Right, gentlemen, as I see things we have one good suspect in Joseph Isenschmid. The man's description is very much like that of the bloodstained man seen in the Prince Albert at 7am on Saturday morning. However, due to medical reasons we haven't been able to arrange an identity parade to confirm the matter. As for all other leads, I gather that alibis are being proved and that we are gradually hitting dead ends; so all our eggs look to be in the one basket. If Isenschmid is our man, that's all very good, but we are going to have to prove that he was in that yard sometime between the hours of four-thirty and six in the morning. However, that could be a problem for us, as the only eyewitness who remembers seeing anyone close to 29 Hanbury Street is a Mrs Elizabeth Long, and the man she saw doesn't match Isenschmid's description. Her statement says that she saw the deceased in the company of a man at five-thirty in the morning, standing very close to number 29, the two of them disappearing very suddenly. This would lead one to assume that the couple she saw left the main street and went into the back yard of number 29. Mrs Long has some credibility as she has attended the mortuary and positively identified the body of Annie Chapman. Even though she says she only saw the man from the side and back, she has described him as having a dark complexion and looking like a foreigner, meaning that he was of Jewish extraction. Now at some stage Mrs Long will be called to give evidence at the inquest, when she does the press will no doubt drop their stories about 'Leather Apron' and start writing stories about Jews in general. When that happens, we will no doubt be flooded with reports relating to dark complexioned Jewish looking men. And therein lies our problem, gentlemen. As Isenschmid, our most promising suspect, has a pale complexion, red-brown hair and a red to ginger moustache. Now that's going to take some squaring with the men of the press. So it would be very helpful to our case, if one of you can find a witness who saw a man, with a ginger moustache, in or around Hanbury Street between 4am and 6am on the morning of the murder."

The officers went on to provide Abberline with progress reports which he included in his telegrammed status report to CI Swanson at Scotland Yard.

⸙ ⸙ ⸙

Reid should have been at home with his wife and family but wanted to take a look around Pearl and Great Pearl Streets before calling it a day. Pearl Street was full of down at heel people and the buildings had seen much better days. Certain streets in Whitechapel were dangerous places for police officers to walk through and Reid found himself in one of them now. He wore plain-clothes and although he didn't spend vast sums on his attire, in thoroughfares like Pearl Street the cut of his cloth stood out and his presence immediately caught the eye. To Reid's advantage the men most likely to consider robbing or attacking him were likely to recognise him as being a policeman, but that couldn't guarantee his getting out of the area totally unscathed. There were a few groups of children in the street and doubting that he would get to speak to all of them, he walked slowly by them, listening to their conversations as he went.

Then he heard one call out 'Watch out, 'ere comes a masher!', then another one shouted 'Nah, he's a rozzer!'.

Reid knew very well that 'masher' was a slang term used to describe some of the less savoury gentleman slummers - men who frequented rundown areas to indulge in illicit activities involving alcohol, gambling and sex. He wasn't sure what he was looking for but hoped that his detective's instinct would kick-in if he came across something out of the ordinary. All the children appeared to be dirty and undernourished, with the last group he saw on leaving the street looking very much like the first.

Great Pearl Street to all intents and purposes looked a replica of Pearl Street. Again there were groups of children scattered about the place and he heard all the same catcalls as he slowly made his way along the dilapidated road. Then, finally, he noticed something out of the ordinary.

Two of the children, a boy and a girl, were different to the others; they were cleaner, much cleaner. Their clothes were dirty rags but the bodies looked spotless. The two children were sitting together and as he got closer to them he noticed that they both looked quite unwell. This disturbed him more than it might usually have done as the little boy reminded him of his son Harold. He walked past them and went to the end of the road, thinking about what he should do. He decided to take a chance. The children didn't look like they were planning on going anywhere, so he left the street and headed for the Spitalfields market. On arrival at the market he located a stall selling multicoloured beads, bought two sets and quickly made his way back to Great Pearl Street. He was in luck, the children were still there.

Reid walked slowly towards the children, being careful not to make eye contact with them. He stopped next to where they were seated and pulled out the two set of beads, inspecting them in the fading light of the day. The children, despite being distressed by their horrible experience in Finch Street and still nauseous from their drug-laced cocktails, looked in wonder at the shiny coloured beads dangling from the man's hands.

"Beads are wonderful things, don't you think children?" he asked.

The children immediately looked away from Reid. They had been taught to be wary of strangers and the horrible events they'd just experienced had made real the numerous warnings they'd received over the years.

"Such things are of no use to me but I'd like to give them a good home."

The girl was the first to raise her head back in the direction of the Inspector. She had taken a liking to the beads as soon as she saw them and couldn't stop herself stealing another a look at them.

"What, mister, you be giving them away?" she asked.

"Yes, young lady. Would you and the boy like them?"

"We ain't doing nothing for 'em," said the boy, with an angry tone to his voice.

The boy's response spoke volumes and it was obvious to Reid that the children had recently endured some horrible ordeal.

"There is no need for you to do anything for them, young man. If you and the girl would like them they are yours to have. Would you like them?"

"Alright mister, we'll have 'em," replied the boy.

Reid handed the each child a set of beads and started to walk away. Then he paused, turned round and walked back to them.

"Actually children, you might be able to do me a service, I am new to the area and am trying to find my way to the Spitalfield market. Do either of you know it?"

The children gave Reid and each other sideways glances as they played with their beads. They both shared a feeling that there was something about this man they could trust.

"Course we do, mister, it be a short walk across the way," replied the boy.

"Which way would that be?" asked Reid.

"Head down that way and ya can't miss it."

"Thank you, children, that is most helpful of you. I've been walking all day and am need of a little rest. Do you mind if I stop here with you for a short while?"

"Please yourself, mister, ain't no business of ours." replied the boy who was now engrossed in his new toy.

"I hear that they sell many wondrous things in the market, have you ever been there?" asked Reid, thinking that he might make some headway with them.

The girl thought for a while before replying. "Yeh, we've been there, but there's not much there for the likes of us."

"I'm after something special, I've heard it said that a man there takes photographs."

The children sat bolt upright, fixing Reid with cold,

piercing stares.

"Wot ya be wanting with things like that, mister?" the boy asked Reid.

"I have two children. A son, younger in years than your good self, and a daughter, older in years than your friend. My wife would like to have photographs taken of them. I am told that a man in the market can do this for a fee. Have you ever seen such a man?"

The little girl started to cry. Reid knew that he had struck a chord and hoped that he'd clumsily found a way to get the children to confide in him.

"What's wrong, young lady?" he asked.

"We knows a man who takes them photographs alright, but you won't do right taking your kin to him," said the boy.

"What do you mean? There's no harm in photographs. I've seen them taken many times, they pose no danger to anyone."

"Maybe the machine don't do harm, but the man that works it does," replied the boy.

"What do you know of photography?"

"We had our photos taken this very day and 'ave seen wot arm can be done."

"BILLY, TELL 'IM NOUGHT," shouted the young girl.

"I am sorry to have troubled you children. I will be on my way to the market now, so there is no need for you to get upset."

Reid's mind had been so fixed upon the children that he did not see the group of men assembling across the road from him.

"WOT'S YOUR GAME MISTER, YOU SOME SORT OF MASHER OR WOT?" shouted a man from across the street.

Five men then ran over and surrounded Reid on the pavement. The ringleader stood in front of him and waved a clasp knife in his face.

"Like I said, wot's your game, mister?"

"I was just asking these children for directions to the market."

"Looks like you been doing a lot more than that. Wot is it you want with 'em?"

"I'm just looking for the market. The children have given me directions and I was just about to get on my way."

"Wot's your business 'ere?" said the leader of the men, continuing his line of questioning. "You don't talk like no slummer, so wot's you after from the little uns?"

"As I've already explained, I'm looking for the market. Now that I know what direction it is in, I'll be on my way."

"Billy, this man been bothering you?" the lead man asked the boy.

"No Alfie. Like he said, he's just looking for the market. Seems like he's lost his way."

Alfred Matthews was a dockside labourer by trade. He was a large powerfully built man and took it upon himself to maintain law and order in his manor, which included Pearl and Great Pearl Streets.

"Alright, mister. Seems like you be telling us the truth. Be on your way whilst you 'ave the chance."

The Inspector considered informing the men that he was a member of Her Majesty's Constabulary but thought better of it. The men were clearly not intent on robbing him and he didn't want to lose the trust of the children. He was sure that the children had suffered some form of evil abuse, but decided that his best course of action was to leave the street as the man named 'Alfie' had instructed him to do.

Reid considered his options as he made his way home. He could return to the street on his own and try again to strike-up conversation with the children, hoping that they might unburden themselves of the details of their ordeal. Then again, he could return with a group of uniformed officers, grab the children and formally interview them down at the station. He didn't think that the former would work and thought the latter would cause the children undue distress. Then he hit upon another tactic altogether, one that might be of the greatest benefit to him and the children. In the end he decided to sleep on the matter and make a final decision about what to do in the morning.

CHAPTER FIVE

Mortuaries and Money Men

REID WOKE EARLY on Thursday 13th September and prepared his own breakfast. Emily was already up and about when Reid awoke and was sharing her time between household chores and playing with their son, Harold.

"Emily."

"Yes, dearest."

"Emily, I try my best not to involve you in my work but on this occasion you might be able to assist me."

"What is it, Edmund?"

"I have need to interview two children about a very delicate matter and do not wish to cause them undue distress by using usual policing methods."

"What sort of children are they?"

"They are street urchins. I am not sure how they live, but they are children nevertheless and I need some information from them."

"And how can I help you in such a matter?"

"I first made contact with them yesterday evening, which is the reason for my late arrival from work. I have since been thinking how I might get to speak more candidly with them and feel that in order to do so, I must first build-up a level of trust with them. This is not something I feel able to do as a policeman. Also, they are currently residing in Great Pearl Street, a street I might easily be assaulted in."

"Are you asking me to accompany you to such a street?"

"No, my dear, I would never ask such a thing of you. However, you have friends at the Christian Mission on Folgate Street. I believe that staff at the Mission and their volunteers are well known to the communities living to the north of the market."

"That is so, Edmund."

"Well, my dear, what I am asking is if you could introduce me to someone at the Mission whom you think might be willing to accompany me to the Great Pearl Street to help gain the confidence of the children. As I have said, the matter is most delicate and the person must be able to act with the greatest discretion. Do you know of anyone that could help me in this matter?"

Emily thought for a short while. She was aware that the staff at the Mission were well known for their assistance of the poor and needy, and were free to walk the rougher streets unmolested. She was also secretly pleased that her husband had been able to move on from the angst of being excluded from the Whitechapel Murder Squad and was focused on a new case. Even if the foul deed involved children.

"Yes, I know a lady who might be able to help, a Mrs Jackson. Am I able to meet you at the station when I have made arrangements?"

"Yes, dearest, I will be there all morning, barring emergencies. You remember that I am on the late shift tomorrow and will be working late into the night?"

"Yes, dear, I remember".

With arrangements in train, Reid finished his breakfast and set off to work. He had scheduled a meeting with Sergeant Leach and a few of the constables, where he intended to discuss arrangements for the raids on Friday night's dog fights and robbery of the Mad Sailor at the Ten Bells public house. He was beginning to feel quite pleased with himself, having made good progress in all three of his major cases. The week had started very badly with the arrival of Abberline, but he was now into his stride and had hardly given his conversation with Dr Phillips much thought. He knew that Abberline and the team had their hands full and that a lot of time was being wasted attending the Chapman inquests, the third session of which was scheduled for later in the day. Inspector Chandler and Sergeant Baugham were due to give evidence at it. Reid was annoyed as Baugham's involvement in the case as he'd wanted to involve the sergeant in the raid of the gambling den. After Sergeant Thick, Baugham was the next officer that he trusted to accompany him on arrests that might involve acts of physical violence.

❦ ❦ ❦

Abberline met Chandler, Helson and Baugham at the Working Lads' Institute for their now usual pre-meeting, which they used to discuss their main case. He wasn't aware of any new leads and was concerned that all they had revolved around Isenschmid.

"Morning, gentlemen," said Abberline.

"Morning, sir," the men replied in unison.

"You will be glad to hear that Coroner Baxter has planned to hold a brief session this morning and will adjourn until Wednesday of next week. He will take our evidence but is going to defer taking Mrs Long's until the next session. Are any of you aware of any new developments?"

"No, sir," the men again replied in unison.

"Now that the furore has died down we should start receiving fewer people into the station reporting new suspects. This should allow us time to investigate new lines of inquiry. I will go into the fine detail later this afternoon but my plan is that we should start investigating the local hospitals. I am keen to know if there are any mentally unstable members of the medical staffs who might also be experienced in the performance of surgical procedures. Our primary focus still remains with the local slaughter men and butchers but I would like someone to make inquiries at the hospitals, starting with the London Hospital."

Abberline's proposal seemed sensible and reasonable to his men, but they were already snowed under with work and could not see how they were going to make the time to interview staff at the London hospitals. But they relegated such thoughts to the back of their minds as members of the press and public started to pack into the hall.

Finally the Coroner, Mr Wynne E. Baxter, entered the hall and all was quiet. He already appeared to have a bee in his bonnet about something, so Inspector Chandler was none too keen when he was called-up as the first witness of the day. However, all went smoothly and Sergeant Baugham was the next person called to the stand. Baugham informed the court that it was he who conveyed Chapman's body to the mortuary, which he described as being an old dilapidated shed. Baxter was keen to verify that all the deceased body parts had been taken with her in the ambulance and that nothing of the woman was left in the yard or lost in transit. Baugham confirmed that this was indeed the case.

Next up was the mortuary keeper, Robert Mann, an inmate of the Whitechapel Union Workhouse. It was now that the cause of Baxter's irritation became known. Mann stated that he opened-up the mortuary at 7am and remained with the corpse whilst two nurses undressed it, and was still there when Dr Phillips arrived to perform a post mortem examination. Baxter listened as Mann gave his account of his actions that morning. Mann was a person with very poor communication skills and appeared to have quite limited intelligence. Baxter's face flushed as he listened to Mann explaining that he was responsible for both the mortuary and the deceased. Baxter looked around the hall, it was packed with reporters from all of London's leading publications. He ceased questioning Mann and started to address the court with his views on the standards of facilities and personnel provided to deal with suspicious deaths.

"The fact is, that Whitechapel does not possess a mortuary, that place is not a mortuary at all. We have no right to take a body there. It is simply a shed belonging to the workhouse officials. Juries have, over and over again, reported the matter to the District Board of Works. The east end, which requires mortuaries more than anywhere else, is most deficient in them. Bodies drawn out of the river have to be put in boxes and very often they are brought to this workhouse arrangement all the way from Wapping. A workhouse inmate is not the proper man to take care of a body in such an important matter as this."

Baxter hoped that the reporters had recorded his every word and would repeat them in their lengthy articles on the inquest. He expected to receive a reprimand for making such a public statement, but thought that it would be worth the trouble if public pressure were to result in better funding of facilities. He then recommenced questioning his unreliable witness.

"Were you present when the doctor was making his post-mortem?"

"Yes," replied Mann.

"Did you see the doctor find the handkerchief?"

"It was taken off the body. I picked it up from the clothing which was in the corner of the room. I gave it to Dr Phillips and he asked me to put it in some water, which I did."

"Did you see the handkerchief taken off the body?"

"I did not. The nurses must have taken if off the throat."

"How do you know?"

"I don't know."

"Then you are guessing?"

Mann had to admit that he was guessing and Baxter's temper flared again.

"That is all wrong, you know. He is really not the

proper man to have been left in charge."

With that, Baxter dismissed Mann and called-up the next witness.

Inspector Chandler breathed a sigh of relief. He had already had managed to annoy Baxter with the errors he'd made into the investigation of Chapman's murder and thought that Baxter would have torn into him if he had followed Mann up onto the stand.

Dr Phillips was eventually called to give evidence. At the end of his graphic description of the murder scene he made the following comment.

"I went to the yard of the Whitechapel Union for purpose of further examining the body and making the usual post-mortem investigation. I was surprised to find that the body had been stripped and was lying ready on the table. It was under this great disadvantage that I made my examination."

Chandler squirmed in his seat as he saw Abberline glaring at him out of the corner of his eye. He had forgotten that he had asked the nurses to clean-up the body before the arrival of the doctor. He had asked them to do so because he thought that it would be easier for the doctor, allowing him to get straight into the examination of the body, rather than waste time cutting off the unfortunate's ragged clothes. Chandler was a competent officer and was not prone to making mistakes, but he had just finished his nightshift when he was called to the murder scene. His shift ran from 10pm until 6am and he was dog tired and looking forward to going home to bed when the call came. He had spent the next four hours coordinating the early investigation into a very high profile murder. He could have chosen to return home, leaving the investigation to the next Duty Inspector, but he'd been keen to score some promotion points. Now that decision was coming back to haunt him.

The last witness of the session was one of the nurses

called to the 'mortuary' on the morning of the murder, Sarah Simonds.

Coroner Baxter started his usual line of questioning. "You are a resident nurse at the Whitechapel mortuary?"

"Yes, sir."

"Where did you first see the body of the deceased?"

"It was in the ambulance, in the yard when I got there. The body was then taken into the shed and placed on the table."

"And what happened next?"

"I was directed by Inspector Chandler to undress the body. I took all the clothes and placed them in a pile in the corner.

"Did you remove a handkerchief from around the deceased neck?"

"No, sir, I left it where it was. It was next to the wounds and I was scared to touch them."

"You are certain of this?"

"Yes, me and the other nurse took the clothes from her body, but left the handkerchief. We found an empty pocket tied around her waist, and then we washed the blood from the body as best we could."

"Did you notice any cuts or tears in the deceased's clothing?"

"No, sir."

"Very good, you may stand down. Inspector Chandler, please return to the stand."

Chandler made his way back up to the stand, being careful not to look in the direction of the men from the press.

"Inspector, you have heard Dr Phillips express his surprise on finding that the body of the deceased was stripped and laying ready on the table on his arrival. This obviously undermined his ability to fully understand how the deceased came to meet her end. The nurse, Mrs Simonds, has told the court that you instructed her to undress the body. Is this correct?"

"No, sir, I did not instruct the nurses to either undress or wash the body."

Baxter knew very well that the word of a nurse could not be taken above that an officer of the law, especially one of the rank of Detective Inspector; but he was beginning to get fed-up with Chandler and was sorely tempted to hold him to account in front of his peers. However, due to the very high profile and sensitive nature of the murder he decided to let the matter rest.

"That will be all, Inspector. You may stand down."

Chandler returned to his seat. He too knew that no one would take the word of the nurse over his. But he sensed that Abberline would take issue with the matter, especially after his inaccurate record of Richardson's evidence. They were minor errors but this was the most high profile case that he had ever been involved in. He had seen Chapman's death as a rung on the ladder to promotion, now he was beginning to think that he might have inadvertently trodden upon a snake.

Baxter adjourned the inquest to the following week as Abberline had said that he would. That now left the authorities a week to get as much information on their prime suspect, Joseph Isenschmid, as they could.

☩☩☩

Emily Reid had been busy. She had been to the Christian Mission in search of Mrs Jackson but was informed that she was not at work that day and might be found at home. Mrs Reid visited Mrs Jackson's home and was happy to find that she was there and, more importantly, that she was willing to accompany her husband to Great Pearl Street.

Reid was at his desk when they arrived and asked his

wife and Mrs Jackson to accompany him to an incident room where he provided Mrs Jackson with an overview of the situation. She said that she was well known in the area and might even be on personal terms with the children that Reid wished to speak to. Emily left them to it and Reid provided Mrs Jackson with the fine detail of why he wanted to speak to the children. He explained that he was only acting on a hunch and did not have any evidence that the children had been abused in any way. Mrs Jackson was shocked by what Reid told her but was keen to try and help the children in any way that she could. The two of them left the station and set off for Great Pearl Street.

❧❧❧

Harris Marks and Hudson Weatherburn met each other in White Hart public house opposite the London Hospital on the Whitechapel High Street. They were both a little nervous and made furtive glances at the other men in the bar. The men were in the business of buying and distributing counterfeit money and today they were going to meet their main supplier, a man named James Richards. The last time that they had purchased coin from Richards they were robbed and had lost half of the consignment. They were not sure whether Richards had set them up or whether it was just a fluke, but whatever it was, they weren't going to let it happen again. This time they had arranged for two minders be in attendance at the deal, John 'Narky' Fieldman and Philip 'Monkey' Cohen. Buying the services of hired muscle was going to eat into their profit margin, but to their way of thinking some profit was better than no profit at all.

"You are sure that we can trust these men?" asked a nervous sounding Marks.

"Yes, like I said, they are working men and do this sort of thing as a sideline. They ain't interested in getting heavy into crime."

"Richards says he don't want them in on the deal. I think he thinks we mean to rob him."

"I make ya right but he knows we were robbed the last time. He'd be taking us for mugs if we didn't go mob handed."

Just then two large, powerfully built men entered the pub. Whitechapel was a rough area, full of men used to violence. However, all eyes turned towards the men as they walked through the bar, a few of the customers being careful to give the two men a wide berth as they made their way through the crowd. Although many looked, all but two men were careful not to make eye contact with them. Fieldman and Cohen were market porters by trade and looked to be no strangers to heavy lifting. They were not men of violence, preferring to rely on their size and appearance to maintain order. They were both blessed with hard faces, huge heads and square jaws. Even if they had been smaller men, their facial features would have been enough to cause other men to steer well clear of them.

"Are we fine for a swift pint Mr Weatherburn?" asked Fieldman.

"Yes, gentlemen, we are in good time. But can you make it just the one?"

"That'll be fine with us." replied Cohen.

The men got their drinks and the group went through the arrangements. The plan was to meet Richards in Spital Square with Fieldman and Cohen watching proceedings from a respectful distance, standing ready to intervene if anything untoward happened. It had been agreed that they could just walk away if the rozzers turned-up, but were to give a good hiding to anyone else minded to interfere with arrangements. After the completion of the deal, they were to escort Marks and Weatherburn into the Spitalfields market, where the two men planned to disappear into the crowd. Marks and Weatherburn preferred taking their chances on the last legs of their respective journeys, rather than risk their 'escorts' following them all the way home.

The arrangements made, the men set-off for Spital Square.

❦❦❦

Reid was pleased to see Mrs Jackson receiving a few nods of acknowledgement as they walked along Great Pearl Street. It was a strange feeling for the Inspector, who normally relied on the likes of Sergeant Thick to escort him on the mean streets of London. He felt that he had made a good decision and thought that all would go well as long as they could find the children.

Reid was in luck, the two children were sitting in the same spot. They looked much healthier, the ill effects of the drug cocktails having had ample time to pass through their systems. Reid and Mrs Jackson had stopped in the market along the way, to buy bread and cheese, just in case the children were hungry.

As they neared the children Reid was spotted by one of the men who had challenged him the night before.

"Ere, it's the masher, come back for the children! Wot's your game, mister, we told ya to leave off yesterday!"

"This gentleman is with me," interjected Mrs Jackson.

"I knows you. You be from the Mission."

"That is correct, sir, and this man is kindly escorting me through the neighbourhood."

"Well I suppose that's alright then," said the man returning back to his business and leaving Mrs Jackson to break the ice with the children.

"Good afternoon, children. You might know me, my name is Mrs Jackson and I work at Christian Mission. This man is Mr Reid and he has informed me that he discovered you looking poorly yesterday evening. I have come to give you some food."

The children recognised Reid as the man who had given them the beads and thought that they also knew the woman with him.

"Wot ya got us, missus?" asked the little boy.

"I have some bread and cheese, if you would like some?"

"Yes, please," replied the boy again.

The children wolfed down the food, their appetites much restored from the lows of the day before.

"Who looks after you?" asked Mrs Jackson.

"We looks after ourselves," said the boy.

From the look of them Mrs Jackson could not see any sign of the horrors described to her by the Inspector. However, she knew that life was very hard for such children and they had most probably endured many great hardships in their young lives.

"Mr Reid tells me that you might be able to take him to the workplace of a photographer. Do you think that you can help him?"

"No, missus, we ain't helping," said the young boy, remembering that Reid had said he wanted photographs taken of his children. He didn't want any other children to have photos taken like the one's he'd had taken of him and his sister.

"Why not, young man? Don't you know the man that takes photographs?"

"Yes, I knows him, but he's no good."

"I am a lady of the church and would like to see this man. If he is like you say he is, I would like to try and change his ways. If you could lead us to him, I will try to restore him using God's words. Do you think that you could help us?"

The children thought for a while. They had decided that Reid and Mrs Jackson seemed like good people, but then so had the man and lady that had taken them to Finch Street.

"How do we know that these two don't mean us harm?" asked the young girl.

"They ain't like the others. I can tell," said the boy.

"How can ya?" asked the girl.

"I just can," replied the boy.

The boy gave it some more thought. Even though the couple seemed trustworthy, he wasn't going to take any chances on actually going back into the house where the evil had taken place. He'd decided to take them to the door, if he could remember it, and that would be that.

"Okay, missus, we can take's ya to the door of the house that the man works in. But that's it, we ain't going back in there."

"There will be no need for you to re-enter the house. If you prefer you can accompany me back to the Mission where I can arrange for you to receive new clothes and a hot meal. How does that sound?"

"Alright, missus, we can goes there," said the young boy.

"As I said my name is Mrs Jackson and this is Mr Reid. What are your names children?"

"I'm William and this is Mary."

"Pleased to meet you William, pleased to meet you Mary," said Mrs Jackson.

Reid had purposely not spoken a word. He was hoping that the children would bond with Mrs Jackson and all had gone better than he imagined it would. He still didn't have anything to go on, but was hoping that the children might give him more detail as the day progressed.

"Do you still have the beads I gave you, William?" asked Reid.

"I've got them hidden safe, Mr Reid."

"I am glad that you liked them, I hope that Mary has hers as well?"

"I have them. Thank you, sir," replied Mary.

"That's excellent children. Are you ready to take us the

photographer's house?" asked Reid.

The children hesitated, looked at each other and then looked back at Reid and nodded. He let them lead the way through the back streets. When they reached Finch Street the children seemed lost.

"This is the street, Mr Reid," said the boy.

"Do you know the number of the house?"

"No, sir, but it's one of them along there."

"Do you remember which one you went into?"

Reid looked along the line of houses. They all looked very much the same to him and he didn't think that the children would point out the right house.

"Billy, I members being taken ill on the doorstep," said Mary remembering that she had vomited as they were led out of the house.

"Yeh, that' right. You was sick on the door step."

"Look, here's the spot", said Mary, standing outside of number 24.

Reid made a note of the door number and escorted the group to Folgate Street. He had no further use of the children and hoped that Mrs Jackson and the people at the Mission might be able to provide them with some form of poor aid. He thanked the children for their assistance and left Mrs Jackson to attend to them.

The Inspector had some thinking to do. He could obtain a warrant and search the house or he could put the occupants under surveillance. His brief had been to stop the supply of hardcore images to perverted, well to do, west end patrons. Raiding the house would be a quick win and would no doubt stem the flow of such material in the near term. Whereas a surveillance operation might uncover the producers of the illicit material, along with the clients and those involved in the distribution network. But surveillance would use up scarce resources and might delay proceedings, possibly resulting in the exploitation of yet more children. Reid was also concerned that Mrs Jackson would tell people what she knew.

As was his way, Reid decided to sleep on the matter and make a final decision on what to do in the morning. It was then that he remembered that he'd not yet formulated a plan of action for the raid on the gambling den. Something he needed in advance of his meeting with the officers allocated to the operation.

Reid was the first man to enter the briefing room. He thought that, with the right resources, his plan shouldn't be difficult to implement. But he did not think that he had anywhere near enough men to get the job done. He had requested two sergeants and ten constables for the operation and had just been informed that due to other, more important priorities, he'd have to make do with one sergeant and four constables. The Super had not bothered to tell him what the other priorities were, but one didn't need to be a detective to know that all available manpower was being used to try and prevent another Whitechapel murder. Of equal, if not more importance to catching the killer, a very visible police presence was required to demonstrate to the masses that the authorities were taking the murders seriously. Giving the impression that it would only be a matter of time before the miscreant was caught.

Sergeant Caunter was the next officer to enter the room, closely followed by the four constables: Barrett, Mizen, Imhoff and Thompson.

"Gentlemen, as you are aware there has been a surge in illicit gambling over recent months and we have been instructed to implement a crackdown," said Reid. "During the course of my investigation I have received information from a trusted informant – a Michael Riley - that two such events are to take place this coming weekend. Riley states that on both Friday and Saturday nights, dog fighting and the like, will commence from about 8pm in Sprat Alley off of George Yard. I would have preferred at least a dozen men to raid the gambling den, unfortunately, there are only six of us. I am afraid that our already fragile resources are to be stretched further by another task that must be attended to on the same evening. Our source says that one of the big hitters will be robbed on his way to Friday night's event. The man in question is Harry Clements, better known to us Mad Sailor Harry. Ordinarily, I'd be content to let Clements get what's owed to him. However, I've been led to believe he is in possession of a substantial amount of counterfeit coinage, which he intends to make his bets with. My plan is to stop the assault on Clements and then grill him for information on the source of the counterfeit money. Now for this to work, we will need Clements to take a bit of beating, making our arrests after his attackers have wrested the coins from his possession. I plan to come to an arrangement with Clements, offering him immunity if he gives us the name and address of the counterfeiter -"

"With respect, sir, what makes you think that Mad Harry will inform on his colleagues?" interrupted PC Imhoff.

"Let me put it this way. Clements will have been on the wrong end of a beating, mitigated by our intervention. Hopefully, he'll see us as his saviours and feel that he owes us something. Clements isn't a professional criminal, so I'm assuming that he obtained the counterfeit money from somebody else. That somebody being the counterfeiter or a very close associate of his."

"I'm sorry, sir, but how are we to deal with Clements and raid the gambling event on the same night?" asked Sergeant Caunter.

"That is a good question sergeant and it is one that I don't have an answer to. My original plan was for a sergeant and three constables to deal with Clements whilst another team comprising a sergeant and seven constables performed the raid in Spratt Alley. I am afraid that the men

I requested have been assigned to matters deemed to be of greater importance."

"You mean for the murders of the fallen women, sir?" commented PC Imhoff.

"Whatever the reason, I intend for us to perform both tasks. Do any of you have a problem with that?"

"No, sir" came the reply.

Reid was a bit taken aback by their response, as he himself had many problems with the plan.

"Look, gentlemen, we have insufficient manpower to deal with the assault on Clements and raid the gambling den in Spratt Alley. Therefore, I want two men to go to Spratt Alley to obtain intelligence on the ringleaders, a record should be made of the names of anyone deemed to be in authority. With luck, the rest of us will deal with any assault on Clements before joining the men assigned to the gambling den. Then, if possible, we should endeavour to arrest the ringleaders. Is that clear, gentlemen?"

Reid was pleased when after a pause Caunter sought further clarification.

"Sir, are you saying that we might not actually raid the event?"

"No, I'm not saying that. What we will do is be seen and heard to blow our whistles, making it very clear to all that a police raid is in progress. Then if numbers allow, we should endeavour to snatch one or two of the ringleaders. Is that clearer?"

"Yes, sir, but how will we know when to start the raid?"

"I will blow my whistle, then I want the rest of you to blow yours. Hopefully, this will give the impression of there being far more than six of us and we should be able to pick a few of them off without anyone putting up too much of a fight. So I say again, gentlemen, is everything clear?"

Reid looked around at the faces of the men in the room. He could see the recognition in their eyes. Yes he felt sure that they had finally absorbed what he was endeavouring to do, which was to make a token raid on a gambling den and allow Harry Clements to take a bit of a beating at the hands of men intent on stealing his snide coinage. Reid hoped that Clements might be more amenable to turning informant if he thought he owed the officers for saving him from a good hiding. And with luck he might tell him how he came to be in possession of some very high quality counterfeit money. Reid wasn't a man who shied away from risk but he was very aware that if things went badly, both he and his men could get injured trying to execute his plan.

"Gentleman, we are all to dress in plain clothes and will meet in the station at 6pm. Constables Barrett, Mizen and Thompson will then accompany me to the Ten Bells. I want Sergeant Caunter and PC Imhoff to go to Spratt Alley to make a note of the ringleaders, the rest of us should arrive there at about 8.30pm. Sergeant, you are not to make any arrests until the rest of us join you in the alley. If you don't see us, you and Imhoff are to concentrate solely on intelligence gathering. Is that clear?"

Reid assigned Imhoff to Caunter as he considered him the most intelligent of the four PCs. He wanted men in the alley that could think on their feet without blowing their cover.

"Yes, sir. Me and Imhoff are to get into the event, keep a lookout for the ringleaders and wait for you and the lads before making any arrests."

"Excellent, Caunter! Now I have one last thing to make you aware of. My source will be at the event. His name is Michael Riley, he stands about 5 feet 5 inches, has dark hair and a dark moustache and will be wearing a red neckerchief. Please ensure that you do not detain any man matching that description. Is that clear, gentleman?"

"Yes, sir," came back the response in unison.

Reid ended the briefing and the men returned to their duties.

CHAPTER SIX

Mad Dogs and Polish Men

ABBERLINE ARRIVED EARLY at the station on Friday 14th September. He was going to have another long day ahead of him. He had scheduled a meeting with his team first thing, followed by a meeting at the Yard with CI Swanson. At what should have been the end of his shift he was scheduled to brief the new uniformed and plain-clothes men drafted into H-Division to provide additional cover over the three nights of the weekend. The new men were being brought in primarily to bolster public confidence in the authorities. Having them on the streets could only help capture the killer, should he be so foolish as to attempt another murder. Abberline had been less than pleased when he'd heard that he'd lost a few regulars to a gambling case being worked upon by Reid. But the Super, in his wisdom, had been adamant that the opportunity to raid an illegal gambling event warranted the diversion of resources.

As the officers started arriving in the briefing room, Abberline put his thoughts about the Super's policing priorities to the back of his mind. He now had to focus on how he intended to track down and capture the Whitechapel murderer. He had an ever increasing list of suspects warranting further investigation. Men whose names had been mentioned on multiple occasions in reports submitted by working girls in different parts of the borough. He intended to assign officers to the investigation of these men's activities at the meeting. As regards the duties of his two inspectors. He'd decided not to allocate additional suspects to Inspector Moore, who he wanted to start making inquiries into mentally unstable medical staff at the London Hospital. As for Inspector Helson, he wanted him to increase the pressure being applied to the doctors at the Bow Infirmary, forcing them into authorising Isenschmid's participation in an identity parade.

⸸ ⸸ ⸸

Reid rose late that Friday morning but was pleased to find that his wife Emily had prepared breakfast for him. They had decided that it would be a nice day to take a walk in the park and partake in some much welcome fresh air.

⸸ ⸸ ⸸

By 5pm, Inspector Moore was writing his report containing the names of suspects given to him by the staff of the London hospital. They had refused to give him names of doctors but had provided him with details of three medical students. He was formally recording that a more senior officer, possibly the Super, would be required to get details of any 'mad' doctors. As for Inspector Helson, he had made no progress with the doctors at the Bow Infirmary.

⸸ ⸸ ⸸

The man responsible for leading the Whitechapel Murder Squad, CI Swanson, was preparing for a meeting with Commissioner Warren. Swanson was not looking forward to it, as he felt that the early promise shown by Abberline and his team was beginning to fade. Swanson entered the Commissioner's outer office and was asked to take a seat until the Commissioner was ready to see him. Swanson thought that he was going to be in for a rough ride, in view of the negative media coverage and his having made no real progress in apprehending the murderer. At the appointed time he was told to go through to the

Commissioner's office, he took a deep breath and went in.

"Please sit down, Chief Inspector."

"Thank you, sir."

"There are a number of things that I would like to discuss with you but my primary concern lies with the Whitechapel murder case. I'd be grateful if you can apprise me with progress to date and we will take things from there."

Swanson took another deep breath. "Well, sir, as you are already aware, our inquiries are now focused on the pork butcher, Joseph Isenschmid. However, progress has been severely hampered by medical staff at the Bow Infirmary, who have blocked all attempts to have the man attend an identity parade. They won't even agree to his undergoing further police interrogation."

Warren looked at his Chief Inspector and wondered how a man like Swanson would fare if he were an army officer immersed in the conflicts of war. He decided that Swanson would not fare at all well. No, any man who could not force through an identity parade was hardly likely to cope with the life and death decisions taken as a matter of routine by members of the armed forces.

"I take it that you've taken all action within your authority to force the issue with the doctors?" asked Warren with a skeptical tone to his voice.

Swanson was well aware that some of the more left leaning tabloids had not taken favourably to Warren's appointment as Met Commissioner. They liked him even less following, what they viewed as, the heavy-handed policing methods used to break-up the Bloody Sunday demonstration back in 1886. The Star had published many less than complimentary articles about the Commissioner and regularly called for his dismissal.

"Well, sir, not as such. I've left Abberline and the men on the ground to get on with it. I took the view that any hint of interference from above might be perceived by journalists in The Star, and similar minded newspapers, that we were trying to incriminate the first available lunatic that we'd laid our hands upon."

Swanson could see that he'd touched a nerve with his reference to The Star.

"And might not the same said journalists also view any feet dragging on our part to be a sign of incompetence and inefficiency?" asked the Commissioner.

"That might be so, sir. But few will be able to criticize our actions as long as there aren't any more murders and the man we think responsible for committing them is under lock and key."

Warren thought that Swanson was right in his reasoning but was surprised that the man appeared to be unconcerned about the daily stories highlighting the police's lack of progress in the case.

"That is all very well, but surely it would be better all round if the press were made aware that we are very confident in the progress being made in our inquiries and that a dangerous lunatic had been taken off the street, etc, etc?"

"Yes, sir. I'll make arrangements for one of the junior officers to make a few 'off the record' comments to one of the more friendly publications. I'll draft the wording of the comments myself. They will be short, sharp and to the point; in order to minimise any ambiguity as to their meaning."

"Excellent. However, I'd also like you to make it clear to DI Abberline that we require progress with the identity parade…" Warren paused, mulling over whether he had covered all bases. He thought that a few favourable stories in the Sunday papers, together with a weekend without another murder, would make for a much more favourable atmosphere in the week to come. Things were not ideal, but with Isenschmid under lock and key, he still had a few cards to play in discussions with his boss, the Home

Secretary. "Let's just hope that there aren't any more murders. Now is there anything else of note that I need to be aware of?"

When the meeting was over, Swanson lost no time in arranging the 'leak' to the newspapers, detailing Isenschmid's arrest and subsequent detention in an Infirmary.

⸸ ⸸ ⸸

Reid was on the late shift but arrived early into work as he needed to submit a request for a surveillance operation on 24 Finch Street. He did not know much about the science of photography but had decided that such an operation needn't be around the clock, as he assumed that the photographer likely worked in daylight to ensure getting the best images for his clients' photographs. He knew that without the testimony of the two children his request might be rejected. However, even the Super would have to watch his back where abuse of children was concerned. Reid thought that it would take a callous and brave man to put the search of the Whitechapel Murderer above a case like his.

One by one, Sergeant Caunter and PCs Barrett, Mizen, Imhoff and Thompson arrived at the station. They had one final meeting just to be sure that they were all on the same page. Then they departed for what they expected to be a hard night's work. Reid had contemplated requesting use of a firearm, but thought better of it. Thinking that if a mêlée did break out, the weapon could be lost and might even be used against them. In his worst case scenario, Reid had already accepted that he and his men might end up being on the wrong end of a beating.

Caunter and Imhoff went off Spratt Alley, by way of the Nags Head and White Hart pubs, where they expected to find most of the punters getting a few drinks in before taking the short walk up George Yard. As for Reid, Barrett, Mizen and Thompson, they made their way to the Ten Bells and all were hoping that they were not going to end up having ten bells kicked out of them.

When the undercover policemen got to the Ten Bells, they were a little surprised to find Harry Clements already in situ and drinking what looked like his second or third pint. Clements was with another man who none of them recognised. The pub was tiny and it was difficult for Reid's men to maintain a discreet distance from Clements and his friend. Reid hoped that if Clements did notice him, he might ignore him. However, there was always the chance that the man might smell a rat and assume that the police intended to follow him to the dogfight. This was a risk that the Inspector was willing to take, as he wanted to keep a close eye on any other group of men that might be in the pub. His reasoning being that Clements' assailants would likely identify him in the bar before following him out onto the street.

Reid's reasoning proved to be correct, as close to where he and his men stood was another group of four men who were also paying close attention to Clements and his friend. Having identified the men most likely to be involved in the ensuing fracas and needing his men to remain sober, the Inspector instructed his team to leave the pub. There was only one way in and out of the building, so there would be no problem in following the men when they finally decided to leave the bar. The policemen sat themselves down on the steps of the Christchurch church, Whitechapel's largest building, whilst they were waiting. After what seemed like an age but was actually more like 20 minutes, Clements left the pub with his friend, not far behind them were the four men that had been watching them in the bar.

Reid and Barrett followed directly behind the group of four men whilst Mizen and Thompson walked along the other side of the road. Then suddenly without any warning one of the men gave the order for the attack. Clements' friend was immediately knocked to the ground and appeared to be unconscious, leaving four men against one. The gang piled into Clements, but he was a very hard man and was not going to go down without putting up a damn good fight. However, after a couple of heavy blows he slumped into the arms of his attackers. Reid's men were waiting for the Inspector to give them the signal to intervene, but it didn't come.

"HOLD HIM UP AND SEARCH HIM," shouted the leader.

Two of the men held Clements as a third man went through his pockets. The man searching Clements stopped at one of his pockets and pulled out a leather pouch and waved it in front of the leader.

"Alright lads, finish him off," instructed the leader.

With that the two men that had been holding Clements let him go and the three men started hitting him again.

Reid finally gave the signal, simultaneously blowing into his whistle whilst rushing the man with the money pouch. Barrett and Mizen blew on their police regulation whistles to alert Clements' attackers to their presence whilst Thompson tried to tackle the lead man.

"STOP POLICE," shouted Reid, just before he jumped onto the back of the man with the money. The man had been taken by surprise and dropped the pouch but to Reid's great surprise managed to shrug him off with relative ease. A similar fate met the attempts of the other three officers, who were then tempted to take flight in a bid for self-preservation. Fortunately, the leader ordered his men to stand down and make a run for it; leaving the pouch containing the money on the pavement behind them.

"LET THEM GO," Reid shouted to his men.

This was an order that they very readily complied with. Reid addressed Clements, pretending that he did not know who he was.

"Sir, are you alright?" asked Reid.

Clements was in considerable pain, dazed and a bit confused. He thought that he might be either, drunk, concussed or more likely some combination of the two; when he realised that one of the men that had rescued him was none other than the rozzer that had tried to have him banged-up at the end of the last year.

"Ere, I know you, you're that copper, Reid."

"Ah yes, and I know you too, sir. You are lucky that I and my men were passing."

Mizen and Thompson attended to Clements' friend, who was shaken, but appeared not to be badly uninjured.

Reid picked the pouch up from the floor. "This seems to be what they were after," he said.

"LEAVE THAT BE, IT'S MINE," shouted Clements.

Reid opened the pouch and inside it found coins that must have been worth between twenty and thirty pounds. The equivalent of about half a year's wages for a dockside labourer, like Clements.

"Well, what do we have here?" asked Reid.

Reid inspected the coins in the manner of an numismatologist, but in actuality had little idea of what counterfeit coins looked like.

"You're Mr Clements, is that correct?" asked Reid.

"Yes, that I am."

"Well Mr Clements, it looks to me like you've moved up in the world of crime."

"What do you mean, Reid?"

"What I mean is that you appear to be in possession of counterfeit money and I am now going to place you under arrest."

"I need an 'ospital, not prison. That money's mine, it's not snide!" protested Clements.

"We will take you to the station and get a doctor to take a look at you there. If it proves necessary, you'll be taken from there to the hospital."

All the blowing of police whistles had attracted the attention of a large crowd and a few uniformed PCs. The crowd thought for a moment that the Whitechapel Murderer had been caught and started to get quite agitated.

"Leather Apron's been ketched!" went up the cry.

"THEY'VE CAUGHT THE MURDERER! STRING-UP THE BASTARD!" shouted another.

During all the commotion Reid slipped a few coins into his pocket. He then had his men, and the uniformed, officers form a cordon around Clements who was sitting on the floor. Reid then called out to the crowd informing them that a street robbery had been attempted and asked if anyone had seen what had happened. Two men called through the din that they had witnessed the assault and confirmed that it was in fact a robbery. The mob then caught sight of Clements' friend and realising that they were wasting their time at the scene of a mere street robbery - of which in Whitechapel there were many – went back to their business. Reid had the PCs make a search of Clements' associate and after they were sure that he had little in the way of money on his person, told him to make himself scarce. The man didn't need telling twice and sped off into the night.

Reid was keen to get himself and his men to Spratt Alley. So he informed the two uniformed PCs that although Clements was a victim of an attempted robbery, he also appeared to be in possession in a substantial amount of counterfeit money. He instructed the officers to take Clements to the station, get a doctor to assess his medical condition and hold him for questioning. The pouch with the money was to be placed in the station safe. Reid was hoping that by the time Clements had been processed at the station and checked-out by a doctor, he and his men would have returned from their raid and so he himself could take charge of questioning the suspect.

As for the two men that had identified themselves as witnesses to the attempted robbery, Reid instructed the men to accompany the officers and Clements to the station where they were to provide brief statements of what they had seen. The men were not keen on spending their Friday night in a police station, but following brief protests they agreed to do as the Inspector asked.

"I hope that you are not badly injured Mr, Clements. I also hope that you will understand that I am obliged to investigate this matter further, but do not have the time to do so now."

Clements said nothing in response.

Reid and his men dusted themselves down before making their way to Spratt Alley. They then split into two groups of two and arrived in the alley a few minutes apart from each other. They were in luck, the lookouts did not recognise them as policemen and allowed them into the area being used for the dog fights. Where they joined Caunter, Imhoff and about another hundred men who were formed in a circle around two fighting dogs, tearing each other apart in a freshly dug pit.

The officers slowly converged on each other, waiting until the end of the fight before moving to a corner of the yard. No one took any notice of the group of six policemen. There was a lot of activity in the yard, with some of the more fortunate punters busy collecting their winnings, whilst many others were sizing-up the dogs being made ready for the next fight.

Caunter informed Reid that the ringleader was a man well known to the local police, James Batey, and pointed him out from the crowd. Batey was standing with two men who appeared to be his bodyguards. The owners of the next two dogs removed their animal's muzzles and paraded them in front of Batey for his inspection. Whilst Reid and his men were assessing the situation they watched as the four men who had assaulted Clements entered the yard.

Three of them were immediately given crowd control duties, whilst the lead man approached Batey and was seen to give him the bad news, which Reid knew to be that they had been unsuccessful in robbing Clements of his money.

It was now obvious to the Inspector that he and his men did not have sufficient manpower to make any significant arrests. If the four of them could not overpower the four of Batey's men on Commercial Street, then the six of them had absolutely no chance against the eight to ten of them positioned around the yard. So Reid decided to implement his plan B. His men were to stand well clear of the exit of the yard in order to allow Batey and his cronies an easy means of escape. Then they were to blow their whistles, in unison, in the hope of at least apprehending one or two of the dog owners.

The officers' blew into their whistles and Batey and his cronies led the charge out of the yard, closely followed by the hundred or so punters. Leaving some of the older men, who couldn't run, and some of the dog breeders who were hesitant about leaving their dogs behind. The police officers managed to bring down two of these men and everyone else was allowed to go free.

There were to have been five dogfights that night. One had taken place before Reid and the other officers arrived in the yard, another had taken place whilst they were there. Meaning that there were eight fighting dogs left in the yard; comprising six dogs that had not yet fought and two badly injured dogs that had won the first two fights. All eight animals would now need to be destroyed.

Sergeant Caunter took charge of the situation.

"Right, you two are under arrest for aiding and abetting illegal dog fighting. Constable Imhoff, get back to the station and make arrangements for these dogs to be destroyed. Barrett and Mizen, I need you to stay here and guard the animals until Imhoff returns. Are we all clear on what needs to be done?"

The Sergeant's men confirmed that they understood and escorted the two suspected dog trainers to the station for questioning.

On his arrival at the station Reid was informed that Clements most likely had a few cracked ribs, an injury that would not be helped by hospital treatment. So it was agreed that Clements would spend the night in the cells to help soften him up.

Sergeant Caunter started questioning the dog trainers with Reid sitting-in on the interviews. Reid was happy to listen to the suspects pleading their innocence. Each man maintaining that he had been invited into the yard, hadn't laid any bets on the dogfights and had absolutely no connection with the dogs. The men were informed that they were not going to be given their liberty and that further questioning would take place the next day. The two suspects were unknown to each other as they came from different communities, one was Irish and the other Jewish; their names were Paddy O'Rourke and Levi Greenfield.

CHAPTER SEVEN

I Will Make a Deal with You

REID WANTED to make a short day of it on the Saturday 15th September. He had decided to let O'Rourke and Greenfield sweat and wanted to see if a night in the cells would make them a little more cooperative. He wanted to know if either man was willing to testify against the man that he knew, but could not prove, had organised the event, Batey. Reid and Sergeant Caunter interviewed O'Rourke first and as they much expected, found that he was unwilling to name the names of any of the other men involved in the event, even that of Greenfield who he was arrested with. O'Rourke was a local petty criminal and as such was very unlikely to turn evidence against a local kingpin like Batey. However, Reid was hoping that he might make some leeway with Greenfield. Neither he or the sergeant knew anything about this man and assumed that he was new on the Whitechapel crime scene. This time Reid led the questioning.

"Good morning, Mr Greenfield, I trust that you did not sleep well?"

Greenfield had spent the night mulling over his options. He knew that the police officers were not interested in him and were looking for a way to arrest the event organiser, Batey. However, he also knew that to grass on a fellow criminal was frowned upon and to grass on someone like Batey was akin to committing suicide. Being relatively new to Whitechapel he had no loyalty to the likes of Batey, but for the sake of self-preservation had decided that he would have to go to court and most likely do some time in prison. The only thing that he could think of to barter with was his involvement with pornographer Joshua

Engels. However, he thought it very unlikely that officers involved in an illegal gambling case would have any interest in vice.

"You are correct, sir. I did not sleep well," replied Greenfield.

"I trust that you have had time to think about your situation?" asked Reid.

"I have, sir."

"And are you willing to give evidence against Mr Batey, the man we know to be the man in charge of the event?"

"As I explained yesterday, sir. I don't know the man and was only in the alley to see the dogs fighting."

"In that case you will have no interest in knowing that none of the dogs found in the yard last night have been put down. However, arrangements are being made as we speak and it will be only a matter of time before the animals are destroyed."

Greenfield was surprised by Reid's statement. If he understood the Inspector correctly, the man appeared to be offering him back his fighting dogs - in addition to his liberty – if he would testify against the local kingpin. He could not understand how any policeman would have the freedom to make him such an offer.

"It would be a shame to see any animal destroyed, sir, but as I have already told you and the other officers, the dogs have nothing to do with me."

"Very well then, I shan't waste anymore of my time on you. My officers have more than enough information with which to convict you. You will now remain in custody until a hearing is arranged for you to appear before a magistrate."

Reid and Caunter got up to leave the interview room. Greenfield staring a prison sentence in the face decided to chance his arm.

"Sir, I may have something for you!"

Reid and Caunter returned to their seats.

"What is it man?" asked Reid.

"As you know, I cannot inform on the likes of Mr Batey, it would be madness for me to do that. But I have fingers in many pies and can provide information on the activities of a man in an unrelated field."

Reid had no idea what Greenfield was on about but thought that he had better hear the man out.

"What do you mean by this?" asked the Inspector.

"Well, sir, I know of a man that takes photographs of naked men and women and is selling them to influential types, out west. I can give you the man's name and address if we are able to come to some arrangement."

Caunter answered first "We have no interest in such matters, either you give us something on Batey or one of his lieutenants or its prison for you!"

Reid thought for a while before speaking. He had been tasked with stopping the escalation of illegal gambling around the Spitalfields area. Now that Batey was aware that the police were on to him, Reid felt sure that the man would cease activities for a while until the heat died down. Also, all that he could currently show for his efforts was the arrest of two dog breeders; something hardly warranting the time and cost of an inspector, a sergeant and four PCs. The charge against a known criminal like O'Rourke was very likely to stick, so a second against Greenfield was unlikely to tip the balance in any particular direction. Reid decided that he'd make a deal with Greenfield if he were able to provide him with good information against the Finch Street pornographer.

"As the sergeant says, we have no interest in any other vice other than gambling. But since you have mentioned the matter, I will listen to what you have to offer. However, please bear in mind that one photographer is much like another, so if you have nothing special for us, we will leave matters where they stand. Is that understood?"

"Yes, sir, I understand very well. What if I were to tell you that the photographs in question are not like others, but show evil acts being committed against women?"

"As I said, Mr Greenfield, one photographer is very much like another. I am no expert in these matters, but I doubt if the pictures you allude to are so much different than any of the others that can be bought in and around the Spitalfields market," said Reid, his interest waning.

"No, sir. Please trust me on this. Pictures can be very different. I can help get you a man that takes horrible ones, not only of women but of little uns as well, sir."

On hearing that, Reid decided that any arrangement that he might be willing to make with Greenfield was not for the ears of his sergeant.

"Mr Greenfield, are you thirsty?" asked Reid.

"Yes, sir. Very much so."

"Sergeant, can you please arrange for this man to have some water, a cup of coffee and a piece of bread."

Caunter left the room as he was instructed and Reid continued the interview with Greenfield.

"As you can see, Mr Greenfield, you now have my full attention. So what is it you want to tell me?"

"I can give you a name and the address of man that takes bad pictures of children."

"What is your involvement in this matter?"

"Well, I deliver the photographs to the buyers and collects the money from them."

"Have you any other involvement in the sordid matter you are describing to me?"

"Now, sir, you have to understand that I personally haven't taken any children off of the street," said Greenfield. Sensing that he has struck a chord with the Inspector and that maybe, if he played his cards right, he just might be able to get himself out of cells and back onto the streets.

"As I was saying, sir. I ain't taken any children off of the street."

"You have told me that. Please continue," encouraged

Reid.

"But I'll admit that I helped this man get the little uns for his photos."

"Go on."

"Well, I found a couple, a man and woman that model for some of the photographs and these people found the little uns used in the photo sessions."

"So what is it you are offering me?"

"For my liberty, I can give you the name and address of a photographer that's responsible for photographing children in all manner of indecent acts, and the man's done a lot more than that. Like I said, I can give you his name and address and I can give you the names and whereabouts of his models."

Reid already knew the photographer's address. What he wanted to know was whether this man would testify against the man in court.

"If needs be, will you testify against this man?" asked Reid.

"I will testify against this man, but only if I am allowed to go free today, to keep my dogs and to be pardoned for my work for the photographer."

Reid mulled the offer over in his mind. This man was asking a lot from him. However, he had set his mind on getting a conviction against the bastard responsible for the ordeal experienced by the two children he'd found in Great Pearl Street. The man before him obviously played a large part in the sordid acts that Reid thought the children had suffered, but it was the photographer that he was really after.

"You say that you did not personally select the children?"

"That is right, sir. I didn't. But like I have already said, I cannot deny having made arrangements for others to do so. I just want to be clear on this so you knows what to expect if I'm called to a witness stand."

The Inspector did not want this man to get away with his part in the evil acts, but like so many others, Greenfield was just a pawn being used by a man at the top. Reid had not gotten a warrant to search the house in Finch Street, as he suspected that no evidence of criminality would now be found there. However, with Greenfield's cooperation, he felt certain of being able to make full-proof case against his employer.

"Very well, I will make a deal with you. I need to know every detail about the man that you work for, all his activities and names and addresses of his clients. If I am satisfied with the probity of your tale, you will be allowed to walk free from this station this very afternoon and will even be able to take your fighting dogs with you. However, please bear in mind that we now know your face, so your card has been marked. Should you be caught partaking in any future acts of villainy, there will be no deals to be made and you will find yourself in the care of one of the city's jailers. Have I made myself clear to you?

"Yes, sir. Very clear."

Caunter returned to the interview room with a cup of coffee, a beaker of water and some bread for the prisoner.

"Thank you, Sergeant. It appears that Mr Greenfield is able to provide me with significant information relating to another of my cases, the details of which need not concern you at this time. Therefore, I have decided that you should proceed with the prosecution against the other prisoner, O'Rourke. As for Mr Greenfield, I intend to release him after further questioning. He will be allowed to take his dogs with him on leaving the station."

Caunter knew that Reid was a man who got results, if not by always following what one might term 'the correct procedure'. If this is what his Detective Inspector wanted, then he was not going argue with him. They had made one arrest and no doubt caused the Saturday night dogfight to be cancelled. What with the manpower shortage caused by the Whitechapel murders, Caunter thought that there was not much more that could have been achieved.

Reid wrote up his notes on the interview with Greenfield before requesting that Harry Clements be taken into one of the interview rooms.

"How are you feeling today, Mr Clements?"

"Bloody awful, Reid. All I wants is to go home."

"Maybe that can be arranged but that will depend on how cooperative you are."

"Wot you on about?"

"We've verified that the money in your possession is counterfeit. I'm told that the craftsmanship is of extremely high quality. What we would like to do is catch the person or persons responsible for creating the coins. Somehow, I can't imagine that this is something that you are responsible for. I'd be willing to let you go, without charge, if you can provide me full details of how you came into possession of money. So what is it to be, Mr Clements, are you able to help me track down the source of the forgeries?"

Clements was in great pain but felt that he was lucky to be alive. He knew that if Reid and his men had not been passing at the time of robbery he might well have been killed on the pavement.

"Okay, Reid. The ways I sees it, I owes you one but I ain't giving evidence against no one. So I don't see how I can help ya."

"Let me by the judge of what you can or cannot do. Now, if you are willing, please tell me how you came to be in possession of the money?"

"Well, Inspector, you knows me, I ain't a bad man. It's just that I gets into a bit of trouble now and again cos of my drinking."

"Come on, man, just spit it out!"

"Well, one day Inspector, I didn't get any work on the docks and took to drinkin' early like. I was wandering the streets for hours. Anyways, I was sitting down in a square when I sees these men doing some sort of deal. I gets the impression that some monies changed 'ands and cos I'm drunk like, I decides to follow the men I'd seen. Anyways, I'm not sure exactly what happened like but I ends up in a fight with the men and they drops this bag that they was carrying. Next thing I know is that the men have gone and I'm left holding their bag. I looks inside it and it's full of coins. I couldn't believe how much money there was and I'm thinking that it can't be real like. So I uses some of it in a pub and the landlord takes it straight and gives me change out of the money that I gave him. So I'm thinking that maybe it's real money like or as good as real money. Anyway, whilst I'm thinking of ways to spend the money, I hears about some dog fighting and I goes a gambling. I puts on some big bets and everyone's happy to take the money off me. Now as far as I knows, the money is real. I've been spending it without no complaints like."

"So what you are telling me is that you obtained the money in a robbery?"

"No, I'm not saying that. What I'm saying is that I gets into a fight with some men and they drops their money and runs away. I didn't have any way of returning it like, if you gets me meaning?"

"So if I understand you correctly. You are saying that you have no connection with any forgers and that you are not involved in the uttering counterfeit currency?"

"What I'm saying is that I found the money that was dropped and that's all I knows about it."

"I'm willing to believe that, but I'm afraid that I don't see how you can then help me catch the forgers, since you don't know who they are."

"Well, Inspector, I might actually be able to help you with that. I know the name of the man that dropped the money and can give you that if you will let me go. What says you to that?"

Reid paused to think. He was sure that someone like

Clements could not be involved in anything like uttering counterfeit currency, as he lacked the skills or the necessary connections. However, it was highly likely that he did rob some men involved in the business. He knew that Clements would not give this evidence in a court of law, so he was faced with risking letting him go in return for what might be false or inaccurate information. Reid was after bigger fish than Clements and knew that he had nothing on the counterfeiters. He decided to take the risk of letting Clements go.

"Very well, Mr Clements. The way I see things, you owe my men and I a debt for saving you from what looked to be more than an average beating. Now you understand that I cannot return the money to you, because, as a member of Her Majesty's Constabulary, I'm responsible for removing counterfeit money from the money supply. However, if you give me the names and whereabouts of the men who dropped the counterfeit money, I'll be willing to take a chance and let you go."

"Look, Inspector. I've got nought save my health and the men that attacked me have taken that from me. Without that money, I've no way of making a living. I'm thinking that I'd like to help you, but prison might be the best place for me till me ribs heal-up like."

Reid put his hand in his pocket and removed the coins he had picked-up during Clements' arrest.

"You appear to be a lucky man, Mr Clements. During last night's commotion, I placed some of your money in my pocket. There appears to be a few pounds here. I am happy to return this money back to you and hopefully you will be able to use it to good effect, keeping yourself afloat until your health returns," said Reid passing Clements the coins.

Clements did not know what to make of the situation. Inspector Reid, the man who had tried to have him convicted for murder, was now willing to let him go free after nigh-on admitting that he had robbed two men of snide money. On top of that, the man appeared to be willing to return a few pounds of the forged money back to him in order to give him a chance to get himself back on his feet again. Clements felt this was too good to be true, but he was a man with very limited options. He thought that Reid was most likely lying to him and that he would take the money back off of him after he had gotten what he was after. However, being tired and in a lot of pain, he decided to take the chance that Reid might in fact remain true to his word.

"Alright, Inspector. The man that dropped the money is named Harris Marks and you should be able to find him at the White Hart pub. That's where he likes to go for a drink. I don't think he has anything to do with making the coins, I think he just buys them from those that does."

Reid had never heard of Harris Marks, but in a way he thought that was a good thing. It implied that Marks might be a successful career criminal, a big fish. In that case there might some kudos to be had from solving the case and might even warrant a bonus to go with it.

"Very well, Mr Clements, it's a deal. Now I'm not asking you to become a regular informant of mine, but I'd be grateful if you can contact me if you discover any other information relating to this matter. Otherwise, please get yourself cleaned-up and try to stay out of further trouble."

Reid informed the desk sergeant that after questioning, the prisoner was free to go and should be released from custody. He then wrote a report to the effect that counterfeit money was found after he and his men had broken-up a fight between two groups of men, and that the money most likely belonged to the men who had escaped arrest. That done, he left the station to make the most of the rest of the weekend with his family.

CHAPTER EIGHT

Very Violent and Mentally Disturbed

THE LAST WEEKEND had seen its fair share of thefts, fights and prostitution, but as far as the members of the Whitechapel Murder Squad were concerned, it had passed without any incident of note. On the Monday, Inspector Helson, sent another telegram to the Bow Infirmary, requesting that Isenschmid be declared fit to attend an identity parade, and at the end of the day he received the usual response that the doctors did not think him well enough to participate in one. Nothing else of note happened that day.

⸎ ⸎ ⸎

On the morning of Tuesday 18 September Abberline arrived early into the station. He had had a sleepless night, which was the result of his becoming frustrated at the lack of progress made in the case. Monday's newspapers contained many stories of the relief felt by the communities of the east end that no new murders had taken place over the weekend. However, most of the stories were critical of the lack of progress made in apprehending the murderer or murderers. Abberline had solved many crimes over the years but he had never been involved in such a high profile case and the pressure was beginning to take its toll on him. He had decided – following a meeting with CI Swanson - that Helson should waste no more time sending telegrams to the Bow Infirmary and should instead go there in person and demand positive action be taken with Isenschmid.

⸎ ⸎ ⸎

Reid's week started badly, as he was informed that the Superintendent had turned down his request for surveillance on the house of the suspected pornographer. The Super was also beginning to succumb to the pressure generated by the Whitechapel murders. He'd stated that there was insufficient evidence to warrant stationing plain-clothes personnel in Finch Street when their time could be spent more productively elsewhere. Reid would ordinarily have protested against such a refusal, but knowing that he'd be wasting his breath, decided to concentrate his efforts on the dog breeder, Greenfield.

❦❦❦

When Inspector Helson arrived at the Bow Infirmary Asylum he was directed to the office of a Dr Mickle whom he had been informed was the man charged with Isenschmid's care. Helson saw that Dr Mickle was a big fish in the small pond in which he worked. The doctor believing himself to be a very important man; and in truth, in the world that was the Bow Infirmary, that is exactly what he was. The Inspector realized that dealing with the man at arms-length, via telegram, had been a mistake. His feeling was that a man so wrapped-up in his own self-importance would have have had been far more inclined to play ball if he had received a personal visit from the off. It was now too late to change the initial approach made to the doctor, who had clearly dug his heels in, with his refusal to allow Isenschmid to participate in an identity parade. However, the good doctor did at least grant Helson access to Isenschmid, even if he did not authorize his formerly interviewing the man. But Helson's feeling was the Dr Mickle had purposely let him have access to Isenschmid in order that he could see how violent and dangerous Isenschmid had become, and just how valuable to the police's inquiries the man might yet prove to be.

The short time that Helson had spent in Isenschmid's company was more than enough to convince him that the man was potentially very violent and clearly mentally disturbed. However, he could not help thinking how difficult it would be for such a man to lure any woman - no matter how desperate - into the darkness and isolation of a small side street or backyard. He thought that many a man, let alone most women, would be afraid to be alone in Isenschmid's company. Anyway, unable to make any headway with Dr Mickle, Helson returned to the station to give Abberline the bad news.

⸙ ⸙ ⸙

Reid was in luck. Greenfield had not reneged on their agreement and arrived at the station that afternoon to inform him that Engels had asked him to procure models for another photo session being planned for the coming Friday morning. Greenfield stated that Engels had instructed him to hire two or three ladies and one gent for 'artistic poses'. Reid made an immediate request for a sergeant and four PCs to be made available to attend a raid on Finch Street on Friday at noon. The Super paid Reid a personal visit informing him that he expected better results than those achieved on the raid on the gambling den, which had resulted in only two arrests. Reid countered by informing the Super that if he had had sufficient manpower the ringleaders would have been caught, adding that if he did not receive his full complement of officers on Friday, they risked another raid failing to meet expectations.

⸙ ⸙ ⸙

When Helson arrived back at the station he found Abberline in the middle of writing a fifteen-page report on all actions taken to date on both the Chapman and Nichols murders. Abberline and his superior officers were now concerned that with the resumption of the Chapman inquest, scheduled for the next day, Mrs Elizabeth Long would be called-up to give her evidence and in doing so would be asked to describe the man that she said she saw with the deceased just before her death. That man would be described as being about 40 years of age, wearing a brown deerstalker hat and having the appearance of a foreigner, or in everyday parlance, the look of a dark-haired, dark-skinned Jew. He knew that following the publication of this description in the Thursday editions of the London newspapers, his team would be swamped with hundreds of reports concerning suspicious looking Jewish men frequenting the Whitechapel area, of which there were thousands. Also of great concern was that tensions were already high between the different communities, with an undercurrent of anti-Jewish feeling beginning to take hold in the district. It was thought that the situation was at crisis point and that a minor incident might be enough to light the touch paper and generate a full-scale anti-Jewish riot.

The Jewish community were intensely aware of the situation and this may have been one of the reasons behind a reward for information into the capture of the Whitechapel Murderer being offered by the Jewish Member of Parliament, Samuel Montagu, and for the reward offered by the Whitechapel Vigilance Committee. Whatever the reasons, the authorities were expecting trouble. The only good that Abberline thought might come out of Mrs Long's testimony was that, by stating that she thought the perpetrator was a member of the Jewish faith, the public should be put at ease by the news of the arrest of the very Jewish sounding, Joseph Isenschmid. Abberline thought that would most likely last up until they received details of the man's physical description, which would be made available following the outstanding identification parade.

However, with a lot of luck, the masses might ignore the fact that his description in no way matched that of the suspects described in the newspaper stories, with Isenschmid having red hair and a large carroty red moustache.

Abberline rose early the next day and completed his lengthy report before he and Inspectors Helson, Chandler and Bannister made their way to the Working Lads Institute for the penultimate session of the Chapman inquest. At the end of his report, Abberline included the suggestion that either the Chief Surgeon or one of the Divisional Surgeons should be asked to make a personal visit to Dr Mickle asking for Isenschmid to be made available to participate in a line-up. His reasoning being that a request made by such an eminent member of the medical community would be enough to satisfy the vanity of the Bow Infirmary's stubborn doctor.

CHAPTER NINE

False Hopes

THE DAYS HAD FLOWN BY and before anyone knew it, it was Friday 21st September and another weekend loomed, over which the Whitechapel Murderer might choose to strike. Abberline and his team had made absolutely no progress with their case and arrangements were again being made to flood the streets with policemen. As for Reid, his planned raid on the pornographer's house was an unwelcome distraction that everyone said they could well do without.

❦❦❦

Greenfield had made the usual arrangement for the 'models' to attend 24 Finch Street. They arrived at 11am in order to make themselves ready for a photo shoot scheduled to start at midday, when the sun was highest in the sky. Greenfield directed a man and three ladies to the top floor of the building and waited downstairs whilst Engels set-up his cameras. Unbeknown to Engels, Greenfield had already prepared an escape plan for when the house was to be raided by the police, having already sourced an escape route over the rooftops. Reid had informed his men not to chase too hard if they had Greenfield in their sights.

Reid waited until 12.30 before giving the order to raid the house. The officers had a search warrant and knocked very loudly at the front door. That was followed by a shout of "POLICE, OPEN UP IN THE NAME OF THE LAW."

Greenfield immediately ran up the stairs, passed Engels

and the models and made his exit through a skylight.

"WHAT'S HAPPENING, GREENFIELD?" shouted Engels.

"We are being raided by the police, sir. Please come this way and we might be able to make our escape across the rooftops."

The thought of clambering over the rooftops did not appeal to Engels or the models. They heard Reid and his men breaking down the front door and decided to leave Greenfield to make his escape and awaited their own fates at the hands of the policemen that were now running up the stairs. By the time the officers reached the top floor Greenfield was long gone, but they found the models in a state of undress and Engels trying to destroy his photographic plates.

Reid was the first officer into the room. "Everyone stop what you are doing, we are the police and you are all under arrest!"

The Inspector read everyone their rights and had his men search the rest of the house for evidence of wrongdoing. Greenfield had told Reid that Engels was very careful not to keep any incriminating images in the house for longer than was absolutely necessary. So he wasn't surprised, following an extensive search, that no other photographs were found. However, Reid felt that he had enough evidence for a conviction and had Engels and his models taken to Leman Street for questioning.

At the station, Reid had his sergeant interview the models whilst he conducted the interview of Engels.

"What is your name?" asked Reid.

"Joshua Engels."

"And your address, Mr Engels."

"24 Finch Street, Whitechapel."

"And what is your occupation?"

"Photographer."

"Mr Engels, as you are most likely already aware, we in

the police are willing to turn the odd blind eye to people in your profession, as we understand that there appears to be a need for the materials that you and your peers produce. However, now and again it is brought to our attention that wholly unacceptable images are being taken and circulated to the populous. I am afraid that when that happens, we are unable to sit idly by and action must be taken. Our intelligence leads us to believe that you have crossed the line of common decency and are the creator of an unacceptable class of evil images, and it is my intention that you will receive no clemency for your acts. If what I have been told is true, the grotesque images seized today are but tame in comparison to your most vile works. What says you to this, Mr Engels?"

Engels did not know what to say. He knew that he was in a lot of trouble. He also knew that the officer was speaking the truth and that he had truly crossed the line of all decency, and by doing so the authorities were going to try and lock him away and throw away the key. In a way he considered himself to have been lucky. In that the images he had taken that day were quite tame in comparison to those that included the children, but even so, he was afraid and did not want to go to prison.

"What can I say, sir? I am a photographer. You and your men have entered my house today and found models and photographic images. All that I can give you is the name of another man who was in the house with me. He made his escape over the roof tops. I assume that you have no other evidence against me other than the plates you found at the house today? In which case, sir, I will accept whatever punishment I am due."

Reid was silent. Engels was right, they had no more evidence against him than the images seized that day. However, as was his way he decided to let Engels sweat for a while. It was usual for prisoners to provide all sorts of information when trying to barter for their freedom or a reduced sentence. In this case, Reid had already made his mind up that he did not want to play ball with the man in front of him. He felt great hatred towards Engels for having exploited children for his personal gain, but he had to maintain his professionalism and go through the motions, letting the due process of the law take its course.

"Very well, Mr Engels. I am going to leave you for a while in order that you can decide if you want to furnish us with any further information regarding your vile business. There may be some lessoning of the charges should you decide to help us with our inquiries, but I will make you no promises. My sergeant is currently interviewing your models and they no doubt will provide us with the name of your accomplice, should you choose not to do so. Please bear in mind that we are aware of your other misdeeds and will request that you receive the maximum penalty that the law is able to impose upon you."

Reid left the interview room, made himself a coffee and sat at his desk whiling away his time organising his in-tray. It was difficult for him to concentrate on anything as the station had started to become jam-packed with policemen, with a lot of additional men arriving for their briefings in advance of that weekend's Whitechapel Murder watch.

From the interview room, Joshua Engels could overhear the conversations of the men arriving for weekend duty, most of the talk was about the Whitechapel Murderer. Then he remembered something, something that might be a straw with which to cling to, something that might get him out of the hole which he had dug himself into.

Reid touched base with the sergeant who had been interviewing the models. They had informed the sergeant that they had been contacted by a man working for Engels, but said that they did not know the man's name. In fact they didn't even know Engels's real name and had referred to him as Mr Smith.

Reid decided that he had given Engels enough time to

ponder his fate and returned to the interview room.

"All right, Mr Engels, have you anything else to tell me?" demanded Reid.

"Actually, sir, I may have something that I can tell you."

"Well, what is it?"

"I could not help overhearing the conversations of the officers arriving into the police station. I believe that they are here in order to try and catch the man referred to as the 'Whitechapel Murderer'."

The Inspector remained silent. He wanted to see where Engels was going with his bid for freedom.

Engels continued, "I cannot offer any excuse for the images seized by your men today and for those that you think that I have taken in the recent past. However, I have not always been a purveyor of such sordid materials. I am afraid that over time, men of a certain disposition started offering me large sums of money if I would provide them with images like those taken today. At first I refused but one day, when I found myself in financial difficulty, I finally agreed to produce them. Then over time, without my even being aware of it, I slowly moved into a realm where I produced the most evil images, for whom I can only assume are the most evil of men. Anyway, that is not of interest to you; however, I believe that I might know something that is. Last year I was approached by a man who has a taste for what could be described as photographs of women in various forms of distress. Over the course of the year his requests became more specific, until I was finally producing images of what I can only describe as assaults on single woman by men brandishing all sorts of medical implements -."

"What has your tale got to do with the situation that you find yourself in today, Mr Engels?" interrupted an impatient sounding Reid.

"Well, sir, if you allow me to finish. What I am saying

is that I believe that you and your men seek a man that has been slashing the throats of women of the lowest class and cutting them to pieces. Well, what I am saying is that the images I took for this particular client bore a great resemblance to the murders that I have been reading about in the newspapers…" Engels hesitated for a moment, realising that it sounded as if he had been photographing actual physical assaults. "I am not saying that I photographed women being physically injured in any way, but one could very easily imagine them having been so. Over the course of a year I have produced images of ever greater violence, and feel that this client has descended further and further into the depths of depravity."

"I am afraid that I still do not understand what you are telling me, Mr Engels. My primary assignment has been to stem the flow of the evil images produced by you and others like you. Having captured you, I feel that I completed this task successfully. So what do I care for the perversions of the men that you do your vile business with, now that I have eliminated one source of their cravings?"

Engels was beginning to think that Inspector Reid must be a bit slow and saw his lifeline slipping out of his hands.

"Look Inspector, what I am saying or more clearly, what I am offering you, is the name of a man who lusts over images of women being assaulted by an assortment of medical implements. Including what I can only describe to be large knives, the sort that a surgeon might use."

Engels finally had Reid's full attention. But Reid was careful to only look partially interested in he had heard.

"Now let me see if I understand you, Mr Engels. What you appear to be telling me. Is that having found yourself in this police station, staring a prison sentence in the face, you want to barter for your freedom by offering me the name of a man you believe might be the Whitechapel Murderer?"

"Well, if those are the terms in which you wish to put

it? Then yes, that is exactly what I am offering you."

"Mr Engels with all due respect, the authorities have not sanctioned any reward for information leading to the capture of the murderer. As for the newspapers, they carry many stories of private individuals and organisations willing to pay a reward for such information. To name but one, the Whitechapel Vigilance Committee, who have offered a reward in excess of £100. What I would like to know from you, sir, is whether you have approached any such organisation and offered them the information that you are now offering me?"

"No, sir, I have not."

"So you have little interest in reward money or the removal of a madman from our streets?"

"I do, sir, but have only this minute truly given the matter much thought."

Engels response seemed quite reasonable to Reid. Who was starting to think that he might have stumbled across a means of exorcising the ghost of Abberline and capturing the killer.

"Very well, Mr Engels. So if I take you at your word. You claim to be able to provide me with the details of a man whom you suppose might be inclined to have committed the horrible murders of recent weeks. However, my superiors will require more than your word, sir, they will insist on some form of evidence. Do you have any evidence with which to substantiate the claim you are making?"

Now it was Engels' time to think. He was stuck, he genuinely believed that one of his clients might be responsible for committing such evil deeds but he had not kept any copies of the photographs that he had taken for the man. He had always been most careful to destroy every trace of his work, just in case the police ever raided his house.

"I am afraid Inspector that I have no proof of what I

tell you. The most that I could do is to try to get the models that I used for the photographic sessions to describe the images that they helped create."

Reid had no intention of helping Engels in any way. In a way he was pleased that the man could not provide him with copies of the images he had taken, as he wanted Engels to go to prison for the vile acts he had committed.

"Very well, Mr Engels, I need to think some more about this. As things stand I can do nothing for you, as you truly have nothing with which to barter. But please tell me some more about your business?"

Engels knew that he sounded like a desperate man, willing to say just about anything to get himself off of the hook for what he had done. He thought that he had nothing to lose by talking a bit more about his business. As long as he did not reveal his client's name, he might still have something to trade with.

"Most of my gentlemen clients correspond with me through third parties. However, I also deal with a few private individuals directly, the man I have in mind is one of those. I noted his requirements, arranged the photo shoot, sent him the photographs and the photographic plates."

"So you personally delivered the materials to this man?"

"No, I did not. I have a man who makes deliveries for me, the gentleman who escaped from your clutches."

"So your delivery man has seen the photographs and met with your client?"

"No, that is not the system that I have in place. My man arranges the models for the photographic sessions, but does not witness the sessions. I give him sealed packages, which he then delivers to the client. He has most likely been able to guess the contents of the packages, but to my knowledge has never seen inside of them."

"But he will have met with your client?"

"No, I am afraid not. This particular man was most careful in his dealings with me. The arrangement was for my man to deliver the packages to the Regents Park, leaving them at agreed locations for collection. I have met with the client but no one else has."

"Do you have the man's home address?"

"No, I do not".

Reid sat in silence, sifting the information in his mind. So far as he could tell Engels had a client with a taste for images showing assaults on women. He had the man's name but no address for him. Reid thought that any man that went to the trouble of hiding his address would go to the trouble of providing a false name. In short, Engels very likely had nothing that he could use. Even Greenfield was unlikely to be any use in the matter, as Engels was certain that Greenfield had neither seen the images nor met the client. Reid decided that there was nothing further that could be done with Engels. He would make a report to the Superintendent informing that further progress might be made by obtaining the details of some of the clients and agents that Engels dealt with, but otherwise Reid was pleased with a job well done.

"I trust that it is your plan to provide me with the name of your client in return for our mitigating the charges that have been levied against you?"

"Yes, sir. That is what I am proposing."

"Well then, tell me this Mr Engels. Do you in all honesty believe that your client gave you his real name?"

Engels finally saw his lifeline slipping from his grasp. "No, sir. I don't suppose that he would have."

"In that case, Mr Engels, please feel free to provide me or my colleagues with the name of your client, but you will get nothing from me for it. I intend to make my report and we will no doubt see each other again in a court of law. Do you have anything else to say, sir?"

"No, I do not."

Engels was returned to his cell and Reid set about writing up his report.

CHAPTER TEN

Tethering a Goat to a Stake

ANOTHER WEEKEND PASSED without incident for the Whitechapel Murder Squad, but in a way it only contributed to the pressure being felt by the individual team members. They had reached Monday 24th September and still had nothing concrete with which to work. The only silver lining, in the cloud surrounding them, was that the murderer had not struck again because he was sitting safely tucked away, in the Bow Infirmary Asylum. As had been anticipated, there had been a surge in reports of suspicious 'foreign' looking men following the publication of Mrs Long's description of the man she reported seeing outside of 29 Hanbury Street on the morning of 8th September. It transpired that most of these new suspicious looking men were in fact plain clothes police officers who had recently been drafted into Whitechapel to beef-up police numbers.

⸙ ⸙ ⸙

Reid had spent an enjoyable weekend with his wife and children. He wanted to make the most of it as he was on the rota for afternoon/evenings that week and was on the duty roster for night duty over the coming weekend. Ordinarily he dreaded the weekend night shift as it threw out his sleep patterns and disrupted his family life. However, the Whitechapel murderer had now not struck for a several weeks and Reid had a feeling in his water that the man would soon strike again. Reid had quite a bit of time over the weekend to reflect on his conversation with Engels. Engels had told him that he had witnessed one of his less than savoury clients sink to ever new lows in his taste for violent pornography. Reid wondered if there could be a link between the killer's physical actions and his mental fantasies. He decided that he'd make another call on Dr Phillips to seek the man's views on the matter. In the meantime he had to decide on what progress, if any, could be made with his illegal gambling case.

He now knew who was behind the dogfights and hoped that his raid would force Batey and his cronies to lie low for a while. However, he also knew that the Super had not been pleased that the gambling raid had only netted a couple of dog trainers. What he needed was another bone to throw his superior's way, to help keep the man off of his back.

As for the forgery case, Clements had given him the details of a man who might transpire to be the main snide-pitcher. If that man could be brought to book, Reid would most likely find the master forger and stem the flow of the bad money at its source.

❦ ❦ ❦

Abberline had arranged to meet his team at two o'clock. He was pleased that the weekend had passed without incident, strengthening his belief that the perpetrator was tucked away in an asylum. However, the failure to get Isenschmid into an identity parade was a cause of deep frustration to him. Abberline was starting to think that he was spending as much, if not more time, managing relationships and playing politics than he was hunting down the killer; a case in point being the police's relationship with Coroner Baxter. He had purposely kept Inspector Chandler away from the last Chapman inquest as he felt that Chandler's presence might be a cause for further irritation to the Coroner. He had achieved that by allocating Chandler to interviews of local hairdressers. Hairdressers were under suspicion, as it was known that a significant proportion of these men had basic medical knowledge and had experience of minor surgical procedures. Abberline expected progress to be slow and would definitely be a valid reason for Chandler not attending the final session of the inquest scheduled for Wednesday.

Abberline started the meeting a few minutes after two, by which time most of the core team of the Whitechapel Murder Squad had settled into the room.

"Right, gentleman, I have some good news and some bad news. The good news is that another weekend has passed without incident. The bad news is that the powers that be have not been able to influence Dr Mickle, of the Bow Infirmary, into authorising our prime suspect's attendance in a line-up. What I would like to do today, gentlemen, is go through progress made in the search for the doctors and medical students, and interviews with male hairdressers, butchers and slaughter men."

Inspector Moore was the first up.

"There is not much that I can report on gentlemen, other than to inform that the London Hospital has provided us with the names of three medical students who failed to complete their training due to mental incapacity. Unfortunately, the whereabouts of these men have yet to be determined."

Inspector Chandler spoke next.

"I am afraid to report that slow progress is being made with the interviews of hairdressers. A large number of the men in the Jewish areas have a poor command of English and are being less than forthcoming about any surgical experience that they might possess. However, further inquiries are being made into the whereabouts of six of these men on the mornings of Friday 31st August and Saturday and the 8th of September."

Chandler looked about the room, nobody looked like they had any questions, so he returned to his seat.

Next up was Inspector Beck. He had been assigned to

butchers and slaughter men.

"Just to concur with Inspector Chandler, I too have experienced quite a bit of resistance from the men that I have interviewed. In many cases it has been like trying to get blood out of a stone. However, I will say that many of the men who tried to play it dumb, hiding behind their supposedly poor command of the Queen's English, were a good deal more lucid after I'd threatened them with a trip to the station to finish their interviews…" Beck paused for a moment whilst scratching the back of his head. "That said, I'm finding that the men from the press are causing the greatest hindrance to my inquiries. I am being followed by at least one reporter everywhere I go. This is having an unsettling effect on the men being interviewed, none of which is keen to become the next 'Leather Apron'. And to tell the truth, I can't blame them."

Many of the men in the room were seen to agree with Beck as the Inspector returned to his seat. A few other officers took their turn at the front, until it was Inspector Abberline's turn to conclude the meeting.

"I just wish to thank all those who have reported to us this afternoon. Now I know that progress has been very slow and that the press reporters are becoming a major nuisance, but we cannot slacken in our efforts. If we are in luck, the reason for the lack of progress is because we already have our killer behind bars. However, it is still far from certain whether Isenschmid is the man responsible for the murders. If he were to fall through the net, the top brass will want to cover their backs by looking for gaps in our own efforts. Should that happen, I want to be able to provide them with reams of reports, detailing the painstaking inquiries that we have made and are yet to make. As for Inspector Beck's comment about the newspaper reporters, I agree that they are a hindrance, but I am afraid that this is something that we will just have to learn to live with."

❧❧❧

Reid called again at the house of Dr Phillips and was again in luck. The doctor was home and agreed to speak with him.

"Good to see you again, Inspector. What can I help you with today?" asked Dr Phillips.

"As you know I am not part of the Whitechapel Murder Squad which is under Inspector Abberline's charge. However, I am involved in another case which might have some bearing on the matters in hand."

Dr Phillips remembered his last conversation with Reid and was very interested in knowing what the Inspector had to say.

"Pray continue, Inspector," said the doctor.

"Without going into too much detail, I have arrested a man responsible for producing pornographic materials. During questioning, he informed me that he has a client with a taste for images of women being assaulted by a man or men using various weapons, mainly large knives and implements of a surgical nature. What I would like to know from you doctor, is your opinion on the likelihood of such an individual committing actual physical assaults on women? The way that I see it, many things might go through a man's mind, but in the main they are likely to remain there."

Dr Phillips mulled over what the Inspector had told him, his bright eyes darting about in their sockets. He had himself spent many hours thinking of the motive for the murders, trying to gain an understanding of what drove the murderer to commit his sordid acts. He had come to the conclusion that the man must be harbouring a secret fantasy, something that that had gradually consumed his waking hours until one day he crossed the boundary separating fantasy from reality.

"This is very interesting, Inspector. Have you seen any of the images prepared for this man's client?"

"No I have not".

"Are you aware of there being any progression in the baseness of the materials?"

Reid's expression changed upon hearing the question and the doctor caught the change with his sharp, intelligent eyes.

"My understanding is that there has been such a change in the nature of materials".

Dr Phillips paused again. He was a doctor of the body and not of the mind. But he was friendly with doctors in the field of psychiatry who had expressed their views on the mindset of the killer.

"The majority of my medical colleagues believe that we are dealing with some maniacal surgeon, medical student or butcher; namely a man with some experience in, for want of a better word, dissection. However, I have also discussed the case with peers in the field of psychiatry who believe that it is equally likely that we are dealing with a man with no hands-on experience of surgery, but who might instead fantasise about performing such acts and has most likely done so over a number of years. If such a man exists, it is possible that he has now moved from the realms of fantasy and is now making his dreams an evil reality."

"So if I understand you correctly, doctor, you are saying that my colleagues may be looking in the wrong places for the killer?"

"Yes, that is exactly what I am saying. However, it would be a brave man to divert resources away from searching for the miscreant in the more obvious occupations. I take it Inspector Abberline has been given the name of the photographer's client?"

"I am afraid not doctor. The man went to extreme lengths to maintain his anonymity."

"Has anyone given any thought to how one might trap

the individual?"

"What do you mean by that, sir?"

"I am not a policeman but as I understand matters, many men are being drafted into Whitechapel from other police divisions in an effort to catch the man in the act of murder."

"That is correct."

"Have plans been hatched with the aim of luring our man into a trap?"

"None specifically, but some steps have been taken in that direction."

"Even though a very risky endeavour, might it be feasible to try and find a means of tethering a goat to a stake and waiting to see if the beast's uncontrollable urges force him into an attack?"

"As you know doctor, we have no female officers. A few of the smaller male officers have been deployed onto the streets dressed-up as ladies in the hope of flushing out the killer. However, even in our foggy, poorly lit streets, it is none too difficult to discern that these women are in fact poorly disguised policemen."

"Well, my advice, strictly off the record of course, would be for a woman or women to be used for such activities. I am sure that some of those from the unfortunate class would be keen to be used in this way, should the right financial inducement be offered to them. Also, I can imagine that as word of such activity got around, the killer might even be deterred from frequenting Whitechapel to commit more crimes, as he would never know if he was in fact being lured into a trap. My peers and I have given much thought to the detail of such a trap. We feel that the man's preferred method of murder is to slash the left-hand-side of his victim's throats, so it would make sense for a decoy to wear some sort of iron collar, acting a protector of the carotid arteries and windpipe. Protection to the body could be afforded by say a whalebone corset and more iron protectors could be worn over the wrists. Such body armour would be far from foolproof but would, with luck, protect any woman from serious injury, during the time taken for the assailant to be brought down by arresting police officers."

"That is an interesting suggestion doctor and something that I intend to bring to Inspector Abberline's attention."

"Before you go, Inspector, I have one other thought that I would like to enlighten you with. Have you identified the killer's first murder victim?"

Reid looked perplexed, as he didn't know what the doctor was getting at by asking this.

"What do you mean by that, sir?"

Dr Phillips had a feeling that Reid might take what he had to say next with a pinch of salt.

"My understanding Inspector is that the Nichols murder is being treated as the first of its kind, with the Chapman murder being the second in the series. However, you yourself were the investigating officer in the Tabram murder. Do you have an opinion as to whether that murder was committed by the same hand as the other two?"

Reid thought that the good doctor already knew the answer to his question, but he gave the man an answer out of politeness.

"I have nothing more than instinct to go on, doctor, but I believe the Tabram murder to be the first in the series."

"What led you to that conclusion?"

"There are parallels in the murders. Even though the mode of dispatch was completely different, in that Tabram was stabbed 39 times and that the deathblow for both Nichols and Chapman was the slashing of their throats, the ferocity of all three murders was similar in magnitude. Also, in all three cases, the bodies of the women underwent some form of mutilation. Tabram receiving multiple stab wounds to the abdominal region, whilst Nichols and Chapman were cut open in the same region. Therefore, it is not inconceivable that mutilation was motive for all three of the murders. On the assumption that it is very unlikely that two men intent on mutilating dead or dying women should appear, within weeks of each other, in the whole of England, let alone the district of Whitechapel, I can only conclude that the same man is responsible for all three murders."

"That is very good, Inspector. Now I will give you my final thought on the matter. We may be dealing with a man who has spent months, possibly years dreaming of performing surgical acts. I'm assuming that one day his fantasies became reality, when he was presented with a very easy opportunity to kill. The implication of this being that our man has spent a large amount of time, trawling the streets of Whitechapel, building up the courage to make his first kill; or that the first murder was committed in his own neighbourhood, somewhere close to his home."

"Can you further explain your thinking, sir?"

"What I mean is that, if the man had been trawling the streets of Whitechapel, the Tabram woman could have been his first victim, a clumsy first attempt at fulfilling his fantasies. The murders of Nichols and Chapman were committed after he got his first night nerves, so to speak, out of the way and so were performed in a style more consistent with those of his dreams. However, it is also possible, and quite probable, that the first act was committed far closer to his home, possibly having taken place during the day. Our man may well have known his first victim quite well and may have seen her on a fairly regular basis, say at a place of work or even at a weekly church service. There may have been something about the woman that aroused our man's appetite for murder and mutilation. If the opportunity to kill her suddenly presented itself, he might well have taken it, crossing the boundary of fantasy to perform his first act of real murder."

"I admit to having some difficulty in following your line of reasoning. Please correct me if I am wrong, but you are suggesting that the first murder victim may not have been of the fallen class and might have occurred, in an area, well away from Whitechapel?"

"That is correct, Inspector. What I am proposing is that there may be at least one unsolved savage murder, likely committed in London, not six months before the Tabram murder."

Reid was not directly linked to the case but he had good information on how the investigation was proceeding. As such, he was certain that there were no unsolved murders committed within the whole of Great Britain matching the savagery of the Whitechapel murders. However, he knew that the emphasis had been placed on murders of women suspected of being prostitutes. He decided that he needed to speak with Sergeant Thick and possibly, the Bank Manager, about this.

"I must thank you again for your thoughts, doctor. I intend to follow-up the ideas discussed in our conversation with Inspector Abberline's team. However, before I go, I am curious in knowing why you are willing to provide me with your private thoughts on this matter?"

"I would have thought that would be obvious to you, Inspector. I believe you to be a very competent investigator. And yet, your superiors, when dealing with one of the most high profile murder cases London has ever witnessed, have chosen not to include you in their murder squad. Now I am no detective but this leads me to believe that your superiors do not trust you, and by this I mean that they do not trust that you will do exactly what they tell you to do. It is my view, Inspector, that ordered logical reasoning will prove to be insufficient in capturing the miscreant. The murderer, though most likely a very intelligent man, does not adhere to the same rules of logic as normal men. No, this man's thought processes are governed by the irrationality of madness. So to my mind, our best chance in capturing a man who does not follow the normal rules of behavior, is to aim, if you pardon my expression, a 'loose cannon' in his direction. If I know you as I think I do, Inspector. Then you may possess the mindset required to capture a man such as the Whitechapel Murderer. Unfortunately, Inspector Abberline, for all his intelligence, is a man steeped in logic and procedure. And therefore, in this particular case, most ill-equipped to get into the mind of the murderer. I wish you very good hunting, Inspector!"

⸙ ⸙ ⸙

When Reid arrived at the station he was pleased to see that Sergeant Thick had been allocated to the same afternoon/evening shift as himself. He had not yet had an opportunity to speak to the Bank Manager, so decided that he would try to get an update on events from Thick.

"Good afternoon, sergeant."

"Good afternoon, sir."

"How are you progressing with our main case?"

"In truth things appear to be grinding to a halt, sir. There has been much activity, but little end result. We have been swamped with details of would-be suspects. None of whom, apart from the lunatic being held at the Bow Infirmary, showing much promise."

"Well, sergeant, maybe you already have the right man behind bars."

"That could well be the case, sir, and I hope that it is."

Reid could sense some doubt in the sergeant's words. He knew that the sergeant was one of the few to have seen the main suspect with his own eyes, so thought it would be good to get his thoughts on the man.

"I believe that you have seen this man, Isenschmid?"

"Yes, I have, sir. I saw him soon after his arrest in Holloway and a very dangerous lunatic he appears to be."

"But you have your doubts about the fellow?"

"If I may speak candidly, sir?"

"Go ahead, man. I currently have no part in the investigation and would just like to know what real progress is being made with the case. I, like you, am a family man and have a wife and a daughter. As such, I would like to know whether the streets are safer for them to tread now that Isenschmid has been safely locked away."

"Off the record, sir. I am not sure that Isenschmid is our man. Mad, violent and dangerous he certainly is and all of our families are the better off for his being taken off of the streets, but the look of the man is all wrong."

"What do you mean by this?"

"Well it's not just me, sir. I have heard Inspector Helson say the same. The Inspector is like me in thinking that no woman, no matter how desperate, would have willingly walked, with such a deranged, ferocious looking man as Isenschmid, into the yard at the back of 29 Hanbury Street. I myself, sir, would not have felt confident in tackling such a fellow without assistance."

"So, your feeling is that our man is still out there?"

"Yes, sir, it is. However, I've heard a whisper that the longer that goes by without another murder taking place, the greater the chances of Isenschmid being fingered for the killings. Inspector Abberline is ever more certain that Isenschmid is the man that the eyewitness, Mrs Fiddymont, saw in the Prince Albert on the morning of the murder. Rumour has it that the top brass are preparing to feed Isenschmid to the dogs of the press."

"And what if we then have another murder?"

"I don't know about that, sir. All I know is that there haven't been any other killings and the top brass want the press and the boys from the Home Office off of their backs."

Reid had now made up his mind that he was going to let Abberline know his thoughts on the case. His gut feeling was that Isenschmid was the wrong man and the same feeling told him that the murderer would soon kill again. Possibly, over the coming weekend.

ℰ ℰ ℰ

Abberline was on the day shift and had been in the station from 8.am, he was looking tired when Reid caught his eye later that afternoon. He could sense that the 'Bank Clerk' was keen to speak with him.

"What can I help you with, Inspector Reid?"

"I can see that you are very busy, sir, but is there any chance that you could spare me ten minutes of your time? I have some intelligence that might be of relevance to your case."

"Very well, Inspector, meet me in interview room two in half an hour."

"Yes, sir."

Although no progress had been made in the case, Abberline was becoming a little more relaxed about events. He was still very frustrated with the absolute lack of progress being made with Dr Mickle of the Bow Infirmary. However, that aside, the press had started to become bored with Whitechapel murder stories and more mundane events were starting to fill the pages of the newspapers. This had appeared to ease the pressure on Chief Inspector Swanson and it was beginning to look like the dots would slowly join around Isenschmid and he could finally get back to his post at Scotland Yard. Abberline was aware that two of Reid's cases involved gambling and pornography, so he assumed that Reid's information might be something that he stumbled upon during the course of the pornography case.

"What do you wish to discuss with me, Inspector?" asked Abberline.

"Firstly, I'd just like to inform you that we have a man in the cells, a Joshua Engels, who might have information of relevance to your case."

"How so?"

"Engels is a photographer and has been arrested for producing pornographic images. However, under interrogation he informed me that he has a client with a liking for images of violent assaults on women using various types of surgical implements; including surgeons' knives."

"Has Engels given you a name and address of his client?"

"No, sir. I have nothing and the name he is likely to furnish me with will most likely prove fictitious, in that his client has most likely provided him with a false name."

"Then how is this of any use to me and my case?"

"Engels might not know his client's name and address but he has met his client and so is able to provide a description of the man. He is seeking to make a deal regarding the length of his prison sentence."

"As you may already know, Inspector, there are no official rewards or pardons on offer by the state, so I have nothing to barter with. However, you say that Engels is currently incarcerated in the station?"

"Yes, sir."

"In that case I will speak with Engels in the hope that his conscience allows him to furnish us with a description of the man. Is there anything else, Inspector?"

"There is something, sir. I know that it is not my place to make any suggestions in regard to your case, but during the course of a conversation with a medical man, a suggestion was put to me regarding a possible means of capturing the killer. I informed the man, who wishes to remain nameless, that I would endeavour to pass-on his suggestion."

"And what is, this medical man's, suggestion?"

"I am aware that some of the smaller male officers have been tasked with patrolling the streets dressed as ladies."

"Yes, that is correct, Inspector. Are you offering me your services for this work?"

"No, sir, I am not. What I was going to say is that a suggestion has been passed onto me, by one of the local doctors, proposing that real women be used as bait to lure the beast out into the open. He suggested that we might try hiring woman from the fallen class. He also suggested that they might be furnished with body armour for their protection. Comprising of: iron collars for their necks, whalebone corsets for their bodies, and iron bracelets for their wrists."

Abberline didn't like the idea of an officer, not formally part of his murder squad, discussing details of the case with third parties. But he decided to take the suggestion seriously and think through what Reid had taken the trouble to tell him. He knew that Reid was a good detective, even if he was not what could be described as a company man. Also Reid, as his successor in H-Division, most probably had the best grass-roots intelligence of all the Whitechapel officers, except perhaps for Sergeant Thick. As such, Abberline decided that he should be seen to actively take onboard the Detective Inspector's suggestion, as he did not want to deter Reid from passing on any other intelligence that he might receive during the course of his enquiries.

"Very well, Inspector. Thank you for your information and for passing on the unnamed doctor's thoughts on the matter. The idea of female decoys is interesting but I cannot envisage anyone at A-Division sanctioning such a proposal. Ultimately, such an operation would require authorisation from the Home Office and I am sure that they would never endorse such a risky venture. However, that said, I promise to put your suggestion to the CI, in private and off the record. Needless to say, I will not be at liberty to report back to you on the CI's decision, so take it that your idea has been rejected if you do not see it in action by say, the end of October. Is there anything else, Inspector?"

"I am on night duty over the coming weekend, sir. Is there anything that would be useful for me to know in advance of operations?"

"No, there is nothing that would be useful for you to know at this moment in time. All the information that you will need to know will be provided in the usual Friday afternoon briefings."

"Thank you, sir. I have nothing else to report."

"Thank you for your information, Inspector, we might speak again at the briefing. Good day, to you."

Reid thought that his conversation with the Bank Manager had gone better than expected. He didn't hold high hopes that Dr Phillips' suggestion would be acted upon but he was pleased that Abberline had not immediately rejected it. He returned to his desk and made ready to start patrolling the streets of Whitechapel. He was still searching for Harris Marks and intended to take a walk to the White Hart pub, hoping that he might find Levi Greenfield somewhere along the way.

Reid had no luck in his search for Marks or Greenfield. He'd expected Greenfield to be lying low and would not have been surprised if the man had left Whitechapel altogether. Towards the end of his shift he found himself walking through Flower and Dean Street, a street full of buildings and people that had seen far better days. The street was one of the first to be built around the original Spittal Field back in the seventeenth century. Landowners Thomas and Lewis Fossan commissioned builders John Flower and Gowan Dean to complete the works. The Fossans had another of the adjacent streets named after them but, over time, its name was changed from Fossan Street to the more memorable Fashion Street. The houses in these streets had become larger and larger as the silk weaving industry developed and Spitalfields, as it came to be called, became a wealthy hamlet on the outskirts of London. Over time the hamlet had been subsumed by the ever-expanding city. As the silk industry buckled and bent under the weight of foreign competition, the houses and the people living in them suffered similar fates. The area had descended from one of grandeur into a London slum and was now noted for its high rates of crime. Halfway along the old dilapidated street Reid came across Sergeant Thick and a couple of PCs. The sergeant and his men had been called out to deal with a domestic incident at one of the common lodging houses. A woman had been quite badly beaten, but her 'other 'alf' was nowhere to be seen.

Reid made his way over to his colleagues greeted the men with a "Good evening, gentlemen."

"Good evening to you, sir," the three officers responded back in unison.

"Anything that I can assist you with, sergeant?" asked Reid.

"No, sir. This is just a minor domestic, we will be on our way soon."

As they were speaking Reid noticed a well-dressed short man leaving one of the other doss houses. He watched as the man walked a few yards along the street before proceeding to enter another building. The man seemed familiar to Reid, but he only saw him clearly from the side and back.

"Sergeant, do you know that man?"

"Yes, sir. That is the good, Dr Barnardo."

"Ah yes, so it is," said Reid.

"He's out early tonight. I hear that he is going from lodging house to lodging house lecturing the inmates on the poor treatment of children in such places. I think that's helped cause the incident that we are dealing with now, sir."

"Thank you for letting me know, sergeant. I am soon

to return to Leman Street, so we might speak later on."

"Yes, sir, I am stationed there tonight. Good evening, to you."

As Reid walked slowly through the streets he reflected on what he had just seen. It occurred to him that a man like Dr Barnardo or workers at the Christian missions had free reign to walk the streets of Whitechapel. They were seen by everybody, but noticed by few. It was also not unusual for such people to roam the streets very late at night and in the early hours of the morning, in search of the most destitute of adults and children; those individuals who had not been 'lucky' enough to find their way into the workhouses. Reid could not help but think that a man, like the good doctor, was free to roam where he liked and was unlikely to be molested by villain or policeman alike. Such a man, he thought, might also possess medical knowledge and the trust of the fallen women of Whitechapel. Such a man might easily approach a woman, on a lonely poorly lit side street, and encourage her into the backyard of a house.

⸸ ⸸ ⸸

Sergeant Thick returned to the station shortly after Reid. It seemed to him that the assaulted woman had not been badly injured. So he left her at the lodging house and hoped that she and her partner could resolve their differences in a more peaceful manner.

"Sergeant, if you have some time, I would like a word with you?" asked Reid.

"I have time now, sir."

The two men found an empty interview room in which to talk.

"What is it that you would like to know, sir?"

"How many men do you currently have under surveillance in connection with the Whitechapel Murder Case?"

"I don't know the exact number, you would need to speak with Inspector Abberline to find that out. However, I believe that there are about five men in all. If you don't mind my asking, sir, why are you interested in knowing this?"

"Well, sergeant, we have, have we not, just witnessed not thirty minutes past, a man walking the streets of Whitechapel with all the freedom of an Alderman of the City of London?"

The sergeant looked puzzled. Then it dawned on him whom Reid was referring to. "Ah, you mean, the good doctor."

"Yes, I do. It strikes me that he and a number of other men are currently at liberty to wander the streets of Whitechapel throughout the night without any restriction made to their movements."

"Well, sir, since you put it that way, I'd say that you are right in your thinking."

Reid paused, so as to give his words greater effect. "Tell me Sergeant, what type of man are you hunting in connection with the murders?"

"I'd say that he'd be some sort of lunatic."

"Is there anything else about the man?"

"Well he appears to have it in for women of the fallen class, knows how to handle a knife and walks the streets like a ghost, leaving no trace of his movements in the fog."

"Very good, sergeant. I agree with everything that you have said. Now tell me, what sort of man is the good doctor?"

The sergeant then understood Reid's reasoning.

"Ah, I see, sir. Well, Dr Barnardo is obviously a medical man, so most likely has an understanding of the human body and might be trained in the use of a surgical knife. Also, he is known and trusted by all in the community, including the police."

"And does he not, spend much of his time lecturing

woman of the fallen class on the errors of their ways?"

"He does that, sir."

"I understand that you don't know the full facts, but how many men of the good doctor's class are currently under suspicion for the murders?"

"Well, none that I know of, sir."

"So it is safe to assume that we also have none under surveillance?"

"That is most likely correct."

"Well, sergeant, this is only a suggestion. But might it make sense to use a few of the many men loaned to us for night duty to follow men, such as the good doctor, as they go about their nightly crusades?"

"Yes, sir, that would seem to make good sense to me. I will be sure to broach the subject with Inspector Abberline."

With that said, Reid let the sergeant get back on with his work. It was getting close to the end of each man's shift and they spent their time attending to their paperwork before heading off home to their respective families.

CHAPTER ELEVEN

He Planned to Play a Little Game

FRIDAY 28TH SEPTEMBER had been a cool, clear day but the sun had long since set when Reid arrived at the Commercial Street police station. He was thirty minutes early for the 9.30pm briefing that had been arranged for officers working the nightshift that ran from 10pm until 6am in the morning. As the other officers slowly started arriving for duty, Reid noticed that many looked tired and unlike himself, looked far from keen to be spending the next few nights patrolling the streets of Whitechapel. Reid was feeling fresh, alert and looking forward to being on duty over the nights of the coming weekend. He still had a feeling in his bones that the Whitechapel Murderer would strike again, and soon, and he was ready for him if he did.

ꝺ ꝺ ꝺ

A number of men, including Dr Barnardo, were out late wandering the streets of Whitechapel that Friday night. Unbeknown to them they were being followed by plain clothes officers of H Division. Three weeks had passed since the murder of Annie Chapman and the fallen women were no longer walking the streets in fear. The weather had been bad all year and this was the beginning of what would turn out to be a cold wet weekend. However, the night passed slowly, without any incidents of note.

ꝺ ꝺ ꝺ

Saturday 29th September was colder and wetter than Friday had been. Reid felt that there was likely to be much less demand for the services of the ladies of the night in view of the inclement weather. He did not imagine that many men would relish spending their hard earned cash getting soaked in a back alley with a woman who had seen far better days. And so it was that a lot of the costermongers and street traders decided to shut-up shop early, the rain resulting in a poor night for business.

Unfortunately, for most of the working girls, they had no such option, they were faced with earning themselves four pence for their doss or spending the night out in the open air. One of these women was a Swedish immigrant, Elizabeth Stride, known locally as Long Liz. Liz had an on/off relationship with a drunken dockside labourer named Michael Kidney. She and Kidney had fallen-out that week and Liz had decided to spend a few weeks going it alone. She was well aware of what life without Kidney's support meant for her but she had become tired of the man's brutal ways. She was not lazy and spent her days charring and had even earned herself six pence earlier that day for cleaning rooms in her Flower and Dean Street lodging house. However, she was never going to be able to earn enough money through legitimate means to get herself some food, a few drinks and a bed for the night. Unfortunately, for Liz, she had acquired a liking for strong drink and would always spend her money on that above all else. She used alcohol to help her cope with life, which had always been hard, starting back in her teenage years when she earned a living as a prostitute in her native Sweden. Liz was a clever woman and could speak Yiddish in addition to English and her native Swedish. She had tried her best to rise above a life of destitution and was at one time the owner of a coffee shop, a business she started from a small sum of money inherited from her mother. However, her efforts were to prove to be of no avail and she inevitably got sucked into the vortex which was Whitechapel, and now found herself touting for business on Berner's Street, on the south side of the Commercial Road. Berner's Street, although quieter and so with less access to 'business' than roads on the north side of the main street, was relatively safer as it was outside the area known as the Wicked Quarter Mile. Streets in the quarter mile included Dorset Street, Thrawl Street and Flower and Dean Street where she was currently lodging on a pay per night basis. She had found a good spot in which to work, Dutfield's Yard, next to the International Working Men's Educational Club. The club was predominantly frequented by Polish and Russian Jews, and was a loud friendly place on weekend nights with singing and dancing going on until the early hours. The club members weren't up for any 'business' but they made no objection to Liz earning a living in the yard. It was a foul night and it hadn't stopped raining until about 11.30pm. However, this wasn't so bad for the street women, as they didn't get most of their trade until after the public houses closed at 12.30am.

❦❦❦

Whilst Liz Stride was busy downing drinks and walking the up and down Berner's Street, another female of the lowest class was lying in a cell in the Bishopsgate Police Station in the police district of the City of London. Catherine Eddowes was also a woman who enjoyed a drink, or three, and had been found by officers of the City Police lying drunk, on the pavement of the Aldgate High Street at about 8pm. As was standard police practice, they had taken Catherine off to the cells to sober-up, with the intention of releasing her, and other drunks, back onto the streets after the pubs had closed.

Catherine had had a bad week. She and her partner of seven years, John Kelly, had tried their luck at hop picking in Kent that week but had returned to Whitechapel because there was not enough work for them, the summer's poor weather having resulted in a poor hop harvest. Kelly had been forced to pawn his work boots, so that the couple had enough money for food. However, the money from the pawning of their worldly goods didn't stretch to the luxury of their being able to afford to sleep together. So the couple had spent their last night apart. Catherine sleeping at the Casual Ward in Shoe Lane whilst Kelly slept at Cooney's, their regular common lodgings house at 55 Flower and Dean Street. But things weren't all bad and the couple had shared a hearty breakfast at Cooney's earlier that morning. Catherine then left Kelly at the lodging house, whilst she went off to her sister's to see if she could borrow some money from her. Hoping to get enough for Kelly to retrieve his boots from the pawn brokers.

However, things had not gone to plan and Catherine did not make it to her sisters. Instead she'd been propositioned by a man on Commercial Street and immediately spent the money that she'd 'earned' on alcohol. One thing lead to another and she managed to make herself enough money to get herself more than a few drinks, in various Whitechapel pubs, and forgot all about trying to get her partner's working boots back from the pawn brokers. She had been quite successful in her early evening endeavours, with a lot of men seeking a bit of female company before the heavens opened. Catherine eventually lost all control of her senses and, by the time she'd regained them, she found herself locked away in a cell in Bishops Gate police station. However, she knew the process by heart; knowing that she'd have to wait until about 1am before the desk sergeant would let her get on her way. She was a lady with a cheerful nature, so whiled away the time singing songs, much to the irritation of the station staff.

⸸ ⸸ ⸸

Most Londoners were not best pleased at having to

endure yet another cold, dank, Saturday evening. The summer having started late and now appeared to be ending early. However, the poor weather came as a blessing to one man. He had wanted an excuse to wear his long dark coat, not wanting to wear anything that would make him standout from the crowd; in short he wanted to blend in. He had spent the last few weeks walking along the roads of Whitechapel and had noticed that most of the hysteria caused by the recent murders was concentrated in the area north of the Commercial Road, with life in much of the rest of the district continuing on pretty much as normal. He had read stories in the newspapers that implied that the killer was a member of the Jewish community and he had hatched a mad plan to add more fuel to what he expected to be a large fire.

The previous weekend a woman had caught his eye and he'd watched her as she paraded along Berner's Street before taking her clients into a narrow gated yard adjacent to a Jewish social club. He'd wanted an excuse to remain in the road and had purchased a bunch of grapes from a fruit seller's kiosk that was situated a few doors down from the club. He slowly ate the grapes whilst observing the woman at her work. The name above the club had read 'International Working Men's Educational Club' and it was soon obvious to him that nigh-on all the club's members were Jews. The whore had picked-up a client and led him into the narrow yard where they conducted their business. After a few minutes the man left and was followed a short while later by the woman. She adjusted her dress and popped what looked like sweetmeats into her mouth, no doubt in an effort to freshen her breath. Right on cue another man appeared, and, after a brief exchange of words, he too entered the yard. Whilst the whore and her client were in the yard, a man of Jewish appearance walked into the yard off Berner's Street, only to leave it a few seconds later and access the club through its main entrance. The man, who was soon to become known as 'The Ripper', deduced from the Jewish man's actions that there must be two entrances to the club. It appeared that most people used the front entrance on Berner's Street, with a few using a side entrance, when it wasn't being used for 'business' by the local prostitutes. The man had seen enough to feed his fantasies and planned to return back there a few days later, during daylight hours, as he wanted to take a look inside of the yard.

⸙⸙⸙

On the Wednesday night the Ripper returned to Berner's Street. He bought himself another bunch of grapes and stood eating them across the road from Dutfield's Yard. It was about 6pm in the evening and not a whore was to be seen. He watched as people entered and left the Jewish club by both the main entrance at 40 Berner's Street and through the door on the side of the building, which was accessible from the yard. He decided to take a look inside the yard. He crossed the road and stopped to read a notice affixed to the club entrance. It was advertising a forthcoming discussion themed 'Why Jews Should be Socialists' to be held that coming Saturday night from 10.00pm until 11.30pm. He then stopped in front of the gates to the yard and read a notice affixed to them, which read 'A. Dutfield, Van and Cart Builder'. The Ripper then stepped boldly through the open gates into an area that felt more like an alley, being about ten feet wide and ran the entire length of the buildings on either side of it. He walked along the alley, past the side entrance of the club, to a point where it opened out into the yard proper, which housed a double-roomed office and what looked to be a disused stable and disused workshop. He determined that the workshop had once been the business premises of the man named Dutfield, who seemed to have long since ceased trading there. As he walked back through the alley he finished eating the last of his grapes and threw the stem into the gutter. He took a right out of the yard back into Berner's Street, after a few strides he reached the end of the road and took another right into Fairclough Street, a road that he knew took him toward the City of London.

⸙⸙⸙

The next few days seemed to pass like weeks to the Ripper. He had not been able to concentrate on anything other than the yard next to the Jewish club and had spent many hours fantasising about what he intended to do to his next victim there. Everything he did was being driven by the need to mutilate his victims. However, he did not consider himself to be some common butcher, no, his incisions were performed with skill and precision. He thought that few men, even accomplished surgeons, would be capable of working with as much such skill in the conditions that he had to work in. Who else could operate in such poor light and at the speed that he did? He'd taken the womb from his last victim and had decided that he wanted more from the next one. He planned to take a kidney from her; something that he might eat, should he get the urge to do so.

Tonight the Ripper entered Berner's Street from the Commercial Road at about midnight and was pleased to see the same whore, parading her wares, close to the Jewish club at the far end of the street. He crossed the carriageway and walked slowly along the way. He noticed that the fruit seller had shut-up shop for the night. Even from the other side of the road he could hear singing coming from the club, the serious discussion of the night had no doubt ended and those that remained in the building were now spending their time, drinking, singing and dancing. He did not loiter in the street this time but continued on, turning into Fairclough Street at the end of the road. He planned to get into the yard unobserved and wait in the disused stable until his prey walked into his trap. He had been pleasantly surprised to find that reading about his work in the newspapers brought back much of the excitement he'd felt when cutting into the flesh of the whores' bodies. He was annoyed by the stories constant references to 'foreigners', by which they meant members of the Jewish sect, as he knew that this made it more dangerous for him to perform his work. Tonight he would play a little game with the men from the newspapers and leave them and the police a cryptic message. He intended to write a message on the yard wall, just above the body of his next victim. He double-checked that he had the stick of chalk in his pocket and then prepared for his work.

Liz Stride walked-up Berner's Street towards the busy Commercial Road where there was more chance of her attracting the attention of a customer. The Ripper watched her go and quickly made his way into Dutfield's Yard, walking to the end of the yard and standing in the disused stables. He was surprised by how many club members were using the side door, resulting in more activity than he would have liked in the yard. But he was out of sight, standing in the dark and decided to stick to his plan. After a while he could see his intended prey standing a mere 30 feet in front of him, as the whore flaunted her wares from the doorway. He had planned to wait for her to bring a client into the yard and then take her before she returned back onto the street. However, the anticipation was beginning to overwhelm him and he found himself edging closer to her. Just as he reached the yard door something unexpected happened, something that even he, for all his planning, could not have anticipated. Two men entered Berner's Street from the Commercial Road, they were not together and one of the men was walking about twenty paces in front of the other. The first man walked as if drunk and was staggering along the pavement. The other man walked behind him and was considering crossing over to the other side of the road to pass him. After about 45 seconds the first man reached Dutfield's Yard and without any warning, he grabbed hold of Liz Stride and threw her to the ground. She was too shocked to do anything other than make a few quiet screams for help. The second man, Israel Schwartz, was a Hungarian Jew who spoke very little English. He had no idea what was happening but it looked to him to be some kind of domestic dispute. He was afraid for both himself and the woman, but his instinct for self-preservation forced him to cross the carriageway to the safety of the other side of the road. He looked across the road at the man standing over the woman, catching his eye. Just then, a second taller man appeared on the pavement next to him. The first man gave a shout of 'Lipski', which Schwartz, even with his pigeon English, understood to be form of racist anti-Jewish abuse. He understood this to be a warning, intended to discourage him from interfering in the assault that was taking place before his eyes. He decided that he was best placed leaving the couple to rectify their differences and started to walk quickly up the road. On looking over his shoulder he was startled by the sight of the other, taller man, walking close behind him. Fear got the better of him and he broke into a run and didn't stop running until he was certain that the tall man was nowhere to be seen.

The first man had thrown Liz Stride to the ground proceeded to rough her up before demanding money from her. Liz did as she was told and lifted her skirts to reveal the pocket where she kept her cash. She emptied its contents onto the pavement and watched as the man picked up all the coins, which amount to eight pence. The man looked pleased with himself, eight pence would get him a night in a lodging house and a hearty breakfast. He staggered the few short steps that took him into Fairclough Street and disappeared into the night.

Stride slowly picked herself up and brushed the mud off her clothes. She was annoyed at being robbed, but was glad that she hadn't been badly injured and that the ground was quite dry, despite the earlier heavy rain. As she reached into a pocket with her left hand to get some sweetbreads she caught sight of a man in the yard doorway. She raised a smile and bade him goodnight, in Yiddish, believing him to be one of the club members. She then noticed the wild look in his eyes, she had been attacked once already and wasn't about to let herself get caught unawares for a second time. However, before she had a chance to react, the man grabbed at her neck scarf, pulling the knotted end tightly into the side of her throat. He dragged her into the yard and pushed her up against the wall. She couldn't breathe but tried to fend the man off with her right hand as she still had hold of the sweetmeats in her left hand. However, her brief struggle was all in vain. Her attacker was very strong and by now was becoming well practiced in the art of murder. Holding the neck scarf tight in his left hand he pulled Liz to the ground, whilst taking hold of a large, razor-sharp knife with his right hand and pulling the blade, with lightning speed, across the side of her neck. The blade cut into the flesh under Liz's left ear, and he drew it all the way around and through to her windpipe, using the top of the scarf as a guide for his deadly incision. He would now have to wait a while before making his 'trademark' second cut to the right side of his prey's neck; the blood spurting from the wound at high force over the yard floor. He was careful not to get splattered with blood and intended to let the whore bleed for a while before getting to work on her.

Seconds later the Ripper became aware of his second

surprise of the night, when he heard the distinctive sound of a pony and trap making its way along the street. He listened carefully whilst holding the whore down by her scarf as she continued to bleed into the gutter. Her blood flowing along the wall, down and away from the yard gates. The Ripper could not believe what happened next - the cart slowed down and stopped outside the yard. He was totally unprepared for this; he knew that there were stables at the end of the yard but they looked to have been unused for many months. The Ripper let go of the whore, whilst the cart driver unlocked the gates, and slowly walked back further into the gloom. The cart driver remounted the vehicle and proceeded to drive into the yard. The pony, sensing that all was not well, slowed and pulled to its left, away from the body of the dying woman. The cart driver, the club steward named Louis Diemschutz, also sensed that something was wrong. He could just make out the shape of a bundle in the darkness, so he reached for his horsewhip and prodded at it. He had a feeling that the object was a person but could not be sure. So he climbed down from the cart, struck a match and then saw that the bundle was in fact a women lying in a pool of blood. His first thought was for his wife, the club stewardess. He ran from the yard in fear and panic, entering the club through its main entrance; hoping that he would find his wife safe and sound inside of the building.

The Ripper had watched the scene unfold from the shadows. It took a while for the red mist of murder to clear from his mind, but as it did so his first thought was not for his own safety but that he had not finished his work. He hadn't even managed to cut the whore's throat correctly. Let alone complete the plans he had for her womb, ears, kidney or the message he had wanted to chalk on the wall, above her body.

All hell then broke loose. Diemschutz found his wife in the building, so was much relieved to know that she was unharmed. However, he was sure that there was a dead or dying woman out in the yard. So the alarm was raised and men ran off in all directions to try and summon the police. The first police officer on the scene was PC252H, Henry Lamb. The constable had been alerted to the murder by a man named Morris Eagle, who had chaired that night's discussion. PC Lamb shone his bull's-eye lantern in the direction of the dead woman; the lantern generated enough light for him to see the massive cut made into the woman's neck, that stretched from under her left ear, round and through her windpipe. Lamb's first thought was that he was dealing with another victim of the Whitechapel Murderer. He asked if Eagle knew his way to the police station and then asked him to run there to summon assistance. Lamb doubted whether the killer was in the crowd of people surrounding the body but thought that any man found with blood on his hands or clothes would more than likely be treated as a prime suspect. With that in mind, he ordered everyone to step away from the body and to keep clear of the stream of blood that was still flowing from the jagged wound in the woman's neck.

❦❦❦

Reid was normally based at the Leman Street police station but had been assigned to Commercial Street for nightshift duty that weekend. It had been a quiet night, by Whitechapel's standards, most likely the result of the heavy rain. He didn't have a beat to patrol, so he stepped out of the station for some fresh air. He was willing something to happen. This only served to make him feel very bad about himself. As there he was, an officer of the law who had vowed to protect the public, secretly hoping, against hope, that one of their number might meet a ghastly end at the hands of a maniac. And why did he wish this? It was because he wanted to be the first Detective Inspector at the scene of the crime.

The only thing allowing Reid to take solace from the situation was that: although another woman would likely have to die, it was the only way in which he, and his colleagues, were going to make any progress in the case. Reid shook his head from side to side before returning back into the station and trying to concentrate on some paperwork.

⸎⸎⸎

Inspector Reid was not the only officer of the law anticipating another attack by the Whitechapel Murderer that weekend. Acting Chief Inspector, John West, had volunteered for night duty and based himself at the Leman Street station in the expectation of trouble. West was actually the senior officer who'd first suggested that Abberline be recalled from A-Division to deal with the case. He had wanted Abberline with him on duty over that weekend, but had settled on Inspector Pinhorn, when it was made clear that Abberline would be best served catching-up on some much needed sleep.

At about 1.10am Morris Eagle burst into Leman Street Police station shouting for urgent assistance; CI West, Inspector Pinhorn and five PCs hastily followed Eagle back to Dutfield's Yard. Before leaving the station CI West instructed the desk sergeant to telegram all the other London police stations to alert them to the possibility of another slaying by the Whitechapel Murderer. When the officers arrived in Berner's Street they found the entrance to the yard being guarded by PC Lamb. Dr Frederick William Blackwell was in the passageway examining the body. West assumed that the killer was long gone but was pleased that they had such a fresh crime scene from which to work from.

"Constable, what has happened here?" asked CI West.

"I think that the killer's struck again, sir. A woman is lying dead in the yard and her body is being examined by Dr Blackwell. Her throat's been ripped but I didn't see any other wounds."

"Do we have any witnesses?"

"Yes, there are about 30 people in the club here, including the man who found the body."

"Whom does the cart belong to?"

"A man named Louis Diemschutz. He's the man who discovered the body."

"Have you spoken to him?"

"Yes, sir. He says that he is the club steward. He said that he found the body in the yard when he returned from a market at the Crystal Palace. He thought that something might be afoot when his pony shied away from entering the yard. He says he did not see anybody other than the victim."

"Has the area been secured?"

"Yes, sir. I gave the order that everyone found in the yard be held in the club. A number of people were in the yard when I arrived and it is possible that a few of the men will have a little blood on their person on account of their being so close to the body. I did my best to keep people away from the body and the blood."

"That is excellent, constable. What is your name?"

"Thank you, sir. My name's Henry Lamb."

"Excellent work, Lamb," repeated CI West.

West instructed Pinhorn to conduct a house-to-house search of all buildings in the street, using four of the officers who had accompanied them to the murder scene. West and few other PCs then entered the club, he located Diemschutz and had him accompany them in their search of the building. They searched every room for signs of the murderer, starting from the basement. When he and his men had finished searching the top floor rooms they noticed a ceiling hatch.

"Where does that lead?" asked Pinhorn.

"To the roof, sir." responded Diemschutz.

Have you ever been up there?"

"No, sir."

"Do you have a ladder?"

"No, sir."

Pinhorn instructed one of the constables to get a table. He climbed onto the table and pushed at the hatch, it was stuck fast. He did not have the strength to open it. He then instructed the largest of the PCs to force it open. The PC forced the hatch as instructed and Pinhorn was the first officer to go into the loft. What he found had no explanation, the hatch door had been bolted closed from the inside, yet there were no other doors or windows in the loft, so Pinhorn could not understand how the person who had bolted the door had been able to get out. Not seeing how anyone could have gotten into the room in the first place, he decided that the loft was probably a red herring but made an entry in his notebook to record the anomaly, just in case it might prove useful later on in the investigation.

❦ ❦ ❦

Whilst West and Pinhorn were searching the Jewish Club, a telegram was received at 1.25am in the Commercial Street Police station. Reid had been kicking his heels almost in the hope that the murderer would strike again and was on his way out of the door in within seconds of reading the alert. He had hoped to be the most senior officer on the scene and was disappointed to find that West and Pinhorn had gotten there before him.

West then found himself in a bit of quandry. He was well aware that Reid had purposefully been sidestepped in the investigation for the murderer, but Inspector Pinhorn had had absolutely no involvement in the case up until that point. West was loath to let Pinhorn start directing operations in Abberline's absence and also knew that Reid was the Force's eyes and ears in Whitechapel, so it made no sense for him to be given such a minor role in the overall investigation. His gut instinct told him to let Reid get stuck into investigating the crime scene, so he instructed Pinhorn to get Reid up to speed on what had been done prior to his arrival. Pinhorn first took Reid see the body and then led him to the top floor to show him the mystery of the loft. After that he left Reid to coordinate the interviewing of the witnesses.

All the occupants of the club, the women as well as the men had their names, addresses and occupations recorded as part of the statements collected by Reid and his men. After that Reid went into the passage to investigate the crime scene. By then it had been flooded with lanterns and was brightly lit. He was interested in how the body had been left by the murderer. He noticed that the killer wound was very large and deep and looked to have been the work of someone who knew what they were doing. He was already thinking that this was the work of a butcher, doctor or a soldier. However, apart from the tightness of the victim's neck scarf, there were no signs of a struggle and the body appeared to have been laid down much like one would a sick child. It had been placed close to the wall, with Stride's head facing the wall with her feet pointing to the gates. There were no cuts to any of her clothes and her skirts had not been raised. Reid then made a thorough inspection of the walls of the passage and was surprised to find very few splashes of blood upon it. He knew that blood should have spurted several feet from the wound in the carotid artery and wondered how the killer had managed to direct the flow of blood in the dark.

At 4.30am it was agreed to take Stride's body to the mortuary. Having nothing further to do, Reid decided that it was late enough in the new day to call at Coroner Baxter's house to apprise him of the murder. Than done, Reid went to the mortuary to make his own inspection of the body. He guessed the woman to be aged about 42 years of age, 5ft.2 in. tall, with pale complexion and dark brown curly hair. He opened Stride's mouth and recorded that she had lost her upper front teeth. He then made a record of the clothes that she was wearing and returned to the station. The first thing that he did upon his return to Commercial Street was to instruct the desk sergeant to send a telegram to all London police stations with a description of the deceased. It was only then, at about 5.15am that Reid found out that this was not the only murder committed by the Ripper that night, there had been another, far more gruesome murder committed in Mitre Square, in the City of London.

CHAPTER TWELVE

Ripped-Up Like a Pig in the Market

AT ABOUT 1.20AM THE RIPPER had crossed the boundary into the district of the City of London. He knew that he was far from safety and wouldn't be safe until he got himself off the streets of London. What he was not to know is that in response to his other gruesome murders in Whitechapel and Stepney, the acting Commissioner of the City Police, a Major Henry Smith, had taken the precautionary measure of increasing police numbers on the eastern edge of his division by about 20 percent. So although he had not noticed many of them, the area he was currently walking through was crawling with policemen.

By now the Ripper had driven himself into a frenzy of bloodlust. He was seething that the driver of the horse and cart had interrupted him in his work, as he had had so much that he'd wanted to do. Then he took the decision that was to greatly enhance his reputation as the most infamous murderer to have ever walked the earth. He looked about him and noticed that the whores in that part of the City looked much very much like those in Whitechapel. He walked up Mitre Street and turned into a large, poorly lit, quiet square, named Mitre Square. He walked quickly around the square's perimeter, surveying its suitability as a venue of murder. There were three entrances to it, the carriageway that he had used to access it, which was in the south and two small passageways, one to the west and the other to the north. Then he saw something that convinced him that a higher power must have sent him to that place to commit murder. At the north end of the square was large Kearley and Tonge warehouse. He thought back to the morning of Friday 31st

August and remembered the name of a large warehouse in Buck's Row; it was another one owned by K & T. He didn't know how he had gotten there, but yet he'd decided that Mitre Square would be the place to finish his night's work. Now all he needed was a willing victim.

As luck would have it, at exactly 1am, Catherine Eddowes had been judged sober by the officers' of the Bishops Gate police station and was let back onto the streets of London. Having spent all the money that she had 'earned' that day on drink; she decided that there was nothing for it but to 'earn' some more so that she could get herself a bed for the night. She had taken a left out of the police station and after a few minutes found herself in Houndsditch, heading further into the City of London and further away from Whitechapel, the area that she knew as home. Catherine decided to keep on walking and was soon in the backstreets bordering Mitre Square. Shortly after arriving there she was approached by a man in a long dark coat. There was something about the man that she liked. She was much taken by his bright alert eyes and casual manner. Catherine thought that the man made a welcome change from the usual punters of Whitechapel and decided that she should try to spend more time 'working' in that part of the City.

As the Ripper and Catherine Eddowes slowly made their way down one of the narrow passages that led into Mitre Square they were overtaken by three men who were on their way home after spending the night in a local club. One of the men turned to take a closer look at them, but the Ripper was quick to bend his head and felt confident that the man did not catch a glimpse of his face. The couple then walked through the passage into the square. There was a single lamppost in the northwest corner, so the Ripper led Catherine to the southeast corner, where it was darkest. It was dark, but afforded more light than Dutfield Yard had. The Ripper thought it to be almost a perfect spot in which to go to work; as the square offered privacy, seclusion and three exits should he need to make a run for it. However, he still wanted to leave a cryptic anti-Jewish message at the scene of the murder. The Ripper would have liked to have written it on the ground next to the soon to be dead prostitute, but the ground was still wet from that night's rain. However, he had more pressing matters to be getting on with and took a moment to have one last look around the square before getting to work.

Eddowes noticed the instant that the man's body stiffened and the look in his eyes changed from one of mischief to one of murder, but it was too late for her to react. The Ripper grabbed her around the throat and watched as she struggled to draw a breath. It took about a minute for the whore to pass-out and then the Ripper lowered her gently onto the rain sodden ground before taking out his knife and cutting into the left-hand side of her throat. He severed the woman's left carotid artery and drew the knife round her neck and through her windpipe, cutting all the way back to the bones of her spinal column. He waited about 45 seconds, watching as the blood sprayed out of the artery, being careful to direct the spray into the ground. As he watched, the volume of blood exiting the wound decreased as the whore's blood pressure dropped and her heart ceased to beat. He then made the second of his trademark double incisions; cutting through the right carotid artery and again pulling the knife through the woman's flesh and round to the wound that he had made to the windpipe. This time, blood only trickled from the new wound. The Ripper then lifted the woman's skirts and got to work on her abdomen. In a few short minutes the Ripper had transformed Catherine Eddowes from a happy go lucky, gracefully ageing woman, into the dead carcase of a slaughtered animal. Her intestines had been cut away and placed over her shoulders, her face mutilated and her left kidney and womb cut from her body. The Ripper had plans for the body parts and placed them carefully into a leather pouch. He looked down to admire his work; at the whore's body with its legs raised and the gaping hole that once housed her intestines. He turned the woman's head to one side and hoped that whoever found the body would get a good look at her mutilated face, thinking that it made a sight that would long live in the finder's memory. He was still not sure about the message that he wanted to leave. Then he had an idea, and took his knife and cut away a large section of the woman's apron. He used the piece of cloth to wipe the blood from the knife and his hands and placed the cloth in the leather pouch that contained the woman's body parts. Just then he heard the familiar sound of a beat officer making his measured two and half miles an hour march over the cobbles of Mitre Street. The Ripper walked swiftly to the north end of the square, entered the passage and was away, just as PC Edward Watkins – number 881 of the City Police - entered the square from the south side.

It was 1.44am and PC Watkins repeated the actions that he had performed only 15 minutes earlier. He unfastened his bulls-eye lantern and swept an arc from left to right. The square had been empty before and appeared to be empty again now. However, this time his lantern illuminated something lying in the gloom. Watkins took a few steps to his right and then saw a sight that all his twenty years in the force had not prepared him for. In front of him lay the body of a woman, who as he would later tell a journalist, had been 'ripped-up like a pig in the market'. For a few moments the officer was paralysed with fear but then he composed himself and sounded the alarm. Minutes later the City Police, like their counterparts in Whitechapel were running through the dark foggy streets of London stopping and searching every suspicious man in their sights.

In the midst of the panic caused by the two murders, one man had kept his head whilst all those about him lost theirs. The Ripper took his time, carefully walking through the backstreets as he made his way across the invisible border back into Whitechapel. He found a water fountain and cleaned himself up. He then thought about where he could leave his message. Goulston Street held a daily market, just like the one held in the adjacent Middlesex Street, which was better known as Petticoat Lane. However, the Ripper reasoned that more Jews lived in Goulston Street, so it would make a better place to continue his little game. He stopped just inside the ground floor of a stairwell, took the chalk from his pocket and wrote his cryptic message on the wall. It read:

> The Juwes are
> The men That
> Will not
> be Blamed
> for nothing

He then took the leather pouch from another pocket and removed the piece of bloodstained apron that he'd cut away from the whore's skirt. It was smeared with blood and faeces, and glinted in the darkness. He then placed the rag on the floor just outside the stairwell. He had hoped to use the body of a whore in the yard next to the Jewish club to draw attention to his message but now felt that the stairwell might prove to be a better location, as more people were likely to see it.

Now he had to get back to his home base. He assumed that by now the body in the square would have been found, so he reasoned that the police were now searching for him in the streets to his left and right. To his left were the City Police and to his right were the officers of Whitechapel's H

Division. To the killer's south lay the Whitechapel High Street, so he decided to head north. It would be hours yet before first light, so he had plenty of time to make his way to safety.

CHAPTER THIRTEEN

The Return of Reid

REID RETURNED HOME at about 6am. He woke Emily and told her about the murders and that he was now re-involved in the case. Coroner Baxter had informed him that he would hold the first session of the inquest into Dutfield Yard murder at 2pm that afternoon, so Reid needed to get himself some much needed sleep. He hoped that he'd be able to sleep through until 10am, planning to arrive at the station for about 11am. He knew that Abberline would want to debrief him as soon as possible and he hoped that nobody would be sent to wake him.

❦ ❦ ❦

Abberline arrived at the station at 7am. He had been hoping that another weekend had passed without incident so that he could finally get to work on Isenschmid. Now he received the news that two new murders had been committed and that the murderer had left a clue in Goulston Street. This was a disaster for him in so many ways. Firstly, it meant that his prime suspect, although insane, violent and dangerous, was clearly innocent. Secondly, it meant that he had lost all his earlier kudos and would now be seen as having made absolutely no progress with the case. Thirdly, the second murder of night had been committed in the City of London, so now there would be a race with the City Police to see who would be first to catch the killer. Fourthly, just to cap it all, somehow the 'Bank Clerk' had wormed his way back onto the case. In fact Abberline had been informed that Reid would be the Met's sole representative at that afternoon's first session of the inquest into the Dutfield Yard murder. He had also been told that Reid did not return home until 6am, so he resisted the urge to have the man summoned to the station, deciding instead to scan the reports from the other officers in his unit and those telegrammed through from the City Police, before making his way to Berner's Street. He had arrived an hour early into work, so expected to be well acquainted with the facts by the time that Superintendent Arnold joined him at the station.

Just then CI Swanson arrived at the station. Swanson normally worked out of Scotland Yard but had decided he would be better placed being at the heart of the investigation.

"Good morning, Abberline."

"Good morning, sir."

"I am glad that you are here, we have a lot to do. I am going to be stationed in Superintend Arnold's office this morning. However, I have not yet been to the murder sites. Arnold will be arriving shortly and I would be grateful if you would accompany us to them."

"Yes, sir."

"This is one awful mess. Commissioner Warren has himself been out since 5am and will soon be meeting Sir Henry at the Home Office. He informed me that he wants new lines of enquiry made and wants suggestions from us about possible new measures that can be employed to catch the murderer. Basically, he wants a better plan than the City Police are likely to come up with."

Abberline responded positively to his superior officer. He pictured in his mind the game soon to be played-out between the Met and the City police forces. On the face of it the two organizations would be seen to be working together as a team to catch the murderer, but beneath the surface they would really be in fierce competition with each other. And with that would come the muck raking and the playing of politics.

Next to arrive at the station were acting Chief Inspector West, Inspector Pinhorn and Superintendent Arnold. It was decided that they would have a quick catch-up before going to the murder sites.

CI Swanson started the meeting.

"Gentleman, we have much work to do today. The Commissioner wants to meet me later this morning, following his meeting with the Home Secretary. Before then I want two lists of suspects. One from eyewitness statements and another collated from our own detective endeavours. Now I'd be grateful if CI West can provide a summary of this morning's events."

"As you may be aware, Inspector Pinhorn and I were based at Leman Street last night and were there when a member of the public, under instruction by the officer at the murder scene, burst into the station alerting us of the murder. Pinhorn and I were at the scene in minutes. A very capable fellow by the name of PC Lamb already had Dutfield's Yard locked-down by the time that we arrived there. About ten minutes after that Inspector Reid arrived at the scene. Since he is Whitechapel's most senior Detective Inspector; I instructed him to take charge of witness interrogation and the search of the surrounding buildings."

"Are you sure that was a wise decision, John?" asked Swanson.

"Look Donald, we just haven't got the manpower to keep up with all the leads and other intelligence coming into the team. No offence to Inspector Abberline, whose efforts have been admirable, but I feel that he has become sucked-in at too low a level. Activities such as the attendance of the inquests have eaten into his workload. I can well imagine that Coroner Baxter will now hold at least three inquest sessions into last night's murder and I think that Reid can be trusted to handle those without supervision."

Abberline could only agree with that. He had been working 12 hour days for three weeks in a row and had even taken to wandering the streets when off duty, during the early hours of the morning in an attempt to catch the killer. Something had to give, so it made sense to assign Reid to the inquests, even if it did up the man's profile.

CI West continued, "There are two other items that you need to be aware of, Donald."

"What are they?" enquired Swanson.

"Firstly, the acting Commissioner of the City Police, Major Smith, was on the scene directing operations himself from the early hours of the morning. Partly in response to this, Commissioner Warren was at this station at 5am and then went on a tour of both murder sites and the site where the blood stained rag was left."

CI Swanson could see where this all leading; there being no way that Commissioner Warren was going to accept the City Police catching the killer before the Met did. Swanson's team might have been under pressure from the press and the Home Office before now, but the case had just jumped in importance by a few orders of magnitude.

"The second item relates to actions taken with regard to the clues left in Goulston Street. A piece of the apron worn by the lady murdered in Mitre Square was left, most likely deliberately at the foot of a stairwell of a building occupied largely by members of the Jewish community. Also at the foot of the stairs was some freshly written graffiti. I personally found the text to be highly inflammatory and felt that if seen by members of the public, could easily have sparked off anti-Jewish rioting. Commissioner Warren arrived in Goulston Street at close to 5.30am, just before sun up and agreed with me that the writing should be obliterated by means of a damp sponge."

CI Swanson bit his lip, as he was not pleased with what he was hearing. He had been led to believe that the message had been photographed for the record but from

West's tone he now realised that it had not been. Swanson asked a question that he thought he already knew to the answer to.

"My understanding is that a photographer was called upon to photograph the writing, did this in fact take place?"

West paused before answering, sensing the irritation in his superior officer's tone.

"No, Donald it did not. I am afraid that a mob was already gathering close to the stairwell and the men were having difficulty keeping them back. We did not think that it was worth the risk of waiting for the photographer to arrive, just in case the crowd broke through the ranks after sun-up and so could see and read the message."

"I see," said Swanson. Although he didn't see at all; he felt that this was a bad decision, forced upon Warren by pressure of time.

West continued, "There is another small matter. A few of the City Police had heard about the clue and were at the scene when the Commissioner arrived. One the men actually had the gall to protest that we shouldn't take any action without Major Smith seeing the writing first."

Swanson actually thought that would have been the most sensible course of action to have taken, but the chance had obviously been lost to them. He now imagined that their 'colleagues' in the City Police would forever use the Met's actions that morning against them.

West carried on "The good news is that one of Warren's men is a dab hand at transcription and recorded the writing, quite closely matching the hand that wrote it."

Swanson broke in. "At least we have something to work with. I think that you and I had better discuss the content of the message outside of this meeting."

CI Swanson was a mid-ranking Freemason, as was acting CI West and most of London's senior policemen. Swanson wanted to discuss the message's contents privately with West as he thought the cryptic message left by the killer might be related to Masonic ritual. If so, their man was likely to be a fellow mason, something that he thought might throw some much needed light on the maniac's motives.

Swanson continued, "John, you can provide me with your thoughts on the message content in a private meeting but for now I think that it would be wise if we get on with a quick tour of the crime scenes."

⸎ ⸎ ⸎

Commissioner Warren had arrived at the Home Office at 8am for a meeting with Home Secretary Matthews. He was surprised to find that the acting Commissioner of the City Police, Major Henry Smith, had arrived there before him and was already waiting in the Minister's outer office.

"Damn awful morning, Sir Charles," said the Major.

Warren thought that it had not been improved by his now having to spend time with his opposite number from the City Police. It was well known that the City Police's actual Commissioner, Sir James Fraser, was due to retire and was now spending his time working in the background whilst the Major got on with the business of actually running the force. As luck would have it, Sir James was on his annual leave, so Major Smith would now have full control over the investigation into the murder in Mitre Square.

"Yes, it is that, Major," replied Warren.

"My man, Detective Halse, informed me this morning that he had tried to stop you having the Goulston Street writing destroyed. He said that he'd suggested waiting for the photographer to arrive or at the very least for my own arrival on-site. He added that you sanctioned its destruction as you and your men were worried that its presence might be the catalyst for an anti-Jewish riot."

"Your man has provided you with a correct account of

events. Did he also inform you that I had one of my men transcribe the message, keeping close to the style of the hand that wrote it?"

"Yes, he did and I would very much like to see a copy of it. However, I will make it a matter of record that I feel that it was a mistake not to have photographed the message."

"So be it. However, that's all in the past now, I think that we would be better placed getting on with the business of trying to decipher what the maniac is trying to tell us," replied Warren.

"I have been told that an inquest is being arranged for later today into the Berner's Street murder. We in the City are not planning on holding one into the death of the wretch in Mitre Square until later in the week, when it is hoped that we have obtained the full facts of the case."

Warren was tired and was becoming very irritated by what he was hearing from his opposite number.

"Look, I have no jurisdiction over Coroner Baxter. It is his want to start proceedings into such matters at the earliest opportunity. I and my men are forced to work around his timetable as best we can."

The door to the Minister's office finally opened and both men were called into the room. Warren noticed that the man from the Secret Department was in situ along with one of the Minister's aids.

"Please take a seat, gentleman," said the Minister.

Warren was expecting a barrage of questions to which he knew he would have few, if any, answers. He was hoping that Major Smith would fair no better.

Matthews continued "I've just come off the telephone from a call from the Palace. Her Majesty has heard the news and has passed on her extreme displeasure in your offices' inability to catch the perpetrator of these foul murders. I informed her that no stone will be left unturned in our investigations and that it is apparent that insufficient manpower has been made available to patrol the streets of this nation's capital city, something I want rectified immediately. What I would like to know from both of you is whether you have any firm leads into the identity of the murderer. Sir Charles, if you would like to go first."

"As you know, sir, we have a man in custody whom we thought very likely to be the murderer. Obviously, the events of this morning have demonstrated that we have arrested the wrong man. To date my officers have been tracking down a combination of insane medical students and doctors, they have also been checking the whereabouts of butchers, slaughterers and hairdressers on the nights of the previous murders. We had about five men under surveillance, but they too can now be disregarded. I am afraid that we have had insufficient time with which to obtain any eyewitness accounts of this morning's murder and no weapon or even a footprint was left at the scene. The killer did leave an item of the deceased's clothing from the Mitre Square murder in our district and might possibly have scrawled a cryptic message on a wall close to where this item of clothing was found."

"So, as I very much suspected, you have absolutely nothing?" replied the Minister.

"Yes, sir, I am afraid that you are correct in thinking that, sir," replied Warren.

"And what about you, Major Smith, do you have anything?"

"As you may not know, sir, I took what I thought to be a wise precautionary measure in increasing the City's manpower on nighttime patrols on our border with Whitechapel following the murder of the Chapman woman."

"No, I was unaware of this. By how much was the increase made?"

"We increased the capacity of the nighttime patrols by 20 percent, Minister."

"This is very good to hear but your action has made absolutely no difference to the situation that we now find ourselves in. "

"Unfortunately not, Minister. I am afraid to say that we to have no eyewitness accounts and did not find a weapon or footprints at the murder scene in Mitre Square. However, I will now instruct my men to make investigations into all medical personnel, butchers and hairdressers in the whole of the City of London."

"That's good to hear, Major. Right, what I would like from the both of you, starting today, are daily reports to be submitted to this office at the end of each day. My intention being to read them on my arrival at the office at the start of each morning. Until I tell you otherwise, I consider these murders to be our number one priority; is that clear gentlemen?"

Both men replied in the affirmative.

"I expect both your offices to work in unison on this matter, with full disclosure of your activities. As regards manpower; I expect the number of men patrolling the streets to be increased immediately, with a good proportion of them in uniform. Plain clothes officers might prove to be more useful in apprehending the murderer, but our immediate priority must be to maintain, and restore, public confidence. We need to make a visual demonstration to the public that we are using every resource at our disposal to protect them."

"Yes, sir," the two men again replied in unison.

"There is one last thing before you take your leave, gentlemen. Sir Charles, I understand that the Assistant Commissioner had been out of the country convalescing after his recent illness, is this still the case?"

"That is so, Minister. I have already instructed him to relocate from Switzerland to Paris in order to be closer to events."

"Well Paris is not London. I think that it's high time

that Dr Anderson returned to duty, don't you?"

The Major allowed himself a sly smile and the Commissioner blushed slightly; it was definitely one nil to the City Police.

"Yes, sir. I will instruct him to return post haste," replied Warren.

"Thank you for your time gentlemen."

Warren and Smith left the Minister's office. They were both extremely tired; Smith more so than Warren as he had been woken at about 2.30am and very much wanted to go home to bed. However, he had another boss to answer to before he would be allowed to get any rest, and now had to attend a meeting with the outgoing Lord Mayor of London.

CHAPTER FOURTEEN

What Help the Irish?

MONDAY 1ST OCTOBER was a fine autumn day. Reid woke at 10.30am, he'd managed to get about three hours sleep and felt shattered. However, he knew that he would be wanted at the station, so he cleaned himself up, had some breakfast and made his way into work. On his arrival at the station the desk sergeant informed him that he should ready himself for a meeting with the Chief Inspectors to be held in the briefing room. The desk sergeant then went to the Super's office to notify CI Swanson, CI West and Inspectors Abberline and Pinhorn of Reid's arrival. Reid read through the report he had submitted before going home earlier that morning and waited in the briefing room for the most senior Whitechapel Murder Squad officers to arrive.

As usual CI Swanson led the discussion. "Good morning, Inspector Reid."

"Good morning, sir."

"CI West has informed me that he assigned you as the lead detective responsible for investigating last night's murder in Dutfield's Yard. We are now all aware that a second, much more gruesome murder took place within forty-five minutes of the first, in Mitre Square in the City. In addition to the murders, the perpetrator of these savage acts appears to have left us a message in Goulston Street. Is there anything else that you wish to add at this juncture?"

"No sir, other than to inform you that we now believe the dead woman to be named Elizabeth Stride, but we have not yet had sufficient time to arrange for any formal identification of the body."

Swanson continued. "So far none of the leads provided

by the public has borne fruit. We are making systematic enquiries into the activities of recently released mental patients, medical students, doctors, butchers, slaughterers and hairdressers, so far without any success. We have also flooded the streets with additional officers in the hope of deterring or catching the miscreant in the act; this has also met without success. What I think we need to do now is to think of a means of entrapping our man. Has anyone got any thoughts on this?"

Abberline had given this much thought over the last few weeks and one thing that he thought might have proved useful at the most recent murder scene was the use of hunting dogs, that might be able to follow the killer's scent back to his lair. By coincidence, on that very day the Times newspaper carried an editorial in which it informed its readers that in 1876 the murderer William Fish had been detected with the help of a bloodhound.

Abberline spoke first. "Sir, I believe that if my memory serves me correctly, many years back a murder case was solved by the use of a hunting dog that helped track down the killer. I am aware that London is a massive city and that thousands of people and horses frequent our streets, but I cannot help but feel that if some form of tracker dog were available, it could be used to track the movements of the murderer."

Everyone, including Reid thought this to be a very good idea. Two fresh murders had been committed in the early hours of the morning. The city never slept, but there had to be a realistic possibility that dogs could have followed the miscreant's scent through the relatively empty streets before the masses woke at the start of another working day.

"Excellent suggestion!" exclaimed CI Swanson "Now we are thinking gentleman."

Reid hesitated for a few moments. He wanted to pass on some of the ideas raised during his conversations with

Dr Phillips but wasn't sure that this was the time or place to do so.

"If we want to trap the man, sir, then we need appropriate bait with which to whet his appetite," said Reid finally filling the silence.

"What are you suggesting, Reid?" asked Swanson.

"Well, sir, I am aware that we are using men disguised as street ladies to patrol the streets. Could we not employ the services of a few real women, not in a patrolling capacity, but instead as targets? Much like a sheep tethered to a stake?"

This suggestion gave Abberline a bit of a start, as he had already approached the CI with Reid's proposal and had it turned down.

"A good idea, Reid, but unfortunately Inspector Abberline has already brought such an idea to my attention. I decided against it on the grounds that the involvement of civilians would undermine the public's confidence in the constabulary."

"Then I am afraid that I personally am at a loss as to how else we might flush the man out. We then are forced to return to the nigh impossible task of trying to deduce the location of his lair from the logic of our inquiries," replied Reid with a hint of disappointment in his voice.

"You are most probably correct in that Inspector but we don't want to take any action that might foster any form of civil disorder. Has anyone any ideas on how we might locate the maniac's hideaway?"

Reid spoke-up again. "I have given this matter some thought, sir. I recently had a discussion with a man in the medical profession whom suggested that it is a possibility that the killer's first murder might have taken place close to his home. So if we could identify the first murder victim, we would have a zone in which to concentrate our search."

Abberline was starting to wonder if Reid was trying to play politics with him and had chosen this moment to try and wrest control of the investigation from him.

"So which is the first murder, are you suggesting that it was the murder of Tabram and not Nichols?"

"No, what I am suggesting is that the first murder might have been committed even before that of Martha Tabram. The medical man whom wishes to remain nameless was of the opinion that our man may have been fantasising about committing these acts for some considerable time, maybe even for a good number of years. The doctor thought it possible that the killer might have had regular contact with his first victim, his choosing to murder her because she might have inadvertently placed herself in a position where he could kill her with minimal risk of detection."

Everyone thought for a good while about what Reid had said.

"So are you saying that the killer might for instance have had regular contact with his first victim, say in a public house or even a common lodging house?" said Swanson.

"Yes, sir, that is a possibility, but the doctor suggested that the killer might have known his first victim from sharing a workplace or even a regular church service with her. He might for instance have had contact with her during the day and so might even have murdered her during the day. As such, the woman need not have been a woman of the lowest class."

Swanson continued "Very well, Reid, I'll accept that as a possibility, in which case is anyone aware of any violent murders of women of the higher classes?"

All the men in the room gave this some thought. There had been a few violent murders over the years, but none that anyone could think of where the victim had her throat cut and her body mutilated. They all remained silent, which encouraged Reid to continue.

"What I would ask you gentlemen to think about are murders where the lady was murdered by means most savage. The killer may not have mutilated his first victim, as he would have been new to his art. If we include Tabram as being one of his victims, it becomes clear that he is perfecting his method of murder each time he kills. It is the violence of the attacks that may distinguish him from his peers."

Swanson liked this idea, but it did not seem to be bearing any fruit, so he moved on. "I like your suggestion, Inspector. If anyone comes across such a murder, be sure to let Inspector Abberline and me know about it. As it happens I have a few of my own suggestions gentleman. Firstly, we are now likely to receive a significant increase in manpower; I propose using some of these men to make in-depth inquiries into the movements of all sailors at the London docks. Initially, they might focus on the whereabouts of men on cattle trading ships but their enquiries should in time be expanded, time and resources allowing, to cover the movements of all sailors. Secondly, I am aware that Mr Lusk and the members of his Vigilance Committee have submitted another proposal regarding incentives to be offered to possible accomplices of the murderer, in order that if any such person should actually exist, they might be incentivised into turning the man in. Namely, they are proposing that in addition to, or instead of a reward, accomplices to the murderer should be granted a free pardon for their part in the crimes. I am going to suggest that Commissioner Warren lobby the Home Office to have this proposal accepted."

Following that there was not much else for the men to discuss. There were now some pressing matters, such as formal identification of the woman murdered in Dutfield's Yard. As for Swanson, he now had a few ideas to include in his report to the Commissioner. Abberline had liked Reid's suggestion about the killer's first victim being known to him. Abberline was of the opinion that the first victim was Mary Ann Nichols, so he thought that it might not be such a bad idea to check J-Division's list of prime suspects.

❦❦❦

There was another meeting held that day which had a bearing on the matters in hand. Five members of the senior committee of the Irish Republican Brotherhood met in the upstairs room of a Whitechapel pub. Their purpose for the meeting was to discuss the murders taking place in and around the streets of the Irish communities of the east end of London. All the men in the room had been born in Ireland in the early 1840's and had come to London when their families had had to emigrate to escape the potato famine. It was widely felt by the majority of Irish people and definitely by all the men on the IRB committee that the English had done precious little to help feed the starving people of their homeland. The men in the room had joined active service units in the 1870's which had been established to try and secure independence from British rule and a return to a united Ireland. All had been involved in the English bombing campaigns of the early 1880's. Some had had relatives captured by the police and English secret service and seen them sentenced to penal servitude or worse.

Patrick O'Driscoll spoke first. "Right, fellas, you all know why we are here. We need to decide if we should help the English catch this murdering bastard."

The group had met shortly after the murder of Annie Chapman and decided then that word should go out to their people that they should not help the London police in any way in the capture of her killer. Now that another two murders had taken place and with the killer mutilating his victims, the group decided that they needed to review that decision.

A man named Steven O'Brien spoke next. "You know

my views on this matter and they have not changed. Anything that rubbishes the reputation of the English is good for us. Our informants have told me that there are plans afoot to pack rozzers into Whitechapel from the other Met Police divisions, this should make it easier for us to get to work in the rest of the city."

Joseph Regan was the next one to speak. "I didn't agree with you before and I don't agree with you now. This maniac doesn't care who he kills, so far we've been lucky that none of our girls has come into harm's way, but he is sure to take one from the Emerald Isle before too long. We've got our own eyes and ears on the streets and I don't want to be the man responsible for their staying blind whilst a madman is prowling them."

O'Driscoll was the most senior man on the committee. Having allowed the others to air their views he proposed a motion.

"I agree with O'Brien that this maniac is helpful to us at the moment but I too don't want the slaughter of any of our women on my conscience. I've already passed word to the English that our people might be able to help the police if they lose Inspector Abberline. I too don't want that bastard taking any credit for catching the killer. However, they don't want to play ball with us. So as it stands, I propose that we stand our ground and hope that this lunatic carries on butchering English whores."

No one else had any other comment to make and with that the motion was passed; the IRB would maintain their policy of silence on the identity of any potential murder suspect that their informant network might uncover.

☙☙☙

Reid was very tired but hoped that he could remain alert looking throughout the whole first session of the inquest into the murder of the woman he thought to be

Elizabeth Stride. He stopped on his way to the Vestry Hall, Cable Street to buy a drink of very strong coffee from one of the numerous street vendors. He got to the hall early but it was already packed to the rafters, with some members of the public trying to force their way into the building. Reid knew that there was nothing much for him to do that day, as he had already informed the Coroner, Mr Wynne E. Baxter, that the body had not yet been formally identified and Baxter agreed that he would forgo confirmation of the dead woman's name until the second session of the inquest scheduled for Tuesday afternoon. So the order of the day was for three eyewitnesses to be called the stand: William Wess, Morris Eagle and Louis Diemschutz.

Wess was responsible for the printing office based in Dutfield's Yard, he affirmed that he had neither seen or heard anything untoward and had left the office for home at 12.15am. Eagle had been the chair of the night's discussion and said that at the end of it he had taken his lady friend home before returning to the club at about 12.40am to indulge in further discussions, singing and dancing. He stated that he had actually re-entered the club through the side door located in the passage leading to the yard. He had walked along the centre of the passage, possibly walking past the dying wretch, who would have been lying close to the right-hand wall. However, Eagle was of the view that he would not have missed her had she been there when he walked by. Eagle confirmed that it was he who alerted the first policeman to arrive at the scene and it was he who had been directed by PC Henry Lamb to summon further assistance from the Leman Street Police Station. Like Wess, Eagle informed that he didn't remember seeing anyone in Berner's Street or in the yard. As for Diemshutz, he was the club Steward and was the man who found the body. He had been selling jewellery off his portable barrow at a market in Crystal Palace that day and had returned home earlier than usual because business had been slack due to the bad weather. The only complication at the inquest was that Reid refused to formally identify the body. This confused the foreman of the Jury who was aware that someone had already come forward to identify the woman as Elizabeth Stride. However, it was agreed that the lady's identification could wait and the inquest was adjourned until the next day.

⸸⸸⸸

After the inquest Reid returned back to the station to find a Mrs Mary Malcolm waiting to see him. Reid spent a few minutes checking his in-tray before speaking with her in one of the interview rooms.

"Good afternoon, madam."

"Good afternoon, sir."

"I have been informed that you are able to identify the woman found murdered in Dutfield's Yard in the early hours of this morning, is that why you have come to see me?"

"Yes, sir, my name is Mary Malcolm and the dead lady is my sister Elizabeth Watts."

The effects of the caffeine in Reid's coffee had worn-off and the Inspector did not immediately understand what the lady was telling him.

"Malcolm is your family name?"

"Oh no, sir, it is not."

"Are you familiar with the surname Stride?"

"No I am not sir, why do you ask?"

Reid was almost certain that the dead woman was a known prostitute named Elizabeth Stride. However, he now had a witness that was adamant that the dead woman was her sister, who went by the name of Elizabeth Watts.

"Well Mrs Malcolm, I'm afraid to have to inform you that we have received conflicting information about the identity of the women that you believe to be your sister. I would like to check some information with my sergeant. Would you mind waiting for a few minutes?"

Mrs Malcolm couldn't understand what the Inspector would need to check, but was so upset by the situation in which she found herself that she didn't feel like moving from her chair in the squalid little interview room.

"I have no problem with waiting, sir. I'm very tired and am happy to have the weight taken off my feet," she said just before placing her head in her hands.

With that, Reid verified with the desk sergeant that Mrs Malcolm had been taken to the mortuary and had formally identified the body. It transpired that Mrs Malcolm had been unable to verify that the dead lady was actually her sister on her first sight of the body and she had to take another look at the corpse before saying that she was certain that it 'definitely' was the body of her sister. Reid noted that the lady was clearly very distressed and he was certain that she was mistaken in her assertions. He imagined that he would have to put some considerable effort into demonstrating to her that she was wrong, something he neither had the time or inclination to do.

"Mrs Malcolm I'm sorry to have kept you so long."

"As I said, sir, I'm in no hurry and am glad for the rest."

"Clearly, this horrible event has upset you greatly. I'm afraid that the next few days will be equally upsetting for you. However, as I told you, we have not yet formally identified the body of the woman lying in the shed that makes for our mortuary. The conditions in that building are very poor and the light is known to play tricks on people's eyes. I believe that you yourself had some difficulty in recognising the lady as your sister when you first saw the body -."

"It's my Lizabeth, I'm sure of it Inspector!" interrupted Mrs Malcolm.

"I apologise for upsetting you, my dear. However, I am

faced with the task of assisting the coroner in formally identifying the dead lady. I have many years' experience in these matters and it is not unknown for people to change their minds after having time to adjust to the shock. There is another session of the inquest being held tomorrow afternoon and you will be required to confirm to the coroner and a jury that you are absolutely certain that the dead lady is your sister. I would be very grateful if you could try to get as much rest as you can and hopefully after a night's sleep you will be in a better frame of mind with which to make a final statement, under oath."

"Well, Inspector, I know that the light in the mortuary was poor and my sight's not what it once was, but I'm sure that it's my Lizabeth that's in there."

"Who am I to say any different, my dear? However, hopefully things will be clearer after you've had a good night's sleep. The desk sergeant will provide you with details of tomorrow's hearing. Would you like to take some refreshment before you leave?"

"I'd be glad of some water, sir."

"I'll have one of the constables bring you a cup my dear. I am afraid that I must leave now, but you should see me tomorrow at the inquest."

"Thank you, sir. Good day to you."

❦ ❦ ❦

After Mrs Malcolm had left the station Reid made ready to go to a common lodging house at 32 Flower and Dean Street, where he had been informed that several people were willing to testify that the dead lady was none other than Elizabeth Stride, aka Long Liz.

Abberline was in the station and was aware of the confusion being caused by Mrs Malcolm's statement. He was still a bit miffed at the Bank Clerk's return to the case and his not being required to accompany him at the inquest, even if he did appreciate that his attendance at the sessions would be a waste of his time. As Reid was leaving the station Abberline caught his attention.

"Welcome back to the case, Inspector! I'd like a report summarising the witness statements on my desk first thing tomorrow morning. Hopefully this will allow you sufficient time to finally identify the murder victim?"

"Thank you, sir. I will complete my report before departing for home this evening. However, my feeling is that it may take a few more days before I will be able to formally confirm the victim's name as we have received conflicting information from a witness named Mrs Malcolm, who is adamant that the dead woman is her sister and went by the name Watts."

"I'm sure that you will do everything that you can Inspector. I might see you on your return to the station. If not, we will speak again tomorrow."

❦ ❦ ❦

Reid and Sergeant Thick then left the station and made their way to Flower and Dean Street. The first person that they met at the lodging house was the deputy, Mrs Elizabeth Tanner. It transpired that she had been at the mortuary and was one of the first witnesses to have formally identified the body. Unfortunately, she only knew the woman by the name Long Liz. The officers then spoke to two other witnesses, a charwoman named Catherine Lane and a barber named Charles Preston. Mrs Lane also only knew the deceased as Long Liz, but fortunately more progress was made with Preston.

"We have been informed that you have been to the mortuary today and have been able to identify the body Mr Preston. Is that the case?"

"Yes, sir, I have done so. The dead woman's name is Elizabeth Stride."

"And you are absolutely sure of this?" asked Reid.

"I am certain of it, sir."

"What do you know of this woman?"

"I understood it that she was originally from Stockholm in Sweden and came to England in the service of a gentleman. She had previously been married, her husband and children all being drowned on that ship that sunk in the Thames, the Princess Alice."

"Did she ever mention that she had a sister, a woman now going by the name of Mrs Malcolm?"

"No, sir, she never mentioned any sister."

"When did you last see the deceased alive?"

"On Saturday evening in the kitchen of this lodging house, I think it was between six and seven o'clock. I remember the time because she asked me if I would lend her a clothes brush as she was getting ready to go out for the evening."

"And did you let her use your brush?"

"No, I did not, sir. I am particular about my possessions and likes to keep them close by and in good nick like."

Reid ended his questioning and he and Sergeant Thick returned to the station. So far he only had one witness's word against that of Mrs Malcolm. Then he finally received some good news. Whilst they had been away from the police station a waterside labourer by the name of Michael Kidney had arrived there in a highly intoxicated state. Although very drunk, he managed to inform the officers that he had had a long on and off relationship with the dead woman, whom he knew as Elizabeth Stride, adding that they had lived together for several years in various common lodging houses. Kidney had formally identified the body and had said that he had last seen his partner alive on Tuesday night. He had not been concerned by her absence as he said that they were in the habit of separating for weeks at a time and he thought that this was just another one of those. The rest of his statement corroborated the details about Stride provided by Charles Preston. The officers thought Kidney to be a bit mad as well as drunk and had his alibi checked out whilst he was at the mortuary, thinking it possible that he might be responsible for killing his partner. However, Kidney's details checked out and he was thanked for his information and instructed to appear at the next day's session of the inquest.

Reid wrote up his report for Abberline, in which he stated that the disputed statement of Mrs Malcolm could now be disregarded. He then made his way home for his supper and some much needed sleep.

CHAPTER FIFTEEN

The World Learned the Name 'Jack The Ripper'

ON TUESDAY 2ND OCTOBER Commissioner Warren found himself reading Swanson's report that included the recommendation of utilising hunting dogs to try to catch the killer. The Times newspaper had published a letter by one of its readers, a Percy Lindley, a breeder of bloodhounds, who by coincidence had extolled the virtues of using the breed for just such a purpose. Home Office officials had also picked-up on the bloodhound stories and contacted Warren for his view on the matter. Basically they were all in agreement that it was an idea worth trying. Warren was especially keen on the proposal, feeling that the Met Police needed something to rival the actions being taken by the City Police. It was agreed to acquire two bloodhounds, and Warren, who was not slow to see the positive publicity that might be had, stated that he would be personally involved in putting the animals through their paces. Two dogs were found and trials arranged to test their suitability for the task in hand, the dog's names were Barnaby and Burgho. The first trial was scheduled for Tuesday 9th October and Commissioner Warren had agreed to play the part of the hunted man.

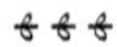

Reid's week was largely taken up with the attendance at sessions of the Stride inquest, there being four sessions in all that week. In addition to that, he had to play his part in sifting and following-up the ever increasing reports that were flooding-in from frightened members of the public. None of this was to be helped by what was to become a major turning point in the case.

❦ ❦ ❦

For David Matthews, Tuesday 2nd October was much like any other working day. Matthews was one of the clerks responsible for processing letters received by the Central News Agency, an organisation that acted as in intermediary for the nation's press agencies. At about 2pm Matthews picked-up and read a postcard that was the most readily accessible item in his in-tray. The text of the postcard dated 1st October read:

I wasnt codding Dear old Boss when I gave you the tip.
You'll hear about Saucy Jackys work Tomorrow double event this time number one squealed a bit couldn't finish straight off. Had not time to get ears for Police
thanks for keeping last letter back till I got to work again.

Jack the Ripper

Matthews, just like everyone else working in the press, was well aware of the 'double event', with both murders being attributed to the Whitechapel murderer . He was also aware that the killer was thought to have been disturbed during the murder of the first of his victims. Matthews' eyes fixed upon the words 'double event' and 'couldn't finish her off straight'. He sat thinking for a while, there was something about the pen name 'Jack the Ripper' that was familiar to him. Then he remembered it, he'd seen the name before and only a few days past. In the corner of his office was a large table on which sat two boxes of letters, labeled 'Monthly Archive' and 'Rubbish'. He searched through the box named Monthly Archive and soon found what he was looking for, a letter dated 27th September. The letter was covered in finger and thumb prints, stained in red ink, and its text read:

Dear Boss,

I keep on hearing the Police have caught me but they won't fix me just yet. I have laughed when they look so clever and talk about being on the right track. Thc joke about Leather Apron gave me real fits. I am down on whores and I shan't quit ripping them till I don get buckled. Grand work the last job was. I gave the lady no time to squeal. How can they catch me now. I love my work and want to start again. You will soon hear of me with my funny little games. I saved some of the proper red stuff in a ginger beer bottle over the last job to write with but it went thick like glue and I can't use it. Red ink is fit enough I hope ha ha. The next job I shall clip the ladys ears off and send to the Police officers just for jolly wouldn't you. Keep this letter back till I do a bit more work, then give it out straight. My knife's so nice and sharp I want to get to work right away if I get the chance.

Good luck,
Yours truly
Jack the Ripper

Don't mind me giving the trade name
Wasn't good enough to post this before I got all the red ink off my hands curse it. No luck yet. They say I'm a doctor now ha ha.

Matthews saw it immediately, both documents had been written in the same handwriting and both were signed 'Jack the Ripper'.

⸙ ⸙ ⸙

At 4.45pm CI Swanson was informed that the senior editor of the Central News Agency, Arthur Kemp, had arrived at Scotland Yard and wished to speak with the lead officer in charge of the Whitechapel Murder Case. At 4.50pm Kemp found himself sitting at Swanson's desk. Swanson had had dealings with Kemp in the past in regard to press releases made for general circulation to the London newspapers with quotes and information relating to some of the higher profile cases that he had taken charge of. Swanson assumed that Kemp had come to see him in order to complain about the lack of information being circulated to the news agencies in regard to his current big case.

"What can I do for you, Mr Kemp?" asked Swanson wearily.

Kemp eyed Swanson cautiously, then without speaking he carefully placed a letter and a postcard on the CI's desk. Then he spoke.

"Earlier today one of our clerks became aware of receipt by our news agency of the two items that I have placed before you. The letter is dated 27th September and the postcard the 1st October. Now before you read them, I am well aware that both of our organisations have received more than its fair share of bogus correspondence in relation to the Whitechapel Murders. However, there is something about the documents laid out in front of you that leads me and my staff to believe that they are both authentic and highly relevant to your case. So much so that I have brought them here myself for your attention."

Swanson read the letter and then the postcard, then he studied the handwriting on both documents. He paused for a while, his eyes focusing on the postcard and the words 'double event' and 'couldn't finish her off straight'. His eyes then fixed upon the words 'Had not time to get the ears for the Police'. He was aware that Catherine Eddowes' right ear had been cut through and that her earlobe had come away from her body during its transit to the mortuary.

"Mr Kemp, I can appreciate that you obviously believe these documents to be the work of the killer, but what would you have me do with them?"

"To my mind the author is clearly a man of some education, there are also a number of Americanisms included in both texts; in that they include sayings that are in common parlance on the North American continent. Such as 'give it out straight'. As such, I am minded to suggest that facsimile copies be made of the documents and they, at a minimum, be placed on posters outside of every police station in the metropolis. One might even consider publishing them in all of the nation's newspapers."

Swanson glared at Kemp from across his desk.

Kemp continued unperturbed, "Look, Chief Inspector, I only suggest this because the writing, even if the author has taken the trouble to try and disguise it, is quite distinctive. As such, the whereabouts on the nights of the murders of every man that writes in such a hand, resident in London, if not the whole country, should warrant investigation by the authorities."

"Now look here, Mr Kemp. You are well aware that we are already receiving between ten and a hundred letters every month, if we in the police were to do as you propose, it would surely open the floodgates. As it is, we are struggling to thoroughly investigate all the correspondence that we have received to date. How will it look to you men in the press if in six months' time we are no nearer apprehending the miscreant and have a team of twenty men sat at desks, devoted to reading letters, when they should be out on the streets physically searching for the man?"

"Chief Inspector, I would not be here if my organisation did not take this correspondence extremely seriously. As such, I give you my word that should the authorities' make these documents known to the general public, there will not be a single article written that even hints of police inefficiency in relation to the work involved in the behind the scenes activities that you must perform. Obviously, any ineptitude by your rank and file officers will not be tolerated and the members of the press would continue to remain duty bound to report on it. However, publish copies of these documents and we at the CNA will guarantee more favourable news coverage going forward.

"Who are you, to come here and try to threaten me into taking actions that will clearly be very beneficial to the circulation of your peers' publications!" said Swanson as he got up out of his chair, and thumped his desk with one of his massive fists.

"Alright, Chief Inspector, I am not here to try and pressurise you in any way. Is it not the case that we could already have arranged for every major publication in London to be sent copies for publication? These documents have been sent to us and are our own property to do with as we please. I am here because my colleagues and I truly believe that the madman prowling our streets could very well be the author of the correspondence and as such we would prefer you to arrange for the contents to be made public. Now, sir, I have handed the documents over to you and leave it for you to decide what is in the best interests of the nation to do with them. I can tell you now that should you in fact decide to do nothing with them, no publication in the land will be informed that you ever received them. All that we want is for right to be done."

Swanson sat back down and took a few deep breaths whilst rereading the two documents. Suitably composed, he lifted his head to face Kemp.

"In that case, Mr Kemp, I promise you that the Commissioner will be shown the documents as soon as can be arranged and that every effort will be made to identify the author. I cannot promise you that their contents will ever see the light of day but full consideration will be given to publishing copies as you have suggested. It only remains for me to thank you for bringing the documents to us and I would be very grateful if any further correspondence received from this man, the 'Ripper', is sealed and sent directly to me and me only."

"Very well, Chief Inspector Swanson, I can ask no more of you, sir."

❦❦❦

Commissioner Warren, much to Swanson's surprise, was very keen to publish the correspondence laid before him, and he and his CI requested an urgent meeting with Home Secretary Matthews. At 7pm they were granted access to the minister. For his part, Sir Henry was pleased to see the men from the Met as he hoped that they were about to inform him that they had finally solved the case.

"Please be seated, gentlemen. Time is short, so I would be grateful if you can get straight to the point."

Swanson knew that he would only be required to speak if his commissioner required him to fill in any blanks, so he left it to Sir Charles to make their pitch to the Home Secretary.

"Sir Henry, I have with me two items of correspondence received by the Central News Agency, the documents are purported to come from the Whitechapel Murderer. The Chief Inspector and I are of the opinion that the detail included in the documents is different from anything we have received to date and we both feel that there is a strong possibility they have been authored by the killer."

Commissioner Warren placed the correspondence on the desk for the minister's inspection. Matthews read the letters, he was a man used to reading dry lifeless ministerial briefs but felt the hairs on the back of his neck rise as he read what he thought could be the words of the maniac who was fast becoming a thorn in his side. Sir Henry was both at once thrilled and disappointed. He had hoped that he would be given the name of the murderer, but the possibility of having the killer's words in his hands sent a shiver down his spine.

"Right, gentlemen, there is obviously something that sets these items apart from the other letters being processed by your staffs. So what is it that you propose we do with them?"

"The CNA has proposed making facsimile copies and publishing them in the press and having posters made that could be placed outside every police station in the metropolis. They have promised that our accepting their suggestion will result in much more favourable copy going forward. Now I for one don't have the slightest intention of being held to ransom by some down at heel newspaper hacks, but I am of the opinion that the benefits of publishing the documents outweigh the externalities that will surely follow."

"Pray tell me, Commissioner, what are the benefits?"

"Well, sir, as I see them they are three fold. Firstly, as you can see the handwriting is quite distinctive, so if authentic, we will no doubt receive the details of men that write in a similar hand. Secondly, the promise of less critical press coverage would be most welcome at this juncture, it would definitely be much better to get the press on our side; and thirdly, I sense that public confidence in the authorities is very low and would be given a boost by such an unusual breakthrough."

The minister considered his options; more favourable press was always good for an elected representative but he was concerned that the decision to publish could come back to bite the man that approved it. However, he would only be acting on the advice of his Commissioner and any blame should surely lie with the Commissioner and not himself. He could foresee many externalities resulting from the publishing of the documents, not least a flood of copycat correspondence, but then the Commissioner and his underlings would have to deal with that.

"Very well, proceed with the suggestions made by the CNA. However, no action is to be taken until I receive a written request from you clearly stating the benefits as you see them. Obviously, one would not expect to see much in the way of 'externalities' as you choose to call them. I'd like your request waiting for me on my desk on my arrival in the office tomorrow morning. Good evening to you, gentlemen."

And with that a legend was born. Sir Henry approved the publishing of the documents and within days the world learned the name 'Jack the Ripper'.

The public had previously gone into a frenzy over the stories of the infamous 'Leather Apron', but their response to those articles was as nothing in comparison to their reaction to the Ripper news stories. The police and the press had combined to create a phantom menace, the likes of which had been unheard of since the days of the mythical 'Spring Heeled Jack'.

ᵻ ᵻ ᵻ

Abberline, Reid and the rest of the Whitechapel Murder Squad kept an open mind about the authenticity of the Ripper correspondence, but the feeling in the camp was that publishing the documents would cause more harm than good. In that they were proved right, as before long, imitation letters started flooding into newspaper offices and police stations all over the country. All of them required processing and wasted many precious man hours.

ᵻ ᵻ ᵻ

The pressure on the Met Police's Whitechapel Murder Squad was also not helped by the actions of their colleagues in the City Police. Commissioner Warren had done his best to try and get the Home Office to authorise a Government reward for information leading to the arrest of the killer. Yet the Lord Mayor of London in corroboration with the assistant Commissioner of the City Police immediately sanctioned a reward of £500, this was more than four year's wages for a Met Police Inspector like Edmund Reid. They also held a short sharp inquest into the murder of the woman found murdered in Mitre Square, Catherine Eddowes. They even had the City Solicitor, Mr Henry Homewood Crawford, represent them at the inquest to thoroughly interrogate every witness. By delaying the inquest, there was also none of the comedy of errors that faced Reid with the identification of Elizabeth Stride's body, all of the deceased details were well known in advance of the hearing. It was found out that Eddowes had been living in common lodging houses, her usual abode being at number 55 Flower and Dean Street. It was also discovered that she had spent the last seven years living with a man named John Kelly, after being married to a man known as Thomas Conway. In short, the City Police were running a very professional looking investigation and were making the Met look slack in comparison.

⸸ ⸸ ⸸

On the evening of Friday 5th October, police stations in H and J Divisions and those in the eastern edge of the City of London were jam-packed with police. There were a lot of new faces, with men being drafted in from many of the country's other police forces. The Met had been lucky, as it actually had a reserve of manpower its disposal. Commissioner Warren had anticipated a repeat of the attempted riots that had taken place in the autumns of 1886 and 1887, and so had arranged for a few hundred officers to be made available for riot control in the autumn of 1888. These men thought that they would spend their time on the day shift performing crowd control duties in the salubrious centre of the city. They were now none too pleased to find themselves placed on night duty patrolling the dilapidated streets of Whitechapel. Police numbers were being increased on all days during the week but it was felt that the Ripper, as the killer would now be known, was more likely to strike over a weekend. The major concern was that the uniformed officers might waste much of their time following and apprehending the new plain-clothes men, in effect chasing their own tails. However, identification of these men was to prove far simpler than anticipated, as they all automatically walked their beats at a pace of 2.5 miles an hour in their regulation hobnailed boots, holding themselves like military men. This even applied to a majority of the men that were supposed to be masquerading as women.

CHAPTER SIXTEEN

The Death of Lucy Clark

TO EVERYONE'S RELIEF there were no new killings over the weekend. Abberline had arranged for a briefing to be held at ten o'clock on the morning of Monday 8th October. He had spent the last week trying to think up new ways of pinpointing the lair of the man they now called the Ripper. He had thought long and hard about Reid's theory that the first murder was the key in locating where the killer lived or worked. Abberline had decided that it was very likely that the man they sought either lived locally or was a sailor, as he could not understand how a bloodstained man could spend so much time walking the streets without gathering the attention of a policeman. He thought that the man must have some local bolt hole or was able to quickly make his way to the docks and disappear onto a ship. Abberline imagined in his mind's eye the murderer making a kill and then quickly travelling back to his home base to clean up. He could not see how a bloodstained man would be able to do this in a common lodging house or workhouse, as all the inmates would be on the lookout for any suspicious bloodstained men. In short, Abberline thought that if the man was not a sailor, then he most likely lived locally, on his own in his own private accommodation.

Abberline had fixed a large map onto the wall at the front of the briefing room. On the map he had placed markers at all the murder sites and in Goulston Street where the bloodstained apron and the writing on the wall had been found. His intuition told him that the killer must live somewhere in the midst of the markers and he had drawn a large circle around the points. He had a feeling that Reid would object to his ignoring the Tabram murder but even adding a marker for her murder made no difference to the location of his circle. At close to 10am the officers of the unofficially named 'Ripper Squad' started to arrive in the briefing room. Reid noticed the map straight away and also noticed the lack of a marker in George Yard, the location of the Tabram murder.

The lead Detective Inspector started the briefing shortly after ten. "Good morning, gentlemen. I am pleased to report that no further murders were committed over the weekend. A number of suspicious characters were arrested but most have now been released following confirmation of their alibis on the nights of the previous four murders. Law and order has been restored to our streets but unfortunately none of this has resulted in any further progress being made in the capture of our man. Today, all Inspectors will report on progress made into their investigations. However, before hearing these reports I would like to draw your attention to the map on the wall behind me."

All the officers in the room looked at the map.

Abberline continued "The map shows the locations of the four murders and the location where the blood-soaked apron was found. The circle around these points depicts the area where I think we are most likely to find the home base or workplace of our killer. Now gentlemen, I want you to keep an open mind as to the occupation of the murderer; I myself am of the opinion that the man that we seek is not the type to live in a doss house or a workhouse. This, gentlemen, implies that the man we seek either has regular employment, might be a sailor, or has some other means of support. In short, with this in mind we can effectively eliminate thousands of men living within the area enclosed by the circle. This unfortunately leaves many thousands of others. However, I agree with a theory put forward by Inspector Reid that our man might live close to the location of the first murder. So I am glad to see that Inspector Helson and his colleagues from J-Division are here, as it is possible that the killer lives in Stepney, in the vicinity of Bucks Row. Has anybody got any comments about the map and the reasoning used to eliminate possible suspects?"

Reid was first to comment. "No disrespect meant by this, sir, but I've noticed that you have no marker for the Tabram murder."

"That is correct, Inspector Reid, the Tabram murder is of a different order to the others and I have been advised by a number of doctors based at various lunatic asylums to ignore it."

Reid broke in again. "Okay, sir, I can accept that the Tabram murder is different to the others, in that the killer did not cut the victim's throat but can we be sure that the Nichols murder was the first?"

"That is a good point, Reid. Does any man in this room know of any other murder that is even remotely like the four we believe to be committed by the Ripper?"

There was silence in the room. Many officers thought that Abberline was asking rhetorical question, as it was obvious to all of them that if there had been such a murder, the people in that room were most likely to have remembered it.

However, Reid spoke-up again "Well, Inspector, I have discovered such a murder."

All eyes were now on Reid. Even the men who had purposely sat at back of the room because they were tired, were sitting bolt upright and looking at him now.

Reid continued. "In the week commencing 16th January of this year a lady was savagely murdered just off the Marylebone Road, at number 86 George Street, Portman Square. There were two possible causes of the woman's death; her head had been bashed-in with a blunt instrument, but more importantly her throat had been cut all the way back to her spine, leaving a notch on the bone. I personally only know of one man that has cut his victim's throats in such a manner."

Most men in the room did not know what to think. They were at a loss to see how Reid could know of a murder that none of them had any recollection of.

An officer who had recently been loaned to H-Division from D-Division spoke next.

"I am Sergeant Brown of D-Division, Marylebone. I believe that Inspector Reid is referring to the murder of a lady named Lucy Clark. If that is the case, although technically an unsolved murderer, everyone in my division believes the lady's murder to have been committed by her two nephews; who were subsequently arrested, tried and acquitted. Also, with no disrespect to the Inspector, the lady in question was of a completely different class to the women being slaughtered by the Ripper. She was a self-employed maker of high quality ladies dresses and the motive for her murder was very clearly one of robbery."

"Sergeant Brown, you do not dispute that Lucy Clark's murder remains unsolved?" asked Reid.

"No, I do not, sir," replied the sergeant.

"And is it true that part of the reason why the jury did not agree on a guilty verdict was because they could not believe that members of the lady's own flesh and blood could have dispatched her in such a violent manner?"

"That is also true, sir."

"Then is my suggestion not reasonable, that our killer could in fact have committed this murder?"

"Well I suppose looked at your way, it would not be an unreasonable suggestion to make."

"There is one other thing, sergeant. Is it not also the case that if the prime motive was robbery, the robber or robbers were somewhat lax in their endeavours? My understanding is that the 'robber' left behind gold, silver and banknotes worth more than £11 and £250 in stocks and share certificates. Why would any robber not have taken away at least the items of jewellery?"

"I believe that that was the case, sir, but surely you must see that it would be quite easy for an amateur burglar to make such elementary mistakes, especially in the wake of committing such a savage attack," countered the sergeant.

"I do not wish to go into the fine detail of the case, but I genuinely believe that this murder should be included in our case as it sheds light on another possible location for the murderer's home base. As such, I propose that our killer might equally live in Marylebone or in Stepney."

Abberline finally spoke. He was caught totally unawares by Reid's comments and wondered whether the 'Bank Clerk' was again purposely trying to undermine him.

"Thank you for your comments, gentlemen. However, with the greatest respect to Inspector Reid, I am afraid that we could all dig up a whole host of other murders that might have tenuous links with the four that we are faced with solving today. So in the interests of efficiency, I would like all of you to take account of my map of murders when performing all further inquiries."

Reid stopped listening to the rest of what Abberline had to say. He had no proof to back up his claim that the Lucy Clark murder should be treated as the first Ripper murder. However his gut instinct said that it should be and in all the years that he had been a policeman, he had rarely found his instincts wanting. At that moment Reid reverted to type; once before in his career he made a decision to pursue a case without the authority of his superiors, he was now going to do so again.

After the meeting Reid was approached by Sergeant Thick.

"For what it's worth, sir, I think that you have a point about the Clark murder. However, if you don't get anyone from D-Division on your side, I can't see how any progress can be made in connection to that murder."

"Thank you for your support, sergeant, unfortunately I must agree with your opinion."

❦❦❦

Later in the day Abberline had a meeting with his boss, CI Swanson.

"How did the briefing go this morning, Frederick?"

"On the whole it went well, but I could do without Reid's meddling."

Swanson studied his lead detective inspector. He had been expecting tensions to occur between Abberline and the man that had stepped into his shoes at H-Division and thought that Reid might have started to rebel against his new boss.

"What do you mean by that, Frederick?"

"I've put a lot of thought into where we should concentrate our investigative efforts and today I wanted to get the men to start expanding their thinking into the background of our killer. I think that they are all too fixed upon the idea of finding our man in a common lodging house or workhouse, when I think it more likely that he either has his own private accommodation or might be a sailor living on a boat moored in the docks."

"I'm aware of that Fred and I agree with your line of reasoning, so how has Reid managed to muddy the waters?"

Abberline's brow furrowed.

"Well, sir, in addition to my telling the men that the murderer most likely has his own accommodation, I also informed them that he most likely lives and or works in an area enclosed by the four known murders. With the first murder likely to be that of the woman Connelly, committed on J Division's patch. Reid then proposed his own new theory that a further murder has been committed -"

"Alright Fred, I see no problem with Reid bringing up the Tabram murder."

"Well that's just it, sir, he didn't"

Swanson found himself confused. He had personally

reviewed the case notes of all the murders which had been committed over the last year, in and around the East End and the City of London. There had been the odd throat slashing but nothing that matched the savagery of the Ripper murders.

"What do you mean by this, Frederick, has Reid dug up some murder in another part of the country?"

"No, sir. He provided the men with the details of a murder that took place in January of this year in Marylebone. A dressmaker by the name of Lucy Clark was bludgeoned to death in her home and the place ransacked. The long and short being that the lady had two nephews, both of whom were arrested and tried for her murder. Well it turns out that the jury didn't find them guilty, as they couldn't believe that the lady's own kinsfolk would despatch her in such a brutal fashion. So Reid is technically correct in having found an unsolved murder in another part of the city."

Swanson found himself confused again.

"You say that this lady, Lucy Clark, was bludgeoned to death, so what possible connection is there to our case?"

"Well, sir, in addition to her killer or killers beating her around the head, she also had her throat cut all the way back to her spinal column. It was this that is thought to have convinced the members of the jury that the nephews were innocent of the crime."

Swanson gave his detective inspector a wry smile.

"Well Frederick, we can't fault Reid for imagination and endeavour, can we?"

"No, sir, but I think that he's in the business of producing red herrings just to undermine my authority."

Swanson paused for a while. He had full trust in Abberline and was content to let him allocate his resources where he saw fit. However, he didn't want him to discourage his men from proffering new ideas, no matter how ridiculous they might seem on first inspection.

"Look Fred, Reid's a good man, a bit unconventional and certainly not someone to bet your house on, but like you he gets results. So by all means keep the fellow in order but try not to extinguish the spark in him in the process."

Abberline scratched the back of his head. He was irritated that the Chief Inspector should even give Reid's ideas the time of day.

"Very well, sir, but I might find myself having to put him in his place if he comes up with too many outlandish ideas."

"You're the boss, Fred, so I'll trust you to keep the blinkers on our wild pony."

Swanson thought a little more about Reid's proposal and decided that he'd request the case notes into the Clark murder, just in case Reid had valid point in wanting to include it in the Ripper investigation. Then he brought up the matter that he actually wanted to discuss with his detective inspector.

"Anyway enough of Inspector Reid. I've another more pressing matter that I want to discuss with you. The boys at the Home Office are concerned about a letter published in the Times by Dr Thomas Barnardo, the gentleman who runs the ragged school. It transpires that he wrote a letter published in the Saturday 6th October edition of the newspaper, in which he stated that on the night of Wednesday 26th September he had visited 32 Flower and Dean Street, the common lodging house frequented by the murdered woman, Elizabeth Stride. Supposedly the doctor says that he remembered seeing the woman Stride in the kitchen, along with a number of other inmates who were listening to a lecture he was giving on some scheme he'd devised for saving children from contamination of the evils of the lodging houses. The doctor said that he took note of all the women in the room because instead of mocking his scheme, they all seemed to very much support it. He went on to say that he remembered one inmate then making reference to the recent slayings, saying, and I quote, 'We're all up to no good, and no one cares what becomes of us. Perhaps some of us will be killed next!' Now Fred, the Minister would like to know why the good doctor would have recorded such a detailed account of his visit to one of many establishments that visited that night."

It was Abberline's turn to smile.

"What's so funny, Frederick?"

"I have good news for you, sir."

"What do you mean by that?"

"One of my men noticed Dr Barnardo out on his rounds that Wednesday night and commented to me, and I quote, 'That such a man could walk the streets of Whitechapel largely unmolested by robbers and the police alike. Gentlemen like the good doctor, being effectively hidden from all whilst remaining in plain sight'. As a result of that conversation, I made the decision to place the good doctor under surveillance and am most happy to report that he was under our watch on the night of the last two murders, remaining at his family home the whole night."

"This is most excellent news, Frederick. You know how it is. Some official at the Home Office has read the letter and immediately informed the Commissioner's office that the doctor could well be the murderer. I will be very pleased to report that the good doctor can be discounted as a suspect due to our proactive policing methods. Tell me, are we monitoring any other men of note?"

"No, sir, none of the other men's names should warrant any similar inquiry."

"I trust that we have all the relevant paperwork showing how we came to place the good doctor under surveillance? You know what these civil servants are like with their procedures."

Abberline wasn't at all sure that there was a paper trail detailing the doctor's inclusion in the surveillance watch lists but intended to ensure that there was, immediately following the meeting.

"I cannot be absolutely sure that all is in order sir, but I will double-check, just in case someone has neglected to dot an 'i' or cross a 't'."

⸎ ⸎ ⸎

Reid had liked the Bank Manager's murder map and decided to make one of his own. He knew that he would not be allowed to use a wall map, so made do with a standard sized map of London. He marked off the locations of the four murders thought most likely to have been committed by the man they were now calling the Ripper, adding markers for the location of the Tabram and Clark murders, and the site where the bloodstained apron was found. Reid looked at the marks on his map and thought that from this new perspective it was quite possible that the first murder had been the Marylebone one. If so, the Ripper most likely knew the lady Lucy Clark and as the doctor had said, might not have planned her murder. It was likely that Clark's was an opportunist killing, the result of which was that the killer had now crossed the boundary separating his murderous fantasies from reality. Reid then imagined that the murderer, his appetite wetted, would then have planned his next murder. It made sense for the man to choose Whitechapel prostitutes, as they were easily accessible, could be lured into secluded locations and no one much cared whether such women lived or died. As it was, no one raised as much as an eyebrow if such a woman was turned-out of a lodging house in the midst of winter to die of exposure. To Reid there was no difference in the way any of these women died. Was it really worse for them to have been slaughtered at the hands of a maniac than to die half-starved from hypothermia?

Reid thought long and hard about the Tabram murder.

That lady did not have her throat slashed, but did have nine stab wounds to her neck. Unlike the other murders, hers was in a relatively public place, the first floor landing of a stairwell of a model dwelling block. Even though the woman died between 2am and 4am in the morning, the stairwell had been in regular use throughout the night. Reid wondered if Tabram realised that there was something odd about her client and so deliberately led him to an area that she thought might provide her with greater security? If so, the killer might have felt less in control of the situation and so might have lashed out at her in anger, resulting in the killer wound being made to the victim's chest as opposed to the more technically difficult severing of the left carotid artery. Upon reflection, Reid decided to include Tabram's murder in with that of the others. It seemed quite possible to him that the killer might have broken away from his modus operandi in response to the circumstances that he found himself in. Reid thought that as the killer had grown in confidence, so had the ritualistic nature of the mutilations. It was as if the man was following some set technical procedure, with the two deep cuts to the throat being made all the way back to the spinal column and the removal of body parts. It was almost as if the man imagined himself to be a surgeon, imitating surgical procedures or maybe even a priest following the ritual of some heathen religion. However, Reid was a detective, not a psychiatrist and knew that he could never hope to fully understand the motives of an insane murderer. For all that, he felt with some certainty that he did know something about the man he sought; that the man would kill again and that the depravity shown in the mutilations committed so far were very likely to get worse.

The Inspector did not want to dwell too long on the fate that he thought awaited the maniac's next victim. He just hoped that someone would capture the man before he was able to kill again. Also, Reid had other more pressing matters to concern himself with. He had been tasked with finding the sister of Mrs Malcolm in order to lay to rest any possible fears that the police had incorrectly identified the body of the woman murdered in Dutfield's Yard. He also hadn't made any progress with his fraud case. He had been given the name of Harris Marks by the waterside labourer Harry Clements and was yet to make any progress in locating him.

CHAPTER SEVENTEEN

We Know Him as 'The Preacher'

ON THE MORNING OF TUESDAY 9TH OCTOBER Commissioner Warren, CI Swanson, DI Abberline and an official from the Home Office watched as two bloodhounds, provided by Edwin Brough, a dog breeder from Wyndyate a village close to Scarborough, were put through their paces in London's Hyde Park. The dogs passed every test asked of them. Their final trial was to track none other than Sir Charles himself through the park under the watchful eye of a few specially selected newspaper reporters. The dogs, Burgho and Barnaby also completed this task with flying colours. Warren was extremely pleased and made sure to let the reporters know that he had had the idea of using tracker dogs before the Times article alluded to it on 1st October.

Arrangements were then made for the dogs to be stationed in London and to be on-call for use by the Whitechapel Murder Squad 24 hours a day. Mr Brough left the dogs with a London based friend of his, a Mr Taunton. However, even though Warren had secured funding for the use of dogs from the Home Office for the remainder of the year, it was far from clear what services were actually payable by the Met Police. Mr Brough wasn't too concerned by any of this, as he incorrectly assumed that over time the public servants would get their act together and some form of financial remuneration would finally find its way to him.

ቆቆቆ

Reid had volunteered for the evening shift that day, as

he was having no luck locating Harris Marks in the White Hart pub during the day. As luck would have it, Sergeant Thick was on the same shift that evening and Reid arranged for the sergeant to accompany him on his search for Marks. They made numerous trips along the Whitechapel High Street with Reid nipping into the White Hart and Nags Head pubs on his own, as the sergeant, who was in full police uniform, drew attention to the pair everywhere they went. Unbeknown to Reid, Levi Greenfield was also in the area and decided out of curiosity to follow the two men. Greenfield's interest had been caught, by what seemed to him to be the strange sight of a plain-clothes detective working the streets in unison with a fully uniformed sergeant. Reid and the sergeant were having no luck in their search and then, just to pass the time a little differently they decided to cut through to Wentworth Street using a little used narrow thoroughfare named Castle Alley. The two men had gone as far as the junction with Old Castle Street when they encountered what looked like a street gang in the process of attacking a woman.

The woman saw the uniformed policeman and hoped that she might be saved from whatever fate the men in the gang had planned for her.

"PLEASE 'ELP ME, THESE MEN MEAN TO 'ARM ME," she screamed.

Reid stepped up, there were five men in the gang but he felt confident that he and the sergeant would be able to deal with the situation.

"Right gentlemen, whatever you might have had planned for the woman ends here. Leave her be and walk away or else you will face arrest."

The largest of the men stepped up. "Wot's it got to do with you mister. If you knows what's good for ya, you'll make yourself scarce."

Reid responded. "I will give you one more chance; now walk away whilst you are still able to do so."

"We'll see whose able, mister," and with that the man lunged at Reid.

Sergeant Thick, anticipating violence had made ready with his truncheon and flew at the two men standing closest to him. However, they were too fast for him and managed to get hold of his arms whilst a third man ran behind him and began hitting him with a club. The initial blows were deflected off the Sergeant's police issue helmet, but they then set about aiming blows at Thick's back and shoulders.

Reid and the gang leader had locked horns, but the fifth man had circled around the back of him and kicked him in the back of the knee. Reid's leg buckled and he started to fall to the floor. The woman, sensing all was lost started screaming again.

Greenfield had watched the fight start from his vantage point at the beginning of the alley. He'd given Reid the pornographer, Joshua Engels, in exchange for his freedom but decided that since the officer had been good to his word, he would further repay the man's kindness in a manner better befitting his capabilities. He swiftly ran up the alley and with just two punches felled the two men who were attacking Reid, each was almost unconscious before hitting the ground. Fortunately for the men, they weren't too badly injured as their landings were cushioned by piles of horse manure that filled the alley. Greenfield then set about the men attacking the sergeant. These men fought like professional fighters and Greenfield then understood why they had chosen to attack the larger of the two policemen. The four standing men then reached a standoff.

With the two officers' still lying on the ground, Greenfield spoke. "Today's your lucky day, gentlemen. For attacking an officer of the law you could spend a lot of time at Her Majesty's pleasure but I'm going to make you an offer that I hope you don't choose to refuse. Why don't you leave off now, pick your mates up of the floor and be off? What says ya to that?"

The woman had stopped screaming and hoped that now all would end peaceably. With their leader still down on the ground, the other gang members were not sure what to do. Not feeling confident of being able to take this third copper down they decided to take up his offer before he changed his mind. They helped their two mates off the floor and then made off up Old Castle Street, entered into Wentworth Street and disappeared into the back streets of the wicked quarter mile.

Reid was still on the ground nursing his bruises. "Are you alright, Sergeant?" he asked.

Thick responded with an "I'll live, sir." But he was actually quite shaken, as it had been more years than he could remember since the last time anyone had gotten the better of him. He directed his attention to the man that had just saved him from a severe beating.

"My thanks to you, sir," said the sergeant.

"Think nothing of it," replied Greenfield.

Then the attention of all three men turned to the woman. She clearly had the look of a prostitute and they thought that maybe one of her punters had lured her into the alley to rob her or worse, sexually assault her.

"Are you unharmed, my dear?" asked Reid.

"Yeh, I'm fine thanks to you and your men. They'd 'ave done me if you 'adn't come along when ya did."

"What's your name, my dear?" asked Reid.

"I'm Ellen Holland, sir."

"I'm Inspector Reid, this is Sergeant Thick and this gentleman is Mr Greenfield."

"It's a pleasure meeting ya all," said the woman. "Excuse me, sir, but I knows your name. You're the man that they say is after him, the Knife."

"If you mean the man they are now calling the Ripper, then yes, me and my men are trying our best to get the villain."

"I hope's very much that he is ketched. I was a friend

to Polly Nichols, the lady he's killed in Bucks Row. I'd do anything I could to help get 'im"

"How did you find yourself to be in this alley?" asked Reid.

"One of them men's conned me like. I don't know wot they would have done, as I ain't got a penny to my name."

Reid did not know the woman, but she was obviously one of Whitechapel's fallen women.

"Where are you living, my dear?" asked Reid.

"I lodge mostly in Thrawl Street, sir. Number 18 is me regular."

Reid reached into his pocket and pulled out eight pence.

"Now, my dear, please take this and get yourself off to Thrawl Street. You have enough for a bed for tonight and some supper, I hope that you choose to spend the money wisely."

With that, the men walked the lady to the Whitechapel High Street and bade her a good night.

"Mr Greenfield, it would appear that the sergeant and I are in your debt," said Reid.

"Well Inspector, I can see that you are a good man and you was true to your word with me, so I'm glad to have been able to help you out. Although knowing a man like you makes it a bit difficult for a man like me to earn a living, if you understand my meaning?"

What Reid understood was that in the last few weeks, Greenfield had lost both Joshua Engels as an employer and the income he would have gotten from his fighting dogs. He wondered if Greenfield was offering himself up to be some sort of paid informer.

"How are you doing for money these days?" asked Reid.

"Actually, I'm doing alright. I likes to keep busy and I've got certain skills that some around here are willing to pay me good money for."

Then Reid remembered that Greenfield might know the identity of Engels's client, the man with a sadistic taste in pornography.

"Mr Greenfield. I have another favour to ask from you."

"Look, Inspector, there's a limit to what a fellow like me can tell men like you and the sergeant."

"Yes, I understand that. I am not seeking information about any of your associates. I am keen to learn more about one of Mr Engels's customers. How much did you see of his work?"

"Not very much, sir, I had no interest in seeing the photographs he was taking. My job was to help find his models, deliver the pictures and collect the money owed. Mr Engels was always careful to wrap the pictures up, so I never saw what was to be delivered. I preferred it that way."

Reid's experience of Greenfield was that he appeared quite open and honest for a member of the criminal class, so he had no reason to disbelieve what the man told him. Unfortunately this meant that in this particular case he had come to a dead end. However, he decided to pursue the issue, just in case he got lucky and stumbled upon something useful.

"Okay, if you never saw the pictures, did you have an inkling of the images captured?"

Greenfield now became a little uncomfortable with Reid's line of questioning, especially as the fully uniformed Sergeant Thick was witness to every word that he said.

"Look Inspector, no disrespect to the Sergeant, but I can only answer questions like that in private like. If we could speak out of earshot of the Sergeant, I'll answer you as best I can."

"Okay Mr Greenfield, that sounds reasonable to me. Sergeant Thick, me and Mr Greenfield will finish our conversation further along the alley."

"That is fine by me, sir," said the sergeant, who had no interest whatsoever in seeking to find a reason to arrest the man with the Inspector.

Reid resumed his line of questioning. He thought that Greenfield must know something about the content of the photographs. "I ask you again, sir, were you aware of the content of the images?"

"Well it was obvious what sort of thing was going on when the little uns were brought in."

Reid cut in "This is not about what happened to the children. I have no interest in the part that you might have played in obtaining them for Engels. I am instead interested in one of his clients. During questioning Mr Engels referred to a client that he considered having unusually violent tastes in the images that he purchased. Were you aware of any images that were different in that way?"

Greenfield thought for a while about the question. To his mind all the images were 'different in some way', but then he remembered Engels comments about one particular man.

"Like I said, I did not see the pictures but there was one customer that I remember Mr Engels talking about. Yes, early last year I remember him commenting on one of the packages I was due to deliver. He said something about how he was glad that he was a single man, without a wife or daughters, knowing that men were out there that had a mind to hurt them. I don't think that those pictures had anything to do with children, as I didn't get any of them for him until early this year."

"Did you deliver the photographs directly to this customer or was the delivery made through an agent?"

"Well, yes and no. The man did not purchase the pictures through an agent, as he was very careful like."

"What do you mean by this?"

"I was told by Mr Engels to take the package to

Regent's Park and leave it in some bushes for the client to collect. The client paid Engels directly. We had no such arrangement with anyone else."

Reid's brain now went into to overdrive. He had already made-up his mind that this man with a passion for seeing women attacked in photographs might himself be driven to attack them in real life and Regent's Park was close to Marylebone; the home of Lucy Clark. Reid was already thinking that Engels' client could very well be the monster that half the police in London were looking for.

"So you never saw the man?" asked Reid.

"Actually, sir, I did see him. A man so secretive was interesting to me you see. After leaving the package in the bushes, I left the park as instructed, but then returned very quickly by way of a fence so that no one would see me. I saw the man collect his package and even followed him to what must be his home address. So I can even tell you where the man lives, if you have an interested in knowing that?"

"Do you know that man's name?"

"No, but like I said I followed him to where he was living."

It was now about 9pm in the evening. Reid and Sergeant Thick's shift was due to finish at 10pm and each had some paperwork to do before they could go home.

"Are you able to take me there now?" asked Reid.

"Yes Inspector, I'll show you on the condition that you can stand the fare of a Hansom."

Reid was not in the habit of returning late from his shifts. In this he was very unlike Abberline, who although married, was renowned for spending many extra hours in the station and patrolling the streets when trying to solve particularly difficult cases. The Whitechapel Murder Case was a classic example of how Abberline worked. Whereas most of the men would return home at the end of an evening or night shift, Abberline was known to spend an extra hour or two of his own time wandering the streets in the hope of catching the Ripper red handed. As for Reid, he tried not to get sucked into cases and as a rule would return home to spend as much time with his wife and children as his job allowed; even with its sometimes unsociable hours.

The two men walked back down the alley to where the sergeant was waiting for them.

"Sergeant, I have a line of inquiry connected to the identity of the Whitechapel Murderer, but must take a trip outside the boundary of H-Division to follow it up. As such, I suggest that you return to the station to complete your duties," said Reid.

"Very well, sir. Would you like me to stop by your house to tell Mrs Reid that you are held up at work?"

"Yes, Sergeant, that would be most helpful. I fully expect Mrs Reid to be waiting for me to return home before retiring to bed. However, please don't knock at the door if you don't see any lights lit."

"I will do, sir. Good night to you. And thank you again for your help tonight, Mr Greenfield."

As a rule Reid did not carry much money with him, but that evening he had enough on his person to give eight pence to the unfortunate and have enough left over for hansom cab fares that would take him to Marylebone and back. He expected to get his money back for the hansom fares from his police expenses, although that was a notoriously hit and miss process. However, word had gotten round amongst the officers that money was currently no object where the Whitechapel Murder Case was concerned, so he was more hopeful of being reimbursed for his personal expenditure than usual.

Greenfield informed Reid that the address he was interested in was a block on the Marylebone Road, very close to the junction with Baker Street. The two men then left Whitechapel by hansom heading for the Marylebone

Road.

❦❦❦

The Inspector wanted to know more about the character that Greenfield had seen in Regents Park.

"You have seen the man, please describe him to me?" asked Reid.

"I'd say that he is about 5 feet 8 inches in height, of medium build, with red/brown hair and when I saw him, he wore a large carroty moustache."

"You say that you don't have a name for him?"

"Engels never said what it was. There was no need for me to know. I only had to know where in the park to place the package."

The cab stopped about 50 yards before the entrance to the building that Greenfield said he remembered Engels' client entering. The Inspector informed the driver that he was on police business and instructed him to wait for their return.

"That is the building, Inspector. I think that it is a block of apartments."

Just then someone opened the front door and stepped out onto the road. Even in the low artificial light provided by the street lamps, Reid could see that the man had a carroty moustache. Both he and Greenfield walked-on up the road trying not to look at the man as they passed him. After about fifteen seconds Reid signalled Greenfield to stop and both men turned slowly to watch the man with the carroty moustache, who was now standing in the street. Reid then noticed that the man had what looked like a small leather holdall with him. He directed Greenfield to cross the road, as he hoped that this would drew the man's attention away from them. Just as they reached the other side of the road another hansom pulled-up, the man entered it and it started off up the road, heading towards east London. Reid had Greenfield run to their waiting cab.

"DRIVER" shouted Reid.

"Yes, sir, what is it that you want?" responded the cab man.

"I want you to follow that cab and be quick about it. Make sure you don't lose sight of it," instructed Reid.

"I'll try to, but I've got to turn us round first. I'm afraid that we might lose it guv," explained the driver.

Reid watched as the other hansom disappeared into the distance. His hansom driver's horse had been spooked by the two men when they ran up to the cab and it took him an age to turn the cab the right way around. By the time the driver had the horse back under control, it was too late the other cab was well out of sight. Reid's mind was racing, everything seemed to be moving in slow motion, everything that is except the other cab. He could not believe that Greenfield had led him to the killer, who looked for all intents and purposes like he might be off to commit another murderer. But Reid reasoned that if the man was the murderer, then he was most likely heading for Whitechapel.

"Driver, take the most direct route back to Whitechapel and be damned quick about it!" demanded Reid.

The carriage sped-off and Reid hoped that they were going in the right direction. Reid's next problem was that one carriage looked very like another; he knew that he would have difficulty in recognising the one containing the suspect with the red moustache, even if they did manage to catch up with it. What Reid didn't appreciate was that the driver of his hansom would remember one of his competitor's cabs. In the world of hansom cabs, many of the drivers knew each other, they may have been competing with each other for business, but the men considered themselves to be like members of a large extended family.

"Got him, guvnor, he's just ahead of us. Wot do you want doing?" asked the driver.

"You're sure it's the same one?" responded Reid.

"I'm certain, guv, what do you want done?"

"Just follow it. When it stops I want you to drive past it and stop about five carriage lengths further along the road."

"Will do, guv."

The other hansom had stopped in Aldgate High Street, on the boundary between the City of London and Whitechapel. Reid's cab passed it and also stopped. Reid told Greenfield to remain seated, as he did not want to risk the moustached man recognising them.

"Mr Greenfield you have been extremely helpful but this is police business and I'll take things from here."

"Are you sure, Inspector? As I'm willing to help you further. Just in case there might be some trouble."

"That won't be necessary, but tell me is there anywhere that I can try and reach you?"

"I'll be in the Ten Bells tomorrow evening from about 6pm if you want to speak to me."

"Excellent, I might see you tomorrow."

"Oh, Inspector, there is just one thing."

"What is that?"

"Can you please ensure that you don't come calling for me with any of your friends dressed in a police uniform?"

"Don't worry, Mr Greenfield, I wouldn't be so foolish as to do such a thing."

Both men remained silent as the man with the leather bag walked past their cab heading for Whitechapel. Reid thanked and paid the driver, bade Greenfield goodnight and watched as Greenfield walked-off into the night. There was something about the way that Greenfield walked that caught Reid's attention. He couldn't put his finger on it, but there appeared to be something unusual in the way the man moved. But Reid didn't have time to ponder over such trivialities as his mind was focused on the man with the red moustache. Reid walked slowly along the road, being sure to keep a distance of about 40 yards between himself and his suspect.

❦❦❦

The Inspector followed the man with the red moustache as he entered the area known as the Wicked Quarter Mile. He passed a few constables on point duty and Reid was surprised to see that none of them gave the man wearing a long dark coat, a hat and carrying a holdall as much as a second glance. Reid himself hoped that none of the officers would acknowledge him, as he wanted to remain anonymous. However, one of the officers on point duty did recognise him but was careful to give Reid the subtlest of nods by way of a greeting, sensing that the Inspector was walking the streets on police business. Reid was pleased to see that at least one of the PCs was on the ball and regained some of the confidence that he was fast losing in the skills of his colleagues. He then watched as the man he was following entered Dorset Street, a street of about 100 yards in length that housed six lodgings houses and three pubs. It was quite a busy thoroughfare, especially at that time of night when the bulk of lodging house inmates were making their way from the pubs to their beds. The man he was following then approached a lady that looked very much like a prostitute out for a bit of business. Reid could not believe what he witnessed next; the man appeared to have forced the woman close to a wall and started to open his holdall. Could it be that the killer had gone completely mad and was going to start slaying every unfortunate that he encountered? Reid reached for his police whistle, just in case the man intended to draw a knife from his bag and was surprised when the man took out what looked like a pamphlet. Realising that he was overreacting, Reid tried to calm himself down. He placed the whistle back into his pocket and slowly walked-up closer to the couple to try and catch their conversation.

"Now I've told ya, mister, leave off, I'm not interested in any of your rubbish," said the woman.

"But my dear, I am trying to save your soul. Can't you see the error of your ways?" replied the moustached man.

"All I can see is that it's late and I need money for me doss. So sod off and let me be," continued the woman.

Before the man with the red moustache could reply, Reid interrupted the conversation.

"Is everything alright here, madam?"

"Wot? Yeh, except for the preacher 'ere bendin me ear."

The man with the red moustache stopped and looked at Reid. Reid's face was bruised from blows he had taken in the fight Castle Alley. His clothes were not those of the typical doss house dweller, but he looked a bit of a ruffian no less.

"There is no problem here, brother," said the man with the red moustache.

"Let me be the judge of that. What is it that you have there, sir?" responded Reid.

"These are pamphlets produced by our church, to help ladies such as this one, see the errors of their ways."

"Would I be able to have one, sir, as I think that we could all benefit with learning a few lessons from the Lord."

The man was a little wary of Reid. He was trying to determine what Reid's business could be in the streets of the wicked quarter mile. He smiled and although obviously irritated by Reid's interruption, seemed pleased to have found a like-minded individual in such a lawless street.

"Yes brother, please take this one."

Reid read the pamphlet. It was aimed at fallen women and contained a few sentences requesting that the reader see the error of their ways and seek redemption from the Lord. At the bottom was an address; it read the 'Portman Church, Marylebone'.

"Thank God for good men like yourself, sir, but aren't you a long way from home? Your church is a good way off."

The speed at which Reid had read the pamphlet surprised the moustached man. Most people he met in the streets of the wicked quarter mile could not read and those that could, tended to read very slowly.

"Thank you, brother. It is true, my church is a long way off, but no disrespect meant to the good lady here, but there are many more sinners in this locality than in our parish. There are many more souls that need saving in these streets than those in the area around my church."

The prostitute broke in "Listen mister, money is wot will save us, not your words, so leave the likes of me be." With that she walked to the end of the road and disappeared off into the night.

Reid continued. "You are most probably right, sir. There are many fallen souls around these parts. They are like moths attracted to the light, are they not? However, as the woman said, lack of a secure income can make it difficult for many to stick to the good life."

The man with the red moustache was studying Reid intently. Reid's accent indicated that he was from the lower classes, but his look and way with words indicated that he might have a sharp mind, in spite of the bruises to his face.

"Let me introduce myself to you brother, my name's George Crawford."

"And my name is Edmund Reid, a pleasure to meet you, sir."

"If you don't mind my being presumptuous, what is it that you do for living Mr Reid?"

"I'm what you might call a local businessman and you sir what is your occupation Mr Crawford?"

From the look of him, Crawford assumed that Reid might be a local slum landlord. The bruising on Reid's face indicated to him that the chap might have received them whilst attending to some dispute with a tenant. The local landlords' employed deputies and doormen to service their properties and this tended to keep them above the daily disputes involving overdue rents and ejections from lodging houses for non-payment of the daily doss money. So it was rare for them to become personally embroiled in arguments over money, but sometimes they got caught-up in a dispute and might receive an injury for their trouble.

"I am also a businessman, I run an import/export business from my London office. I consider myself fortunate in having sufficient time and funds to help those less fortunate than myself. It has been my pleasure to meet you Mr Reid but I have much to be getting on with. I have only just arrived here in Whitechapel and have much to do tonight."

The Inspector wasn't happy to let the man go just yet.

"If you don't mind me asking, sir, where are you from? I'd say from your accent that you are an American by birth."

"That is correct, Mr Reid. I made my fortune back in my homeland, but business is much better in England. Now as I said, sir, I have things to do."

Reid watched as Crawford approached a small group of woman standing outside a lodging house. After a brief exchange it was clear what the women thought of the do-gooder intent on telling them the error of their ways. Crawford went through similar exchanges all the way along Dorsett Street until he reached the Britannia pub at the junction with Commercial Street.

The Inspector walked past Crawford and turned into Commercial Street where he felt sure that he would find a constable. He was surprised to find that there wasn't an officer to be seen, but then he spotted two burly young men walking slowly along the road. Reid instantly recognised their methodical 2.5 mile an hour pace and their police regulation boots. He did not know the men but was correct in assuming that they had been drafted into Whitechapel to perform the night-time plain clothed patrols.

Reid flashed his badge at the men. The men stopped and stood almost to attention.

"What can we do for you, Inspector?" asked one of the officers.

"I trust that you fellows are in this district in order to assist us in the capture of the Whitechapel Murderer?"

"Yes, sir. That we are," replied the first man.

"Good. Now you see that man. The one with the red moustache, carrying the holdall and standing close to the pub?"

"Yes, sir, I see him."

"I want you to follow him for next hour or so and watch what he does, as I have found him to be a most suspicious character. Now this is important. The man does not live in Whitechapel and at some point he will leave the district in order to return home. Before he leaves this police district I want you to stop and search him. You are to arrest him if you find a knife or similar weapon upon his person. Be sure to check the lining of his coat in addition to his bag. Are you clear on this?"

"Yes, sir. But what are we to do if he isn't carrying a weapon?"

"Then apologise for troubling him and let him get on his way home. Be sure to write a report on all that you see, I will expect to be able to read it on my arrival at Leman Street at 10am tomorrow morning."

"Yes, sir, it will be ready for you, sir."

"What is your name Constable?"

"I'm Constable Pearse, 37R from Greenwich division."

The Inspector left the two men to get on with the task he had set them. He then passed back through Dorset Street and made his way back to the constable he had seen on point duty.

"Constable, if I might have a word with you?"

The police officer stood to attention. "Yes, sir, do you require some assistance?"

"Tell me, earlier when you saw me walking past you earlier, did you not see a man carrying a bag?"

The constable thought for a moment and then he remembered the man.

"Yes, sir, I did. I trust you mean the man with the red moustache?"

"Full marks for observation, constable. Yes that is the man that I am referring to. Why did you not stop and speak to him? Aren't you under orders to stop any suspicious men seen walking around Whitechapel after nightfall, especially those carrying bags?"

"Yes, sir, we are. But I recognised the man, we know him as the preacher. He often comes round these parts, telling the working girls to give up their evil ways. He's harmless enough and has never done anything more than speak to the women."

"And you know what he carries in his bag?"

"Yes, sir. He has a batch of church pamphlets inside it."

"How do you know that?"

"I have stopped the man on one occasion past and searched him as we are instructed to do. In fact I stopped and searched him after the two murders that occurred the other week."

"Okay, that is very good, constable. You have been most observant. We can only hope that the rest of the men are as diligent in their duties as you are."

"Thank you. Goodnight, sir."

Reid then returned quickly to Dorset Street. Crawford and the two plain-clothes men were nowhere to be seen. He decided to return home. He was on the evening shift again the next day but decided that he would pop into the station in the morning to read the report on Crawford's activities that he had just instructed the plain clothes officers to record for him.

CHAPTER EIGHTEEN

Without Real Hard Evidence

WEDNESDAY 10TH OCTOBER started out cold and wet. Fortunately Emily was asleep when Reid arrived home battered and bruised. She woke before him, noticed the bruises and could not stop herself from waking him up to find out what had happened to him. Reid explained that he and Sergeant Thick had had a spot of bother in a back alley, adding that neither of them were badly injured, he then fell back to sleep. Emily was careful to take the children out of the house before Reid finally woke-up and prepared himself for work; she would have to tell them later that day that their father had been involved in a fracas in the line of duty. She had planned to give her husband a bit of a telling-off for staying out late at work but she forgot all about that when she saw his injuries.

Reid arrived into the station at 10.30am. The two plain-clothed officers had done what Reid had asked and followed Crawford as he harangued the fallen women of Dorset, Flower and Dean and Thrawl Streets. The undercover men had noticed that Crawford was oblivious to the threats of violence that hung on every street corner. Crawford's advantage over the two officers was that his face was well known to the local people of those dilapidated streets, the inhabitants of which were more inclined to try and keep out of his way, rather than rob him or beat him up. The officers had waited about an hour before they stopped and searched the man. He offered up no resistance and did not protest when they ordered him to empty his bag and remove his coat. The officers realising that Reid thought the man to be a possible Ripper suspect, took no chances and thoroughly checked the lining of his coat and searched his person for any knives. But all the man had in his possession were church leaflets.

The Inspector asked the desk sergeant if Abberline was in the station and was informed that he was, but was currently unavailable as he was in a meeting with the Super. Reid then asked the desk sergeant if he could inform the Inspector that he would be grateful for 10 minutes of his time, preferably sometime before midday. After that Reid set about writing his report on the preceding night's events. So far, all he had was hearsay evidence that Crawford had purchased sadistic pornography. However, he included in his report details of Lucy Clark's unsolved murder and the theory that her death might possibly have been the first known killing by the Whitechapel Murderer. Reid was getting to the end of his report, and was just penning his request for Crawford to be placed under night-time surveillance by the officers of D-Division, when Abberline appeared at his desk.

"You wanted to speak with me, Inspector?" Abberline asked Reid.

"Yes, sir, if you could spare a few minutes of your time I'd like to discuss a matter relating to your case? We could use one of the interview rooms."

The men entered an interview room and Reid told Abberline all the details of how his investigation into the source of the hardcore pornography had led him first to Greenfield, then to Engels and finally to Crawford.

"Look, Reid it's not that I don't appreciate the effort and commitment that you are showing in trying to catch the beast responsible for these murders, but we have been inundated with reports of possible suspects and quite frankly I think many of them warrant a higher priority than your man Crawford. I read all the overnight reports relating to the case and was interested in knowing why you had diverted two officers from their allocated duty of patrolling Commercial Street and Whitechapel Road. I then read the report made by Constable Pearse and have since taken the liberty of checking into Crawford's background. From the little that I could find about the man, he appears to be a successful businessman with connections to gentlemen in high places. The man does not have a criminal record and is well known to the beat officers of this division for his church related activities. Without real hard evidence against the man I cannot request that D-Division place him under surveillance. As I understand it, Crawford has a quite distinctive appearance. As such, I will ensure that his description is included in the list of suspicious persons that is given to all men participating in the night watch activities. I am afraid that any more than that I cannot do for you."

As Reid listened he tried to place himself in Abberline's shoes. Abberline's team currently had about fifteen men under surveillance, however, most lived within the police districts covered by H and J Divisions. Following the murder of Catherine Eddowes a few men living in the eastern portion of the City of London had been added to the watch lists. As far as Reid was aware, nigh on all of these men had a history of mental illness, violence against women or a combination of the two. Reid decided that if he were Abberline he would most likely have taken the same decision. What Reid needed was some hard evidence against Crawford and he was determined that he would find it.

"Okay, sir, I can see that we have no evidence against the man but I'm sure that in the course of my investigations I -"

Abberline stopped Reid in his tracks. "Now listen to me, Inspector! There is one thing I want us to be clear on. You are a good man and a fine detective, but you've got to learn where to draw the line with your authority as a policeman. We are all extremely busy and no doubt we will get busier still, so I don't want you to spend any more time investigating Crawford. When he comes into Whitechapel his presence will be noted and he will be monitored accordingly. If his conduct warrants it, then and only then will a decision be made on whether or not to perform further investigation into his nocturnal activities. Have I made myself clear?"

Reid bit his lower lip. Although he could see things from Abberline's perspective, he was sure that the man was mistaken in his analysis of the situation. However, he thought it wise to agree with his boss and let the matter rest.

"Very well, sir, I understand and will act accordingly. Thank you for sparing me some of your time," said Reid.

"I believe that you aren't supposed to be here until 5pm today. Please go off and make the most of your afternoon," instructed Abberline.

Abberline then returned to his desk and Reid returned home to his wife and family.

On his way home Reid thought more about what the Bank Manager had told him. It was obvious to him that Abberline was party to the details of the reprimand he had received in 1887, from none other than the then Assistant Commissioner, James Monroe. Reid determined that Abberline had been instructed to keep a careful eye on his activities, just in case he should again try to cross the legal boundaries constraining the activities of one of Her Majesty's policemen. The thing was, Abberline was right to do so as Reid often bent the rules to suit his purposes and would go to extreme lengths to get his man. Now he was stuck, his gut feeling told him that Crawford was a man that definitely warranted further attention, but the man lived in another police district. Reid's only possibility of contact with the man would be when he was on duty on the evening and night shifts. Abberline had guessed correctly, that if D-Division did not place Crawford under surveillance, then Reid was planning on devoting a significant portion of his work time in tracking the man's activities. However, what Abberline probably didn't know was what prompted Reid over step the mark back in 87. It wasn't in Reid's nature to become overly obsessive about a case; back then it was the protection of his own family that drove him on.

CHAPTER NINETEEN

An October from Hell

THE WEEKS FLEW BY. Elizabeth Stride's funeral had taken place on Saturday 6th October, with her being buried in a pauper's grave in the East London Cemetery. Catherine Eddowes' funeral had taken place on Monday 8th October, with her being buried in the City of London Cemetery, Ilford. The final sessions of the Eddowes' inquest ended on Thursday 11th October and that of Stride on Tuesday 23rd October. In the interim period there had been a bit of a storm created by George Lusk, the chair of the Whitechapel Vigilance Committee, who had received half a human kidney through the post, around which was wrapped a letter. The letter read:

From hell

Mr Lusk

Sor
I send you half the kidne I took from one women
Prasarved if for you tother piece I fried and ate it
Was very nise I man send you the bloody knif that
Took it out if you only wate a whil longer

Signed
Catch me when you can Mishter Lusk

Lusk originally thought the gruesome package to be a hoax, but was more than a little shaken after being informed by Dr Thomas Openshaw of the London Hospital, that the kidney was not only human, but also a kidney from the left-hand-side of the body. This troubled Lusk, as Catherine Eddowes the woman killed in Mitre Square, had her left kidney removed by the murderer. The likelihood of the half kidney being Eddowes' only increased after Major Henry Smith, acting Commissioner of the City Police got in on the act and requested a report on the origin of the kidney from Dr Henry Sutton. Dr Sutton went on to pledge his reputation upon the kidney having been immersed in spirits within hours of its removal from the body; something very unlikely to have occurred in a late 19th Century mortuary.

Other than the mystery of the human kidney, the police had no prime suspects and the press gradually ran out of Ripper related stories to sell their newspapers with. By the end of the month life had pretty much returned to normal in Whitechapel, meaning that the working girls had returned to their old haunts. Looking on the bright side, even the smog that had enveloped London for most of the month finally began to disperse. As for Abberline and his team, they had decided that if the Ripper was still at large, there was a good chance that he would now seek out another victim in the first week of November, as the final day of October was a Wednesday.

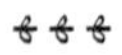

Amidst the all the quiet on the Whitechapel Murder front, a battle was raging between Commissioner Warren and Home Secretary Matthews. The pressure from the press might have abated but the ruling elites knew that public confidence in the authorities would never be restored until someone was caught and convicted for the murders. The next best way of placating the masses would be for senior heads to roll and neither Warren nor Matthews wanted it to be theirs.

The new Deputy Commissioner of the Met, Dr Robert

Anderson had been out of the country recuperating from an illness for much of the investigation. He had left the country on the 8th September and had not returned until early October, and then only on the command of his boss Warren. On the 6th October he found himself being placed in overall command of the investigation with Warren and Matthews trying to get him to accept in writing that the role made him directly responsible for the apprehension of the murderer; something that Anderson was canny enough not to do. So as the weeks went by, Matthews, Warren and Anderson got caught-up in a sophisticated game of catch; the first one to drop the ball would pay for it with his job and his reputation in society.

In the midst of the battle amongst the elites, a strange state of affairs started to manifest itself on the streets of London's east end. The streets were now full of policemen in an evening, so criminal activities such as robbery and burglary were at an all-time low, however prostitution was rife. Warren had proposed dealing with the problem by arresting any woman caught soliciting. However, Councillors of the more salubrious districts which bordered the east end had started to complain that their boroughs were being swamped by women of the worst type, who were plying their sordid trade in what they deemed to be safer neighbourhoods. So instead of a police crackdown on soliciting, what happened was that the ever increasing numbers of police officers turned a blind eye to the illegal activities of the unfortunates, with the justification that it would be easier to catch the killer if all the goats were tethered in the one location and not spread out about the whole of the city. Warren did not like this one bit as it left him open to attacks of incompetence. However, he and Dr Anderson were left with no other choice other than to provide the fallen women of Whitechapel with a police guard for their illicit activities.

Partly because Warren became caught-up in the heat of

this battle, he forgot all about Barnaby and Burgho, the bloodhounds provided by Edwin Brough. Warren had gone to great lengths to secure Home Office approval for the funding of bloodhounds for Metropolitan Police use for the rest of that year and for the whole of the next. However, no payment terms were agreed with Mr Brough and Warren was under the misapprehension that Brough had provided his dogs for free. So by the time a request was finally made for use of the dogs by officers from Leman Street Police station to try and track a burglar, Brough had almost reached the end of his tether, with his having seriously considered reclaiming his animals. Then Brough learned from his friend Mr Taunton that the police had finally made a request for the use of a dog in order to try and track down a burglar who had robbed one of the grander houses in Whitechapel. The problem was that the burglary had taken place many hours before and no one thought to get a dog on-site until after numerous officers had blundered throughout the premises in their size ten boots. Needless to say, that through no fault of its own, the dog did not perform at all well and the policemen ridiculed Taunton for the animal's failure to pick-up a scent. Taunton for his part responded by telling the policemen to stick their truncheons where the sun didn't shine and stormed off home. Unsurprisingly, Brough blew a gasket on hearing this news and feeling that he was in a no win situation, recalled his animals. Barnaby and Burgho were to leave London, never to return. None of this comedy of errors was relayed to Warren, Swanson, Abberline or any other man in the Whitechapel Murder Squad.

❦ ❦ ❦

Abberline for his part spent most of the month chasing shadows. He watched as his superiors tied themselves up in knots as they followed-up false leads provided by members of the press and one from a totally unexpected source, Her Majesty's Ambassador at Vienna, Sir Augustus Paget. It appeared that the Ambassador had been approached by a man professing to belong to a left-wing Socialist International group that had established itself in order to fight against the forces of capitalism using methods of terror, assassination and propaganda. The informer told the Ambassador that a former disgruntled agent belonging to the group was at large in London and had taken to murdering poor unfortunate women in a bid to discredit the organisation. The informer professed that if he and one of his superiors could be paid to travel to England, they would track down their man in short order and so put an end to the slaughter. The Ambassador was so convinced by the story that he paid his informant 200 florins from his own pocket so that the man could start making the necessary arrangements that would result in his proceeding post haste to London. In what turned-out to be a very convoluted process, the informant returned to the Ambassador requesting more money before he was willing to set to work. The Ambassador wary that he might have trouble getting his money back from the Government based in London, refused to pay out any more money without a guarantee from London that all his costs would be met. On receipt of the Ambassador's request, Government officials refused to pay-up and the whole affair died a death. This was not before Commissioner Warren got embroiled in discussions with various government offices over who was responsible for reimbursing Sir Augustus his 200 florins. In the end Warren, to his great irritation was instructed to find the money from Met funds.

❦❦❦

Reid was becoming ever more enmeshed in the hunt for the killer. He completely lost sight of Harris Marks and had not seen Greenfield since the night that the two of them had followed Crawford to Whitechapel. He had not seen sense after his talk with Abberline and was now spending some of his off-duty hours wandering the streets of Marylebone. He'd been to the Portman Church, where Crawford was an active member, and had found out that it was also Lucy Clark's local church. Reid was informed that she had attended most Sunday services there before her death in January. He'd also visited George Street and stood outside her old place of residence. He was sorely tempted to track down and interview her two nephews in order that he might judge himself whether they might have actually have murdered her. However, he held himself back from doing that, thinking that it might be a step too far and would most likely result in his receiving another reprimand.

ꟿ ꟿ ꟿ

By the evening of Friday 2nd November, it was a case of all hands to the pump and Reid found himself in a packed briefing room at the Leman Street station, along with about 50 other men who would be on night duty over that weekend. Although Reid had not made any progress with the fraud case, he had been commended by the Super on the fine job he had performed in stemming the flow of pornography from Whitechapel into the city and for the cessation of street gambling. Since his raids there had been no recorded incidents of either activity. However, Reid thought that the lack of gambling might have had a little less to do with his raid and a little more to do with the streets having been flooded with policemen, but he was not going to take the shine off his apparent success by drawing anyone's attention to that.

Nothing of note happened that Friday night and Reid and the other nightshift officers went home to their beds at 6am in the morning and hoped to get some sleep before rising in the late afternoon for some downtime before the next night's shift which was due to start at 10pm.

The time passed quickly and before the Inspector knew it he was on his way back to the station for his Saturday nightshift duty. On his way there, Reid finally bumped into Levi Greenfield.

"Good evening, to you, Inspector Reid. Long time no see."

"Good evening to you, Mr Greenfield."

"I am glad that I caught you, Inspector. Grateful if you could tell me have you arrested the man you were seeking when we last met?"

Reid thought that Greenfield was making reference to their pursuit of Crawford.

"Now, Mr Greenfield, I thank you again for the assistance that you provided me and my sergeant with but I cannot discuss police business with you."

"Please accept my apologies for asking, Inspector, I won't do it again. It's just that I have seen Harris Marks out and about and was wondering if you'd ever managed to interview him?"

Reid changed his mind; maybe he and Greenfield could discuss police business after all.

"Ah, you are referring to Mr Marks. No, unfortunately I have not yet had the pleasure of interviewing him. Are you telling me that you know his whereabouts?"

"It just so happens that I do. I have seen him this very night in the Princess Alice pub on Commercial Street."

Reid was keen to get hold of Marks but wanted to be on time for the start of his shift at the station.

"I tell you what, Mr Greenfield, I am keen to see Mr Marks but don't have time right now. If you think that you are able to assist me I can get to the Princess Alice in say half an hour's time. You would be doing me a service if you could go there now and keep an eye on the man."

"For you, Inspector, that would be a pleasure. I'll go

there this instant, sir. However, it would be grand if you could stand me a pint of two for my trouble."

With that Reid made his way to Leman Street and Greenfield went off to the pub.

Reid thought about what he could do with Marks. He did not want to arrest him as he was unlikely to be carrying much in the way of money on his person and it was also quite possible that the money he did have in his possession was legal tender. Instead Reid wanted to see what the man looked like and hopefully have him followed back to his home address. He decided that he would request the services of two plain-clothed constables and instruct them to follow Marks and any of his companions from the pub. He was hoping that Marks might return to his home address, so that he might have the premises placed under surveillance. Abberline had slapped his wrist the last time that he had re-assigned plain-clothes men away from duties relating to the Ripper murders and he fully expected him to be less than happy when he found out that he had done so for a second time in as many months.

Reid looked around the station, he was pleased to see that constables Barrett and Imhoff were on duty. He spoke with the desk sergeant and informed him that he needed two men to immediately accompany him on a surveillance exercise. The desk sergeant put-up a little resistance before finally agreeing to reassign two men allocated to Ripper Duty to Reid's charge.

"Imhoff, Barrett, interview room number 2 if you please," instructed Reid.

The men followed him into the room. At first they thought Reid wanted to speak to them about the gambling stakeout that they had participated in, but soon discovered that he had other plans for them.

"Right, gentleman, I know it's all hands to the pump this weekend with the Ripper watch and all, but I've received intelligence this very evening that a man I have been trying to locate in the uttering of counterfeit coinage has been sighted drinking in the Princess Alice. The man's name is Harris Marks. I have never laid eyes on him before and as far as I know he is unknown to the police in general. Therefore I intend to go to the Princess Alice where I have an informer waiting to point the man out to me. Once his face has become familiar to me I intend to return to my duties at the station. However, I want one of you to follow Marks for the rest of the night. I am hoping that he will return to his home address in order that I can then have the building placed under surveillance. I want one of you to follow him back there and record the address for me. I do not know how many other men are with Marks in the pub, but I want the other one of you to follow the most senior man in the group back to his home address. Have you got that gentlemen?"

Imhoff was not sure if anyone was to be arrested, so clarified this with Reid.

"Inspector, so we are not going to arrest Marks?"

"No, I don't know if he is in the possession of any counterfeit money. I just want to find out where the man's home base is and hopefully the home base of one of his associates. So is everything clear now gentlemen?"

"Yes, sir, very clear," said Imhoff, "If it's alright with you Barrett, I'll take Marks?"

"Yes, I don't care who I follow," responded Barrett.

The two men were quite pleased at the prospect of their new assignment. Hunting the Ripper had made for a pretty boring night's work. The prospect of being reassigned to a pub on a Saturday night, without the supervision of a more senior officer, was much more to their liking. No doubt they would be forced to sink a few ales in order to stop their cover from being blown!

The three men left the station and were soon at the Princess Alice public house. Reid spotted Greenfield sitting in a corner, close to the bar on the left-hand side of the pub. The man was with what looked like a fallen women. Reid thought that to be good undercover work on Greenfield's part, for as part of a couple he would not stand out from the crowd. However, Greenfield's was an easy task to perform in Whitechapel, as many of the unfortunates were alcoholics and would get chatting to any man in a pub in the hope of having a drink or three bought for them.

On seeing Reid and his men enter the pub, Greenfield gave his 'escort' a few pence so that she could buy herself another drink and she went on her way. He had expected Reid to come on his own and was not happy to see what he knew to be three policemen heading in his direction. His thinking was that as a group they stood out and were much more likely to be recognised as policemen, men that it would not be good for him to be seen speaking with.

"I didn't know that you were going to come mob-handed," said Greenfield in very hushed tones.

"Don't worry, we aren't planning on arresting anybody and I will be leaving promptly. Which one's our man?" asked Reid.

Greenfield pointed to a group of four men standing toward the end of the right-hand side of the bar. "Your man is the small skinny fella in the brown jacket."

Harris Marks was with his business associate Hudson Weatherburn. The two men were in the middle of agreeing terms for a counterfeit coinage deal with another would be dealer.

Reid observed Marks for a few moments and after he thought that he'd memorised the man's features he said his goodbyes to his men.

"Can I walk with you, sir, as I have no other business here?" Greenfield asked Reid.

"If you like," responded the Inspector.

So the two men left the pub and chatted as Reid made his way back to the station. Reid put his hand into his pocket and pulled-out a half crown that he intended to give to Greenfield for his trouble.

"There's no need for that, Inspector. I quite like the idea of helping you out now and again."

"Okay Mr Greenfield, as you wish. However, you should be careful. It will only be a matter of time before the wrong people see you in my company. Becoming known as a policeman's nark may well result in your having to leave Whitechapel."

"I'm willing to take my chances with that."

"And what would you do for money should that happen?"

Greenfield laughed. "I can't very well tell you that, Inspector. However, it's become very hard to make a living round here these days, with the likes of you and so many of your sort standing on every street corner."

"Yes, it's going to be like this for a few months yet. The only night off for a lot of the men will be this coming Thursday. It's all hands on deck for the Lord Mayor's show on Friday and our top brass don't want to see the streets lined with sleepy policemen."

"Well I suppose that it's got to be done. Even the men in my line of work can see the sense of it and aren't complaining too loudly about you fellas getting in the way of our trying to earn a living. We are all just looking forward to the day when everything goes back to how it used to be."

"Sorry to talk business again but just to be sure, the man in the brown jacket back at the pub was Harris Marks?" asked Reid.

"Yes, I'm certain of it and I'm sure that you'll find that he's got a lot to do with the spread of the bad money."

"Thank you again for your help, Mr Greenfield," said Reid and on that note that two men parted company.

The Inspector made his way to the station to complete his shift, whilst Imhoff and Barrett kept a close eye on

Marks and his associates. The men did not leave the pub until the official public house closing time of 12.30am, at which time Imhoff followed Marks back to what he hoped was the man's home address. However, Barrett met with less success. It turned out that the men who had come to do business with Marks were from another police district. Barratt followed them across the Met boundary into the City of London, but decided to give it up after they started to head northwest towards Camden.

Both the officers reported back to Reid on their return to the station and he was happy enough with their efforts. Reid's main priority had been to identify Marks' home base. Now he had an address he was hopeful of finally making some real progress in his fraud case.

CHAPTER TWENTY

Followed by a Sadistic Serial Murderer

REID ROSE SHORTLY AFTER 1PM on Sunday 4th November, Emily had gone to the park with Elizabeth and Harold and he met them there shortly before 2.30pm.

"Good afternoon, dearest."

"Good afternoon, Edmund. You should have slept for longer, you are looking very tired."

"Don't worry about me, I am fine dearest."

"There are no new stories in the newspapers, so I trust that you had a quiet night."

"Yes, I was able to make some headway with one of my priority cases."

"Do you wish to rest Edmund, as I and the children were just going to make another circuit of the park?"

"No dearest, as I said I am feeling fine, I will walk with you."

They had only walked for a few minutes when Reid saw someone out of the corner of his eye that made his blood run cold. About 40 yards to his and his family's right was a man with a red moustache. Reid hoped that Crawford had not noticed that he was now aware of his presence, and Reid and his family continued to walk around the perimeter of the park. For one of the few times in his life, Reid felt afraid. He was not afraid for himself but for his wife and young daughter. It was clear to him that Crawford was following him and his family as they walked through the park. How long the man had been in the park, he did not know, but what he did very much want to know was whether Crawford was following him or whether he had an eye on his family.

Two years had passed since Reid had felt similar

feelings to those he was experiencing now. Back then he had overacted to the situation and his actions resulted in his almost losing his job and his receiving a reprimand. However, he'd vowed then that if he was ever again faced with a similar situation, he would not hesitate in dealing with it in the same way. Reid did not want to alarm his wife by informing her that she and her daughter might be being followed by a sadistic serial murderer, so he tried to indulge in small talk with her whilst continuing to watch Crawford out of the corner of his eye.

"Emily, my dear, have you had much contact with Mrs Jackson of the Folgate Mission?" asked Reid.

Reid's wife had been thinking about the two children that very day.

"Yes I have. The two children are still under the care of the Mission. Mrs Jackson says that they seem very happy there," responded Emily.

"I think that Mrs Jackson and her kind do excellent work and it is good to know that there is some hope for the poorest in our society," commented Reid.

Emily continued "I met another of her kind only this morning. There is a man from church based in Marylebone who informed me that he had been distributing food to some of the unfortunate women that are forced to sleep in the park,"

Reid bit into his lower lip and his mind started to race.

"How did this man happen to speak with you my dear?" asked the Inspector.

"I can't recall, Edmund. I saw him handing out some bread to some of the women and just caught his eye. He insisted on my taking a pamphlet published by his church."

Do you still have the pamphlet as I'd be interested in reading about the man's work?"

Mrs Reid gave her husband the pamphlet and Reid was not surprised to see that it was a publication commissioned by the Portman Church, Marylebone.

"This man, what did he look like my dear?"

Reid realised his mistake immediately, but it was too late to do anything about it. Emily stopped and looked about the park for the man that she had spoken to earlier that day and pointed at Crawford when she saw him.

"Why, Edmund, it's that gentleman standing over there."

Crawford was looking over at the family when Emily pointed him out to her husband; Crawford took this as an invitation to approach Reid and his family.

"It is Mr Reid, is it not?" asked Crawford.

Emily was surprised that the man knew her husband's name. "You know this man, Edmund?"

"We have met once before my dear. This is Mr Crawford."

"Yes, I am. It is good to see a man out with his family. If there were more decent god fearing men like you, there would be much less need for the services of men like me."

Emily Reid was slightly on her guard, as she did not know whether her husband had met this man through the course of his work or in a social setting.

"How do you know my husband, Mr Crawford?"

"We met one evening when I was distributing leaflets to some of the less fortunate ladies of the borough."

Reid broke in "You appear to spend much time in the east end. Does your local parish not require your services?"

"Yes, it does, but there are so many more unfortunate souls living in these parts. I feel that I am able to do more good here than I could ever hope to do back in Marylebone. I am hoping to devote a few nights to God's work during the coming week."

"How do you decide on which nights to venture out?" asked Reid.

"I try to arrange my charitable work around my business activities. I have a slack day on Wednesday and intend to watch the Lord Mayor's Show on the Friday. So I will most likely venture out on Tuesday and Thursday nights."

"Then I hope that this fine weather continues through the week for you, as there has been so much rain and fog of late," said Reid.

"Yes, the weather this summer has been very poor, but it does not appear to have dampened the enthusiasm of those that stray off the righteous path intent on committing immoral acts."

Reid had heard all that he needed to from Crawford.

"Well it was good to meet you again, Mr Crawford. No doubt we will meet again. I hope that you have a good day sir."

"Good day to you, Mr Reid, Mrs Reid."

Reid decided to walk the perimeter of the park again. Now he had the excuse of being able to look over at Crawford at will. Crawford for his part left the family to their own devices and started to concentrate his efforts on some women that looked decidedly worse for drink.

"How do you know, Mr Crawford, Edmund?" asked Emily.

"It is like the man said, I saw him circulating his literature to the fallen women one night."

"He does not seem to address you as one might a policeman. Is he aware of your occupation?"

Emily had found it unusual that Crawford had been at ease in the presence of her husband. Rarely did Reid's professional world crossover into his personal family life, but when the two did meet there was usually a tension in the air.

"That is very observant of you, my dear. No, Mr Crawford is not aware that I am a policeman."

Emily could see the tension in Reid's face as he talked of the man. There was something about this seemingly law abiding charitable man that seemed to have set her husband on edge.

"So he is not a man that I and the children should be wary of?"

Reid thought for a moment. He did not want to unduly alarm his wife but he did wish to warn her that Crawford was a man that she should keep her distance from.

"In times like these dearest, I think that it is best to be on your guard against all strangers. For my part I have only witnessed Mr Crawford trying to perform good works in Whitechapel, but I do not know the man and currently I view all strange man in these parts with suspicion. So my dear, I would be grateful if you can keep any future contact with Mr Crawford to a minimum."

Emily sensed that her husband did not want her and the children to remain in the park, so she simply followed his lead when he then suggested that they return home.

Reid had been keeping a careful watch over Crawford. When he was certain that the man was sufficiently distracted with a group of unfortunates, he ushered Emily, Elizabeth and Harry out of the park and walked them back home. On the way he decided that he needed to make clear to his 15 year old daughter that she should be wary of Crawford and his kind.

"Elizabeth."

"Yes, father."

"The man I spoke with earlier, Mr Crawford."

"What about him father?"

"I just want you to be clear, that the man is not a friend of mine or your mothers. He is an acquaintance, as such should you ever meet him again, please be sure to treat him like you would any other stranger."

"I will do, father, but where should I meet him again?"

"I don't know, Elizabeth. Who knows what causes people's paths to cross, but I repeat, please be sure to treat him in the same manner that you would any other stranger."

Reid's daughter thought it strange that her father

should make such a request of her but thought it best to confirm that she would do as he asked of her.

❧ ❧ ❧

Reid then spent the rest of afternoon thinking about what could be done with Crawford. He wished that he knew whether the man had been following his family because he had recognised Reid from their encounter in Thrawl Street or whether it was because Crawford had set his sights set on his wife and daughter. Either way, it made his skin crawl that this man had had any contact whatsoever with his family and he did not want it to happen again. He remembered Crawford saying that he intended to visit Whitechapel on Tuesday night. He was determined that he would do his best to shadow the man's movements when he arrived in the district.

On his arrival at the station he submitted an immediate request to work the nightshift, stating that he needed to work from 6pm until 2am. He gave the fraud case as the reason, with his wanting to investigate the movements of a possible distributor of counterfeit money. He added that his main suspect, Harris Marks, appeared to be most active in his dealings late at night. He also added a line about the lack of cover on Thursday night that had resulted from the need to provide men on the morning and early afternoon to cover the Lord Mayor's show.

CHAPTER TWENTYONE

The Missing Girls of West Ham

INSPECTOR REID WAS OFFICIALLY on the dayshift on Monday 5th November but had been told that he should aim to arrive at the station at about midday. He was hoping that his request to work nights would be approved in order that he could try and track the movements of Crawford, whom he thought would be prowling the streets on Whitechapel from the Tuesday night onwards. The Whitechapel Murder case had now become very personal to Reid and he had spent many hours thinking how he might track and entrap the man he believed to be the Ripper. So far, all that he had planned to do was be in the Aldgate High Street between 10pm and 12am on the night of November the sixth, in the hope of intercepting Crawford's hansom cab, should one deliver him there.

The Inspector had had an average of four hours sleep on each of the last three nights, but didn't feel even remotely tired; he possessed the energy of a fanatical man on a life and death mission. When he arrived at the station he was pleased to find that his request to work the nightshift had been approved, the desk sergeant suggesting that he should go straight home before Abberline or the Super spotted him. However, before leaving the station he bumped into Sergeant Thick. He was keen to speak with somebody about Crawford and thought that the Sergeant might have some additional information on the case as the man worked quite closely with Abberline.

"Good afternoon, sergeant. How was your weekend?" asked Reid.

"It was very good, sir. I was not on duty and managed to catch most of the fine weather with my wife and family."

"Do you have a few minutes to spare?"

"Yes, I have some time now, sir."

With that the two men found an empty room and sat down for a chat. Sergeant Thick had read the updates relating to the Whitechapel Murder case and had seen Reid's report relating to Crawford and the note raised by Abberline for all men on the nightshift to monitor the actions of men matching Crawford's description.

"I'm assuming that the man that Greenfield took you to see was a Mr Crawford, sir?" asked the sergeant.

"Yes, sergeant. As soon as we arrived at the man's address he was off in a hansom and headed straight for Whitechapel. I have to admit that I thought that lady luck had given the murderer over to me. Having followed him for so short a time, I have not yet decided what to make of the man. However, there is something about his manner that makes me think that his intentions are not honourable and even if he is not the man that we all seek, I feel that he is best kept off our streets."

"You know that the instruction has been given to the men on night duty keep to a watchful eye on men matching Crawford's description. So whatever the man might be up to, we should have a good chance of catching him at it," commented the sergeant.

"Yes, sergeant, that is something, but I wanted the man to be placed under surveillance and Inspector Abberline does not believe that this would be the best use of our resources."

"As you know, sir, I served under Inspector Abberline for many years before his departure to the Yard and your arrival as his replacement. I have found the both of you to be very able men and have no favour for either of you. All I can say from how I see things, is that the Inspector appears to be making a good fist of the investigation. I am certain that he would have placed Crawford under surveillance if the man lived in our manor. But Crawford doesn't seem to have done anything that warrants men from another division keeping tabs on him. Word is out that the top brass are looking for a scapegoat and the Inspector needs to watch his back, sir."

"Yes, sergeant, I can see your point. However, yesterday afternoon, I noticed Crawford following my wife and children through the park. You are a family man sergeant, I hope that you can appreciate how such a thing could affect a man."

The sergeant was taken aback by Reid's candidness, as he had never really spoken so openly with him. He also could not understand why a wealthy man like Crawford would be spending so much of his time in and around the east end of London. As for Crawford following Reid's family, well if that was what he was doing, then the Sergeant thought that the man was lucky not to have been assaulted by the Inspector. As a barrier appeared to have been broken between the two men, the sergeant took the opportunity to ask Reid about the reason for his transfer from J Division. Word had it that it was to do with Reid's over stepping the mark and personally harassing a prominent local businessman. As far as he could tell, history was about to repeat itself.

"It probably isn't my place to say this, sir, but I believe that we all need to be careful in such matters. It can be very easy for men in our position to do things that we later come to regret. Word has it that you had some trouble sometime past with a prominent local man in Stepney."

The Inspector thought for a moment. He could see where the sergeant was coming from. Yes, a civilian would most probably get away with assaulting a man that he thought responsible for interfering with his family, but not so a policeman.

"What do you know of my time at J-Division, sergeant?"

"I know very little about it, sir."

"But I believe it to be common knowledge that my transfer from J-Division was the result of a reprimand that I'd received there."

Thick was aware that he had caught his Inspector at a moment of weakness and felt it best to try and leave the matter rest where it was. He didn't want the Inspector looking back sometime in the future and regretting disclosing some personal information to him.

"That much is known, sir, but none of the men knows or needs to know the details of the incident, sir. We all know you to be a good man. At first we were a bit wary of working with you like, in that we didn't know how much we could trust in your judgement. But those days are long gone now and no man that I know of has a care to what brought you to our Division."

Reid could see that the sergeant was trying to help him, but he liked and trusted the man and so continued with his story.

"What do you know about the disappearance of young girls in West Ham?"

The question took the sergeant by complete surprise. He thought for a while and then he remembered that a few young girls had gone missing from the area in the early 1880s.

"By this, do you mean the young girls that went missing about six or seven years back?"

"Yes, I do."

"Well, to be honest, sir, I don't know much about them. Memories fade with the passage of time."

"I too once knew little about them, but they are a continual itch to the men of J-Division. All new officers are informed as part of their induction of the girls' disappearances, in the hope that one day the mystery might be solved. Anyhow, I took up post as J-Division's local Detective on 31st July 1886 and like all other men was given details of the unsolved case into the disappearances of the missing girls. The story goes that a 13-year-old girl by the name of Emily Huckle disappeared in February 1881, with a 14-year-old named Mary Seaward going missing in April of the same year. Then a 12-year-old girl named Eliza Carter was said to have disappeared in January 1882. None of the missing girls has since been found and it is hoped that they all simply ran away from home, but we in our business often think of the worst outcomes of such situations. Anyhow, having a young daughter, Elizabeth, who was 13 at the time, initially put me on my guard for her safety. But you know how it is, after a few months I forgot all about the long past case."

The sergeant was now feeling a bit uneasy in his chair. He very much hoped that Reid was not going to inform him that something terrible had happened to his daughter.

"It sounds a terrible business, sir. I did not know that the men of J-Division took the matter so seriously."

"I am glad and I believe fortunate that they do. You see my wife Emily is an active member of the church and after a few months was heavily involved with the activities at our new local church, with Elizabeth accompanying her, attending to trivial tasks about the parish. However, a prominent local businessman, who will remain nameless, was also quite heavily involved in the church's business. This man had connections in high places, in point of fact a man who appears to have far greater influence in the world than his status should rightly have granted him. It appears that the man even knew Mr Monroe, our last head of the Detective force. However, not unlike our Mr Crawford, I developed grave suspicions about the man's motives for working with the church and the access it provided him to the local community. All that I can say is that he appeared to make an attachment to my daughter and I found things out about him that put me on my guard. My detective's instinct told me that he was a wrong'un. I had nothing concrete on him, but after a while I warned him to keep away from my wife and family. Ultimately, I lost my temper with him one day and found myself assaulting the man in the high street. He pressed charges and I thought it likely that I would lose my job. In the end a compromise was reached whereby he accepted that I be moved from J Division, probably assuming correctly that my family would move out of Stepney. Both he and I could not have supposed that I would only be moved into the neighbouring police division of Whitechapel, but the agreement had been approved, so I found myself here as Inspector Abberline's replacement. This was an outcome far better than I could ever have imagined at the time. Now, I tell you all this because I have no regrets for the actions I took back then, as I was only trying to defend my family. Needless to say, that the man is still at large, his reputation unblemished, without one shred of evidence against his name. Now Sergeant, I appear to have unearthed another supposed 'man of the church', whose motives I am beginning to find equally suspect. Now, I may be just being more than a little paranoid, but I'll tell you this. Seeing Mr. Crawford following my family yesterday caused me great distress and I don't intend to rest until I've uncovered what his true motives are."

The sergeant did not know what to say. He could see that Reid had been greatly affected by Crawford's actions. But he also knew that the Ripper Case was bringing to the police's attention a great number of men who he thought much more likely to be a danger to the families of Whitechapel. However, from the way Reid was speaking, the Sergeant was certain that his Inspector was intent on taking some form of action that he would later come to regret.

"I know not what to say, sir. It sometimes troubles me that one day a villain might choose to take his revenge against me by harming my family but I try to push such thoughts out of my mind. The man that we seek in the

Whitechapel Murder case only appears to want to murder the easiest of targets. Even if Crawford were this man, I cannot imagine him taking a chance of killing during the day. The man we seek likes to hide in the shadows, in the late hours. Thankfully our families are safely tucked-up in their beds when he performs his evil deeds. To my mind sir, you have to try to let the business with this man go. As I said before, the men on nightshift have been instructed to keep a lookout for anyone matching his description. From now on sir, Crawford will be walking the streets in the glare of a hidden lantern."

"Thank you for listening, sergeant. You are a good man. Don't be concerning yourself that I will take any unwarranted action. I trust that this conversation will stay between us?"

"Rest assured that it will, sir."

❦❦❦

Reid left the station shortly after his conversation with Sergeant Thick. He decided to take a long walk around Whitechapel whilst he tried to think things through. He was considering changing his request to work the late shift, thinking that the sergeant was right in that Crawford posed no direct threat to his family. He would have to trust that his colleagues would be watching Crawford more closely from now on and would probably catch the man committing any unsavoury act that he might chose to perform. However, he was then left with the problem of explaining why he suddenly didn't need to investigate Marks' nocturnal activities. Whilst he was pondering his best course of action, he caught sight of the fallen woman that he, Sergeant Thick and Greenfield had saved from assault in Castle Alley.

"Good afternoon, Mrs Holland, I trust you are well?"

"I remember you. You're the copper that 'elped save

me. Yes, mister, I'm good thanks ta you. I can't helps but think about how Polly must 'ave met her end. She woz most probably done to death similar like."

A crazy idea then entered into the mind of the Inspector. He had suggested that Abberline try to arrange for real women to be used as bait to draw the murderer out into the open. He felt sure that the idea might work. He also thought that it much more likely to work if the bait could be dangled in front of a few selected men, to see if any of them would bite. Well he was nigh on certain that he had identified the right man, so he thought that is should be a relatively simple matter to lay a trap for him.

"How are you doing for money, my dear?"

"I make do."

"How keen are you to help catch the man that murdered your friend Polly?"

"I s'pose I'd do most anything to 'elp ketch 'im like. Why do ya ask?"

"Say I said that I thought I knew who the killer might be but needed some assistance in laying a trap to catch him. Would you be interested in helping?"

"I would that, sir. But you're a rozzer, so why would ya need the likes of me to 'elp ya get 'im?"

"I have a way of catching the man but it needs the services of a brave lady. A task I would be willing to pay for, say two shillings for a few hours work, if you were interested?"

Ellen Holland's eyes lit up. Two shillings was nigh on a week's doss money. She didn't have a clue what Reid was on about, but the man's heart seemed to be in the right place and she trusted that he would try to do the right thing by her and the memory of her recently departed friend, Polly Nichols.

"Yes, sir, I'm interested. Wot is it ya want me doing?"

"Which lodging house do you live in again?"

"18 Thrawl Street, you can find me there most

mornings until 10 o'clock."

"If all goes well, I might call on you to help me with my plan to catch the murderer. But remember this, everything that I tell you must remain a secret. There can be no other way, if you truly want to help me catch the man that murdered your friend. However, be warned that the activity I have in mind will take place late at night and will place you in great danger."

Ellen Holland laughed. "That's no bother to me, sir. Sounds a lot like wot I does most nights anyway."

❦ ❦ ❦

Ellen Holland had given the Inspector some confidence that his mad scheme might actually work. His mind was racing again. He wanted to be able to use the woman to try and entice Crawford into attacking her, but so many things had the potential to go wrong, not least that the woman would blab to all that would listen to her. He was trying to weigh-up in his mind whether his plan was worth losing his job over. He had to admit to himself the harsh truth that he didn't know or really care for any of the murdered prostitutes. Yet he did very much care that a monster was lurking in the shadows of Whitechapel. If he did nothing, it was likely that the maniac would kill again. As things stood, Abberline and or a few other senior officers would be blamed for failing to catch the man; which in the long run might be good for his own prospects of promotion. Yet, if Crawford was the killer, how easy might it be to catch him if a vulnerable woman was waved under his nose? If he got the right man, no one would care how he did it.

Reid tried to unpick the problem. If Crawford were the murderer, he would be tempted to attack the lady he intended to use as bait. He might seriously injure her or even kill her in the process of such an attack. Even if he did not manage to harm her, she would have to be the primary witness in court and if she blabbed about the trap laid for the killer he might be sacked. Yet, if Crawford was caught with a prostitute in the dead of night carrying a long-bladed knife and didn't have alibis on the nights of the other murders, Reid would be famous. He would have caught the most notorious murderer in the history of London.

Having weighed-up all the possible outcomes; with a heavy heart Reid finally decided that as a family man he couldn't take the risk to his reputation and livelihood. When he had attacked the businessman in West Ham it had been because he thought that the man posed a direct threat to his family. However, in Sergeant Thick's view Crawford didn't pose such a threat and for that reason Reid saw sense and made a decision to try and forget all about his hair-brained scheme.

At just after 7pm that Monday night Inspector Reid took a walk around Whitechapel in the hope that he might find Harris Marks and his associates. He walked down the Whitechapel High Street, popping into the White Hart and the Nags Head pubs as he went. There was no sign of Marks in either establishment, so he tried a few other pubs as he made his way to 27 Chicksan Street, the place Constable Imhoff had recorded as being Marks' home address. He was disappointed to find no signs of life at the property and spent a few minutes thinking about whether there was anything that he could usefully do before returning to the station. As he was now a fully-fledged member of the Whitechapel Murder Squad, he decided that he would spend about 45 minutes walking the Whitechapel Murder sites; starting from George Yard, the murder site of Martha Tabram.

As he walked he thought more about Crawford and

what if anything he could do about the man. He found it strange that Crawford should even have told him when he would next be on Whitechapel's streets. As far as Reid was concerned Crawford still thought him to be a local businessman. So why would the man, he thought to be the Ripper, want to advertise the nights he spent in the area? He could only think that Crawford was trying to reinforce in people's minds that it was normal for him to be on Whitechapel's streets at all hours of the day and night. He thought that it might be the man's way trying to cultivate an image of being someone that everyone sees but nobody remembers.

The Inspector walked from Bucks Row, where Polly Nichols was slain, onto Hanbury Street, where Annie Chapman met her end. He then entered Commercial Street with the intention of walking down to Berner's Street and Dutfield's Yard, the site of Elizabeth Stride's murder. As he passed Thrawl Street he thought about Ellen Holland and his stupid plan to try and entrap Crawford. He stopped at the road junction and looked about him at the misery and deprivation that was at the heart of his patch, H Division's Whitechapel. He then caught site of Levi Greenfield walking in the opposite direction, on the other side of the road to him. Greenfield was another man he could not fathom. An up and coming hoodlum no doubt, but also a man whose heart appeared to be in the right place. Reid mused that in another life, Greenfield would have made a fine policeman.

Greenfield walked a little further along Commercial Street and then entered a pub named the Britannia which was on the corner of Dorset Street. Dorset Street was one of the most notorious streets in the whole of Whitechapel and was a street that uniformed beat officers were forced into patrolling in pairs, so as to reduce the risk of being attacked by the local street gangs. Reid decided to take a walk past the pub to try and catch a glimpse of Greenfield and anyone that he might be sharing a drink with. He might not know what line of criminality Greenfield was currently engaged in, but thought that Greenfield's associates might shed some light on how the man was making a living. As he walked slowly past the pub's dirty windows he could just make out Greenfield chatting at the bar with what looked to be a prostitute. Just then it started to rain, so Reid thought better of completing his murder mile and instead headed off to the relative comfort of the Leman Street Police station.

When Reid arrived at his desk he was informed that a burglary had been reported in a house in Steward Street, one of few salubrious streets in Whitechapel. On the assumption that that the property was occupied by one of the more prominent local residents, Reid was told to pay the property a visit to demonstrate to the occupant how seriously the police were treating the incident. It was not every day that Whitechapel's most senior local Detective was called to investigate such a relatively insignificant crime. Reid did not expect to discover any more than the constables, but knew that his involvement made for good public relations at a time when confidence in the force was low.

After the last fiasco with the bloodhounds, none of the station staff thought to try and use them again. So all the officers, including Reid remained unaware that the dogs were no longer available; Barnaby and Burgho having long since been recalled to Taunton. The rest of the night passed quickly and without incident. Reid made a few late night/early morning patrols, the only person of note that he encountered was a Barnardo staffer wandering the back streets looking for ragged children that he might take off the streets and place in a shelter. This only served to remind Reid that Crawford might also be on the streets 'persuading' fallen women to see the error of their ways.

CHAPTER TWENTYTWO

No Harm in Having a Little Fun

WHEN REID ARRIVED AT WORK on Tuesday 6th November he hoped that there was nothing sitting in his in-tray that might keep him away from Aldgate High Street between the hours of 10pm and midnight. There was a report of a serious assault in White's Row that required his attention, so he decided to go straight to the scene in the hope of sorting it all out before he expected Crawford to make his appearance in Whitechapel. Reid had taken all the details and had ordered a search for the attacker by a few constables by 8.30pm, leaving him plenty of time of attend to his paperwork before venturing out in what he recorded in his work log as 'a search for the suspected dealer in counterfeit coinage - Harris Marks', but was actually his planned surveillance of the nocturnal activities of George Crawford.

At 9.45pm the Inspector was on the Aldgate High Street. He automatically moved into the shadows at the sight of every hansom cab that came clattering along the thoroughfare. This continued for about 45 minutes until a cab stopped and out stepped a man wearing a long dark coat, dark hat, and carrying a leather holdall. Reid couldn't see the man's face in the gloom but felt sure that it was Crawford. He followed the man along the High Street and up into Goulston Street, the street where Catherine Eddowes' bloodstained apron had been found. The man walked slowly up Goulston Street and turned into Wentworth Street and then turned into a very narrow thoroughfare named Hort Street. Reid knew that the street led into a very quiet, poorly lit square, named Cox's Square. The Inspector followed the man as he entered the square, which turned out to be completely deserted. These were notoriously dangerous streets for a police officer to tread and Reid in his plain clothes felt more than a little vulnerable to attack. He watched, as the man seemed to be surveying the area and then followed him when he exited the square, making his way to Sandy Lane. The man was moving quickly now and it was here that Reid saw the man approach what appeared to be one of the 'unfortunates' out trying to earn her night's doss. Reid watched, as the man in the long dark coat led the woman underneath a lamppost, opened his holdall, and as Reid expected, pulled out what appeared to be a leaflet. Then something unexpected happened. Reid noticed that the woman had started to caress the man's arm. The man then replaced the leaflet into the bag and then gave the lady something that looked like money. The couple then started to head in Reid's direction, back towards Cox's Square.

The Inspector moved quickly, making his way back into the still deserted square and hid in the shadows. Two people entered the square just as he had found himself a place to hide. Reid's heart was racing and he was not sure what to do. If the man was Crawford and was about to slaughter a woman, he would be carrying a large razor sharp knife. Reid did not think that he would be able to tackle a knife wielding maniac on his own, so he reached for his police whistle and decided that on the first sign of trouble he would blow it, sounding the alarm. He looked-on as the woman led the man under a lamppost which was close enough for him to overhear their conversation.

"Come this way, deary, I won't bite. You preacher types are all the same, you likes a bit of female company as much as the next man."

The man made a reply and Reid instantly recognised the voice as Crawford's.

"Please God, forgive me the evil that I'm about to commit," Reid thought he heard him say.

The Inspector placed his whistle to his lips in expectation that Crawford meant to attack the woman, who looked very unconcerned by the danger that Reid thought her to be in.

"Wot's evil about a little slap n tickle? No 'arm in 'avin a little fun in life is there?"

Crawford placed his left hand on the lady's throat.

"Oi, what's your game? You a rough one or what? Keep your 'ands 'orf of me or else I'll scream for a rozzer!"

Crawford pulled his hand back. "No forgive me, I did not mean anything by it," he said softly.

Reid then looked-on very uncomfortably as Crawford proceeded to make a connection with the woman. When it was over the woman left the square the way she had come and Crawford sat on the floor close to the lamppost. He looked distraught and was muttering to himself. Reid did not know what to make of the situation. Clearly Crawford had a liking for dangerous liaisons, but then did not appear able to live with his actions. Crawford got up and walked out of the square. Reid followed him as he walked back to the Aldgate High Street, where he hailed a hansom and went on his way. Reid assumed that Crawford would now return home to the Marylebone Road.

The Inspector had just witnessed first-hand how difficult it would be to catch the killer. In less than a quarter of an hour, Crawford had selected a deserted quiet square, picked-up a prostitute and taken her there to have sex with her. All this had happened out of sight of any of the now numerous police officers patrolling the streets of Whitechapel. If Crawford were the Ripper, he would have had ample time to slaughter the prostitute in the same fashion that Catherine Eddowes had met her end in Mitre Square.

Reid did not know what to make of Crawford. The opportunity to commit murder was there if he had wanted to take it. Crawford had looked very upset after committing the sexual act and the Inspector wondered whether the man would now go home and spend a few days brooding over the event, blaming the evil prostitute for his sinful ways. Would he then return to the streets in pent-up fury and reap vengeance on the evildoers? All this was just speculation, but even Reid without any understanding of psychology could see how such a scenario could play out in a mind like Crawford's. Then he decided to take a real look for Harris Marks before returning to the station.

CHAPTER TWENTYTHREE

A Very Risky Plan

HAVING SLEPT on the events that he had witnessed the night before, Reid decided to return again to his very risky plan. Crawford had said that he would return to Whitechapel on Thursday night, the day before the Lord Mayor's Show. Reid thought that the man would very likely be walking the streets in a state of pent-up anger and as such, was highly likely to assault a woman. Reid also knew that Thursday night would see minimal police cover as many men had been given the night off in order that they might get some much needed rest in advance of their participation in crowd control duties required for Friday's Lord Mayor's Show. The Inspector thought that all this would make for a perfect storm, greatly increasing the chance that Crawford could attack another woman and get away undetected as a result of the minimal police presence on the streets. Reid had finally made his mind up; he was going to contact Ellen Holland to see if he could get her to play the part of the tethered goat in his trap. He would also pay a visit to a Blacksmith's, as he wanted a lightweight iron collar and cuffs made for the woman's protection. His wife Emily had a few whalebone corsets and he decided that he would take the shabbiest for the unfortunate to wear as the final part of her body armour.

❦❦❦

As Inspector Reid set about making plans for Thursday night, he would have been oblivious to the battles going on between Commissioner Warren and Home Secretary Matthews. Matthews was to finally receive some information that might prove useful in nudging Warren into what he considered the right direction, namely proffering his resignation.

On his arrival at his office, the Minister was presented with his daily pack containing his appointments for the day, along with the supporting documentation required for each of his meetings. On the top of the pile was a note attached to an article from the latest edition of a periodical named Murray's Magazine. Ordinarily the magazine would have contained little that would have interested the Minister, but that month's issue contained an article penned by none other than Metropolitan Police Commissioner, Sir Charles Warren. The article was entitled 'The Police of the Metropolis'. The note attached to the article made reference to a little known Home Office ruling that dated back to 1879, that forbade all officers connected with the Department from publishing anything without express permission of the Home Secretary. Matthews saw many pieces of paper throughout each of his very busy days, but he certainly had no recollection of authorising Warren's article. Sir Henry's Private Secretary had a broad smile on his face that morning, as he expected that his boss would be very pleased with the contents of the note.

"Who found this article?" asked the Home Secretary.

"One of my aides, sir. A keen-eyed chap by the name of Frederick Jenkins."

"The ruling of 1879 still stands?"

"Yes, it does, sir."

"In that case I think that I will write to the Commissioner in strong terms about his breach of discipline."

"I've already drafted a letter for you, sir. I trust that it has been worded strongly enough?"

Matthews read the draft letter, he was most pleased with its tone, drawing attention to the 1879 ruling and instructing the Commissioner not to repeat a similar act of

MISCONDUCT in the future.

"Yes, this is excellent. Get this typed-up as is, I want this to go to the Commissioner's Office this morning."

"Yes sir, I'll see to it immediately."

"Right, what else have we got on this fine day?" asked a jovial Secretary of State.

The Minister and his PS went through his diary and planned out his day. When they had finished, a copy of the approved letter was given to Matthews for signature and then sent on its way to Scotland Yard.

⸙ ⸙ ⸙

For Inspector Abberline it was just another hard day at the office. He and his men had been swamped with information and were in the process of investigating the whereabouts of at least twenty new suspects. He had noticed a change in the air in the streets with most things having returned back to normal. It had been five weeks since the last two murders and there were rumours circulating Whitechapel that 'The Knife' had moved from London to Newcastle. This lackadaisical atmosphere was beginning to feed through to his weary men, who had been rotating the nightshifts amongst themselves to try and minimise the ill effects that the shifts were taking on their sleeping patterns. Abberline had decided that his men needed a pep talk. He had a feeling his water that the killer was still at large in London and might strike soon, possibly over the next weekend. He didn't want his men slackening off just when they should be at their most alert. He'd arranged a briefing for 10am which included officers from both the neighbouring police districts of J Division and the City, which he hoped would act as an energiser. Inspectors Helson and Halse had been invited to represent their respective Divisions.

Abberline opened the briefing,

"Good morning, gentleman. I've gathered you here today in order that our colleagues from J-Division and the City can apprise us with their investigative endeavours. I'm hoping that we can use this meeting to gear ourselves-up for the extra efforts that will be required over the next few weekends. As you know it all hands on deck for the Lord Mayor's Show on Friday, so we are short of cover on Thursday night. Let us hope that our murderer also takes an early night in advance of the day's fcstivities."

There was laughter in the room.

Abberline continued, "Now gentleman, I intend to hold briefings with nightshift officers at various stations tonight and tomorrow night, informing the men on duty on Thursday night to be extra vigilant due to our short numbers. I've noticed a change in the atmosphere in the streets over the last few weeks, since word has spread that 'The Knife' as they are referring to him, has moved to Newcastle. Now for those of you that don't know it, this rumour started after an article appeared in the 2nd October edition of the Newcastle Chronicle, stating that a man calling himself Mr Duncan is our killer. Well I've personally investigated the matter and found that the man in question is named John Davidson and that he has cast iron alibis for the nights of the murders. So take it from me, 'The Knife' hasn't moved up north and is very likely still with us in old London Town. I'd be grateful if you and your colleagues can make this clear to people during the course of your duties. Inspector Halse from the City will now provide us with an update of the situation in the City, following-on from the murder of Catherine Eddowes in Mitre Square."

The rest of the meeting was used to go through details of numerous men who had been placed under surveillance and to highlight the most promising snippets of intelligence gleamed from the streets. Overall, Abberline was pleased with the content of the meeting and more importantly the attitude of the men. The weather had been bad most of that year and he was expecting a long cold hard winter ahead of them. He wanted to ensure that his men didn't lose their focus and was pleased that see that they were all still determined as ever to catch the man they now all referred to as 'The Ripper'.

❦❦❦

Reid had made his way to the common lodging house at 18 Thrawl Street. He entered the premises and made his way to the kitchen where he was pleased to find Ellen Holland.

The Inspector greeted the woman with a "Good morning, my dear."

"Morning, sir, wot can I do ya for?"

"I'd like to speak with you for a few minutes. Can we take a walk out in the open?"

"Yes, I'll be with ya in a jiffy."

Reid and Ms Holland took a slow walk along Thrawl Street.

"You informed me that you would do anything to catch the man responsible for murdering your friend, Polly, is that still the case?"

"Yes, Inspector. I'd do anything I could."

"I have a plan. It requires the utmost secrecy and is very dangerous."

"I'd be willing to give something a try. You can trust me well, sir. I won't go blabbing."

"Right, I believe that I may have identified the man responsible for murdering your friend Polly, but have absolutely no proof to back up my feeling. I have now thought of a way of drawing the killer out into the open, and so allowing us to catch him in the act."

"But word about is that 'The Knife' has moved up north."

"Trust me my dear. The reports that he has moved on to Newcastle are false. If he is anywhere, he is most likely still at large here in London."

"Why ain't you arrested 'im then?"

"Unfortunately, many men might be the murderer and so far all of our suspects have provided us with good alibis. However, I know of a man that often comes into Whitechapel to preach God's good works. The man is by all accounts the most honest and law abiding of citizens, so there is some difficulty in our simply arresting him. Therefore, I want to place this man in a trap. My plan being to see how the man reacts when drawn into a secluded spot with a lady in the dark of night."

"Wot's that got to do with me, Inspector?"

"What I need for my trap to work is a woman willing to walk the streets in order to tempt the man into accompanying her in a secluded spot under the cover of the darkness. The woman would wear body armour, much like the knights of olden times and would remain constantly under my protection."

"So I'd be this lady?"

"Yes, what you would need to do is walk the same streets as this man in the hope that he proposes taking you to a quiet spot in order to perform a connection with you. Once out of sight, off the main streets, I imagine that the man would then try to attack you. It is then that I intend to come to your aid and arrest him. Now what I'm proposing is very dangerous, but you would wear body armour to help protect you. You would only have to speak with one particular man, as I have no interest in any others. Do you think that you could do this?"

"Hold on, mister, I said I'd help ya as best I could, but it sounds like you wants me to be murdered!"

"No, that is not what I plan. The killer first strangles his victims before cutting them with a knife. My plan is to wait for him to try to strangle you and then bring him down. At the first sign of his attacking you, my men and I will rush him. If he does brandish a knife, your neck and wrists will be defended by a set of metal collar and cuffs, and I have a whalebone corset that you will wear to protect your body. I am not saying that there would be no chance of injury, but the chances of incurring a serious injury will be much reduced by the body armour. I understand that what I ask is very dangerous, but I believe it to be the only way that we have for drawing the monster out into the open.

Ellen Holland thought about what Reid had told her. She knew that her friend Polly and the others had been done-up badly by The Knife and she was scared that she could end up the same way. However, she also knew that none of the women attacked so far had had any form of protection; they had gone to their deaths like lambs to the slaughter. She'd have body armour and would remain in sight of the rozzers. She could be hurt, maybe even killed, but she trusted in Reid to protect her.

"Alright Inspector, I'll do it. What needs to be done?"

Reid went through the rest of the plan, explaining that she should only be required to go out on one night, the next night, and would deal only with the one man. Then it struck Ellen that the man might not be the murderer.

A smile spread over her face and then she asked, "Inspector, wot happens if 'e ain't your man?"

"What do you mean?"

"Well what happens if I leads him to a quiet spot and he ain't up for killing, but is only after a bit of slap and tickle, if you gets my meaning?"

"If you mean if he is only after a connection. Then by all means complete the act. The money that he gives you will be yours to keep."

"And I still gets the two shillings?"

"Yes, you will get that money regardless of whatever else happens."

"But it will be awkward, sir. It's a thing to earn me money in private, but quite another knowing you'll be watching it all like."

"Yes, I can understand that but there is nothing else for it. Now if you are willing to give this a go, I'd be grateful if you can accompany me to a Blacksmith, as we need to sort out your body armour. Now, I'll say this one last time. What we do must remain a secret and can never be told to anybody. Are you clear on this?"

"Yes, Inspector. You're a good man and I want to do right by Polly. I'll keep me gob shut."

Reid's next port of call was to a Blacksmith.

"Good morning, sir, I wonder if you can help me?" asked Reid.

"Good morning to you, sir. Wot's it that you want 'elp with?" replied the Blacksmith.

"I have a most unusual request. I am an officer of the law and am seeking some special body armour that can be worn by this lady."

The Blacksmith looked bemused. "Wot's that all about mister?"

"What I would like sir are lightweight metal guards that this woman can wear on her wrists and around her neck. The woman is to help me in the training of hunting dogs and the guards will be used to protect her from bites to her arms and neck."

"Wot, like a suit of armour like?"

"Yes, exactly like that. I was thinking that they could be made from thin plates of iron."

"I could make such things, sir. How many does ya need?"

"I would like two wrist guards, say four inches wide and one neck protector, say four inches wide at the back and two inches wide at the front, so as to follow the shape of the lady's jaw."

The Blacksmith thought for a while until he was sure

that he thought he knew what the gentleman for after.

"I can make such things sir, but they will make difficult wearing for a woman."

"Could you allow a little room for some padding, so as to protect her skin?"

"Alright mister, I'll make 'em. When do you want 'em?"

"I want them by tomorrow at noon. Can you do this?"

"Yeh, I'll do that for ya guvnor, but they won't come cheap."

Reid agreed a price for the protectors and then walked Ellen Holland back to Thrawl Street.

"Thank you very much for agreeing to do this. Now I will meet you here again tomorrow at 11.45am and we will then return to the Blacksmith to collect the guards."

"Alright, Mr Reid, I'll sees ya tomorrow then."

With that Reid retuned home. He wanted to rest up before his nightshift. He was seriously worried that he had just made a grave error of judgement, but he could not stop himself now that his plan was in motion.

CHAPTER TWENTYFOUR

Matthews Wins the War

WHEN SIR CHARLES WARREN ARRIVED at his office in Scotland Yard on Thursday 8th November he noticed a Home Office letter sitting at the top of his pile of papers. It was marked 'Private and Confidential' and was from Sir Henry Matthews, Minister of State for the Home Office. What he read sent him into a blinding rage. He immediately dictated a letter to his secretary and when it was ready he signed it and headed straight off to the Home Office.

⸙⸙⸙

Reid was surprised that he had managed to get a full night's sleep. He took it as an omen that he was doing the right thing, even though his actions contravened his responsibilities as a member of Her Majesty's Constabulary. He had thought long and hard about trying to involve more men in his trap to capture Crawford but had decided that he couldn't take the risk of anyone talking. However, he still had a nagging doubt lingering in the back of his mind; could he, one man alone, tackle a psychopathic murderer?

Then it struck him, that as an Inspector he was licensed to carry a firearm. He had carried guns on duty before now but only on the most dangerous of arrests. Having determined that he would arm himself with a firearm, he needed an excuse to sign one out of the strong room. He decided that he would file a report containing fictitious intelligence that Harris Marks was thought to carry a gun, justifying his carrying his own firearm in order that he might arrest the man. He also thought that once Ellen

Holland saw the weapon her own nerves would be calmed as she should feel more confident in his ability to protect her.

❦❦❦

Warren was informed that the Minister was in back to back meetings all day and could not be disturbed until the afternoon. Warren, who was still in a furious temper, insisted on seeing Matthews immediately, stating that he was needed to discuss a matter of the utmost importance. Within the hour Warren was finally allowed into the Minister's office.

Matthews knew why Warren was there to see him but decided to play the innocent.

"Good morning, Sir Charles. What matter is so urgent as to have caused me to cut short my meeting with the incoming Mayor of London?"

"I think that you jolly well know what the matter is."

"Ah, this is about your article in that publication, Murray's Magazine."

"Yes it bloody well is."

"Now look here, Sir Charles, you mind your language in my presence, you are not on the parade ground now."

Warren did all that he could to hold his tongue and then gave Matthews the letter that the Minister had been longing to receive for weeks.

"What's this, my man?" he asked in all innocence.

"I'm not your man, Minister, but all will be made clear when you read the letter."

Sir Henry scanned the letter; it made no mention of the Commissioner's failure to catch the Whitechapel Murderer, but would suffice all the same.

"This is a bit strong, is it not? You are an army man are you not? Surely you are used to receiving a rap across the knuckles from time to time?"

"Call it what you will, but I am not a child and I will not come running to the likes of you when I feel the need to write an article in the press. If I'd have known that the post allowed so little latitude, I'd never have taken the job on in the first place."

"I see, but you do understand that less discerning minds than ours may interpret your resignation as a result of your office's failure to catch the Whitechapel Murderer?"

"Yes, I am sure more than a few will think that and I somehow imagine that this office will not be slow in providing them with fuel for the fire."

Matthews chose not to get into an argument with his Commissioner. He had what he desired and decided to accept the man's resignation immediately, just in case Warren should have second thoughts and have a change of mind.

"Look, you've caught me at an awful time. My diary's packed full all the way through to the weekend. I'm afraid that I'll have to reluctantly accept your resignation, if that is your choice. Arrangements can be made for a formal statement to be issued to the press on Monday. I am afraid that you will have to excuse me as I have a meeting with the Prime Minister at Number 10 which is scheduled to start within half an hour."

"I trust that arrangements for my final day in office will be worked out next week," commented Warren.

And with that the Commissioner of the Metropolitan Police strode out of the Minister's Office and headed off to St James' Park to take in the air and ponder his future before getting back to the outstanding business of his day.

As for Sir Henry, he called his PS back into the office and instructed the man to prepare statements to the press that were to include lines about the 'Home Secretary reluctantly accepting the Commissioner's resignation and the matter having absolutely nothing to do with the Met's failure to capture the Whitechapel Murderer, etc, etc'. Then the Home Secretary left for his meeting at number 10, where he would 'reluctantly' inform the PM of the Commissioner's decision to resign.

❦❦❦

Reid met Ellen Holland at 11.45am and as agreed he took her to the Blacksmith's to collect the metal collar and cuffs that had been especially made for her protection. A few minor adjustments were made before Reid paid for them and accompanied Ellen back to her Thrawl Street lodging house. Once there he sought out the deputy, as he wanted her to place the whalebone corset under her care, as he could not trust that Ellen would not have it stolen from her or sell it for drink before nightfall. He decided to keep hold of the protectors, intending to give them to her later that night. The preliminaries out of the way, he took Ellen to the Aldgate High Street as he wanted her to be familiar with the streets that she would be walking under the gloom of the streetlamps.

"Now, my dear, you know where to meet me tonight?"

"Yes, on the corner of Middlesex Street and the Aldgate High Street."

"And at what time?"

"Nine o'clock, by the bell of the church."

"That's fine. Now I'll provide you with the protectors when we meet but you must be sure to wear the corset. Also, I can appreciate that you will be a little afraid, but try to keep away from the drink. I will bring along a tot of rum to help calm your nerves but until then try not to have too much."

"Don't ya worry, Inspector, I knows wot needs doing."

"One last thing. You are only to go with the man I describe to you tonight and no other. You are to tell any other man that approaches you that are waiting on a friend and are not after any male company or some such tale. The man that we seek professes to preach God's word and will have a bag with him. He will most probably start by telling you to give up your evil ways. What you need to do is try to tempt him to go with you into Cox's Square. Once there, I will be waiting and will apprehend him should he try to harm you in any way."

"Yes, Inspector. I already knows all this. Don't you worry; I think I knows how to get a man into an alley, if ya gets me meaning?"

"Very well, until tonight and keep away from the drink."

❦ ❦ ❦

Reid returned home and spent a few hours reading a book in order to divert his mind away from the ordeal that awaited him. He then made his way to the station at 5.45pm to initiate the first part of his plan. As he expected, there were far fewer men on the nightshift as most of the men had been given the night off so as to be available for duties relating to the Lord Mayor's Show. Reid spoke to the desk sergeant.

"Good evening, Sergeant Jenner. Is the Super in his office?"

"No sir he has gone home for the day. Why do you need him for something?"

"Well it would have been good if he were here, but no matter. I am going to be placing a man under surveillance tonight and it has been brought to my attention that he can be quite dangerous and is in the habit of carrying a firearm. Therefore, I will need to sign-out a pistol for my own personal protection. I would have preferred the Super to have countersigned the form, but I have sufficient authority to self authorise it."

"Do you want me to get you a weapon from the gun cabinet right away?"

"On no, that will not be necessary, I'll sign for it just before I go out on my rounds. I won't need it until about 8.30pm."

"Very good, sir. I'm on from now until 2am, so just give me the word and I'll get it for you."

Reid completed the requisition form and handed it to the sergeant for processing. He then went to his desk to check his in-tray.

Sergeant Thick should already have gone home as he was on the dayshift, but was still in the station when Reid made his request for the gun. On his way out of the station he paused for a quick chat with Sergeant Jenner who had been stuck on the nightshift.

"Everything OK, Brian?"

"It sure is William."

"I hope that you are in for a quiet night."

"Me too, but who knows what might happen. The Inspector has just put in a request for a pistol."

"What, Inspector Reid! He doesn't usually carry one of them. What does he want it for?"

"According to his F20 form, he needs it for a surveillance job."

"Can I see the form?"

Sergeant Thick looked at the F20. It all looked above board, but Reid had written that he needed it for protection because the suspect he was investigating, Harris Marks, was known to carry a gun. Thick had heard a bit about the man Marks over the last few weeks and everything that he'd heard about him didn't point to his being the kind of man that would carry a gun. The sergeant decided that Reid must have another reason for wanting a weapon. Then it struck him what that reason might be.

"Well I'm sure that it will all come to nothing. Although, you've just reminded me that I have a message that I was supposed to pass onto the Inspector, I'll tell him now, whilst I remember it.

"OK then, William. I'll catch you later."

Thick walked through the station until he saw Reid sitting at his desk.

"Inspector Reid, can I have a quick word, sir?" asked Sergeant Thick.

"Yes, what is it that you want, sergeant?"

"Can we speak in an interview room, sir?"

"Yes, that's fine."

The men entered interview room number 3.

"Sir, the DS has just informed me that you've submitted a requisition for a pistol. It's none of my business but grateful if you can tell me what you want a gun for?"

"You are right, sergeant, it is none of your business."

Reid paused for a while. He felt that he could trust Sergeant Thick and knew that by unburdening himself, he would allow himself one last opportunity to call an end to his mad scheme.

"You remember our speaking about the man named Crawford?" continued Reid.

"I do, what of him, sir?"

"Well, I have thought-up a plan to try and trap the suspect in the act of murder and intend to put the scheme into action later on tonight."

"I see, sir, and who else have you assigned to help you take the man down should he turn out to be the killer?"

"There is nobody else. It will be me and one of the unfortunates, the woman we saved from the mob the other week."

It was the Sergeant's turn to have a think. What Reid told him sounded like madness. If Crawford really was the Ripper, he might prove very difficult to take down, even with a gun. If the weapon failed, which they were known to do on a quite regular basis, Reid would be forced to tackle the man with nothing more than a truncheon. The Sergeant thought that his inspector was taking a massive chance by trying to capture the man on his own. As for involving a civilian in his plan, Thick thought that Reid might just as well hand in his notice before leaving the station.

"Look, sir, what you are planning sounds like madness to me. Even if you are able to catch him in the act, how will it stand-up in court using such a woman as bait?"

"You are right, Sergeant. A great many things might go wrong, but I've always regretted not sticking to my principles in the West Ham case. I should have resigned then, rather than have allowed a man I thought to be a child murderer to walk the streets. I now have the same feeling about Crawford and I intend to do something about him, even if I lose my job in the process."

"And what happens if the lady is murdered and Crawford gets away from you? It will be your word versus his and the woman would have lost her life for nothing."

"That is a chance that I am willing to take."

Very well, Inspector, I can see that there is no talking sense into you. Look, I've just finished my shift, but I can come back to the station later tonight to help you entrap the man. It would all be off the record. Would you like my help with this?"

Reid knew that by acting alone he was courting disaster. He didn't want to involve the sergeant or eat into a fellow family man's rest time but he knew that not accepting the offer would truly be the act of a mad man.

"Okay, sergeant. I will take you up on your kind offer. I don't know how I will ever be able to repay the debt and I most probably never will."

"That's fine with me, sir. So what time do you want me back here?"

"I think is best that we don't meet at the station. I have planned to meet the unfortunate on the corner of Middlesex and Aldgate High Streets at nine o'clock. We could meet a little after 8.45pm."

"Very well, sir, I'll meet you there. I'll be wearing my civvies, but will have my whistle and truncheon."

"There is one last thing."

"What is it, sir?"

"Do you have soft-soled boots?"

"Yes, sir, I have those rubber boot covers that they recently gave us for night duty. I'll make sure to wear them."

"Excellent, sergeant. I will see you later."

The sergeant left the station and returned home for his dinner. Reid now felt much calmer. The sergeant's involvement should make everything that much easier. Reid now hoped that nothing of note happened before 8.30pm, the time he planned to leave the station to embark on his mad scheme.

❦❦❦

Nothing of note did happen that evening and Reid collected a pistol from the desk sergeant and made his way to the rendezvous. He got there at 8.40pm. Sergeant Thick arrived bang on 8.45pm by the chimes of the church bells.

"Good evening, sir."

"Good evening, sergeant."

"I've been giving your plan some thought sir and was wondering where you intend to trap Crawford?"

"On Tuesday night he picked-up a woman in Sandy Row and took her into Cox's Square and I am hoping that he will repeat the same pattern tonight."

"Okay, sir, but how are you intending to keep the streets around the square clear of other women?"

"I hadn't thought about that. But the last time he checked that the square was deserted before returning back there with a prostitute, so he is likely to do the same tonight."

"I was just wondering whether we should have a few

uniformed constables make a sweep of the area to clear away any other whores and would be robbers?"

"No, I think that we will proceed as I've planned. You are correct in wanting to clear the area, but in doing that we might create an unnatural atmosphere that might arouse the man's suspicions."

"Very well, sir."

Just then Ellen Holland came into view. She was true to her word and had barely touched a drop of alcohol the whole day. However, she needed some to function properly and very much hoped that Reid had brought some rum with him.

"Good evening, my dear. I trust you remember Sergeant Thick?" said Reid.

"I do, sir."

"And you are wearing the corset?"

"Yes, it makes for a good fit. Sorry to trouble ya about this, but it's awful cold today and I could do with a shot of rum to 'elp get rid of the chill from me bones."

"Ah yes, I have some in a hip flask. Please go gently with it as we might have a long night ahead of us."

Ellen took a sip of the liquid in the flask. Reid was good to his word and had filled it with high-quality rum.

"Thank ya kindly, Inspector. I can tells that this is the good stuff."

Reid was all business, and was now highly focused on the task ahead of him.

"Right, we will stand in the archway over there. Our man should arrive in the street by way of a hansom cab. He is about 5 feet 8 inches in height and is clearly recognisable because he wears a large ginger/red moustache."

The church bells rang out every fifteen minutes and there had been no sign of Crawford as the bells chimed to mark 10.30pm. However, there was nothing that could be done other than to wait and see if the man alighted there as Reid expected him to do. The trio made small talk to pass the time. Reid and Thick were wary of giving away too much information to someone they might have to arrest at a future date. However, Reid made sure to tell Ellen that he had a gun and ensured her that he would not let anything bad happen to her.

"Sorry to trouble ya, Inspector but I needs ta take a leak," said Holland.

"Okay, but please try to be quick about it," replied Reid.

Ellen moved back into the darkest corner of the archway, where she hoped that Reid and the Sergeant couldn't see her. Then as is always the way with events, the two men spied a hansom cab coming their way. It stopped on the other side of the road, about 200 feet from where they were standing. Even from that distance and in the low lights of the streetlamps they could make out the red moustache of the man that departed the carriage.

Reid was a little agitated that Ellen Holland was otherwise engaged, but tried to keep his composure as best he could.

"Right, my dear, if you can try to hurry along as we will soon be in business. Our man has just arrived."

"Be with you in a mo, sir."

Crawford was looking edgy and soon spotted the two men lurking in the shadows of the archway. However, there was nothing unusual about such a sight and he was just glad that he had not chosen to walk on the other side of the carriageway. He turned into Goulston Street, taking the same route as he had done on Tuesday night. Holland had finished her business and was able to catch sight of the back of a gentleman in a long dark coat, black hat and carrying a brown bag in his left hand. The three of them then moved off slowly, turned into Goulston Street and kept back about 150 feet from the target in the long dark coat who was slowly making his way up the road.

Crawford looked over his shoulder just before he

turned into Hort Street and was relieved to see a woman with the two men he'd seen in the archway, as he assumed that a gang of robbers would not include a lady.

"Right, he's following the same route he that took on Tuesday. He's most likely going to survey the Cox's Square before making his way to Sandy Row. Sergeant, give it five minutes and then proceed to the square and hide there. We will enter Sandy Row by the main carriageway and I will follow Miss Holland and our man back into the square."

Reid and Thick had been careful not to use Crawford's name, just in case Ellen should accidently use his name when speaking with him.

"Very well, sir. I hope to see you shortly," said the sergeant as he watched Reid and the unfortunate walk to the end road and turn right into Sandy Row.

The Inspector dropped back so that the prostitute was walking about 50 feet ahead of him.

Ellen Holland walked hesitantly up Sandy Row and positioned herself midway between two side streets that led from Cox's Square and waited. However, Ellen wasn't the only woman selling her wares in Sandy Row and it wasn't long before one of them was on to her.

"Ere wot's your bleedin' game? I walks this patch. Now sling ya hook," said a rough looking hag.

Before Ellen could respond, a man entered Sandy Row from one of the thoroughfares leading from Cox's Square. It was Crawford and he immediately intervened in what he thought was an argument between two fallen women.

"Please calm yourselves, ladies. There is no need for shouting."

"WOT'S IT GOT TA DO WITH YOU MISTER?" shouted the disgruntled Sandy Row regular.

"I am here to do the Lord's work, do please try to remain calm. I have some literature here that will help you see the error of your ways."

"Some wot, you masher? You can both bleeding clear

orff."

Ellen took the man's arm and led him back a little way into the street that he'd just come from.

"Don't be minding 'er mister. See we ain't good readers round 'ere. Can ya read me wots wrote on the paper?"

"Why yes of course, my dear. It is a pamphlet produced by my church."

The other prostitute was not keen on wasting her time with a preacher and left the two of them to it.

Crawford continued, "Well, firstly, it says that women such your fine self should stay clear from committing immoral acts."

Ellen squeezed the man's arm. "Wot would those be, sir?"

"Well, such things might include fornication outside of marriage."

"And would you be a married gentleman, sir?"

"No I am not, but this is nothing to do with me."

"But I thinks that it is, sir. I bets you get all sort of lonely like, 'especially in the long winter nights. Don't ya think that I cuts a fine figure in my new corset?"

Crawford observed the whore, her dress was dirty and tatty, but she did cut a fine figure for a woman of her age. He could feel the passion beginning to course through his veins.

"I've got much more besides me corset under these skirts that might interest a good man such as yourself like," said Holland, as she pulled on Crawford's arm and led him towards the square. "There's a quiet spot back the way ya came if ya wants a bit of company, but it'll cost ya sixpence".

Crawford knew before he had ventured out that night that he would most probably find his way back into Cox's Square. He had spent a good number of hours fantasising about what he intended to do there. He now took control and led Ellen Holland by the hand into the square.

Reid was careful to keep his distance, feeling safe in the knowledge that Sergeant Thick would be on hand to intervene should anything happen before he was able to get himself into position.

Crawford reached into his pocket and pulled out sixpence. "You are an evil one my dear but you have caught me in a moment of weakness."

Sergeant Thick saw a man and a woman enter the square. He assumed that the couple were Crawford and Holland. His pulse was racing and he already had his truncheon and whistle in his hands in expectation of having to take the man down.

As Reid followed the couple, he noticed something about Crawford that he hadn't expected; the man was wearing normal hard leather soled shoes that clapped hard on the cobblestones. The conventional wisdom going about police circles was that the Ripper wore rubber-soled footwear that allowed him to move noiselessly through the shadows. However, Reid had no time to muse over such intricacies at that moment in time. He did not enter the square but chose to stay in sight of the couple, remaining at a vantage point in the alley.

"There's nothing evil about me, sir, I might be a little wicked if ya gets me meaning, but evil I'm not."

Ellen then noticed a change come over Crawford, his gaze hardened and her heart skipped a beat as the reality of her situation dawned on her.

"Wot is it, sir, you alright?"

"I hear that you whores like a little rough treatment. Well you deserve some for leading the innocent astray," said Crawford, suddenly grabbing Holland with both hands and squeezing tightly on her upper arms.

"STOP MISTER, YOU'RE 'ERTING ME," screamed Holland.

Crawford placed his left hand quickly over her mouth.

"Keep your voice down, you harlot," whispered Crawford.

Reid and Thick made ready to take the man down. Thick was waiting for a signal from his Inspector, but he did not get one. Reid was waiting to see the glint of a knife in the gloom, just to be sure that he really had lured the Whitechapel Murderer into his trap.

Crawford proceeded to pull Holland's skirts up. He was more than a little rough with her, but it was obvious that he had other things on his mind than murder. When it was over he pushed Holland away.

"AWAY WITH YOU, HARLOT," he shouted at her.

"Steady on, mister, no wonder you ain't a married gentleman."

"Be gone woman and may you rot in Hell."

Holland was pleased that her ordeal appeared to be over. She slowly walked away from the man who fell to the ground behind her. She passed Reid and made her way back to the relative safety of Sandy Row.

Reid was not sure what to do. On Tuesday night Crawford had settled for a connection and did not attack the prostitute that he had sex with. Reid was tempted to let the man go and try and catch him another night, but curiosity had gotten the better of him. He decided to challenge Crawford and search him for a weapon.

"You there, get yourself up and place yourself under the light of the streetlamp," barked Reid as he entered the square.

Crawford's self-pity rapidly left him as he thought that he was about to be attacked and robbed.

"What is it that you want?" asked Crawford nervously.

"I said on your feet and place yourself under the light," repeated the Inspector.

As Crawford got to his feet he saw two men standing in front of him. Even in the half-light he instantly recognised one of them.

"I know you, you are Mr Reid."

"That will be, Inspector Reid, to you Mr Crawford. Tell me, how did you find yourself to be here at this hour?"

Crawford thought carefully before speaking. He was very surprised to learn that Reid was a policeman, an Inspector no less. However, he reasoned that Reid and the other man would already have arrested him if they had caught him with the prostitute. He tried to think about how the situation might look to two policemen out on their rounds, stumbling across a man sitting a deserted square.

"Mr, I mean, Inspector Reid. You are well aware of my church activities. Did I not tell you on Sunday that I meant to do good works for the Lord on Tuesday and Thursday night of this week? I was passing through this square when I came over all peculiar."

"Yes, he came over something alright, Inspector," quipped Sergeant Thick.

"You are no doubt aware that all the police in Whitechapel are hunting for the murderer of street woman, the man they call the Ripper?" said Reid.

"Yes, I am aware of that Inspector, but what has that got to do with me?"

"Officers are under instructions to search all suspicious looking men found walking the streets of Whitechapel during the hours of darkness. You would no doubt agree that you yourself fall very much into that category tonight?"

"Well, I suppose finding me like this would appear somewhat odd. Search away, Inspector, I have nothing with me other than my words from the good Lord."

Reid was surprised and disappointed at Crawford's readiness to be searched. He knew then that they wouldn't find a weapon on the man.

"Sergeant, please search this man."

Sergeant Thick first emptied out Crawford's holdall, being very careful to check for anything hidden in the lining, but all he found were church pamphlets. He repeated the process when going through Crawford's coat, and even took a look inside the man's hat.

"He's clean, Inspector. What do you want done with him?"

"Stay where you are for a moment, Mr Crawford, I need a private word with my sergeant."

Reid led Thick a short distance from Crawford so that the man could not overhear their conversation.

"Thank you for your help, sergeant, I am now in your debt. You get yourself home and I will take Mr Crawford back the station. I'm interested in seeing how he responds to a night in the cells."

"Very well, Inspector, but is it worth bothering with? By placing him in the cells he might decide to raise a complaint against you? I mean, without a weapon, we have nothing on him."

"That's the least of my concerns now. You get yourself off home, man. I'm going to push ahead with this. Once he's in custody he will have to provide me with alibis for the nights of the previous murders. My feeling is that he will be unable to do so."

"Very well, sir, but I'll take the lady back to Thrawl Street first."

"Thank you for that. I had forgotten about her. Please be sure to reclaim the neck and wrist protectors that she is wearing and can you give her this for her trouble," said Reid handing the sergeant two shillings before bidding him goodnight.

"Now, Mr Crawford, I can appreciate that you have been wandering our streets doing good works for the Lord. However, in my capacity as an officer of the law I am obligated to act on any suspicious activity that catches my eye, and finding you sitting on the floor in this square at his time of night certainly meets that criteria. For that reason I am going to place you under caution and ask you to accompany me to Leman Street Police Station."

"This is ridiculous. It is a clear waste of police time and

taxpayers' money. How long is this all going to take? I intended to rise in good time to see the Lord Mayor's Show."

"It will take as long as it takes," replied Reid, coldly.

Reid led Crawford to Leman Street and had the desk sergeant place his prisoner in a cell. He also returned the firearm, stating that he had not found Harris Marks, but had instead discovered a man acting suspiciously in Cox's Square. Reid then went to his desk to make his report detailing the reason for the apprehension of Crawford. He knew that being an influential businessman there was likely to be consequences for his holding the man at the station, but the way that he saw it he had valid reasons for the action that he had taken. His only concern was the involvement of Sergeant Thick, which he deliberately left out of his description of events in the square. Reid's shift was scheduled to end at 2am, so he decided to let Crawford stew until 1am, when Crawford was moved from his cell into one of the interview rooms.

"I am sorry to have kept you waiting, Mr Crawford, but I had to attend to an urgent matter that arose whilst I was out of the station."

"I will tell you now, Inspector, I am very unhappy about this situation. As I told you earlier, I was hoping to retire early enough to get a good night's sleep before tomorrow morning's festivities."

"Well what was I supposed to do, sir? I discovered you late at night sitting in a deserted square wearing a long coat, dark hat and carrying a bag. If any my constables had stumbled upon you I very much hope that they would have treated you in the same way. Now I'm all for letting you leave here as soon as is possible so that you can get yourself off home to bed. However, I have a few questions that I feel obliged to ask you before doing so."

"Very well, Inspector, if we must. Please fire away."

"Where were you on the night of Monday 6th August of this year?"

"What man, are you raving mad! How am I supposed to know that?"

"In that case what about the night of Thursday 30th August?"

A smile spread across Crawford's face and Reid immediately knew that it meant that he had the wrong man.

"Ah now let me see, yes I can answer that. I was out of the country on holiday in France for two weeks during the summer; I arrived back in London on Sunday 2nd September."

"I trust that you will be able to produce witnesses, if required?" said Reid trying his best to hide his disappointment.

"Well let me put it to you this way Inspector, on Saturday 1st September I travelled by train from Paris to the French port of Calais. This I am sure that I can prove to you as I still have the receipts for the journey. Now do you have any other dates that you would like to check with me?"

"No, in that case Mr Crawford I am very sorry to have interrupted your evening. By all means feel free to raise any complaint that you see fit for my detaining you this evening. But as I informed you earlier I was just doing my job."

"Well from what little that you know of me Inspector Reid, you should know that I am a good Christian man and I can appreciate that we are living in difficult times. So no, there won't be any complaint levelled against you on my behalf. However, I do expect you to arrange for a hansom cab to be called in order that I might return home unmolested."

"Very well, sir. I'll instruct one of the constables to walk with you until you are able to pick one up."

"That will be just fine, Inspector. In that case I bid you goodnight."

Reid asked Sergeant Jenner to arrange for a uniformed constable to escort Crawford to the Aldgate High Street and wait with him until he was able to hail a hansom to take him home to Marylebone. Much deflated, Reid then made ready to return home after a very unsatisfactory night's work.

CHAPTER TWENTYFIVE

Last of the Five

WHILST CRAWFORD WAS LANGUISHING in a cell another man had picked-up an Irish born prostitute on Commercial Street. Unknown to the woman, he already knew that she would suggest their returning to her cramped dirty room in a courtyard off Dorset Street. In fact he knew quite a bit about the lady and her habits as he had been watching her movements for a number of days and nights now. The prostitute was Mary Jane Kelly and she did not know it but the man she took back to her room that night intended to rip her body to pieces. And so it was that in the early hours of Friday 9th November, the Ripper crept out of 13 Miller's Court, the room that he had turned into a temporary Hell, leaving behind him the savagely mutilated remains of a once attractive young lady in the prime of her life. He'd cut-off her breasts, her ears and removed her liver and kidneys, placing them all about her body. He had also wanted something to remember the whore by and carefully wrapped her heart in a piece of clean cloth. Before leaving the room he was careful to turn the woman's head towards the door and placed her left arm across her body, so that her hand fell into the gaping hole that used to house her stomach and womb. The murderer had become interested over recent months in seeing what lay inside a women's skin and earlier that Friday morning he had performed his greatest feat. The killer's lust for murder sated, he entered Dorset Street and when he was sure that the coast was clear he walked-off silently over the cobbled streets and into what remained of the night.

❦ ❦ ❦

At 10.40am later the same morning, John McCarthy, the landlord of the shabby room that was 13 Miller's Court, was having a conversation with his man, Thomas Bowyer, about the 29 shillings outstanding rent owed by his tenant.

"Last night I was in the shop and noticed our Mary Jane making good on her promise to get me some of the rent she owes. I heard her singing until at least 1am, so I want you to catch her before she's up and about and off spending my money in the pub," instructed McCarthy.

"What should I so if she don't answer the door, Mr McCarthy?" asked Bowyer.

"You just keep on banging on the door, she'll open it soon enough. Now get yourself off and remember that I want nothing less than a shilling from her. I don't care what excuses she gives ya, a shilling is what I want from her."

"Yes, sir, Mr McCarthy, I'll get it for you now."

Bowyer did as he was bid and banged hard on the door of number 13. There was no response. He was sure that Mary Jane hadn't gone out as there was only one entrance to Miller's Court and nobody had seen her leave. The woman only occupied a single room, so there was no way that she wouldn't have heard him. Bowyer knocked again, this time very much harder.

"Listen, Mary Jane, I know that you're in there. Mr McCarthy says he wants some of his rent money and he knows that you've got it. So let's get this over with; open the door."

Bowyer had taken a liking to Mary Jane and didn't like to have to scare her into paying-up, but he was McCarthy's man and jobs like this one went with the territory. He walked a few paces along the outside wall, where there were two windows with rotten frames, each containing broken panes of glass. He pulled back an old coat that had been put up over the largest of the windows like a makeshift curtain and peered into the gloom. At first he thought he must be seeing things, but as his eyes adjusted to the darkness he saw the blood and the body parts that had been placed on a table that stood between the bed and the window. He looked again and could see what he assumed to be the body of Mary Jane lying on the bed, her grotesquely mutilated face staring out at the window. Bowyer went white with fright; he knew that the woman in the room was dead and must have been slaughtered at the hands of 'The Knife'.

"Come quick, Mr McCarthy, it's horrible like. The Knife, he's done Mary Jane to death!"

"What's the matter with you, Bowyer, can't you get anything right. All I want is the money that is owed me."

"No, sir, go and see. Mary Jane's been done to death!"

McCarthy was a local man made good. He was one of Whitechapel's success stories, some of the cream that existed within the slops of the heaving masses of the destitute. He knew Bowyer well, so knew that what the man said must be true, so he took a deep breath and peered through the broken window into the gloom. McCarthy, like Bowyer, had liked Mary Jane and now hoped that by some turn of fate that it wasn't her eviscerated body that he saw lying on the bed.

"Right, Thomas, calm yourself down lad. I want you to run to the Commercial Street police station and tell them what's been done. Can you do that for me, lad?"

"Yes, sir, I knows what to do."

Bowyer ran to the station as fast as his legs would carry him. McCarthy, trying to maintain his composure followed the lad at a brisk walking pace. McCarthy decided that he had been right to follow his man to the station as Bowyer had made little headway in telling Inspector Beck what had happened by the time he arrived there.

"Mr McCarthy, what's your man blubbering on about?" demanded Inspector Beck.

"That lad's telling you the truth. The Ripper, he's done another in my room in Miller's Court."

The Inspector had been expecting an easy day, what with most people being upbeat about the holiday for the parade being held in the City of London that day.

"What is it you are saying, Jack?"

"The Knife, he's done Mary Jane in my room at number 13. Come quick and bring all the men that you can spare with you."

Inspector Beck and one of his sergeants followed McCarthy and Bowyer to Miller's Court. The Inspector took a look through the window and almost vomited at the sight that met his eyes. He told his sergeant to run back to the station and get every spare man in Whitechapel round to Miller's Court. He also wanted a telegram sent straight away to all London police stations reporting the atrocity. He wanted it to read 'Another Whitechapel Murder, Urgent Assistance Required, Miller's Court, Dorset Street' and finally he wanted Dr Phillips called the scene immediately. The sergeant did as he was instructed and soon there were constables everywhere. The door to the dead woman's room was locked and McCarthy informed them that he didn't have a spare key. Dr Phillips arrived whilst the men were discussing their next move.

Beck spoke first. "Thank you for getting here so quickly doctor. I'm afraid that he's struck again, I think that this is his worst yet."

"You think that this is the work of the Whitechapel Murderer? Where is the body?"

"She's in number 13, the door is locked but I have seen the body through the window. We were just about to force the door as there is no spare key."

"May I suggest that you and your men take a moment, Inspector?"

Dr Phillips was next to take a look through the window. He had been imagining that the next murder would be worse than the last, but even he had not expected to see the nature of the wounds inflicted on the woman's body. However, being more used to the sight of dead bodies than the others around him, he kept his calm and tried to remain as professional as the circumstances allowed.

"It is plain to see that the woman is dead, there is nothing that medical science can do for her. My recommendation, Inspector Beck, is that the room remain closed and that the bloodhounds be summoned to see if they can pick-up the fiend's scent."

"That's as excellent idea, doctor. Please accept my apologies for having forgotten about the dogs. Dew, you heard the doctor, get yourself back to the station and find that fellow's address where the bloodhounds are being kept. We need them here straight away."

Sergeant Dew didn't hesitate and ran straight off back to the station.

❦❦❦

At about 11.30am Inspector Abberline arrived on the scene. Inspector Beck told him of the decision to leave the room containing the murder victim locked, pending the arrival of the bloodhounds. Abberline concurred that this was the best course of action and instructed that the whole of Dorset Street be sealed-off by the police, he didn't want anyone to enter or leave the street without his say so. At about 1.30pm Superintendent Arnold arrived in Miller's Court.

"What has happened here, Abberline?" asked the Super.

"I arrived here at 11.30am, but Inspector Beck was called to the scene at 11.00am. We fear that the Whitechapel Murderer has struck again. Over there in number thirteen a woman lies savagely mutilated on a bed.

Dr Phillips has seen the body through a window and we have all agreed to leave the room locked until the arrival of the bloodhounds."

"Do we have key for the door, Inspector?"

"No, sir."

"Well in that case I want it forced open now."

"But, sir, shouldn't we wait for the dogs?"

"No Inspector, there seems to be a problem with the use of the hounds. I have this very morning seen an order from the Yard countermanding their use. In short they are no longer available to us."

All the police officers and Dr Phillips looked shocked. None of the assembled men could believe what the Super had said. They had a relatively fresh crime scene that most likely contained only the scents of the murderer and the dead woman. For all the potential pitfalls in the dogs' abilities to follow a scent through a crowded city; all the men, the doctor included, thought that their best chance of catching the killer had just slipped from their grasp.

McCarthy found a wooden club and forced the door to the room. The doctor went in first, followed by the Super, Abberline, Beck and McCarthy. The doctor and the policemen had all seen at first hand the work of the man they called the Ripper. However, McCarthy had only read about the miscreant's evil deeds in the newspapers, now he was face-to-face with what he could only suppose to be the work of the Devil. The officials set to work and McCarthy staggered out into Dorset Street. He walked to the line of policemen blocking the road and asked to be let through.

"Where do you think you are going, sir?" asked one of the constables.

"Look, officer, I'm the landlord of the room where the woman has been slaughtered. I've just seen a sight that would freeze any man's blood. I need a drink. If someone needs to question me, can't it be done in the pub?"

"Alright, I will let you through, but you must return

right back here as soon as you finish your drink. What's your name?"

"I'm John McCarthy, sir, everyone here knows me."

"Constable, escort Mr McCarthy here into the Britannia pub there. Allow him one drink and see that he returns immediately after. Whilst you're in there I want you to note down the man's whereabouts last night and any other usual particulars."

McCarthy entered the pub and the landlady, Mrs Ringer, who knew him well, poured him a double measure of her best rum.

"Have this one on me and may God save the poor girl's soul," she said.

❦ ❦ ❦

Reid woke at about midday. He was feeling a little tense, fully expecting all sorts of repercussions relating to his entrapment of Crawford. However, he also felt that a weight had been lifted from his shoulders, now that he was almost sure that Crawford was not the maniac stalking Whitechapel. He was still concerned that the man may have been following his family in the park, but felt a lot better knowing that he wasn't a savage murderer. However, the down side in not having captured the Whitechapel Murderer was that he now most likely had a lot of explaining to do. He was already imaging Ellen Holland trawling the pubs of Whitechapel telling all of her part in the trap to catch the Knife.

Reid's wife Emily had been up early as she had a few errands to attend to. She had just returned home with the news that was spreading through Whitechapel like wildfire.

"Hello Edmund, did you sleep well?" asked Emily.

"Yes, I did my dear, I slept very well indeed. And how are you today, dearest?"

"I am very well, but I've heard some awful news. The

murderer has struck again, they say this time in Dorset Street."

"Are you sure, my dear?"

"Yes, Edmund. People say that a woman has been murdered in her own bed."

Reid hoped that his wife had made a mistake. He thought for a while, still clinging in his mind to the possibility that Crawford might be the culprit. He imagined that the man would have caught a hansom under the watchful eye of a constable at about 1.45am. Could the man really have then gotten out of the cab somewhere in Whitechapel, met another prostitute and then instead of murdering her in the street, murdered her in her room? This all sounded very implausible to him. Reid jumped out of bed and started to get dressed.

"I am sorry about this, dearest, but I will have to go to the station."

"But why Edmund, nobody has called for you. So they must have matters in hand."

"I am sorry, my dear, you are right. However, as you know, I have been drawn into this case and do not want to be pushed to the sidelines again."

"But, Edmund, is this business worth becoming unwell over? Why not leave Inspector Abberline and the others to it? As I've told you many times before, we have enough money coming-in to tide us over. I have no care whether you were to achieve another promotion."

"I am sorry, my dear, but I must go. It is not the thought of a promotion that drives me on, but of Abberline gaining more glory at my expense. I am a first class detective and I am fed up living in the man's shadow!"

"Very well then, Edmund, you go and do what you feel you must. But remember, I have no care for you to run yourself into the ground. A man should spend time with his family. Elizabeth is all grown-up now and before we know it, Harry will be as well. Children grow fast and all too soon leave the nest to set-up homes of their own. All I know is that you are spending more and more of your own time trying to capture the beast and all it seems to be doing for you is wearing you down."

"Do not worry, my dearest. I promise you that from now on I will place you and the children before my work. However, today I must go. I just want to see the scene of the murder before they take the poor unfortunate's corpse away to the mortuary."

The Inspector grabbed himself something to eat and rushed-off to Leman Street. When he arrived at the station he found it nearly empty, with only a sergeant and a constable in the building. The desk sergeant told him that most of the men were managing the crowds at the Lord Mayor's parade and all the rest had been assigned to duties in Dorset Street. Reid decided to spend a few minutes reading the telegrams relating to the latest murder before making his way to the scene of the crime.

"Tell me, sergeant, can this be true? We no longer have access to the bloodhounds?"

"Yes, sir. We only found out this morning when the call was placed to take them to Dorset Street."

"This is bad news indeed. So yet again, we will most likely have nothing on the murderer. Just to let you know, Sergeant, officially I am on the late shift tonight but consider me on duty from now on. Should anyone want me I will be at Dorset Street."

"Yes, sir."

Reid arrived in Dorset Street at about 2.pm. He was pleased to learn that the corpse still lay where it had been discovered and he made his way into Miller's Court. Abberline was the first to note his arrival.

"Afternoon, Inspector Reid. This is a terrible business, it's the worst yet. A number of men are being held in the main street for questioning. Inspector Beck and a few other detectives are interviewing them, but it would speed things up if you could assist them with this."

"Yes, sir, I'll attend to it immediately. However, before I start, can I first see the crime scene as it may prove useful to me when interviewing the suspects?"

"Yes, go ahead, but prepare yourself before entering the room. No one here has ever seen such a sight."

Reid wondered how bad things could be but even Abberline's words did not prepare him for slaughterhouse that had once been someone's home. He tried to detach himself from the emotions pulsing through his veins and hoped to find a clue, anything that he might one day be able to link to the murderer. The room contained two small tables, a chair, a cupboard and a bed. It had two small windows and a fireplace. The wall next to the bed showed signs of arterial spray and Reid guessed that the killer had cut the woman's right carotid artery so that all the blood would spurt away from the centre of the room and onto the wall. Her clothes were neatly folded over the chair and there was evidence of there having been a ferocious fire in the fireplace, as the spout of a kettle that was over the fireplace had been melted by the heat. The woman herself was almost naked, except for what remained of her chemise. Most of it had been cut away from the body, along with the flesh of her legs and abdomen, which had been placed on the table closest to the bed. The woman's breasts had been cut-off, one being placed under her head and the other under her right foot. He liver and kidneys had suffered the same fate. The woman's face had been savagely mutilated and her ears cut off. She was only recognisable by her long flowing hair and bright blue eyes that still seemed to have some life left in them. Reid tried to get a feel for the mind of the fiend who had committed these acts of depravity, but he gave-up as the thoughts that passed through his mind were too horrible for him to contemplate. He left the room, left the court and got to work with the other detectives in Dorset Street.

⸙⸙⸙

McCarthy's conversation with the constable had been overheard by many of the pub's customers, some of which were of Irish decent. One of these, having recorded the details left the Britannia and quickly made his way to another Whitechapel pub.

John Downey looked about the bar but could not see the man that he sought.

"Is Mr O'Driscoll in the house?"

"Who wants to know?"

"My name's John Downey and I need to speak to him, urgent like."

"You know better than that, John, now what it is you would like to speak with Mr O'Driscoll about?"

"It's to do with the Murders in Whitechapel, there's been another in Dorset Street and they say that this time he's murdered one of our girls."

"You stay here for a moment now and I'll see if Mr O'Driscoll will see you."

The barman ran upstairs. After a few minutes he came back downstairs.

"Mr O'Driscoll has asked me to get you a drink, John. Anything you like, it's on the house.

Downey knew well not to abuse O'Driscoll's generosity.

"That's grand, I'll have a pint of ale if that's fine with himself like?"

"That'll be fine John, now you come with me. My man here will bring the drink up to you."

"Here's the man that wishes to speak to you, Mr O'Driscoll. He's name is John -."

O'Driscoll cut the man short. "I already know his name. Come and sit yourself down, John. Long time no see. What it is you have to tell me about a murdered girl?"

Downey told Mr O'Driscoll all that he had heard McCarthy tell the constable in the Britannia. Downey could see the rage building-up in O'Driscoll's eyes.

"Thank you for all that you have told me, John. You did right by coming straight to see me. Now you get yourself down into to the bar and feel free to spend the day here. All your drinks will be on the house. Next time don't leave it so long. I can always spare a good man like you some of my time."

"I'll do that, sir. I'll be thanking you kindly for that."

O'Driscoll waited for Downey to leave the room.

"Steven, I went you to get O'Brien, Regan and the others here for a meeting at 6pm tonight. And get someone down to Dorset Street, I want to find out all that we can about the murdered girl, Mary Jane Kelly."

"Is there anything else that you want done, Mr O'Driscoll?"

"No, that will be fine for now."

⸸⸸⸸

Dr Robert Anderson, the new Assistant Commissioner of the Met arrived in Dorset Street to see the murder scene for himself. Up until now he had been conspicuous by his absence from all enquiries into the Whitechapel murders. Due to his taking a month off on sick leave, the week after starting in his new job.

"Who is in charge here?" asked Anderson.

Superintendent Arnold was the most senior officer on site, so he replied to the Assistant Commissioner.

"I am, sir."

"What do we know, man?"

"A woman, we believe to be named Mary Jane Kelly was found murdered at 13 Miller's Court at approximately 11.00am this morning. Due to some confusion over the use of bloodhounds, the door to the lady's room, which was locked, was not forced open until 1.30pm. The body is greatly mutilated, with many parts of her body cut out and placed about the room. So far, the doctor has been unable to account for the woman's heart, which the murderer may have taken away with him. A large fire was most probably maintained throughout the woman's ordeal, but the doctor has not been able to find any trace of burnt flesh in the hearth. There was no murder weapon and even though much blood was split, no footprints have been found either in the room or leading from it."

"Very good, Superintendent, is that the room?"

"Yes, sir, but please ready yourself before entering it."

Dr Anderson had never before heard any fellow officer make such a remark but once inside the room he could appreciate why Arnold had given him the warning.

"Right, Inspector Abberline, can you please leave the room for a few minutes as I have a few items to discuss with the Superintendent and the doctor."

Abberline and another of the inspectors left the room as instructed, the door was pulled to so as to give the three remaining men some privacy.

Anderson spoke first.

"Gentlemen, as far as possible, I want the details of this lady's mutilations kept secret. There must be none of the graphic descriptions made at the previous inquests. I'll personally see to it that that showman, Baxter-Phillips, has nothing to do with the inquest into this poor unfortunate's death. I truly believe the morale of the Kingdom will suffer if we allow the detail of this poor women's slaughter to get into the newspapers. Are we in agreement on this?"

The question was really directed to the doctor, as Superintendent Arnold was obliged to comply with any orders given to him by his superior officer. Dr Phillips did not like to be coerced into anything, but he found himself in full agreement with the Assistant Commissioner.

"I promise that unless forced to impart the details by a coroner, the notes that I have taken today will be restricted to only those people that you think fit to see them."

"Thank you very much for you cooperation, doctor. I would be grateful if you could do me one other favour. Are you also able to leave this room for a while as I need to speak the Superintendent in private?"

"Of course, gentlemen, but please try not to be too long." Dr Phillips then left the room as he was bid and Anderson continued his conversation with Arnold.

"What I am about to tell you is to remain in strictest confidence until an official announcement is been made. Sir Charles resigned his post yesterday afternoon, a formal statement will be made on Monday. As you will appreciate, all attention in the case will now fall upon me and Chief Inspector Swanson. My feeling is that Monroe will replace Warren, but until then, this mess is firmly in my lap."

Arnold wasn't totally sure of what the Assistant Commissioner was alluding to but he could see that the man standing before him was not relishing now being the most senior police officer responsible for catching a faceless monster. As for Anderson he was speaking as the thoughts entered his mind.

"My first action will be to make a request to increase the manpower provided to us by the other Divisions, I am sure that Matthews won't quibble over that. In the meantime I can appreciate that the existing men are beginning to buckle under the strain of the late night watches, but we must ensure that every spare man is placed on the streets over the coming weekend. All non-priority operations must be suspended until further notice. Are you clear on what needs to be done?"

"Yes, sir. However, I have one question."

"What is it?"

"What are we to do with newspaper reporters? They will be out in droves following our detectives wherever they go?"

Dr Anderson paused for a moment. Whilst recuperating from illness in Switzerland and France he had received official police reports from Sir Charles, but he had also had access to the English newspapers, so he was well aware of the stories that had been written for the masses over the last few months. Even he, in his lofty position, was aware that many reporters had been a real hindrance to the officers on the street. His personal feeling was any reporter caught interfering with the work of his officers should be locked-up until the miscreant was captured, but he knew that this was never going to happen.

"Off the record, tell the men to make life very tough for any reporter that interferes with them. Have them locked away in the cells for hours at a time whilst their credentials are checked and such like. I want it made very clear to these men that from now on they had better keep out of our way."

"But what if the likes of the Star use this as stick to beat us with?"

"Trust me on this, I want word passed onto the editors that from now on this case is to be treated as a matter of national security. I am all for the democracy and the rule of law, but a tight lid must be kept on this situation from now on."

"Very well, sir. I'll see that the right message is sent to them."

Dr Anderson left the doctor and his officers to get on with their grisly work. On his arrival back at Scotland Yard he was informed that his presence was urgently required in Downing Street. He was instructed to report directly to the Prime Minister in the presence of the Home Secretary. Word had it that the Queen had been made aware of the murder and was communicating directly with the Prime Minister about it. Anderson could already feel himself being drawn into the light and very much hoped that he didn't get his wings burned.

⸎ ⸎ ⸎

At six o'clock that evening O'Driscoll was presiding over the IRB's English Council.

"Thank you for coming at such short notice, gentlemen. However, as you know our worst fears have come true and the maniac has taken one of our own. Now what I propose to do is contact the English and inform them that we will offer them all intelligence our network is able to provide them with. What says you to that, gentlemen?"

Regan spoke first. "You already know what I think, Patrick. If I'd had my way we'd have been helping the English to hunt down the maniac months ago."

O'Brien had been the main dissenter against cooperating with the English authorities in any way and he spoke next.

"You also know my views on helping the English. My nephew was put away by that bastard Abberline, so it hurts me to think that we'd be helping him in any way. How about this fellas, I'll agree to our helping the English, if they take the Inspector off of the case?"

This was actually better than O'Driscoll expected to hear. He had called the meeting with the intention of riding roughshod over any dissenting views. However, even he thought that the English would be hard pushed not to accept their proposal.

"Alright, gentlemen, I can agree to that. What says you all?"

The proposal met with unanimous approval.

"Now I have one other proposal. The English are flooding the streets with plain clothes men from all over the England, many of them stand out like sore thumbs. What I would like to do is call in some of our men from across the water to help patrol our communities of an evening. We will let the English know what we are doing and why these men are here. In return we will give them a pledge that there will be no bombs made or planted until the maniac had been caught."

None of the other men in the room had expected to hear such a proposal and all were very sceptical.

O'Brien commented. "What's to stop the bastards from taking the opportunity to arrest our fellas? I mean if they do that, we know that they'll force confessions out of them and that could destroy everything that we've all worked for over the last few years."

"This situation is worse for them than it is for us. I'm sure that if we call a truce it won't last the winter, but I think that it's in all our interests to work together on this one. I don't want the death of another of our women on my conscience. What says you boys?"

None of the men could find the words to argue with their leader and the motion was passed. One of the lieutenants was instructed to make contact with his opposite number at the Secret Department and report back with their response. In the interim, arrangements were to be made for twenty of their best men to be transferred over from the Emerald Isle.

CHAPTER TWENTYSIX

Could You Identify Him?

REID WOKE LATE on Monday 12th November. He was exhausted, having worked himself to a standstill over the weekend. He was scheduled to meet the Super, Abberline and an Inspector Nearn at Commercial Street police station, prior to them all heading off to the inquest into Kelly's death at the Shoreditch Town Hall. Coroner Hammond and his deputy Hodgkinson had been selected to oversee proceedings. In between interviewing suspects, Reid had spent a lot of his time wondering how he could have been so wrong about Crawford, but that was all past history now and everyone was back to square one. The feeling amongst the Ripper Squad officers was that the case had entered a new level. There were rumours that Warren's head had already rolled, with an official announcement due out later that day.

❦ ❦ ❦

Whilst Reid and his superior officers were at the Inquest, Sir Henry Matthews was chairing a meeting attended by Sir Charles Warren, Dr Anderson, James Monroe and a man representing the Secret Department.

"Gentlemen, it is unfortunate that we are to lose the valued services of Sir Charles in these difficult times, but as you know it has now been agreed that Mr Monroe will be recalled to the Met and is to take over as acting Commissioner. Sir Charles is to remain in charge until 27th November. We have a number of items to discuss today, but first on the agenda is a proposal that has been received by the Secret Department from the London representatives of the IRB. This part of the meeting will be excluded from the minutes and I encourage you all to speak candidly."

The man from the Secret Department took his lead from the Home Secretary and gave them a detailed description of the requests made to the Government by the IRB. In summary, the men had two decisions to make. Firstly, whether to accept the IRB's help in trying to catch the Ripper, by accepting information supplied by the IRB's London based network of informants. However, this came with the proviso that Inspector Abberline be removed from the case. The second decision was whether the authorities would turn a blind eye to a number of IRB operatives transferring over to London from the Irish Republic, in order to work as a Whitechapel vigilance group.

Warren commented first. "I have no idea how many men the IRB have operating in London, so am unable to gauge what contribution, if any this organisation might make to our own investigations. As regards the second item, clearly this is a matter of national security. I will be unambiguous in my view on this. In no way whatsoever do I support our allowing these men to operate in our country. As such, I support neither of the proposals made to us.

The discussion went on for a while, then Monroe spoke.

"As you know, gentlemen, up until very recently I was Head of the Secret Department, so I am in a position to know the real value that the IRB can be to us. My view is that we should accept their first proposal. Inspector Abberline is a very able officer and has a wealth of local experience, but the local intelligence that the IRB can provide us with will more than make up for his removal from the investigative team. As regards their second proposal, as much as I am tempted to accept any help that we can get to remove the maniac or maniacs from our streets, I agree with Sir Charles that we cannot allow any more of their operatives into the country. Each of those men will be a skilled bomb maker with the potential to kill and injure hundreds of our citizens."

Eventually, it was agreed to accept the unofficial support of the IRB in helping to capture the killer, but they rejected any possibility of IRB operatives being allowed to transfer over to the mainland

❦ ❦ ❦

Unlike the inquests into the deaths of the other prostitutes murdered in Whitechapel and Stepney, the inquest into the death of Mary Jane Kelly was completed in a single day. Abberline and Reid had traced a number of witnesses who were called to give evidence and Coroner Hammond determined that the jury had received sufficient information on which to reach a decision. Most of the sordid details were not discussed and perhaps the greatest story, as far as the press was concerned, was that Abberline himself admitted that he was unaware of the order that countermanded the use of bloodhounds. The inquest ended with the now familiar verdict by the Foreman of the Jury of 'Wilful murder by some person or persons unknown'.

On his return to the station Abberline was surprised to be informed that another witness had come forward, saying that he could provide a description of the Ripper. Abberline was very tired but decided that he himself would interview the potential witness.

"Good evening, sir. I'm told that your name is George Hutchinson, is that correct?"

"Yes, sir."

"And are you aware that the inquest into the murder of the prostitute named Mary Jane Kelly has been determined?"

"No, sir, I'm not, but wot's that got to do with wot I wants to tell you about the lady's death?"

Abberline wasn't going to get into the semantics of the law with this man, so he thought it best to move on.

"I am Inspector Abberline, the lead detective assigned to the Whitechapel Murder Investigation. I would be grateful if you can tell me all that you know about the woman's death."

"We'll, Inspector, it goes like this. I knows, I mean I knew Mary Jane very well like. I've known her a number of years now. I know she has for a long time being keeping the company of a man named Barnett. Anyways, I've been acquainted with Mary Jane a number of times and coz she knows me like, she'd sometimes asked me for a few pennies to help tide her over. Sometimes I'd give her sixpence, but other times, especially if I'd been drinking, I might have paid her for her company."

"So you say you were well acquainted with the woman, but what has that got to do with how she met her end?"

"Well, the night she died, I saw her with a man very late like."

Abberline had being feeling very tired, but now he was wide awake and the man named Hutchinson his complete attention.

"This was on the Thursday night?"

"No, it was early in the morning, on the Friday. You see I'd just returned from my time in Romford. I met Mary Jane at about 2am and she asked if I 'ad anything I could give 'er. I told 'er that I'd done the rest of my money in Romford and had nothing for 'er. Anyways she thanks me and then heads toward Thrawl Street where this fella, who must have been some rich slummer -."

"How did you know that the man was rich?" interrupted Abberline.

"From his dress like. All 'is clothes were of the finest type. Then there was this thick gold chain he was wearing. He was a rich man alright, like no local man I've seen, that's how I knew he was a slummer."

"Very well, what happened next?"

"The man says something to Mary Jane and she laughs at what he tells 'er and then they walks right past me going toward Dorset Street, where she was living."

"You say that they walked right past you, so you saw the man up close?"

"That I did, sir. I'd say he was about 5 feet 6 inches in height, about 35 years of age and he was a Jewish fella, with a pale face. As he comes past me he dips his head down but I lent down to catch a look at him. Then I sees his eyes, they were dark, he had a moustache, a thin one, turned-up at the corners."

"What else was he wearing?"

"He had a long coat on, a dark one. It was undone and I sees a dark jacket under it. He had a tie on with a pin in it, in the shape of a horse's hoof. He had a very gentlemanly look, all official like. He was like one of them gents you see at places like the Lord Mayor's Show."

"You seem very sure of all this. Tell me, why has it taken you four days to come forward?"

"Well for the first few days I didn't know it was Mary Jane that had been done. I've come here today coz I now knows that it woz her that's been taken."

"Very well. Now you say that they passed by you heading toward Dorset Street. Did you see them enter the street?"

"I did more than that, sir. I was so surprised by the look of the man, I wanted to see if he'd really go with the likes of Mary Jane, so I followed them into Dorset Street. Then I watched as they stopped outside the court for what must have been a couple of minutes. Anyways, I heard her say 'alright my dear, come along, you will be comfortable'. He then gives Mary Jane a kiss and puts his arm on her shoulder. She said something about losing her handkerchief and he pulls one out of his pocket and gave it to her. It was a red one. Then I follows them as they goes down the court into her room. I waited a while, I'm not sure why, I was just curious like. Then I went on me way."

"One last question, Mr Hutchinson. If you saw this man again, could you identify him?"

"Like I said, sir, I got myself a good look at the man. He had a look that ain't easy forgotten."

There was something about this man that Abberline trusted in. If Hutchinson did see a man at about 2am in the morning, Abberline thought that it must have been very close to the woman's death. What Hutchinson said also tallied with a statement made by one of the witnesses at the inquest; a Sarah Lewis. She had said that at about 2.30am she was standing at the end of Miller's Court and saw a man opposite the court standing alone by the lodging house. She said that the man was looking up the court as if waiting for someone to come out. Her statement now made sense to Abberline, if Hutchinson was the lone man she saw looking into the court. Abberline had to also assume that it was possible that the new witness might be the murderer, but for now he thought it best for Hutchinson to be escorted around Whitechapel in the hope that he might be able to point out the man that he said he saw. Abberline then prepared a report, including the detail of Hutchinson's statement marked 'Urgent', for the attention of CI Swanson and Superintendent Arnold.

CHAPTER TWENTYSEVEN

A Toast to A-Division

ON TUESDAY 13TH NOVEMBER Abberline woke early. He sensed some new hope that he might finally have stumbled on the real description of the murderer, a distinctive description to boot. He knew that there was still much work to do, but if the killer was really a member of the higher classes it was likely that more of the locals were likely to recollect the man's movements in the early hours of that Friday morning. He himself had a number of suspects to interview and had an end of day progress meeting scheduled with his boss CI Swanson and Commissioner Warren. He couldn't understand why he was to make a report directly to the Commissioner, especially as the man had resigned and so was soon to give up his responsibility for the case. He hoped that Sir Charles might want to thank him personally for his work to date, but whatever the reason, it was going to ruin his day as he had many other more important tasks to attend to. Inspector Abberline just hoped that he would remember to go to the Yard at the appointed time.

❦❦❦

Reid also woke early that day. He'd set about the case with renewed enthusiasm, now that the sideshow that was Crawford could be forgotten. He had promised Emily that he would try his best to work his core hours and would give-up using his free time patrolling the streets in the vain hope of trying to catch the killer red handed. He decided that the best way for him stick to his core time would be to apply himself to his maximum ability from the moment he arrived at the station. Reid reasoned that if he worked himself like a dog during his fixed hours he'd be too tired to get himself drawn into any more hair-brained schemes. He'd also decided that it was high time that he made some progress in apprehending Harris Marks and the counterfeiters.

☙☙☙

As Reid arrived at Leman Street for another day at the office, a meeting was already in full swing in room above a Whitechapel public house. O'Driscoll, Regan, O'Brien and a few other members of the IRB's English Council were already discussing action to be taken following the reply from the Secret Department. As was usual, O'Driscoll led the discussion.

"Gentleman, as we might have expected, the English haven't agreed to allow any of our members currently based back home in Ireland to enter the country. However, if we confirm that we agree to pass-on any intelligence relating to the possible identity of the murderer, Abberline will be gone before the week is out. So what are we to do, lads?"

As usual Regan was the potential block on any cooperation with the English. "Look, fellas, I've no reason to get in the way of catching the maniac. My condition was that we do nothing that helps the career of that bastard Abberline. So this is all fine with me."

Redmond, who hadn't spoken in any of the previous meetings, spoke up next. "Now, fellas, I'm all for us helping to catch this maniac, but I want to know something. Are we to allow our people to snitch on any of us?"

"What do you mean by this?" asked O'Driscoll.

"Well, what happens if one of our people informs the police that they think one of the men in this room or one of our boys out in the field is the killer? Can we to allow something like that to happen? I mean if we allow them to provide our details to the police for that, what else might they be willing to report on?"

O'Driscoll responded to that. "I can see your point, Cahan, but to my mind no man in our organisation can be above suspicion whilst the lunatic is on the loose in the City. As for the English, if they take liberties with any of us, then we will go about finding the man without them. What say you gentlemen, are we in agreement on this?"

And so it was agreed that they would put the word out in the Irish communities of the east end of London that details of all suspicious men, no matter who they might be, should be reported to the police. It was also agreed that a few up and coming men from the Emerald Isle should be brought over to London to form an active service unit with a single objective, that of trying to catch the murderer, regardless of the English's refusal to allow it. A messenger was then swiftly dispatched to the IRB's Secret Department contact with their response.

❦❦❦

At 4pm CI Swanson arrived for a meeting with his outgoing Commissioner, Sir Charles Warren.

"You wanted to see me, sir?" asked Swanson.

"Please sit yourself down, Donald."

Swanson sat in front of the Commissioner's desk. He was expecting his boss to give him some details of how the department was to run during the transition period, with his leaving and Monroe's taking over the helm. What he was about to hear was to leave him with a sour taste in his mouth.

The Commissioner continued. "I am sure that what I'm about to tell you will not make very much sense to you, but believe me, I am in full agreement that it must be done."

Swanson could feel his stomach tighten, as he had a

feeling that he was about to be told that he was either to be transferred off the Ripper Case or worse, given some form of reprimand. It made sense to him that Sir Charles carry the can for the Met's failure to capture the Ripper; but now he thought a decision had been made to wield the axe in his direction. He sat and waited to hear his fate.

"Now this is no reflection upon you or anyone else in the team, but I am afraid that Abberline has to go."

Swanson looked at his Commissioner and wondered if he had misheard what he had said.

"What, sir, what has the man done to warrant this?"

"I can't go into the detail, but trust me that the decision has absolutely nothing to do with the man's ability or performance of his duties. I myself am well aware that a more competent and committed man does not exist in our ranks. However, for operational reasons he must go. Arrangements are to be made for him to hand over to one of the other Detective Inspectors by the end of this week; I'll leave it to you to choose his replacement. It has been decided that Abberline will be of greatest use to us working back at the Yard."

"And you are in full agreement with this, sir?" Swanson asked the Commissioner.

"Yes, I am Donald. As I have alluded to, the man has done absolutely nothing wrong. There are reasons, other than his competency, as to why he needs to be removed from the investigation. I would like you to make him aware of the decision this evening."

"So I take it, sir, that Frederick is not required to brief you at 6pm?"

"No, Donald, I just wanted to ensure that he is here at six for the meeting with you."

Swanson reflected for a moment on what the Commissioner had told him. He wondered if Monroe was party to Abberline's reassignment.

"I appreciate that it is not my place to ask, sir, but is Mr

Monroe aware of the decision?"

Sir Charles' gave his CI a wry smile.

"Look Donald, this has nothing to do with my going, Abberline had done nothing to warrant my displeasure. Mr Monroe and I jointly made the decision based upon operational issues in the field. All that I am allowed to say is that the detail is classified, and that's all there is to it."

❦❦❦

At 5.50pm Abberline arrived at the Yard for the meeting he had been told was to be held with Swanson and the outgoing Commissioner Warren. As the church bells chimed six he made his way into the CI's office. He immediately noticed the absence of the Commissioner, a decanter containing what looked like whiskey and two glasses.

"Come in, Fred, take a seat," beckoned Swanson.

"Good evening to you, sir, no sign of the Commissioner?"

"Would you like to join me in a drink, Fred?"

Abberline knew then that the Commissioner wasn't coming. There being no possibility of the CI taking a drink whilst on duty.

"I've finished my duties for the day, sir, so I don't mind if I do," replied Abberline.

Swanson poured himself and his Inspector a drink.

"No Fred, the Commissioner's not coming. I met with him earlier this afternoon and he asked that I give you his thanks for the excellent job you have made in coordinating the Whitechapel murder investigation. However, during the course of our conversation he mentioned that your endeavours have reminded the top brass why you were transferred to the A-Division last year and how they could do with you working back there… So Fred, I don't want you to take this the wrong way but as from next Monday you will be returning to your duties back at the Yard."

Abberline bowed his head and took a few sips of whiskey. He looked about the room before looking the CI in the eye.

"I don't understand, sir. Does Monroe not want me on the case anymore? No disrespect, but who else knows this part of London better than I?"

"Look, Fred, it's like I said. Absolutely nobody has criticised your handling of the case. As I understand it, somehow your involvement in the investigation has complicated the relationship with the local communities. How, I don't know, but there appears to a problem that the top brass thinks is undermining the benefits that you have brought to the case."

Abberline was nobody's fool. He himself had heard the rumours that the Irish community were thought to be withholding evidence relating to the case. He didn't know how things worked in the Secret Department, but thought it possible that with the death of Mary Kelly arrangements might be have been agreed that bypassed an organisation like the police.

"Very well, sir, if that's what's been decided, I'm not in any position to protest. However, I'd like to say off the record, that I think this is a mistake."

Abberline paused, finished his drink and again looked his CI in the eye.

"Tell me, sir, whom is to be my replacement?"

"To tell the truth Fred, I haven't had time to give the matter much thought, but I will most probably choose Detective Inspector Moore."

"Not Reid?" asked Abberline.

Swanson allowed himself a smile.

"No, Fred, Reid comes with his own baggage and the top brass would never agree to his taking your place."

The CI then refreshed the two men's glasses.

Swanson continued, "In many ways I envy you, Fred.

I'd much rather this case went away, so that I can get back on with my life and some regular police work. How about a toast?"

"Why not, sir?"

"To A-Division."

"To A-Division, sir," repeated Abberline.

The two men downed their drinks and laughed.

"Alright, Fred. I'd be grateful if you can be ready to start handing over your work to the new man, whomever he might be, at say 10am tomorrow morning."

"That's fine, sir, I'll be ready by then."

"Goodnight to you, Fred."

"Goodnight, sir."

Abberline rose from his seat, gave his CI a wink and made one last comment as he went out of the door.

"Good luck to you, sir. I don't care if you catch him with or without me, but make sure that you get him."

With that Abberline took a slow walk home, his only consolation being that the Bank Clerk, Reid, had not been chosen to replace him.

ǂ ǂ ǂ

Later that night Patrick O'Driscoll received some unusual information. His most trusted lieutenant, Michael Hodges had been informed that an English prostitute was drunk out of her mind and mouthing off to all that would listen to her or more accurately to all that would buy her a drink, that she had been used as bait to try and catch 'The Knife' in a special police operation.

"Where is this woman, Michael?"

"She's in the Prince Albert pub."

"Can you bring her here to me, as I'd like a word with her?"

"I wouldn't do that, boss. The woman is drunk out of her brains and might kick-off if we try force her out of the bar. I left a couple of fellas to keep an eye on her, so we won't lose sight of her."

"Very well then, I'll go pay this woman a visit."

When they reached the Prince Albert, Hodges had a quick word with the landlord, asking whether the man would be able to do Mr O'Driscoll a kindness in allowing him the use of a private room. William Baxter was an Englishman through and through and certainly no friend to the Irish, but like most people in the pub trade he knew something of Mr O'Driscoll and the consequences of not granting him a favour. Hodges then got chatting to the drunken prostitute and offered to give her a drop of the landlord's finest brandy if she would care to take a drink with him in a private room. Before she knew it, Ellen Holland found herself drunk and in a room with the head of the English division of the IRB. She didn't know who the man was that was asking her the questions, but even in her drunken stupor she could tell that he was not a man to be trifled with.

"Now, my dear, I hear that you have a tale to tell concerning the capture of the maniac that's loose on our streets?" started O'Driscoll.

"Well, sir, I'm not s'posed to say anything about it."

"From what I hear my dear, you've been speaking to a fair few number of people this evening and I'd be grateful if you'd grant me the favour of repeating what it is you've been telling them?"

Holland could sense that by speaking to this man, it was going to cause trouble for Inspector Reid. She had wanted to avenge the murder of her friend Mary Ann Nichols and had taken a great risk with her own life in trying to capture the man that the Inspector thought responsible for killing her. Now she was going to cause trouble for the big-hearted policeman that had tried to capture the monster.

"Take a sip of the brandy, it's a fine drink. There's a

good woman, now tell me what it is you were telling your friends earlier tonight," repeated O'Driscoll.

"Well, sir, it's a long story like, but I 'elped this policeman in luring a man into Cox's Square."

"What's the name of the man that you were trying to capture?"

"I don't know, sir. All I knows is that he was a preacher type and had a big ginger moustache. But it turns out that 'e wasn't the Knife."

"How would you know that, my dear?"

"I woz wearing all this armour, like one of them knights of old, in case the man tried to cut me, but all he woz up for was a connection like."

"And the policeman that you say set-up this trap, what would his name be?"

Holland hesitated. She was tempted to make-up a name but thought that the men before her, might harm her if they found out that she'd lied to them.

"Well the man's name is Reid, Inspector Reid. I think that he works out of the Leman Street nick."

"Now there's a good woman. And I believe that you said that all that you did was very secret?"

"Yes, sir, it was, but I've let the Inspector down. He's a very good man, big-hearted and I can tell that he tries to do well by the women of the unfortunate class, like myself. I wouldn't want the man ta get into any trouble coz of me."

"Don't you be worrying yourself about anything, my dear. Go back the bar now and enjoy the rest of your night, the landlord will see to it that you are alright. Now here's something for your trouble. You'd be doing me a service if you could spend it on some food." O'Driscoll gave Holland a shilling. "As for your lodgings, where is it that you live?

"I live mostly at 18 Thrawl Street, sir."

"Well for being so kind, I'll pay for your lodgings for the rest of this week. Now like I said, please be a good woman and use that money for food. However, I have one last favour to ask of you before you leave, my dear. I'd be most grateful if you can keep all this very secret from now on. We wouldn't want your Inspector friend getting into any sort of trouble, would we?"

"Thank ya most kindly, sir. I'll be sure to keep my mouth shut tight from now on like, no matter how much I 'ave to drink."

With that Holland returned to the bar. O'Driscoll was already working through thc possibilities of what he could do with the Police Inspector, named Reid.

"Michael, if what the woman says is true, we might be able to use it to turn this Inspector over to our side. Tomorrow I want you to find out all that you can about this Inspector Reid. Especially if he's a family man, it will be better for us if he's got something to lose."

"I'll do that for ya, boss. Do you want a special eye kept on the woman?"

"No, that won't be necessary, she'll be easy enough to find if we need her. However, you can get her lodgings paid-up for the rest of this week, she's staying at 18 Thrawl Street."

CHAPTER TWENTYEIGHT

End Game

WHEN REID ARRIVED AT THE STATION on Wednesday 14th November he was informed by the Desk Sergeant that his presence was required in the briefing room at 11am as CI Swanson was coming to the station to make an announcement. Reid decided to get stuck into the items in his in-tray and finish off some outstanding reports.

Swanson arrived at 10.45am with Abberline in tow. Reid assumed that they had come to inform the men of some new initiative relating to the capture of the killer. By 11.15am, both men had left the station, leaving the men in the Whitechapel Murder Unit to ponder what they had been told. Reid couldn't believe his ears, the Bank Manager was off the case. He was pleased to hear that for once in his life, his nemesis Abberline had finally failed to get his man. However, he also felt sorry for the man, having watched how Abberline had put body and soul into trying to catch the murderer. He had seen how the man had put the job before his wife and family life, and now at the drop of a hat he was gone. Reid wasn't surprised or bitter on hearing that he had not been chosen to act as the lead detective in Abberline's place. He knew that Monroe was to be the new acting Commissioner and it was Monroe that had reprimanded him back in 1887. Reid decided to treat the episode as one of life's lessons. There he was, willing to risk his livelihood in an effort try and capture the maniac that stalked the streets of London. Yet the men at the top had demonstrated that a man's efforts counted for nothing as his seniors jostled for position in order to please their new boss.

Reid returned home for his lunch and informed Emily

what has happened. He decided to take a walk around the neighbourhood before returning back to the station. As he walked along Commercial Street he saw a familiar face in the crowd, it was Levi Greenfield.

"Good afternoon, Mr Greenfield, how is life treating you?"

"Good afternoon, Inspector. Life is treating me very well. I'm having good week, despite the best efforts of you coppers trying to stop me from earning a living."

Reid thought for a while and pondered again on how Greenfield was actually earning his living. Whatever it was, it was most likely illegal and seemed to give the man quite a bit of free time.

"Well hopefully our paths will not cross in a professional capacity."

"I'll do my best to ensure that they won't, sir. It is a very bad business with the latest woman to be murdered. I'm guessing that the man I put you in contact with was of no use to you?"

"I thank you again for your help, but alas, no he was not the killer. Our problem is that the man we seek appears to have no motive and leaves nothing at the scenes of the crimes. He could be just about anybody. For instance you yourself might well have supped a pint of ale with the miscreant only last week".

Greenfield looked a little alarmed by what Inspector had said. Reid put this down to the man taking his words literally, his being a policeman and all.

"What do you mean by that, Inspector?" asked Greenfield.

"Only that I saw you drinking in the Britannia pub sometime last week. By all accounts the dead woman Kelly was a regular there and it would not surprise me if the killer had not visited the place at some time or other."

"I take a drink at many a pub but I can't remember ever drinking in the Ringers," replied Greenfield.

Reid paused again, Greenfield did not ever remember drinking in a pub that he knew by its nickname, the pub having received its nickname from the surname of its owners. Reid supposed that Greenfield, a local criminal, was just being evasive out of habit. After all it wouldn't pay him to be too open and honest with a policeman.

"I know what you mean. I frequent many pubs myself, mostly in a professional capacity of course! In that case I saw a man that looks very much like you."

"How many has he done now, Inspector?"

"Including Mary Kelly, we believe it to be five."

"I suppose that you're not including the Tabram woman who was stabbed in George Yard Buildings?"

This time Greenfield had said something that the Inspector found to be very suspicious. Even though Martha Tabram had been stabbed a total of 39 times, most of the lower orders in Whitechapel assumed that she had had her throat cut like all the other murder victims. Reid thought it highly suspicious that Greenfield should know the method of her murder and why it might lead the police to not attribute it to the Ripper.

"That's very perceptive of you, Mr Greenfield. I wish that some of the men in my unit were as well acquainted with the murders as you appear to be."

"Oh, I only really know a bit about that particular murder as I live in George Yard. Very close to the block where that unfortunate woman met her end."

Reid did not possess a poker face and a slight look of relief flashed across it as Greenfield explained how it was that he knew so much about the Tabram murder. However, to those skilled in the arts of body language it was perceptible that he was still a little concerned about what he had heard.

"Ah, I see. I was just beginning to wonder how you would know a detail like that. Anyhow, if you don't mind I'll be on my way. I'm on the lookout for the man involved in the distribution of the counterfeit money, a Mr Marks, and am on my way to the White Hart. I'm going to pass by there on route to the station."

"Very well, Inspector, until we meet again..." Greenfield paused and then looked as if he had just remembered something, "Inspector, sorry to trouble you, but just one more thing."

"What is it, Mr Greenfield?"

"Last week, my previous employer, Mr Engels made contact with me from his prison cell. He wanted me to pick up some of his personal effects. Anyway amongst the belongings at his home in Finch Street was a notebook. My reading isn't up to much but I think that it contains the details of many of Mr Engels's clients, a number of which might be those that have what you might call peculiar tastes. If you are interested I could drop the book into the station for you?"

"Well, I have to admit that my seniors are content for no further action to be taken in the matter, now that Mr Engels has been taken off the streets, but I suppose that it wouldn't hurt to have the book."

"Actually Inspector, I could get it for you right now if you don't mind coming back to my 'umble abode?"

Reid had just that minute made his mind up that Greenfield warranted further investigation in relation to the Whitechapel murders. So he decided that seeing where the fellow lived might provide him with some useful background information.

"Very well, Mr Marks can wait another day. Lead the way, man."

"There's just one other thing, sir. Would it be alright if you followed me, say ten or twenty paces back? No disrespect meant but it won't do my reputation much good to be seen walking along my local streets on friendly terms with a plain clothed policeman."

"Very well, I understand your position. You lead the

way and I will follow, I'll be sure to maintain a discreet distance between us. Trust me on this, following a man at a distance is something that I am most skilled in."

Greenfield led the way and picked what Reid thought must have been the longest route possible to George Yard. As the Inspector followed the man to his home he finally realised what had been troubling him about the way Greenfield walked. Reid's shoes, like most other men's, were hard soled and clanked hard against the cobblestones. Many of the impacts were muffled by horse manure and the other rubbish that filled most roads but every now and again one of Reid's shoes would come into contact with a bare stone and the two hard surfaces were generate a loud clunk. This wasn't the case with Greenfield's boots. They were almost soundless. Reid took a closer look at them and noticed that the man's boots were covered in a skin of rubber. They looked to be covered by the same sort of rubber material that had only recently been issued to the night beat officers and plain clothes men, in order that they could patrol the streets silently during the night watch.

Finally the two men reached George Yard. Reid remembered George Yard Buildings well, as that was the block in which Martha Tabram had met her death. Greenfield entered a small yard and stopped outside the front door of a building whilst he reached for his key.

"Do you want to come in, Inspector, or are you happy to wait in the yard?" asked Greenfield.

"I'll come in, if that's alright with you."

The two men walked through the door, directly into the front room of Greenfield's small ground floor dwelling. It was sparsely furnished with a large table and a few chairs. Reid did not own a pet, but a strong smell of dogs met his nostrils as he entered the room.

"I'll just fetch the book, if you'll wait here for a moment" said Greenfield.

"Yes, that's fine," replied the Inspector.

Reid had left the front door ajar, primarily to let more light into the room but also just in case he needed to make a quick exit. He was now becoming deeply suspicious of Greenfield and thought that he might have made a mistake in entering the man's home alone. He knew that he was no match for the man physically, but curiosity had gotten the better of him and he was interested in seeing inside the man's home. Even so, he thought it prudent to make ready with his truncheon and police whistle. But then before Reid could make another move two fighting dogs stormed into the room. It was all a bit surreal, the animals didn't bark but stood in front of Reid baring their teeth, giving every indication that they would pounce on him if he made the slightest movement. Then Greenfield followed his dogs into the room.

"You are wise not to have moved, Inspector. I've trained the dogs to tear a man to shreds and I can assure you that they will rip you to pieces if you make any sudden movement or even try to shout or scream."

"Now what's this all about, Levi, I have no beef with you! My interest is purely in your former employer, Mr Engels."

"Unfortunately, I only wish that was true. Like you said, that case is closed, but you are actively involved in another."

Reid tried to play the innocent and stall for time whilst he assessed the situation that faced him.

"What! My current case involves fraud and a man named Harris Marks. What has any of that got to do with you?"

"I think that we both know that that case has nothing to do with me but another case just might. Now try to keep very still, Inspector, I wouldn't want to dogs to harm you."

Greenfield approached Reid slowly, he opened Reid's coat and removed the truncheon and the police whistle. He then patted Reid's clothes down in search of other weapons. Once he was sure that his man was unarmed, Greenfield struck Reid across the head with the truncheon. Reid fell to the floor and lay where he fell, barely conscious. He was powerless to do anything as Greenfield hauled him across the floor, through what appeared to be a kitchen and into a back room. The room was bare except for two more chairs and a couple of tables. Reid could make out what looked like pieces of rope on one of the tables. Greenfield hauled him onto one of the chairs and within a few minutes he found himself tied to the chair facing Greenfield and his dogs. Greenfield threw some cold water into the Inspector's face and Reid finally regained his senses. Reid tried to speak but then became aware of the gag that had been placed into his mouth. Greenfield then pulled-up the other chair and sat facing him.

"I've enjoyed our little encounters, Inspector. It is a great pity that things should end this way."

Reid struggled in the chair but was helpless. He couldn't move or speak and assumed that, barring a miracle, in a few minutes time he would be dead. He thought about Emily and his two children and how he would never see them again and they most probably would never find out how or why he'd left them.

Greenfield continued. "You know that it was me that you saw in the Ringer's last week, don't you Inspector?"

Reid reluctantly nodded his head.

"And my slip about the whore Tabram connected a few more dots, did it not?"

Reid nodded again. He tried to speak but the gag was too tight.

"You also know that I mean to kill you. However, before I do that I'll tell you a story. A story I've wanted to tell someone, anyone, for a long time now."

Greenfield spent a few seconds collecting his thoughts as his mind scanned through the evil deeds that he had committed.

Then he continued with his confession "I don't know where to start, but I'll start with my life in Poland. Before my family came to this country my father was a farmer. We used to eat mostly vegetables, but every few months my father would kill a pig or a cow. I am of the Jewish faith and we believe that the blood of all living beings, including people, belongs to God. Anyway, even though I was only a small boy I would follow my father and hide, watching as he slaughtered the animals that we would eat for our suppers. He would always take the animals into a yard, tie them to a wall and then slash their throats. I'd watch as the blood spurted from the side of the animals' necks across the yard. I don't know why, but I liked what I saw. Anyway, one day life changed and we left Poland to start a new life in England. My father had to give up farming, a life that he loved and he and my mother spent many hours away from our home trying to find work in this wretched city. I spent many hours alone in our home and to pass the time I would search our rooms for rats and mice that I might kill. I took pleasure from tying them up and cutting their throats and making patterns with the blood that sprayed from their little necks. I also liked to cut them open to see what made them work. One day when I was older and I became interested in woman, I became friendly with say what we might call a woman of the night. Even though our family was very poor, I had a few pence hidden away and this woman led me along the path into manhood. Anyway, one night I encountered my father with the same woman. It was then that I saw the evil that the whores did and knew that one day I must avenge my mother for their acts against her and all the other mothers of the world. Then one day, the cholera came and took both my mother and father away from me. You see, I am not a bad man Inspector."

As Reid listened to Greenfield's story he could not help but imagine himself to be like one of rats that the man had tortured and killed in his youth, and wondered what horrible games that the man might play with him before he too was slaughtered like an animal. He tried to move his arms, but they were tied tight to the chair, that also caught the attention of the dogs and they both jumped up at him.

"Lie still, boys!" commanded Greenfield and the dogs both lay on the floor. Greenfield then led the dogs into another room and closed the door, locking them inside. He returned and sat back down on the chair facing the Inspector and continued with his story.

"Anyway, time went by and I made a living for myself as best I could. Then one day I started work for Mr Engels and without his knowledge I would steal some of the photographs that he had me deliver to his clients. At first my plan was to sell them, but I grew fascinated by them. In fact I have a number of them on the table over there."

Reid looked over at the table and could see what looked like ten or eleven photographs, a large sharp knife and large jar filled with pale liquid.

Greenfield continued "I found myself drawn to images of the women and got my pleasure from them. Then over time I started to take my pleasure from the local whores. Then one day the idea came to me that I should rid this world of such evil and that I should wipe these women from the face of the earth. Still, committing murder is not an easy thing to do, even for a man like me. As I said, I'm no monster. You remember me telling you that I had to deliver the man's photographs to Regent's park?"

Reid nodded that he remembered.

"Good. Well I was not lying when I told you about that. One day whilst hiding in the bushes waiting for him to collect his parcel I spied a well-dressed women being set-upon by two robbers. I forgot all about the parcel and went to the woman's aid. I fended off the men, who made a hasty retreat. Anyway, the lady, Lucy was her name, was badly shaken and asked me to walk her home. The lady was in no way evil, but instead was very obviously vulnerable. On the way she told me a story about how her nephew had robbed jewels from her home. I don't know why but I got the feeling that I might easily murder the lady and the finger of suspicion would point to this nephew of hers. Once inside the house, I took a hammer and caved the lady's head in, but it's the cutting open of a neck that has always fascinated me and before she was dead I found a large knife and cut her throat from the left and then the right, right down to the bone. Being my first murder, I panicked and ransacked the house to try and make the woman's death look like part of a robbery. There was much blood and I left a great many footprints. Anyway, I got clean away, even though I made the mistake to selling some of her jewellery at a pawn brokers. Looking back, I was very amateur in all that I did. I can only thank the Lord for keeping me safe.

Read gave Greenfield a wry smile. His gut feeling told him that the lady Lucy Clark had been murdered by the same hand as the others and now he had his proof. This helped to take his mind off the fate that he knew soon awaited him.

"You surprise me, Inspector. You find my tale of murder amusing? I thought that you might instead have reacted in horror. However, I'll continue on. My next murder was that of the whore Tabram. She was the first that I deliberately set out to kill. Of course it was only chance that brought that particular woman to me, I let God guide my hand on which one deserves to die at the end of the knife. Anyway, as you know the whore's murder did not go as planned. She was a very aggressive woman and wouldn't let me take her to a spot that I had planned to kill her in. In my frustration I ended up stabbing the woman in the heart to shut her noise. After that I couldn't give over her blood to God, as cutting her throat would have produced very little blood. So I stabbed away at her until my fury subsided. After that, I made sure that I killed all the others in locations that I had chosen to sacrifice them in. And so it was that I made my first proper offering to God. I did the woman Nichols in an open street, but had chosen the spot beforehand. I picked somewhere that I thought a woman would feel safe in but was private enough for me to complete my offering to the Lord. However, working in the open road was risky and I didn't feel comfortable in my work."

Greenfield got up, walked over to the table and picked up the knife.

"This knife belonged to my father. It has been used to kill many animals and one day I hope will have helped to remove an equal number of the lowest form of women from this world. There is much work to do in this great city, but after today I think the time may have come for me to travel to pastures new."

Reid was afraid but also resigned to his fate. He had a feeling that the maniac was intent on telling him his whole sordid tale of mass murder, but was not sure if Greenfield also intended to torture him before he met his end. He could not help but to stare at the knife.

"Yes, Inspector, this knife will soon cut your soul from your body as well. But not quite yet as I have more that I want to tell you. After Nichols, I determined to take a look inside the women that I killed, much like the animals of my youth. And even took some of their body parts away with me. But for this I needed privacy to get my work done. So I decided to study the habits of the foul creatures before I took their souls from them. I saw that the woman Chapman made a habit of using a yard in Hanbury Street for her vile trade. The yard was much to my liking, being very private. However, it was difficult to work in, you wouldn't believe the number of people that frequented the place at all hours of the day and night. In the end I fed the parts that I took from that one to the dogs."

Greenfield paused for a while, his eyes sparkled, as he seemed to be reliving the murder over in his mind.

"Being so close to the market I was seen with the whore by a passing woman. I hoped that she wouldn't remember me, but she knew enough to let you and yours know that the man you sought might be a Jew. When I saw the woman, Stride, plying her trade out of the yard next to the Jewish club I hatched a plan of double bluff. I composed a message that I meant to write in chalk on the wall over her body, but before I could get to work on her, I was disturbed by a man with a pony and trap. I was going to return home that night but took a walk outside the police lines where I didn't think anyone would be looking for me. Then I found Mitre Square and thought it an ideal place to complete my work. I found the whore, Eddowes, in Houndsditch and she didn't take much persuading to get her to where I meant to kill her. Again I was seen, this time by three men who passed us in a passageway, one of them took more notice of me than I would have liked, but it was dark and I was sure that none of them got a good look at my face. I worked quickly and by now was becoming well acquainted with woman's parts, so decided to test my abilities and was pleased to have been able to locate her kidney. That one didn't seem such an evil one to me, she had a very friendly nature and I felt bad at having taken her. I felt far better after I cut her face up; she looked much more deserving of the butchering that I'd given her after that."

Greenfield's face now broke into a smile. Reid could see the pride in the man's eyes as he recollected how he came up with the idea of cutting away some of Eddowes' bloodstained skirts and taking the piece back into Whitechapel to act as a marker for his 'Juwes' message that he wrote in a stairwell of the block in Goulston Street. His plan with the message had been to make it look like someone was trying to frame the Jews for the killings, so implying that the murderer was not in fact a Jew himself.

Greenfield went on to tell Reid that he hadn't written the notorious Jack the Ripper letter, but had actually sent George Lusk half of Catherine Eddowes' kidney in the post. Greenfield had become interested in his pursuers, and had taken to following Abberline, Lusk and Reid around Whitechapel.

Then Greenfield got onto his latest and most gruesome murder.

"Finally, Inspector, we get to my latest offering, the Kelly woman. You were right, you did see me in the Ringers last week. The woman was a regular there. She had something about her that the others did not have, it was more like an arrogance she most likely got from being younger than most of the others of her kind. I followed her back into the courtyard on a few occasions to get a feel for the place. It was busy, but everyone seemed to mind their own business. I felt sure that if the woman didn't scream, too loudly, I'd be able to get my work done unmolested."

Greenfield smiled again at Reid.

"I must take this opportunity to thank you, Inspector, for giving me the tip about the night before the Lord Mayor's Show. I didn't risk going to work in the whole of October because there were too many rozzers on the streets for my liking. Things looked like they'd be easier for me when the rumours started which said that I'd moved onto Newcastle, but I still didn't want to take the risk. It was exactly as you said it would be, I hardly saw a policeman on Thursday night. The woman, Kelly, had a very busy night and I thought I might be wasting my time with her. Then at about 2am she found herself a very well to do looking gentleman, one of them slummers no doubt. He was a strange one. I watched as she took the man to her lodging. She did not know it but they were closely followed by another man who I thought meant to rob the gentleman on completion of his business. Anyhow, this other man gave up waiting in Dorset Street and moved-on before the slummer finally left the whore's company at about 3am. I was determined to make my move, but wasn't sure whether the whore would venture back out onto the streets. But I was in luck as a few minutes later she too left the court. It was then that I pounced. I made acquaintance with her in Dorset Street and soon had her back in her room. I had to play a little game with her and we were both fully undressed before I was able to get the better of her."

Greenfield then walked over to one of the tables and picked up the knife again. He studied it for a few seconds.

"Now, Inspector, I admit to doing horrible things to that whore and the others, but I want you know that none of them except Tabram knew much about what was to become of them. You see I strangled them all first so as to keep them quiet and got to work on them whilst they lay asleep. It was only Tabram that I stabbed whilst she still possessed her senses, as she had annoyed me with her aggressive conduct."

Greenfield paused again.

"As for you, Inspector, I am not keen to take you, but you have given me no choice in the matter. But in a way, just like the whores, you had this coming to you. I've been following you and know that you are a family man with a wife, a fine looking daughter and a young son."

Reid suddenly forgot all about the helplessness of his situation. Lately his instincts had let him down, but they were screaming at him now, telling him that Greenfield had it in mind to harm his family. He did not know how he would do it, but somehow his must stop him.

"If you continue to struggle Inspector I will bring the dogs back into the room and trust me the fate I have in mind for you is far more humane than the one that dogs will give you. So, please remain still. Now where was I? Ah yes, your family. Now Inspector, what is it that drives a man like you to take so many risks with his own life when you have responsibilities for others? I want you to think about that before you meet your end. Your family will never know what has become of you, I intend to feed your body to the dogs and bury what's left of you in the countryside. But how will your family survive without you? I can see a time, in the not too distant future when Mrs Reid might find herself walking the streets of Whitechapel. And what of your daughter, is that the life that you planned for her?"

Reid struggled, trying to free himself from the chair but it was no use, he was bound too tightly and the ropes were too thick and strong. There were tears in his eyes as he thought the worst thoughts about the future of his family and how they might end up at the mercy of the beast that stood before him.

Greenfield's smile was gone and Reid could see murder in the man's eyes.

"Struggle no more, Inspector. I shall end your misery for you now."

Greenfield replaced the knife back on the table, walked slowly over to Reid and placed his strong hands firmly around Reid's neck and began to throttle to life out of him. Reid struggled as best he could, but after about 45 seconds, he like the whores before him, lost consciousness. Greenfield returned to the table, picked up the knife and was about to slice into Reid's left carotid artery when he heard a floorboard creak behind him. Before Greenfield could move, the blade of a dagger pierced his back, passing through his heart and left lung as it made its way through his body. He fell to the floor as four men burst into the room, the man with the dagger was clearly the leader.

"Right, fellas. I'm going to finish this bastard off. Johnny, I want you to get hold of a horse and cart and park outside of the yard, I want it here within 15 minutes. I want you two fellas to clear out these rooms. Don't open that door as the bastard has got a couple of fighting dogs locked in there."

"What are we to do with the policeman, Michael?"

"Get a sack and put it over his head, I don't want him seeing us."

The man stood over Greenfield who lay motionless on the floor. His left lung had been punctured and had quickly filled with blood. His heart, although pierced by the blade of the dagger was still beating, he was struggling to breathe through his right lung. Michael Hodges then pulled out a cosh, bent down over Greenfield and hit him what must have been ten times across the head, fracturing his skull in several places. Greenfields wounds bled slowly as his heart had slowed and soon he was dead.

"THAT WILL TEACH YOU, YOU FECKIN' BASTARD" shouted Hodges at the blood splattered man lying on the floor before him.

After a few minutes Reid awoke, surprised to find that he was still alive. However, the euphoria of knowing that he was alive soon wore off when he realised that he had a sack over his head. He assumed that Greenfield had changed his mind about giving him a quick death and now meant to torture him first. He could hear a lot of movement and thought that the dogs had been let back into the room.

Hodges spoke in what Reid recognised to be a thick Irish accent. "Don't be worrying yourself, Inspector, you are in safe hands now. Consider yourself to be a very lucky man. You see, my boss had me and a few of the lads follow ya today as we was interested in finding out a bit about you like. Well I'm going to be telling the boss that you're a brave but stupid man. Anyways, in a while I'm going to loosen your ropes and I'd be grateful if you could give it a few minutes before you free yourself. Do you think that you could do that for us?"

Reid instinctively nodded his head. He hadn't a clue what was going on and was just glad to be alive. All he knew was that trusted the voice that told him that he was save.

"Now be remembering not to open the door to the other room as the dogs are still in there. Have ya got that now?"

Reid nodded again.

"Right fellas, are we all done?"

The other men all nodded at their leader.

"Okay, Inspector, we'll be on our way now. Before we go though, I'd be grateful of a favour. You don't know me and will never know me, but I've just saved your life to be sure. The man that was going to kill ya is dead and won't be troubling anyone anymore. But ya see, we've taken his body and effects away with us and would prefer that no one else know that he's gone like, as it suits us to keep things that way. Now in payment for your life, do ya think that you can keep our little secret?"

Reid still hadn't a clue what was happening but he had just spent the last few minutes re-evaluating his life and was glad that he somehow seemed to have been given a second chance to make the most of it for himself and his family. He decided that his duties as an officer of the law would take second place to those of his family and he made a vow to himself that he would never again put his own interests ahead of theirs. He looked up in the direction of the voice and nodded.

"There's a good fella, ta be sure. Now you be remembering that the world's a hard place to live in and we can all do without making it any harder for ourselves."

The man loosened the knots on the ropes that held Reid to the chair and then squeezed Reid's shoulder.

"Now you look after yourself, Inspector."

With that the men left Greenfield's tiny lodgings, walked through the yard, climbed onto the wagon that now contained the Ripper's body in a sack and started on their journey out of the city and into the countryside where they meant to dispose of his body.

Reid didn't try to move until he could no longer hear the sound of the horse's hoofs clattering on the cobbles. The knots holding him to the chair had been loosened but he still had to struggle with them for a few minutes before was able to break free. He took the hood off his head and looked around the room. Greenfield's knife, photographs and the jar were gone. In fact there was no trace of him apart from some fresh bloodstains that were on the floor in front of Reid's chair. He could hear the dogs moving about in the other room, so he went back into the front room of the house. He looked around and replayed in his mind, the encounters he'd had with the man he knew as Levi Greenfield. His head was bruised and he still felt very groggy. He wanted to go home, but knew he had to report back into the station, as they would be expecting him to return back there from his lunch. He left the building and walked through the small yard, back into George Yard. He wondered why he and his men had not suspected Greenfield of committing the Tabram murder, but that was all history now. He took a slow walk back to Leman Street, where he informed the duty sergeant that he had been attacked whilst patrolling one of the back streets and that he needed to go home to rest. Emily was at home when he arrived back there. He asked her not to worry about his bruised head, but instead asked her to prepare the family a dinner fit for a king, as he felt famished.

❦❦❦

Reid never did file a report on the fate of the man that was to be known forever more as the 'Ripper'. Instead he went back to his regular policing duties, even managing to track down the elusive Harris Marks and through him he went on to capture the 'King of the Coiners' Thomas Riley, aka, Stephen King, aka, Old Steve, aka, One Armed Steve.

However, never again was he to be assigned to a case that might allow him to free himself from the shadow of Abberline and he was to remain forever more just another east end Detective Inspector. But he didn't care about any of that; he had his family, his health and a secure job with a pension. Reid's daughter Elizabeth went on to marry H-Division's PC Thomas Smith in 1895. Reid transferred from H-Division into London's L-Division (Lambeth) in the same year. However, his time as a member of Her Majesty's Constabulary was soon to end and he went into retirement on 27th February 1896, having had a few thrills and spills along the way.

❦❦❦

As for the hunt for the Ripper, that went on for a few more years before the authorities finally gave-up the ghost in 1891. Although, according to the official figures, five women had been slaughtered at the hands of the unknown monster; the nation's focus on the poverty and destitution in London's east end went on to result in improved policing and over time would also result in improved housing and working conditions of the local people. As is often the case with the Yin and Yang that is life, some good usually grows from the manure of the bad.

Some people are placed on this earth to live eventful lives and Edmund John James Reid was certainly one of those. He kept the promise that he made to himself in that little room in George Yard on Wednesday 14th November 1888. Never again would he senselessly risk his life in the line of duty or by parachuting from hot air balloons. He was content to live an ordinary life, safe in the knowledge that he'd helped in a small but significant way to make the world a better place in which to live.

And so ends one possible tale from the streets frequented by the man they called 'Jack the Ripper'.

INSPIRED BY

Begg, P., Jack The Ripper, The Facts (Portico, 2009)

Chisholm, A., DiGrazia, C-M, Yost, D., The News from Whitechapel, Jack the Ripper in the Daily Telegraph (McFarland & Company, Inc, 2002)

Connell, N. and Evans, S., The Man Who Hunted Jack the Ripper (Amberley Publishing, 2012)

Eddleston, J.J., Jack the Ripper, an Encyclopaedia (Metro Publishing and imprint of John Blake Publishing Ltd, 2010)

Evans, S.P. and Skinner, K., The Ultimate Jack The Ripper Source Book - An Illustrated Encyclopaedia (Robinson, 2001)

Oates, J., Unsolved Murders in Victorian & Edwardian London (Wharncliffe Books Ltd, 2007)

Rule, F., The Worst Street in London (Ian Allan Publishing, 2010)

Stubley, P., 1888, London Murders in the Year of Ripper (The History Press, 2012)

Sugden, P., The Complete History of Jack The Ripper (Robinson, 2002)

Trow, M.J., Ripper Hunter: Abberline and the Whitechapel Murders (Wharncliffe True Crime, 2009)

ABOUT THE AUTHOR

JOSEPH BUSA was educated at Royal Holloway College, University of London, where he took a BSc in Chemistry before going on to study a PGCE in the teaching of science at the University of Southampton. He has had a variety of jobs but hopes that in the writing of books he has found his true vocation in life. He was born and lives in London.

Printed in Great Britain
by Amazon

82812545R00210